BANNISTER'S CHART

ANTHONY TREW has had three careers: sailor, business executive, writer. The first was the sea. Returning to it during the Second World War he served with the South African and Royal navies in the South Atlantic, the Mediterranean and the Western Approaches where he commanded the escort destroyer HMS *Walker*, principally employed on Russian convoys. He was awarded the DSC.

After the war he resumed his work with the Automobile Association of South Africa of which he was Director General and in his spare time wrote the best-selling novel, *Two Hours to Darkness*. On the strength of it he retired early and embarked on a third and highly successful career as a writer.

He now lives in Weybridge, Surrey.

Available in Fontana by the same author

Death of a Supertanker
Running Wild
Sea Fever

ANTHONY TREW

Bannister's Chart

FONTANA/Collins

First published by William Collins Sons & Co. Ltd 1984
First issued in Fontana Paperbacks 1986

Copyright © Anthony Trew 1984

Made and printed in Great Britain by
William Collins Sons & Co. Ltd, Glasgow

ONE

Beyond the windows of his office, high in the building, the long stretch of water from Lukoni down towards Port Reitz shimmered in the heat of the noonday sun. It was a view that had been with him through all the important years of his life and he had not tired of it. Now, watching the small rust streaked ship come slowly into Kilindini harbour, he was moved as always by the sight of her safe return. Known to his friends as Goosam, this balding bespectacled Hindu in late middle age, Jinha Goosammy Patel, was principal shareholder, chairman and managing director of J. G. Patel & Co. Ltd – import/export merchants and owners, among other things, of the Capricorn Islands Shipping and Trading Company. Despite the pretentious name, its shipping operations were confined to this aged coaster.

'Upper works all right,' Patel muttered to himself. 'Hull needs painting next time in.' More expense but it had to be faced. He looked at the wall-clock: ten past twelve. Soon after two o'clock Cassidy would call. It was an occasion to which Patel always looked forward. He liked and admired this larger than life Irishman with his naive, unaffected charm and old world courtesy, so much out of keeping with the times. Over the years they had become firm friends. As *Sunglow*'s captain, Cassidy was an employee, but Patel had from time to time given him enough bonus shares to justify his status as a partner in the Capricorn Company, albeit a junior one.

In recent years more modern vessels had come into the coasting trade and *Sunglow*'s operations had suffered. Faced with taking her out of service or improving the facilities, he and Cassidy had decided to have the passenger accommodation extended and improved. It had been designed originally for carrying creole labourers – the *ilois* – among the islands. The substantial alterations had added a new dimension to the old coaster's activities: 'adventure cruises', the revenue from which, together with the economy measure of running her at ten knots against her normal twelve would, it was hoped, make the ship's operations once again profitable.

The intercom on Goosam Patel's desk buzzed discreetly. 'What is it?' he asked.

'Captain Cassidy's here, Mr Patel,' replied Miss Panjee.

'Send him in.'

Through the doorway came a big man in a tropical suit; his flaxen hair and beard, large cigar, Malacca cane, and Panama hat worn at a rakish angle, suggested someone of importance. To the Hindu, the Irishman was somewhere between Long John Silver and a character from Conrad.

Patel stood up, hand outstretched. 'Welcome Shamus. It's good to see you. How are you?'

'Sure, and not too bad, Goosam.' The Irishman's large hand smothered the Indian's and the eyes, curiously blue in the weathered face, looked down on the small man with friendly amusement. 'I'd be better for a pint of the iced lager.'

Patel smiled, nodded – it was an old joke. 'Tea is coming, make yourself comfortable.'

The big man took off his hat, placed it on a table with the Malacca cane, unbuttoned his coat and lowered himself into an easy chair. There followed the customary enquiries about family: Patel's, for Cassidy had no wife, though he admitted to the possibility of offspring somewhere. ''Well, now,'' he had once explained to Patel, ''A young man that travels the world meets many a fine lass. The more the pity it would be, then, not to have refreshed the blood along the way.'' Patel was never quite sure what that meant, and had preferred not to ask.

6

Miss Panjee, olive-skinned, sloe-eyed, brought in the tea. Patel poured it, passed a cup to Cassidy. 'Now tell me – how was the voyage?'

Cassidy finished wiping his forehead with a large silk handkerchief, put it away, tipped the ash from his cigar. 'Not bad at all. Cargo about average. Fair loads of copra, *boriti* and guano.'

'And the passengers?' Patel cocked his head on one side.

'So so, and not too bad. I'd be thinking that most of the gentry enjoyed themselves.' Cassidy sighed. 'But the usual complaints. Mostly from the women – the old ones of course.' He affected an upper-class English accent. 'Menu too repetitive – smell of copra most unpleasant – ghastly cockroaches and beetles . . .' He shook his head.

Patel made little clicking noises, fiddled with an arm of his spectacles. 'Dear me, Shamus. What do they expect?'

'That's what I tell them. Refer them to the brochure: *A working vessel going about her trade – not a floating hotel.* And who is it that ever heard of a cargo of copra without beetles.'

'The menu complaints? How did you answer them?'

'Indeed, and did I not tell them that Pierre was a French chef.'

Patel smiled. 'He's a Seychellois, Shamus.'

'Well now, and isn't that French enough?'

'The cockroaches?' Patel blinked anxiously behind his spectacles.

'She's an old vessel, Goosam. Bound to collect a few along the way. In any case she's due for fumigation this time in.'

'More expense.' Patel thumbed the pages of a folder which lay on his desk. 'The last quarterly accounts show that *Sunglow* . . .'

'They take in the last cruise, do they?'

'Yes. And the interest on the loan for alterations and additions.'

The Irishman put down his cigar. 'And how would things be looking, then?'

'Just about breaking even.'

'No more than that?'

Patel shook his head. 'The reduction in speed has meant a useful saving on the fuel bill. That and the net passenger revenue after expenses, feeding them and so forth, seem to have stopped the losses. But no more.'

They went on to discuss other things: *Sunglow*'s next voyage, to begin in five days; the cargo to be loaded, the voyage itinerary, the passenger reservations.

All of the ten two-berth cabins would be occupied, reported Patel. 'Three of them with single occupants. Ladies of course. They seem quite prepared to pay a supplement of fifty per cent for the privilege.'

Cassidy leant back in the chair, drew on his cigar, blew a smoke ring and watched it climb to the ceiling. 'Sure, and a miracle it is to me – the money the ladies have.'

'Widows, Shamus. The men die making the money, the widows enjoy it.'

'Would that be why your lot puts the widows on the funeral pyre?'

'That is a most irreverent suggestion. Now, tell me, how is it with the new mate, Mr Scalatti?'

Cassidy was silent, considering the question. At last he said, 'He's not a man I take to, Goosam. Sullen, unfriendly. Uneasy with the men. Sure, and I'd rather have promoted Said Obudo.'

'Said hasn't got a first mate's certificate, Shamus. When he gets one, we can put matters right. In the meantime you'll have to make the best of it. At least Scalatti's got a first mate's ticket.'

Cassidy pulled at his beard with thumb and forefinger. 'I have me doubts about that.'

'Because it's Panamanian?'

'No. I'd rather not say yet awhile. But sure, and it's doubts that I have. We shall see.'

Patel looked unhappy; said nothing. The talk moved to crew leave, ship's stores, the need for more refrigeration space, replacement of the third engineer (a Bengali who wanted to go into business ashore) and other matters. Patel asked about personalities and events in the islands. Cassidy brought him up-to-date.

The Irishman rose to go. Patel saw him to the door. 'There's mail and ship's papers waiting for you in the general office, Shamus. Pick them up on your way out.' It was something he'd said on countless occasions.

'I'll do that, Goosam,' replied Cassidy, playing his part in the ritual.

'Don't forget that Prahud expects you for dinner tonight.'

Smiling at the man he looked upon as one of his closest friends, one for whom he had the greatest regard, Cassidy said, 'My compliments to your lady. Be sure to tell her I'll not be late.'

Bound for Nairobi and Johannesburg, Flight BA 055 was two hours out of Heathrow when Jim Abernethy took the travel brochure from his flight bag and paged through it. He'd done this so often before leaving England that he knew most of its contents by heart; but now, actually embarked on the journey which a few weeks back would have seemed a dream, he felt he must do so again. He turned to the first page. It showed a small ship at anchor off a beach lined with palm trees. Beneath it appeared: *Join a Capricorn Adventure Cruise and revel in the mystery, romance and adventure which await you among the sapphire lagoons and palm-clad atolls of the Indian Ocean – get away from it all and explore these islands set in azure tropic seas. 'Sunglow' is no cruise liner, but a working vessel going about her lawful trade. Little wonder she attracts interesting and adventurous folk, the sort you'd like to meet; those for whom floating hotels hold no charm.*

Another page gave details of *Sunglow*. To Jim she

seemed small, displacement only 1500 tons but it was this he found especially attractive. Diesel-engined, said the brochure, but no speed given. *Accommodation for twenty passengers in two-berth cabins of generous size, ten by eight feet, each with its own shower and WC.* He'd paced that out at home. It was quite ample, really. Would any of the passengers be young? He hoped so. He was seventeen. *Large lounge with cocktail bar,* continued the brochure, *leading onto passengers' sundeck. No pool, but excellent swimming and goggling in the crystal clear lagoons which abound in the islands. Four motorized inflatable boats – skimmers – to carry passengers to and from the beaches, and to explore the coral reefs and lagoons of nature's most beautiful playground.*

'Great,' murmured Jim. 'Really great.' He turned the page: *The coaster 'Sunglow' has for many years traded in the waters of the Northern Indian Ocean, principally along the East African coast and among the Aldabra, Cosmoledos, Farquhar, Amirante and other groups of islands and atolls on that great reach of shoals which stretches from the Equator down to the Tropic of Capricorn. The islands are inhabited by creoles who work the coconut plantations and guano deposits, the principal sources of exports, and catch the fish and turtles which, with the flesh of coconuts, form their staple diet.*

It was marvellous of Aunt Beryl to have invited him on the cruise. Really marvellous. And travelling first class. There was something to be said for a rich aunt – even if she was a bit severe and demanding at times. But what was the mystery bit all about? Why had she said their relationship was to be kept a secret, that he must say they had met for the first time at Heathrow when he'd helped her with her luggage? He was, she said, to call her 'Mrs C', as did all her friends.

'I'll explain later, Jim. But in the meantime you must behave as if we were strangers.' She'd said that with one of those kind but stern smiles which the family called Aunt

10

Beryl's trade-mark. So strangers they were, and that was why they weren't sitting together. He looked back to where she was reading a newspaper, three rows behind, on the opposite side of the compartment.

They must have been somewhere over the Mediterranean when Mrs Clutterbutt took two pieces of paper from the travel wallet in her flight bag. One, fragile with age, was heavily creased where it had been folded. It was a cutting from *The Times*. The other appeared to be a simple, hand-drawn map.

Mindful of the passenger next to her, Mrs Clutterbutt looked at these surreptitiously. Not that she need have worried, for the man had tipped his seat back and was asleep. The faded wisp of paper triggered a chain of pictures which ran through Mrs Clutterbutt's mind like an old home movie: 'Clouds End', the country house in Cornwall overlooking St Ives Bay, where she'd been born and spent most of her childhood. The cold rainy day when, not knowing what to do, she'd gone up to the attic and rummaged through boxes of old clothes, toys and other family bric-a-brac accumulated by generations of Bannisters.

Her great-grandfather, Harvey Bannister, a sea captain, born at 'Clouds End' in 1843, had died there in 1881. She'd never known him of course, but he was a family legend; a Bannister folk hero.

It was while rummaging through an old, rotting, leather trunk that she'd found the Bible in the pocket of a folded oil skin jacket which time had pressed into a sticky slab. In the trunk she'd come across other possessions of her great-grandfather's: a fob watch, a seaman's knife and lanyard, a hand compass, and an old logbook. But it was the Bible which had interested her most. On the inside back cover Harvey Bannister had listed the ships in which he'd served, beginning with his first voyage as an apprentice in the barque *Madeleine* in 1858, and ending with his last ship, the

11

barque *Koolamagee*, which he'd joined as master in 1877.

For Beryl Bannister – then a girl of thirteen – the most exciting discovery was a secret pocket in the Bible. It had been made from end papers which had been glued together. In the pocket she'd found the newspaper cutting and hand-drawn map. She had told her family about the other things, but never mentioned the Bible which she'd hidden away with secret possessions in a box under a pile of old rugs in the attic.

She left 'Clouds End' when she was eighteen, spent the next year at a finishing school in Paris, returned to England in the following year, and married soon afterwards.

It was when she'd read the advertisement for the Capricorn Adventure Cruises that she'd remembered the box in the attic and hurried down to 'Clouds End' to see her brother. There she had found the box, still under the pile of rugs, and retrieved the Bible.

That, she reflected, was really why she was on board Flight BA 055, due to land in Nairobi at six o'clock that morning. That and, perhaps, for one other reason.

She had for some time been worried about her favourite and much adored nephew, Jim. His mother, her sister Hilda, to whom he had been devoted, had died the year before. Mrs Clutterbutt knew that her sudden death had deeply saddened him. He did not get on with his father, Frank Abernethy, who'd married a younger woman just six months later. Mrs Clutterbutt had never liked Frank Abernethy. Pompous, self-opinionated, he was a poor second to his brother John Abernethy, her solicitor and good friend. The advent of the handsome, affected and demanding young stepmother had added to Jim's misery. He had turned, then, increasingly to his aunt with whom he had a close relationship. Only too plainly, she had seen what was happening to him.

It was to get Jim away from his grief and unhappy environment that she had begged his father to let the boy accompany her on the cruise.

It was a happy solution: Jim had been thrilled, his father and stepmother delighted – despite the latter's exaggerated concern for her stepson's safety. For Beryl Clutterbutt it could not have been better: Jim rescued – a strong, handsome young man as escort – and what promised to be an interesting time ahead.

Mrs Clutterbutt replaced the travel wallet in her flight bag. Later, when *Sunglow* was out at sea, she would show Jim the cutting and tell him the story of which he as yet knew little, if anything. Those faded pieces of paper might, she thought, play an important part in what was to come. In any event the mystery they suggested, the family link, added elements of purpose and excitement to the coming voyage. Much, of course, would depend on Captain Cassidy's attitude. If he were prepared to co-operate, well and good. If not . . .? She shrugged her shoulders – at least they'd be spending three weeks at sea in the tropics and for Beryl Clutterbutt that meant a great deal. She adored ships, the sea and the sun, and on top of that they'd be going to strange, out of the way places.

By now Captain Cassidy should have had her letter. She wondered what his reaction would be.

Ali Patel, deputy managing director of J. G. Patel & Co. Ltd, and heir apparent to his father, Jinha Goosammy Patel, had gone to the latter's office soon after Cassidy left. When the problem of *Sunglow*'s future had first arisen Ali had opposed the decision to keep her in service. The decision had gone against him; but now that *Sunglow* was back in harbour, and the latest quarterly accounts available, he was determined that the matter should be reconsidered. Her operations were barely profitable and, in Ali's opinion, that was only because the provision for depreciation had been understated.

'We're throwing good money after bad, Father,' he stressed. 'There's a case for disposing of the vessel. She's too old and too slow. The maintenance charges continue to

13

escalate. The costs of servicing the refit loan are prohibitive. Those two items swallow any real profit.'

Goosam Patel looked up from the note he was making. 'You say dispose of her. How? Sell her for scrap? That would mean virtually nothing by the time we got the vessel to where the scrap could be used.' He pressed his steel-rimmed spectacles onto the bridge of his nose. 'There is another consideration, Ali. I have to think of Captain Cassidy. It would break his heart to scrap *Sunglow*. She is his life.'

'Why scrap her, father?'

'It is you, not I, who have said she should be disposed of.'

Through half shut eyes, Ali watched his father closely. 'You know, month after month, year after year, old *Sunglow* has been threading her way through islands, shoals and atolls. She works in dangerous waters – hidden reefs, uncharted hazards.' He looked out through the windows to the harbour beyond. There was a long silence.

'So?' Goosam Patel regarded his son with a frown of inquiry.

'If she should strike one of those coral reefs, or other hidden danger . . .?' Ali hesitated, a half smile on his lips. 'The accident, the misfortune, would itself have disposed of her.'

'You mean . . .?' interrupted his father.

Ali nodded. 'She is well insured. From the proceeds you could handsomely compensate Captain Cassidy – and it would solve . . .'

'Stop it, Ali.' Goosam Patel half rose from his chair, held up a restraining hand. 'I will not hear of such things. Nor will Captain Cassidy. It is disgraceful that you should even think of them.'

That had ended the discussion, but not Ali's intentions. His father was, he believed, an anachronism, absurdly attached to business principles belonging to another age. Ali had few scruples. For him, being found out was the ultimate sin. It was not the first time that conflicting

14

attitudes towards business morality had led to unpleasant scenes between father and son.

Back in his office, Ali filled a glass with iced water and squeezed into it the juice of two limes. He took it to his desk, sat down, drank slowly, his eyes on the distant harbour, his thoughts elsewhere. Luigi Scalatti, *Sunglow*'s new mate, was prominent in them. Ali, too, had seen the Panamanian certificate, noted the oddity and, with an eye to the future, said nothing. A man with a dubious certificate of competency might well be open to reason.

TWO

During the taxi journey down to the harbour, Cassidy thought about the way in which things had changed since he'd first taken command of *Sunglow*, almost twenty years earlier. The coaster was old then, but she'd been well maintained and the last refit had given her a fresh lease of life. That was when the new passenger accommodation had been built into the ripped-out shell of the old. In many ways he resented the change. Carrying creole labourers in primitive accommodation was one thing; the new accommodation with its refurbished cabins, elegant lounge, cocktail bar and sundeck, was quite another. In place of the undemanding *ilois*, passengers now were wealthy tourists from abroad, people who were anything but humble and undemanding; on the whole a self-important lot who expected constant attention. But at least they helped to keep *Sunglow* in service, so he accepted the change and did all he could to ensure that they were well cared for.

With time, he reflected, everything changed: the island and coasting trade, Mombasa town and Kilindini harbour, and indeed Kenya itself – even he and Patel, so much older now, had changed. How could he hope for an exception to be made of the small ship which meant so much to him.

His thoughts were interrupted by the taxi's arrival opposite *Sunglow*'s gangway. He stepped out, paid the fare, and made his way on board.

He had almost finished changing into uniform when there came a faint double rap on the door.

'Come, Mbolwo,' he called.

A tall thin African, with grave eyes and an aquiline nose, came into the cabin carrying a tea tray. He was shown on the crew list as 'Captain's Steward'. It did not reveal that the Swahili had been with him through all the years he had commanded *Sunglow*, that he was devoted to the big white man whose comfort and day-to-day welfare were responsibilities of which he was quietly proud.

He put the tray on Cassidy's desk. 'Will the Captain be on board for dinner tonight?'

'Not tonight, Mbolwo.'

The African took the discarded white suit from the bunk, arranged it carefully on a coat-hanger, and hung it in the clothes cupboard. He put away the shoes, the Panama hat and the Malacca cane with the assurance of one who had done this many times before. Afterwards, he stood against the door with folded hands.

'Is that all, sir?'

Cassidy, sitting on a chair pulling on socks, looked up. 'Yes, that's all.' He added, 'Better take the next three days off, Mbolwo. Before the passengers arrive.'

'It is not necessary, sir.'

'Sure and it is. There's a family waiting for you. Hassim will look after me.'

'He is not experienced, sir.'

'You say that of all of them. I'm thinking he'll be good enough. It's only a few days. You'd best be getting along.'

'Thank you, sir.' Mbolwo gave the slightest of bows before leaving the cabin. Cassidy settled down to tea and the mail. It was mostly ship's business but there were several personal letters. One from his brother, a farmer in County Mayo; two from passengers of previous cruises; an inquiry from a German about a lost camera; a request from an Indian for information about one of the islands visited. The blue envelope with its United Kingdom stamp and postmark, addressed in a strong, firm hand, he kept to the last. Having opened it, he looked first at the signature: 'Beryl Clutterbutt'.

'Sure and it'll be a strange woman with such a name,' he murmured, turning to the letter's beginning.

Dear Captain Cassidy,
I shall be arriving in Mombasa on the 22nd September to join your ship on sailing day, the 24th. I presume you will have seen my name in the passenger list. The purpose of this letter is to inform you that I am bringing with me something of considerable interest; indeed, it may well influence 'Sunglow's' route, and much else, on her coming voyage.
If you will dine with me on the 23rd September at the Nyali Beach Hotel – where I propose to stay until we sail – I will be happy to explain something that it is difficult, and perhaps unwise, to commit to writing. Unless I hear from you to the contrary I shall assume your acceptance.
Yours sincerely,

Beryl Clutterbutt
PS: 7.30 for 8 – informal dress – I shall be in the foyer.

The letter was dated 12 September, the address embossed upon it a Somerset one. The handwriting was so assured, that Cassidy felt he would be dealing with a woman of considerable character. He wondered what she was like.

The handwriting, the tone of the letter, the imperiousness, suggested a woman used to having her own way; that

17

meant a difficult woman. He pulled at his beard, sighed noisily, put down the letter, and picked up a bulky envelope. It was over printed, *Capricorn Islands Shipping and Trading Company Ltd*. It would, he knew, contain ship's papers, among them cargo manifests and the passenger list. Having found the list he ran his eye down the names – seventeen in all. Goosam Patel had told him there would have been eighteen but for a late cancellation – a Swiss couple. Their cabin had been allocated to a Miss McLachlan from London, previously short-listed. 'We will do well from this,' Patel had explained. 'The Swiss cancelled too late for refund of the fares.'

So Beryl Clutterbutt was a Mrs not a Miss. Widow, he imagined. A woman who wrote that sort of letter would surely have sent her husband to an early grave. And a happy escape, at that. MRS CLUT-TER-BUTT: he rolled the name through pursed lips, stressing the syllables. What was it that he would find of considerable interest? Did she seriously imagine that a ship with cargo, mail and supplies for the islands could be diverted from its course by something she was bringing with her? She'd probably been influenced by the travel brochure's extravagances – *Sunglow's cruise itinerary is a strictly guarded secret, known only when the ship is at sea and the Captain has opened his sealed sailing orders*. Cassidy disapproved of that sort of hyperbole, disliked the charade he had to perform: the opening of sealed orders in the lounge or saloon soon after sailing, the reading of them to the assembled passengers, the emphasis on the names of places of call. Rarely more than two to be announced in advance for it was important, the advertising consultants had insisted, to maintain the atmosphere of mystery, exploration and adventure. The undisclosed itinerary also made it possible for *Sunglow* to vary her ports of call as the voyage proceeded, so accommodating the exigencies of island trading.

But, yes, of course he would accept Mrs Clutterbutt's invitation. While common sense warned that what she was bringing with her was probably of little consequence, Shamus Cassidy, like so many of his countrymen, was naïvely romantic. She just might be bringing something that really *was* important. In any event, dinner at the Nyali Beach Hotel was always a pleasant occasion.

Sunglow's first mate, Luigi Scalatti, was a dark, hairy-chested man with deep-set eyes which reflected the suspicion and resentment of the underdog. On those rare occasions when he smiled, his face was transformed and he became what women might have called an attractively ugly man. Opening the corner cupboard he took from it a bottle of Martini, poured a stiff drink and settled himself on the cabin settee. He wore only shorts and sandals for it was a sultry, humid evening. Cassidy and Said Obudo, the second mate, had gone ashore, so it was Scalatti's turn for harbour duty. A boring business. If the Captain hadn't gone ashore, the Italian would have been on the other side of the island at Ruth's Place, off the Mzizima Road, overlooking the old harbour. The disco had a great rock group – the Coco Jocos – plenty of drink, and girls with strong thighs and fine straight backs. They really knew how to swing it. And other things if they liked you, and you had the money.

With the coaster's arrival back in Mombasa, Scalatti had completed his first round voyage. So far, though she was small, as was his cabin, he liked the routine. Not too much sea-time. Three weeks trading among the islands between the Seychelles and Madagascar, and along the East African coast, then back to Mombasa for five or six days. The passengers made things more interesting; the expeditions ashore, the skimmer journeys, and the beach barbecues. Quite unlike the monotony of the long voyages and quick turn-rounds of his last ship – a Panamanian registered bulk-carrier on which he'd served as third mate until put ashore with malaria in Mombasa. While in hospital there he'd heard that *Sunglow*, still at sea, had lost her first mate.

19

He'd applied for the job, was interviewed by Ali Patel, and got it. He had joined *Sunglow* when she returned to Mombasa a day or so after his discharge from hospital. At the first meeting with Cassidy he'd sensed that the big Irishman didn't like him. Scalatti was not surprised. It was mutual. A matter of chemistry, he supposed. Several times during the voyage he'd clashed with the Captain. On one occasion it was when Cassidy had seen him strike an African seaman for impertinence; on another, on a hot dark night, Cassidy had found him sitting in the chartroom drinking coffee and paging through a copy of *Paris Match* borrowed from a passenger. Cassidy, wearing rope-soled shoes, had appeared on the bridge without warning.

'Drop that magazine, switch off that light, and get off your backside, Mister Scalatti. You're supposed to be on watch – the safety of the ship in your hands.'

Scalatti had resented being told off within hearing of the African at the wheel. But he'd said nothing.

On another occasion, it was the second night out of Mombasa, Cassidy had called him to his cabin. 'I saw you drinking with passengers in the lounge this evening. You're crew, Mister Scalatti. In my ship, crew don't drink with the passengers.'

Again Scalatti had said nothing, just stared at Cassidy in a sullen way before walking off. In the days that followed he'd seen Cassidy at the bar talking to passengers. He'd mentioned this to the second mate. 'Yes,' said Said Obudo, 'The Captain talks to passengers at the bar. But he never drinks there. Only in his cabin.'

It was absurd the way Cassidy acted, as if he were captain of a great liner, not a clapped out old coaster. The Irishman was the only snag in what was otherwise a pleasant job. But Cassidy was captain and that made things difficult. On balance it was worth putting up with him, at least for the time being. The Captain was no chicken, getting on for sixty; it could be that . . .

A knock on the door ended his train of thought. Hassim,

one of the two passenger stewards, came in. 'Telephone for you, sir.'

Scalatti went down to the lounge, picked up the phone. It was Ali Patel, polite, solicitous: How was the unloading going? The new deckhouse awning. Had it arrived? Had Scalatti enjoyed the voyage? Then came the real purpose of the call: 'There is a private matter I'd like to discuss with you. Tomorrow night at ten o'clock. At the junction of the Kilindini and Liwatoni roads. Look out for a grey Mercedes.' He gave the registration number. 'Can you make it?'

Scalatti said, 'Okay. I'll be there.'

'This could be of great advantage to you. Not a word to anyone. Strictly confidential.'

'Okay. I understand.' Scalatti heard the phone click off. He put down the handset, went back to his cabin.

It was certainly strange. Except for the interview for the job, he'd never met Ali Patel. Now he was being asked to a secret meeting with the deputy managing director. What could it be that Ali wanted to discuss? Why the secrecy? Was it something to do with Cassidy? The Italian's interest was excited. This could be the big break. The chance he'd never had. His own command, maybe. A man born and bred in a Naples slum didn't get many chances.

THREE

He was speaking to the receptionist when he saw her in the foyer. She must have guessed it was him, for she stood up and came across: a woman of much his own age, tall, straight backed, with iron grey hair and a commanding presence.

'Captain Cassidy?'

'Yes, ma'am. Is it Mrs Clutterbutt then?'

She nodded. They shook hands.

'Come and sit down, Captain. I'll lead the way.' He followed her into the lounge, to a quiet corner. A waiter came and took their order. For a minute there was silence. Cassidy was aware of stern grey eyes examining him. Not a lady to be trifled with, he decided.

'And how was the flight, then?' he asked.

'Rather boring, Captain. But air travel always is, don't you think?'

'Indeed it is, Mrs Clutterbutt. Nothing like a sea passage.'

'Yes, I do agree. As a girl I often travelled to and from India. P & O of course. Such splendid ships. I had an aunt in Delhi.'

The waiter returned with their whiskies. Mrs Clutterbutt liked scotch, soda and a little ice; he preferred irish, water and a lot of ice.

Their conversation remained formal: the weather, the news, her questions about Kenya, his replies.

It was not until they had gone into the dining room, and been shown to a table near open french windows which looked out into the garden, beyond it the sea, that she mentioned her letter.

'It was good of you to come, Captain Cassidy. When we have dined I shall tell you what caused me to send you that somewhat mysterious letter.'

'Indeed, ma'am, and it greatly interested me.'

She gave him a stern look. 'Please don't call me ma'am. I know that Clutterbutt is rather a mouthful. Call me Mrs C – most of my friends do.'

Cassidy smiled. 'Then Mrs C it shall be.'

Dinner was a leisurely affair during which Mrs Clutterbutt ate sparingly. Cassidy, as always, did justice to his considerable appetite. His hostess, who appeared to know her way through a wine list, had asked him for his preference.

'The wine is not for me, Mrs C. Not in this climate. It's iced lager I'll be having.' He got his lager, and she her half bottle of Riesling.

Dinner over, they went back into the lounge, to the same quiet corner. A waiter came; more iced lager was ordered for Cassidy. The waiter went off. Mrs Clutterbutt said, 'I shall now tell you a story which I trust you may find interesting. Before I do so, however, I would like you to read this.' She took from her handbag a newspaper cutting and passed it to him.

It was from *The Times* of 23 April 1881 – a column of shipping news. The marked paragraph was a report from Durban about the loss of the barque *Koolamagee* in a cyclone in the Indian Ocean while on passage from Bombay to Bristol. Her cargo had, the report stated, included a number of gold ingots. The master, Captain Harvey Bannister, and a cabin boy, the only survivors, had taken to a raft and drifted ashore on a desert island. The cabin boy had died soon after landing. Some time later, a delirious Captain Bannister had been rescued by native fishermen.

Cassidy passed the cutting back to Mrs Clutterbutt. 'Sure, and that's very interesting. But what, may I ask, would be its importance?'

Her grey eyes held his in a disconcerting stare. 'Captain Harvey Bannister was my great-grandfather,' she said.

'Ah well, and that explains much that I have been wondering about.' Cassidy pulled at his beard. 'But there is surely more to the story than that.'

'There is indeed. Let me begin at the beginning.'

Mrs Clutterbutt replaced the cutting in its envelope and put it in her handbag.

'My great-grandfather's ship, the *Koolamagee*, was lost somewhere north of Madagascar a few days after she'd been dismasted in a cyclone. Led by a mutinous first mate, most of the crew had taken to the life boats and were never heard of again, but Great-grandfather, a seaman and a cabin boy, remained on board until the ship sank several days later. The life boats having gone, they made a raft and were apparently provisioning it when the ship overturned. That sudden disaster left them without a chart, sextant or chronometer, and so unable to plot the raft's daily position. They drifted for many days, carried by wind and current, with little food – a small supply of ship's biscuits, my great-grandfather told the family – and no water other than that collected during rain storms.'

She paused, looked out through the french windows into the dark, starlit night. 'The seaman, apparently demented by suffering, disappeared one night shortly before the raft broke up on a coral reef off a small deserted island. Captain Bannister and the cabin boy struggled ashore. They had to swim across the lagoon. A few days later the boy died in the captain's arms. He'd been injured when the raft struck the reef. Almost five weeks later great-grandfather . . .' She paused. 'From now on I shall call him Bannister. It simplifies matters.' Momentarily she seemed lost. 'Now where was I?'

'The lad had died in Bannister's arms,' prompted Cassidy.

'Oh yes. Well, after almost five weeks of privation Bannister, by then in a state of delirium, was found by native fishermen. Almost three months later he arrived in Bristol from Durban, safe but seriously ill. He died not long afterwards.

The waiter returned with the iced lager. Cassidy took a brown leather case from his pocket. 'Would you be minding, Mrs –,' he hesitated. 'Mrs C. There's nothing better than a cigar after a fine meal.'

'As you wish, Captain.' The slight inclination of her head suggested no enthusiasm. 'Some of my bridge friends smoke. I prefer not to.'

Unabashed, Cassidy took out a cigar and began the ritual of its preparation. When it was alight, he leant back in the armchair, blew a cloud of smoke to the ceiling, sighed contentedly.

'There a question I must be asking,' he said. 'What port did Bannister sail from to reach Durban?'

She shook her head. 'It is something we don't know. I could find no record of where the natives landed him – or how he then reached Durban. It would have been a most valuable clue. Remember, all this happened more than a hundred years ago. He was, I imagine, too ill to write about his experiences when he got home. His death soon followed. He must, however, have given members of the family some idea of what happened, or the story could not have been handed down. But nothing was recorded, other than . . .', she directed another of those disconcerting stares at Cassidy, '. . . something which I found in his Bible.'

Cassidy nodded understandingly. 'The Bible was a great place for family information in those days.'

'It wasn't exactly family information, Captain. It was rather more interesting.' Mrs Clutterbutt told him of the box in the attic at 'Clouds End', of the secret pocket in the Bible where she'd found the cutting from *The Times*. 'There was something else in that pocket, Captain Cassidy. Something which explains why I decided to join your ship for the coming cruise.'

In the background of his bearded face, Cassidy's blue eyes twinkled good humouredly. 'And what might that be, I'll be asking?'

'A chart,' she said gravely. 'A simple, hand drawn chart of the small coral island on which he'd survived for all that time. I imagine he drew it while in the sailing ship on his way home to Bristol.'

Cassidy pulled himself up in the armchair. 'Have you the chart with you, then?'

'Not here. You shall see it after we have sailed.' She leant towards him, looked round the lounge, lowered her voice. 'That is, if you decide to co-operate with me. In the meantime all I can tell you is that my – I mean Bannister – has shown the approximate latitude on the chart, but not the longitude.'

Cassidy looked puzzled. 'The native fishermen would surely have known where they found him. Strange it is, he didn't know the longitude.'

Mrs Clutterbutt nodded. 'I thought you might say that. It is something which, initially, worried me. Later, I realized that native fishermen, particularly in those days, would have little knowledge of latitude and longitude. They would, it seemed to me, have worked in terms of direction and distance. But they would certainly have known where they'd put him ashore. And I imagine he would have been told that sooner or later.'

'Ah, and that's good thinking, Mrs C. Very logical.'

Mrs Clutterbutt smiled briefly. 'In the last few weeks I have devoted much time and thought to this, and come to a number of conclusions. For example, if Bannister had no sextant he wouldn't have known even the approximate latitude after a three week drift – yet he shows it on the chart. *Obviously*, even if it were sometime later – remember, he was delirious – he must have known where the fishermen put him ashore. He would, at some stage before reaching Durban, have asked questions about the island. In the light of what he was told, he would have known roughly where it was. So he showed the approximate latitude of Ile Blanche on his chart but deliberately, I believe, omitted the longitude – for reasons, shall we say, of security.'

'Ile Blanche you say, Mrs C. Now if he did not choose to give the location of the island, why then should he be giving the name?'

Mrs Clutterbutt was about to say something, but he interrupted.

'It's a long time that I've known these waters and the islands, Mrs C, but never have I heard of Ile Blanche. When you come aboard I'll be showing you the charts – the Admiralty charts – and you can see for yourself.'

Mrs Clutterbutt shook her head. 'No Admiralty chart of the Indian Ocean shows Ile Blanche, or White Island for

26

that matter. I've checked that very thoroughly. Possibly Ile Blanche was the native name – or Bannister called it that for some reason of his own.' Mrs Clutterbutt sank back into her chair, her grey eyes somehow reflecting the enigma. A long silence followed before she spoke again. 'I very much want to find that island, Captain.'

'What I would be asking, Mrs C – and indeed with respect – is this: why should the matter be of interest to me?' Cassidy's manner was sympathetic, almost that of a parent talking to a child.

Once again Mrs Clutterbutt looked round the lounge. 'Because, my dear Captain . . .' she hesitated, watched him as if making a value judgement, '. . . because of something Harvey Bannister inscribed on the chart. It's *raison d'être*, one might say. That will, I believe, be of great interest to you.'

'And what might that be, Mrs C?' Cassidy spoke casually, raising his tankard and taking a long draught of iced lager; then, with the knuckle of a forefinger, wiping delicately at the rime of foam between beard and moustache.

Mrs Clutterbutt leant towards him. '*Koolamagee*'s cargo included gold ingots, Captain Cassidy. Need I say more?'

FOUR

The grey Mercedes came slowly down the Kilindini Road before turning at the junction with Liwatoni Road. It stopped behind a street light not far from where he was standing. He checked the registration number, walked down towards the car. The door on the passenger side swung open. He climbed in.

'Good,' said Ali Patel. 'I'll head for the Nyali Bridge.

27

There's a quiet spot beyond Kongowea. We can chat there undisturbed. Better that we're not seen together.'

Scalatti said, 'Yes.'

'There'd be charges of favouritism. That sort of thing.' Patel swung the car left, accelerated. Scalatti saw that they were avoiding the busier, well lit streets. There were not many people about.

Before long they had crossed the bridge which spanned the neck of water between the island of Mombasa and the mainland. Soon afterwards the Mercedes turned left off the Nyali road. More twists and turns followed, confusing the Italian who knew little of Mombasa and its environs. The lights of houses grew fewer until they were eventually left behind. The car bumped along a winding sandy track. 'Long time since I was here,' said Patel. A few minutes later they came to a stop in a clearing beneath tall palm trees. Before Patel switched off, the headlights shone across an expanse of water.

'This'll do,' he said. 'Nothing here except an occasional courting couple.'

The Italian laughed. 'That's how you know it, hey?'

'I was young once.'

'Not so old now.'

'I've responsibilities. Outgrown that sort of thing.'

Scalatti detected a hint of reprimand, decided to be careful.

Patel said, 'It's a hot night.'

'Not too bad in here.'

'Air conditioning. Without it we'd have to choose between closed windows and mosquitoes.'

An aircraft passed overhead, its navigation lights blinking like flying stars.

'I suppose you're wondering?'

'Yes – I am, Mr Patel.'

'I think we can drop the misters. My friends call me Ali. Even those who don't like me. You're a seaman, Luigi. You know ships and the sea better than I do. But I know

28

the problems of ship-owning better than you do. It's your advice as a seaman that interests me.'

'I'll do my best.' Scalatti spoke modestly.

'Ship-owners have problems. Ageing vessels is one of them. Inflation over the last decade has made nonsense of the provision for replacement. The money put aside for that in the past can't match the inflated building costs of today. Take your ship, *Sunglow*, for example. She's thirty or more years old. Impossible to operate her profitably. Costs of maintenance, fuel, wages, wharfage . . .' he paused '. . . and insurance. Under present day trading conditions it's virtually impossible to finance her replacement. So what can the poor ship-owner do?'

Ali's voice trailed off on a plaintive note.

It occurred to Scalatti that the new Mercedes didn't suggest undue poverty, but he said nothing. He wasn't going to offend Ali Patel. And he was already disappointed. The drift of the deputy managing director's remarks seemed hardly likely to lead to a suggestion that what *Sunglow* needed was a change of command. Though Patel's last question appeared to be rhetorical, Scalatti felt he should say something, if only to break the silence. He was about to do so when Patel remarked, 'Some ship-owners look to marine insurance to finance new tonnage.' The dry laugh which accompanied the remark suggested a jocular aside, but since it struck Scalatti as good sense he said, 'Why don't you do the same? After all the Capricorn Company must have paid a lot of money in insurance premiums over the years.'

Ali professed reluctance to embark on such a course. 'I know it's done, but we're not those sort of people.'

'Of course,' said Scalatti. 'But you must think of the company. Watch for its interests. I mean, the money would not be for you.'

The discussion continued for some time, the Italian appearing to overcome Ali's resistance to a point where the latter conceded grudgingly that it could be a highly profitable operation; both for the ship-owner and, he stressed, for whoever assisted him.

He said, 'I suppose it's something I really should think about. But there are problems. My father and Captain Cassidy are old-fashioned men. They would not – well, you know – permit anything like that. Their generation is not really familiar with the – shall we say the *methods* of coping with the exigencies of modern ship-owning.'

Scalatti didn't know what 'exigencies' meant but he was determined to press on: 'It is not difficult, you know. To lose a ship in such a way that – okay, you understand – a way that won't cause suspicion.'

Ali appeared casually interested. 'Yes, I suppose you're right. But that, of course, is up to someone on board – someone with authority. I mean, the ship-owner can't do it on his own. It's a seaman's job.'

With that the discussion began to take a more positive line. Ali stressed the need for absolute confidentiality. 'There's only one way to keep a secret, Luigi – that's not to confide in anyone. Silence can't be passed on.'

The question of ways and means was next discussed; obliquely, Ali handling the subject in a sufficiently off hand way to suggest that they were discussing something abstract, an interesting hypothesis, no more. It was the Italian who took the plunge. 'It would have to be done during my watch – the middle watch,' he explained. 'Running aground on a coral reef at ten knots – Jesus! That'll tear the bottom out of any old ship.' In the interest of tact he avoided the name *Sunglow*.

'Casualties? Injuries? Deaths, maybe?' Patel's tone was guarded.

'No. That couldn't happen. In calm weather with the ship close inshore, there's no risk of that one. I wouldn't go along with such a thing if there was. Nothing like that, Ali. You can be certain.'

'You're the seaman. It would be up to you to decide the detail: time, place, weather and so forth.'

'Yes. Of course.'

'One other thing, Luigi. You'd better have a story ready to explain the – accident.' Ali stopped for a moment. 'And to protect *that* – *your* – Panamanian certificate.'

The way the Indian said that, the innuendo in the stressed words, worried Scalatti. But there was, nevertheless, a question he had to ask. 'One point, Mr Patel – sorry, I mean Ali – what is in this for me?'

He heard the Indian take a deep breath. 'You will be well looked after, of that you can be sure.'

'How well, Ali?'

There was silence in the car but for the distant chirping of crickets, a sound partially muffled by the closed windows.

'When the claim was settled you would get your percentage. About fifty thousand US dollars. It's a lot of money.' Patel lowered his voice, though there was no possibility of it carrying outside the car.

Scalatti said, 'It's a lot of risk for me.'

'Not for a man of your . . .' Ali coughed, '. . . your ability, Luigi.'

Scalatti wondered if anything lay beneath that remark. The cough had sounded affected, the tone much the same as when Patel had referred to the Panamanian certificate.

How much did the man know, Scalatti asked himself? He by-passed the question in favour of another. 'What guarantee for me? You know – how shall I be sure to get my percentage?'

'Same as for me, Luigi. How do I know that you will, shall we say, play your part? It's a matter of mutual trust, isn't it? Such arrangements cannot be committed to paper.'

'I suppose so.' Scalatti sounded doubtful.

'Let's shake hands on it.' Ali Patel smiled in the darkness. 'A gentleman's agreement. Like in the days of the Raj.'

Sailing day was a busy one for *Sunglow*: stores and late cargo were being loaded, shipping agents, port, customs and immigration officials came and went. In the early afternoon passengers began to arrive. By five o'clock the last of them had come aboard. A notice on the gangway gave the time of sailing as six o'clock that evening. By way of nautical confirmation a Blue Peter flew from the yard-arm. Among the first passengers to arrive was Jim Aber-nethy, tall, fresh-faced, red-haired, eager-eyed. An African steward took his luggage and showed him to cabin No 2 on the port side. The steward told him that the dining saloon was at the forward end of the passageway; the lounge and sundeck one deck above. Before leaving he drew the young man's attention to the passenger list on the notice-board in the lobby. 'Notice-board important. You look every day. All information there,' he said. The passenger list showed that Jim Abernethy would be sharing cabin No 2 with a Mr Blake.

There was as yet no sign of the man or his luggage. Jim began to unpack. On the assumption that Blake would be the older man, he took the upper bunk, leaving his pyjamas on it as a token of possession. Once unpacked, he decided to look round the ship.

As he explored his enthusiasm grew. It was a surprise to find so much in a small vessel. The bridge, passenger accommodation and sundeck were on an island amidships, the cargo hatches fore and aft of it. Crew accommodation was in the stern, above the engineroom. A squat funnel, black with a yellow band, rose from the after superstructure which it shared with two lifeboats, inflatable rafts stowed on launching racks, engineroom skylight and venti-lators. From these came the hum of auxiliary machinery and the acrid smell of diesel oil.

The crewmen looked like Africans or Arabs, or a mix-ture of both. One of them, a young man in khaki shorts with two gold stripes on the shoulder-straps of his shirt, had shouted, 'Hey, you! Keep clear of the hatchway.' That was when he'd stopped to look down into the after-hold and a loaded cargo sling had swung past his head as the crane

32

lifted it inboard. The man who shouted had come over to him. An African with a straight nose and dark eyes set in a high cheekboned face, his skin shining like polished mahogany.

'Hi,' he said. 'You a passenger?'

'Yes.'

'Keep clear of the hatches while cargo's being worked. You can get hurt, man.'

'Sorry. I was just looking round.'

'Okay. When we're at sea I'll show you round. I'm Said Obudo, second mate.' He held out a hand. 'What's your name?'

'Jim Abernethy.' They shook hands.

'Right. See you later.' The second mate left him.

Jim went up a ladder to the sundeck. It was cooler under the awnings there than anywhere else. A number of passengers, three of whom he recalled having seen on the flight from Nairobi, were already relaxing in deck chairs, among them a youngish couple discussing a camera which the man was holding. Their accents were North American. The woman looked up and smiled as he passed. At the forward end of the sundeck there were sliding doors into a lounge. It had settees, easy chairs, a bookcase of paperbacks, a framed chart of the Northern Indian Ocean, and a small bar in the corner, signposted THE PUB. It reminded him that he was thirsty, but the venetian screen over the counter was shut.

'Bloody typical,' announced a hoarse voice behind him. The owner was a short stubby man with a bearded, perspiring face. His eyes were masked by dark glasses. Grey hair, worn long, showed beneath a blue yachting cap. A T-shirt inscribed MINE'S A GUINNESS in front, and WHAT'S YOURS behind, blue shorts and white plimsolls, completed his wardrobe.

'Perishin' heat-wave and the pub's shut,' said the stubby man.

Jim said, 'I suppose it's something to do with duty-free.

33

Like the cross-channel steamers. You can't buy anything until they're at sea.'

'Where you from?'

'London,' said Jim.

'Great. Can't beat it. What part?'

'NW3. Hampstead.'

'Very posh. Heath an' all.'

There were a number of passengers in the lounge. Two elderly men sitting together were looking at him, smiling. Jim was embarrassed. 'My dad's house,' he said defensively.

'No harm in that. I lived in me dad's house in the Mile End Road until he kicked me out. Wicked old sod.'

'I see,' said Jim gravely, now more than ever aware of the onlookers.

'Be there still if he hadn't. Lazy little bugger, I was. But he kicked me out. That started the career of 'Enery Atkins. Began with a barrer I did, then into scrap metal – *and* what falls off trucks.' His grin revealed stained, uneven teeth. 'The two professions go together, see. Now the mail for Henry Atkins comes to Chester Square SW1 – *Esq* after me name an' all. That's a bleedin' laugh. Tell the truth, I'd rather be back in the Mile End Road. But the wife's got social ambitions. So we had to move. The Cortina used to be good enough for Mrs 'Enery Atkins – but not for Mrs *Henry* Atkins. Now it's a bleedin' Roller. That's your classless society, lad. What's your moniker?'

'Jim. Jim Abernethy.'

'Good. See you later, Jim.' The stubby man hustled away.

Jim heard one of the two elderly men say, 'Mostly what fell off trucks, I should imagine.'

'More likely hard work and native wit,' said the other. 'Amusing little man. Must have made a lot of money. We can't drive Rollers, Dick.'

'Don't know that I want to. What is a Roller, anyway?'

'Good heavens. Don't you watch *The Minder*? In scrap metal circles, a Roller is a Rolls Royce.'

'Really. How interesting.'

Jim went back to the sundeck, leant over the rail on the side overlooking the quay. A taxi drew up and he saw the commanding figure of his aunt climb out. She made for the gangway, followed by the African driver with her luggage.

She looked up and saw him as she crossed the gangway: he smiled, waved, but she gave no sign of recognition. With a shock of guilt he remembered that they were to be strangers.

'It is a busy scene, isn't it,' remarked a pleasantly feminine voice. He turned to a sudden vision of hazel eyes, dark hair, ivory teeth and moist lips. Over it all the fragrance of jasmine.

'Yes, it is.' He smiled shyly, acknowledging to himself that lovely as she was, she was too old for him: at least thirty, he decided.

'I'm Diana Kitson,' she said, putting on sunglasses. 'Are you coming on this cruise?'

'Yes, I am.'

'Oh, how super. I'm so glad. I think it should be marvellous, don't you?'

Her smile and enthusiasm were almost too much for him. All he could manage was a hoarse, 'Yes. I think so.'

'You're very tall.' She looked up at him, smiled again. 'What's your name?'

The personal way in which she looked at him, said things, made him feel he wasn't, perhaps, too young after all.

'Jim Abernethy,' he said.

'Oh, Jim. What a lovely name.'

He felt a strange excitement, as if something wonderful but inexplicable was happening to him. It was going to be a super voyage.

35

In late afternoon *Sunglow*'s gangway was lifted, she man-oeuvered clear of the quay, gave a farewell blast on her siren, *half-speed* was rung down on the engineroom tele-graph, and she headed up towards Likoni and the sea.

Cassidy and the pilot were acquaintances of long stand-ing but, like most sea captains, the Irishman instinctively resented the presence of an outsider giving orders on his bridge, so he crossed to the port side, away from the man.

As he had done so many times in the past, Cassidy watched the familiar landmarks of Kilindini slide by: Liwa-toni Creek, then Mbaraki Creek, after that the Likoni ferry. When the distant bulk of the Oceanic Hotel had fallen astern to port, his spirits began to rise. He and his ship would soon be at sea again, clear of the harbour with its humid heat, the noise and litter of cargo work, and the coming and going of officials of various kinds.

With Fort St Joseph broad on the port bow, course was altered to starboard and *Sunglow* headed out to the open sea. Soon afterwards the engines were stopped, the pilot launch came alongside, a rope ladder was dropped over the side and the pilot climbed down. He waved to Cassidy as the launch turned and headed back towards Kilindini harbour. Cassidy waved back and ordered, 'Full ahead, steer due east.' Said Obudo repeated the order, rang it down on the telegraph. The quarter master spun the wheel and steadied the ship on the new course. The second mate noted in the rough log the bearing of Ras Serani, and the departure time.

Cassidy looked down to where two seamen were clearing litter and hosing the steel deck around the foremast hatch. Scalatti was leaning against the foc'sle bulkhead watching them, his uniform cap on the back of his head, a cigarette drooping from his mouth. The khaki shirt and shorts he wore were sweat soiled and crumpled, the shirt without its shoulder-straps of rank.

'Scruffy devil, the man is,' muttered Cassidy into his

36

beard. On the way to the bridge he'd reprimanded Scalatti for his appearance. The Italian had looked at him with narrow, smouldering eyes. 'The ship has been working cargo, Captain. It is dirty round the holds. So I wear the khaki.'

'In future, Mr Scalatti, you'll be wearing clean uniform while there are passengers aboard this ship. Is that understood?'

Without waiting for the Italian's reply, he had continued on his way to the bridge.

Sunglow drew away from the land, and the south-easterly swell began to make itself felt. The creaking of the superstructure, the hum of auxiliary machinery, the vibrations and throb of the diesel, were pleasant reminders to Cassidy that his ship was again alive.

It was close to sunset, and on the western horizon banks of cumulus cloud, piled high upon each other, reflected the light of the vanishing sun. The wind coming gently from the south-east, bringing with it the fresh smell of the sea, the movement of the ship, rhythmic and predictable, the swish and lap of water along the hull, induced in Cassidy feelings of security and harmony which he experienced only at sea.

Somewhere beneath him in the ship were the passengers. So far he had met two of them, Dr Summers and Mrs Clutterbutt. She was an unusual woman, undoubtedly an interesting character. The doctor seemed a likely enough man. Retired, living in Surrey, courteous and intelligent. Maritime law required that a doctor be carried in ships with more than twelve passengers. It had been Goosam Patel's idea to meet this expensive requirement by offering a half-fare to a suitably qualified passenger prepared to carry out the duties of doctor for the duration of the voyage. The arrangement had worked well and for each cruise so far there had been several applicants. Cassidy wondered what the other passengers were like. Some would be pleasant enough, others not so pleasant, and a few a damn nuisance.

Whoever they were, they'd paid a lot of money to come on the voyage. It was up to him to make it interesting. To create mystery and adventure to order was not as easy as the copywriters would have it, but he'd do his best.

FIVE

The stars faded and the eastern sky grew lighter, tropical twilight giving way to the day. In the east the bright disc of the sun, lifting above the horizon, was laying a gilded path across the sea.

With the dignity of an elderly lady refusing to be hurried, *Sunglow* dipped and rolled to the undulations of the swell, while white horses fanned by the south-easter splashed and slapped against her bows.

For Cassidy the onset of dawn, darkness giving way to light, was always the best time at sea. On this first morning out of Mombasa it had brought him familiar pleasure as he walked his small bridge thinking of the day ahead. For reasons of economy, and because she seldom spent more than two or three consecutive days at sea, *Sunglow* had no third mate. Watchkeeping duties were shared between the first and second mates, with Cassidy himself keeping the morning and first dog-watches. It was an arrangement which suited him well.

He had still to meet most of the passengers, for it was his custom not to dine in the saloon on the first night at sea; nor did he ever breakfast there, preferring the comfort and convenience of his day-cabin to which Mbolwo would bring a breakfast tray. He sometimes lunched in the saloon, and almost always dined there, taking his place at the head of the Captain's table.

As to the day ahead, his real encounter with passengers

would take place in the saloon at 10.30 that morning when he would open and read aloud the 'secret' sailing orders.

There were usually a number of passengers who remained in their cabins on the first day at sea. He wondered how many would do so on this occasion. Sea-sickness was an affliction he found difficult to understand. For him the motion of a ship at sea, other than in exceptional circumstances, was both pleasant and therapeutic. How then, could it make a physical wreck of normally healthy people? Would Mrs Clutterbutt – he corrected himself, Mrs C – be a victim? He doubted it. Too strong a character. A mental picture of her triggered other thoughts: the dinner at Nyali Beach, the way the conversation had gone when she'd lowered her voice and said, 'Gold ingots, Captain Cassidy. Need I say more?'

Playing for time, digesting what she'd said, he'd pulled at his beard, looked absent-mindedly into the darkness from which came the distant sound of the sea. 'And what is it that you'd be wanting of me?' he'd at last asked her.

'Your help in finding White Island.'

'On this cruise you mean?'

'But of course. That is why I'm coming with you.'

Cassidy had nodded sympathetically before continuing the softly spoken conversation. 'And, if that's not too direct a question, what would be in it for me?'

'A very natural question, Captain.' She had smiled impersonally. 'A share of the gold.' She'd whispered the words 'the gold' as if they were slightly improper.

'And what share would that happen to be?'

'Fifty per cent. Half the amount the treasure realizes. It would be for you to decide how to apportion that. As between Mr Patel and yourself, I mean.'

Cassidy had taken a long draught of iced lager, put down the tankard, turned to her with the suggestion of a smile. 'Indeed and that's generous enough, Mrs C. But how would we be getting it ashore? Customs, the law – ownership of buried treasure – disposing of it at the end of the day, and so on. There's many a problem beyond the finding of the island.'

'I am well aware of that, Captain. It is a matter to which I have given some thought. Let me say now that, before deciding on this venture, I did a good deal of research in England. Among other things I enquired about The Capricorn Islands Shipping Company – and its owners, J. G. Patel & Company Ltd – and . . .' she had hesitated then, before saying, very directly, '. . . and of course about you, Captain.'

'Well did you now, Mrs C? And I trust the enquiries were satisfactory.' The blue eyes were lively.

'Yes, indeed. I may say I was reassured by what I learnt. My most useful informant was a friend in Nairobi. It occurred to me, then, that Mr Patel himself might be of considerable assistance. Indian merchants are so competent in matters of this sort, you know.' Mrs Clutterbutt's sweeping glance had encompassed the lounge, as if in search of someone to challenge the statement. 'And I've no doubt a share of the treasure might well encourage him.'

'Ah, would you be thinking, then, that I should mention the matter to him?'

'That is something entirely for your discretion, Captain.'

In the discussion which followed Cassidy had promised his co-operation, subject to Goosam Patel's approval. It was his belief, he'd added, that Goosam would support the search for White Island provided it did not involve the company in extra expense. If a little additional steaming time were necessary, explained Cassidy, he could offset it by tailoring the voyage itinerary; but not by much. For her part, Mrs Clutterbutt told him she had in her possession an agreement drawn by her solicitors which confirmed the terms she'd discussed with Cassidy – namely, half shares of the amount received for the treasure found.

'Before you leave the hotel tonight I shall hand you a copy. I suggest we sign it once *Sunglow* is at sea. When that has been done I shall show you the chart. Not before.' Mrs

40

Clutterbutt's manner had, quite suddenly, become severe.

Cassidy accepted the arrangement, though he'd pointed out that when he and Goosam Patel had studied the documents, amendments might be necessary. Mrs Clutterbutt's reply suggested she thought that highly unlikely. She'd added, however, that she would not close her mind to such a possibility.

Cassidy stopped pacing the bridge, his thoughts interrupted by Mbolwo's arrival with coffee and an apple.

He looked at the wheelhouse clock. 'Six-thirty already, is it Mbolwo?'

'Yes, sir. I put tray in chartroom?'

'Thank you, Mbolwo.'

It was a moment at sea to which Cassidy always looked forward: his steward's early morning appearance on the bridge with coffee and an apple; a routine which never changed.

Sunglow had no ship's broadcast system, information for passengers being disseminated by means of the noticeboard in the saloon passageway, or by word of mouth by ship's staff; usually the stewards.

On this first morning at sea both methods had been used to inform passengers that the ship's sailing orders would be opened by the Captain in the dining saloon at 10.30. Well before that time passengers began to gather in the saloon; by 10.30 most of them were present.

Cassidy came down the stairway from the officers' quarters, followed by the chief steward, and took his seat at the Captain's table. The chief steward, Gaston Pascal, a dark serious man with sleek hair and a neat moustache, was a Seychellois. Like the other officers, he wore tropical rig – white uniform shirt, white shorts and stockings. Cassidy wore white slacks. A man of his age and shape, he would say, had no dignity in shorts: a statement which the bulge at his waistline confirmed. But he certainly was a man of considerable dignity, a bearded giant with a calm and

41

unquestionable air of authority. 'A fine-looking man,' Mrs Clutterbutt had observed to herself when first she saw him.

It was with this air of authority that he now contemplated the passengers who'd gathered in the saloon. To Mrs Clutterbutt, sitting at a small table on the far side, he nodded courteously before saying, 'Good morning, ladies and gentlemen. I hope you had a good night.'

A ripple of 'good mornings' came from the passengers. As always Cassidy found their various interpretations of tropical dress interesting. He often wondered at the way people from different parts of the western world met the challenge of hot weather, but he was seldom surprised.

'Absentees?' he enquired of the chief steward.

Pascal looked at his clipboard. 'Mis McLachlan and Mrs Cawson.'

'*Mal de mere*,' said a small, heavily jowled man with a Scottish accent; presumably Mr Cawson.

'I've seen them, Captain. Nothing serious. They'll be up and about before long.' The speaker, slight, grey haired, with a weathered face and a reassuring smile, sat at the far end of the Captain's table.

'Thank you, Dr Summers.' Cassidy turned to the chief steward. 'Our sailing orders, Mr Pascal.'

The chief steward took a wax-sealed envelope from his briefcase and passed it to the Captain. Cassidy looked at the passengers rather as a conjurer does before producing a rabbit from a hat, broke the seals and took from the envelope a sheet of paper. He considered its contents in frowning silence.

'Ah, so that's it,' he said at last, showing a commendable measure of surprise, observing that he himself had drafted the sailing orders before they were typed and sealed in Goosam Patel's office. Cassidy began to read:

'Having departed Mombasa at eighteen hundred hours on the twenty-fourth of September, *Sunglow* will proceed to the Amirante Isles in Latitude 5°30′ South, Longitude 53°05′ East, visiting Eagle Islet and such other places in the

42

group as may be necessary for the purposes of discharging, loading, exploration and adventure cruising.'

There was a murmur of excitement. Cassidy held up a hand. 'It's interesting, indeed, that we are to visit the Amirante Isles. Now let me tell you something about them.' The chief steward passed him the clipboard.

'I'll quote from these notes of mine,' explained Cassidy. He did not add that they were the work of Goosam's secretary, Miss Panjee, who had spent hours researching the subject in the Mombasa library. 'There are numerous atolls and islands in the Amirantes which lie on a bank of sand and coral extending for some ninety miles in a sou-sou-westerly direction. Most of the islands are inhabited by people working the coconut plantations and guano deposits. The islands themselves tend to be flat, composed of coral, and seldom more than twenty feet high. In addition to coconut palms, many have thick undergrowth, clumps of casuarina trees, mangroves and lagoons with beaches of fine white sand. Some of the atolls and islets you will visit are uninhabited. Where this is not the case, the people are mostly creoles, though the settlement managers are often European or Seychellois.' Cassidy looked up. 'That is people from the Seychelles Islands which lie about one hundred and twenty miles to the east of the Amirantes.'

He put down the clipboard. 'The Amirante Islands are eight hundred and forty miles east of Mombasa. This involves a journey which will have taken three and a half days by the time we arrive off Eagle Islet – by far the longest leg of the voyage which, in all, will occupy three weeks. The night before we reach the islands there will be a briefing session. You will then be told of the programme for the following day, and detailed to your skimmers. The programme and beach landing schedule will be posted on the noticeboard in the passageway outside the saloon. Next to the noticeboard you will find a chart of that part of the Indian Ocean which concerns this voyage.' He picked up the clipboard again, cleared his throat. 'Ladies and gentlemen, the seas through which we will be sailing, and the numerous islands in them, belong to a little known but romantic region of the Tropic of Capricorn. In the seventeenth and eighteenth centuries it was the hunting ground of pirates and corsairs. They were attracted to it by its remoteness and the dangerous nature of its waters,' he looked up for a moment, 'studded as they were with hidden reefs, coral atolls and large numbers of small islands, some of them not charted. Those features hampered pursuit and made possible the concealment of their ships. Not far away lay their target: the great sea-route round Africa, linking the East with the West, a marine highway along which many hundreds of ships were obliged to sail each year.' Cassidy paused again, fixed his audience with a blue-eyed stare. 'Many the ship it was they boarded and pillaged, killing the men and, where there were women, taking them . . .' Cassidy sighed, shook his head, evidently moved by the fate of the unfortunate women.

'Yes,' he went on. 'These remote, historical waters have witnessed savage and terrible deeds – and brave ones, too, for the pirates and corsairs received no quarter from the warships which pursued them. So when you step ashore on these islands, ladies and gentlemen, have a mind to these things, these violent yet somehow romantic happenings of long ago.' Cassidy took out a large silk handkerchief and wiped his forehead.

Mrs Clutterbutt used the opportunity to say, 'Thank you, Captain, for that most interesting and graphic account.'

She had listened to Cassidy in fascinated silence: his manner, his tone and accent would, she'd noticed, change subtly depending on whether he was reading the notes, which he did rather as a schoolmaster might, or using them as a prompt to his memory in which case he became the Irish raconteur. Cassidy put the clipboard down, looked round the lounge. 'If there's questions you'd like to be

44

asking, now is the time. It would be helpful if you could give your name.'

A man in blue shorts and a highly coloured beach shirt introduced himself. 'Dean Carter, Washington, DC. Is photographic gear liable to get wet in a skimmer, Captain?'

'Not liable, but possible,' replied the chief steward who'd taken the question in response to Cassidy's signal. 'Sand also, is damaging. Best to keep cameras in plastic bags. I can let you have these.'

'Thank you, sir. That's great. We – that is,' he glanced at the suntanned blonde at this side, 'Sandra and myself – intend to make a comprehensive photographic record of the voyage. For the folks back home, of course. *Not* for publication.' A snort-like laugh exposed large, gappy teeth. 'I guess I read the small print on your voyage contract, Captain – "All publication rights arising from the voyage, literary, photographic, video, audio and otherwise, shall remain the property and copyright of the Company". Okay, Captain?' The American emitted another snort, grinned amiably, and sat down.

Cassidy tidied his moustache with a forefinger. 'Yes. That is correct. Next question?'

A slight, stooping, pink-faced man, bald with thick lensed glasses, put up his hand. Beneath his safari jacket he wore a clerical collar. 'Reverend Arnold Bliss, Welton-mere, Norfolk,' he announced, his tone apologetic. 'Would you happen to know, Captain, to what religious order the creoles of the islands belong?'

Cassidy stroked his beard thoughtfully. 'Well now, Reverend, it's good Catholics I'm thinking they would be. The French influence and all that you know. It's not a matter I've enquired into, the religion. But I can tell you, Reverend, that they like their poteen. *Calao* they call it. A sort of toddy that is, made from the sap of coconut palms. And they like the women, too, for it's big families they have. Sure, and speaking as an Irishman, I'd be thinking it's Catholics they must be.'

Looking somewhat forlorn, the Reverend Arnold Bliss murmured, 'Thank you,' and sat down.

Next to ask a question was Mrs Kitson. 'I was wondering, Captain, if we can . . .' she hesitated, smiled, appeared embarrassed, '. . . if we can say in what skimmer, I mean in which party – actually I mean, may we choose who we'd like to go ashore with?'

'Space and numbers, and other considerations permitting – yes.' Cassidy's manner was abrupt. 'But they don't always permit. Have a word with the chief steward, Mr Pascal. He's OC skimmers. Next question, please.'

Henry Atkins nudged Jim. 'Quite a dish, that one.' The hoarse aside rumbled through the saloon like the murmur of distant thunder.

'Two points, Captain,' said an elderly man sitting next to Dr Summers. His face was lined, his white hair precisely brushed. 'First – I think one should make a distinction between . . .'

'Your name, sir?' Cassidy interrupted.

'Rollo, Richard Rollo. As I was saying – I think one should make a distinction between pirates and corsairs. The former were bloodthirsty villains for whom murder, rape and robbery were commonplace, whereas corsairs behaved in a comparatively gentlemanly fashion. Most of them in this part of the world were French, their ships flew the ensign of France, and they were recognized by their government. Indeed they were virtually private men-o-war.'

'Thank you, Mr Rollo.' Cassidy sounded anything but grateful.

'*Commander* Rollo, RN retired,' corrected the white haired man who had spoken with the authority of one who knew his subject. He went on. 'If I may continue – I shall be brief – it is worth noting that pirates who operated in these waters often buried their stolen treasure on uninhabited islands. This was usually when under pursuit from French and British warships. There have been various attempts,

46

over a long period, to discover this buried treasure, but there do not appear to have been any worthwhile finds. This, of course, does not mean that there haven't been any. Those who find buried treasure are, I daresay, not particularly forthcoming. Thank you, Captain.' Commander Rollo, evidently satisfied with his contribution, sat back and fanned himself with a copy of the *Financial Times*.

When Rollo got on to the subject of buried treasure, Cassidy had shot a discreet but despairing glance in Mrs Clutterbutt's direction. Feeling obliged to do something to repair the damage, he said, 'If you'd been sailing in these waters all the years I have, Commander, you'd be knowing that the stories of buried treasure are greatly exaggerated. Folk in the islands, the descendants of families who have lived there for generations, will tell you that such stories are myths – legends which have grown in the telling. Like the leprechauns of me own old Ireland.'

Mrs Clutterbutt had nodded approval.

Abruptly, Cassidy changed the subject. 'Any further questions?'

'D'you think there's anything in the buried treasure story?' Jim whispered to Henry Atkins.

'Load of codswallop, I'd say. Banks is the only place you'll find buried treasure, lad.' That the hoarse aside had carried across the saloon was evident from Commander Rollo's sudden frown.

Cassidy and the chief steward dealt with several more questions: a large and cheerful Mrs Van der Karst wished to know what they should wear for beach landings? In reply the chief steward gave his usual warning about too much sun if too little modesty. Her husband wanted to know if there was any danger of malaria? He was assured by Dr Summers that there was none if Maloprin had been taken as recommended in the voyage contract.

A portly German, Kurt Bruckner, with close cropped hair, small eyes and large ears, wished to know what a skimmer was? His German accent made it 'schkimmer'.

47

'An inflatable boat with an eighteen knot outboard engine,' Cassidy told him. 'Glass window in the bottom for seeing beneath the surface.'

A crimson faced Mrs Bruckner, her skimpy sundress bulging with flesh and wet with perspiration, was concerned that the passenger accommodation had no air-conditioning. 'There is not the possibility of sleep,' she protested. Used to such complaints, the chief steward passed to Cassidy a copy of the brochure advertising the adventure cruises.

'*Sunglow* is no cruise liner,' Cassidy read out, 'but a working vessel going about her lawful trade.' He put down the brochure. 'We are in the tropics, Madam, close to the Equator. Passenger cabins are well above the main deck. With open portholes and doors on the latch, there's always a breeze – even if it's only what the ship makes. And each cabin has an electric fan.'

Mrs Bruckner made a grumbling noise. 'In these days, even your vorking vessels must haf air-condition, I am sure.'

Cassidy ignored the remark, made an aside to Pascal, and passed on to the next question.

Seven bells sounded at about the time the last question was dealt with. Cassidy thanked the passengers for their attendance, lifted his considerable bulk from the chair, and made his way up the staircase.

The chief steward stood at the saloon entrance as the passengers filed out. The last to leave was Mrs Clutterbutt. As she passed, he handed her an envelope. 'The Captain asked me to give you this, Madam,' he said.

SIX

After the saloon briefing, Jim went to the sundeck where a number of passengers were stretched out in deck chairs, among them the Van der Karsts and Mr Cawson whom he recognized as having been on Flight BA 055. Much to his disappointment Mrs Kitson was nowhere to be seen. On his way to the sundeck he'd looked for her in the lounge but she was not there either. Disconsolate, he pulled up a chair next to Stephen Blake. A quiet, much reserved man, his steel-rimmed glasses emphasizing his scholarly manner, Blake was more disposed to listen than to talk. Jim had decided that he must be some sort of ornithologist: the two books beside his bunk were *Birds of the Oceans* and *The Birds of East Africa*.

At the far end of the sundeck, Dr Summers and Commander Rollo were leaning on the rail talking. Jim had not known who they were until the saloon briefing. Scraps of their conversation which drifted down to him, suggested that the two elderly men were old friends. The commander was talking about his experiences in the Indian Ocean during World War Two, when the cruiser he served in had been looking for a German raider active in the Mozambique Channel.

'I fell in love with the East African coast and the Capricorn islands in those days,' the commander was saying. 'It was a long time ago, but I've never been able to get this part of the world out of my system. That's why I jumped at the chance of the cruise when you mentioned it.'

'I'm glad you did,' replied the doctor.

Blake's silence was discouraging and, with little else to

49

do, Jim found himself listening again to the nearby conversation.

'The crew, Dick? Strange mixture aren't they?'

'Mostly Swahili I'd say,' replied Rollo. 'They're coast people, you know. Mixed African and Arab origin – the descendants of dhow crews, a lot of them. Fine sailors. That young second mate is a good example. Obudo's an African name, Said an Arabic one.'

Dr Summers laughed. 'Irish Captain, Italian mate, Swahili second mate, Swahili seamen, plus a sprinkling of Seychellois and Indians. A sort of human Ark. What's the *lingua franca*?'

'Kiswahili and English, I'd say. What do you think of our fellow travellers?'

Dr Summers lowered his voice. 'Too early to say, Dick. We'll know more about them in a day or so. Difficult not to under these conditions.'

'The Bruckners, that German couple. Rather ghastly?'

'Yes. Pretty awful.'

'And Mrs Kitson? The lady who seems worried about who she may have to go ashore with? Bit over the top, isn't she?'

Dr Summers smiled. 'Thought you might notice her, Dick. Good looker, isn't she?'

'Very easy on the eye. Rather too much so, I'd say.'

Jim bristled with resentment. Despite the lowered voices he'd heard what the commander had said. Diana Kitson was a super person. She'd probably snubbed the commander. He seemed a bit of a snob.

'That Mrs Clutterbutt's a fine looking woman,' the commander was saying. 'Very much a memsahib. Holds herself so well. Straight back, head high. Like a gunner's mate at Whale Island.'

'Unfortunate name, Clutterbutt.' The doctor grinned. 'Shall we call her Mrs C?' With some glee, Jim decided he must tell his aunt what he'd just heard. That reminded him that he was not to think of her as his aunt. His thoughts

50

were interrupted by something Blake was saying. '. . . out there, see?' He was pointing ahead. 'Isn't that a remarkable sight?'

There was no wind, but the glassy surface of the sea rose and fell gently to the rhythm of the southerly swell, *Sunglow* following its undulations.

Their arched bodies glistening in the sunlight, splashes of white foam marking their passage, a school of dolphins came leaping and diving down the starboard side. When they'd gone Jim said, 'Are dolphins and porpoises the same thing?'

Blake shook his head. 'No. Porpoises have blunt heads, dolphins have beaks.'

Henry Atkins joined them. The stubby Londoner was wearing a floral beach shirt, shorts that were several sizes too large, and the yachting cap he so rarely removed. Jim introduced him to Blake. Atkins at once took charge of the conversation. 'Blimey,' he said, looking hastily round the sundeck. 'I'm in dead trouble.'

Jim looked puzzled. 'What d'you mean?'

'I've got the church after me, haven't I? Me cabin-mate, the Rev. Arnold Bliss. He's on to the reformation spiel. Told him to forget it. Been sinful all me life, I told 'im. Want to stay that way, I said.' Atkins winked, pinched his beard. 'Know what 'e said? The Lord's more interested in the sinners because they need him more than the other lot. So I told 'im, with the greatest of respect I did, that I couldn't reciprocate the good Lord's feelings. That put the kybosh on it. He gives me a cross-eyed look and buggers off.'

Blake looked at his watch. 'I've a date with the chief steward. See you later.'

When he'd gone Atkins shook his head. 'Bleedin' trappist monk, ain't 'e. Never says a word. Friend of yours?'

'We share a cabin. He's a nice guy actually. Very quiet, though. It's just the way he's made, I suppose.'

51

Atkins puffed out his cheeks. 'Well, the way I'm made I could do with a pint. Coming along?'

'Yes. Good idea.'

In his cabin, Gaston Pascal, the chief steward, had before him the seating plan for passengers in the dining saloon. As was usual on the first day at sea, a number of them had asked to be moved. There were three tables in the saloon: the Captain's, which seated ten passengers; the starboard table, which seated eight; and the small table on the port side, reserved for deck officers and engineers.

The first request was from Henry Atkins. He'd asked to be moved from the Captain's table where he had been placed next to his cabin-mate, the Rev. Arnold Bliss. 'Enough's enough,' he told Pascal. 'We share a cabin. Let me off the 'ook at meals, Chief. Put me at the starboard table, can't you. I've a mate there. Youngster by the name of Jim. He's OK.'

Pascal had agreed and was now changing the names on the plan: Atkins in place of Blake; Blake to go down to the Captain's table in place of Atkins. No problem there. Promotion for Blake, *and* he'd be next to the attractive Mrs Carter.

The next problem was Mrs Kitson. She'd asked if she might be moved from where he'd put her at the Captain's table – immediately on the Rev. Bliss's right – to the seat allocated to Miss Jean McLachlan at the same table. Mrs Kitson had asked Pascal for this favour in such a charming manner – leaning over the plan with her heady perfume, her breast lightly nudging his shoulder – that he could not refuse. Particularly when she'd pointed out that Miss McLachlan, laid low by seasickness, had not yet appeared in the saloon and could not therefore complain that she was being moved. Mrs Kitson's request presented no problems. The change would put her between Dr Summers and Dean Carter, and opposite Commander Rollo. Pascal was sure they would be pleased. Miss McLachlan, who'd described herself on the reservation form as 'lecturer', was anything but good-looking.

When Mrs Kitson had gone he took her passport from the bundle in his safe and checked her age. Thirty-nine. It was unbelievable. She didn't look a day older than Mrs Carter, whose passport gave her age as twenty-eight. It confirmed Pascal's belief that men could rarely place the age of women between thirty and forty.

Last to call upon him had been Mr Cawson. He asked that he might change places with his wife; she was not happy sitting next to Mr Bruckner. 'He is a noisy eater, she says. And she dislikes Germans. I'd be glad of your co-operation.' Pascal had found no difficulty in granting a request which he felt was not only reasonable, but said worlds for the unselfishness of Mr Cawson. He gave the seating plan a final look before putting it away. Having read Goosam Patel's letter to Cassidy, he was left in no doubt as to why the Captain had told him to place Mrs Clutterbutt on his right.

It was almost ten o'clock in the morning of *Sunglow*'s second day at sea when Mrs Clutterbutt made her way up the saloon staircase and through the officers' quarters to the bridge. On her arrival there the officer on watch, Said Obudo, took her to the chartroom where Cassidy was waiting.

'Ah, good morning, Mrs C,' he said. 'It's punctual that you are.'

'Your note said ten o'clock, Captain.'

'Indeed. Please take a seat.'

Mrs Clutterbutt lowered herself onto the small settee, adjusted her flowered summer frock, and placed her handbag beside her. Cassidy leant against the chart-table facing her, feet apart, bracing himself against the ship's slow roll.

'Perhaps we should begin by your telling me of Mr Goosam Patel's attitude. I take it you discussed this matter with him.'

'Ah, yes, I did so. The morning after that fine dinner. It was . . .'

Mrs Clutterbutt interrupted. 'And what did he think about it?'

'Sure, and he said it was interesting. He left matters to my discretion, provided I did not involve the company in extra expense. I have to admit that Goosam does not take the matter too seriously. Indeed, he has his doubts. But the idea of searching for a mysterious desert island appeals to him. He sees it as something of unusual interest for the passengers, you know.'

Mrs Clutterbutt's mouth tightened. 'No, I do *not* know. It is essential that this matter be treated as strictly confidential between us. This, you may recall, we agreed at Nyali Beach. Confidentiality is of the utmost importance. I've no intention of allowing a hotch-potch of passengers to butt in. If your intention is otherwise, I shall destroy Captain Bannister's chart.' She gave him a hard look. 'It is, I may say, a photocopy. The original is at home.'

'Now, now, Mrs C. There's no need to destroy anything. Not a word about the chart will reach the passengers, nor what it is we're after finding. All that Goosam had in mind was to interest them, so that we would have more eyes, more look-outs, searching for the island. If you're against the idea, then we shall forget it.'

'I am most certainly against *that* idea.' Mrs Clutterbutt spoke with crisp finality.

The embarrassed silence which followed was relieved by Cassidy's, 'Well, now? Shall we be getting on with the matter?'

The grey eyes challenged him. 'Have I the assurance of your co-operation?'

'That you have, Mrs C.'

'Very well. I shall show you the chart.' She took a linen-backed envelope from her handbag, removed from it a folded sheet. 'I'd better join you at the table,' she said, 'so that we may look at this together.'

54

The photocopy was an excellent one; its high definition revealed every line, mark, scratch and fold of the original. For some minutes Cassidy examined it in silence. He decided that Bannister must have used a mapping pen to draw the chart which had been done with the skill and care he'd have expected of a master mariner in those far off days. The island, narrow-gutted and lying on a north-south axis, was shown to be less than a mile in length. There were various inscriptions upon the chart: one, marked Wreck Reef, indicated where the raft had stranded; another, Castaway Cove, the place where Bannister had made his camp and collected rainwater. There was a neatly drawn compass rose, and a scale indicating ten inches to the nautical mile. Beneath it appeared, *Latitude 9° to 10° S.* There was no reference to longitude.

Many palm trees here was inscribed beneath a shaded area covering the central and southern parts of the island. At its northern end a finger of land jutting into a lagoon opposite Wreck Reef was named, *Lone Palm Point.* From it an arrow led to an inscription in the right hand margin: *Gold buried twenty full paces due east of this palm.* Finally, Bannister had, in the neat copper-plate hand of his genera-tion, written: *Here on Ile Blanche, in the tropic of Capri-corn, with God's aid and much hardship, I survived for thirty-eight days.*

Cassidy straightened up from the chart-table, faced Mrs Clutterbutt. 'Remarkable it is. Poor man, what suffering there must have been behind this.' He handed the chart back to her. 'And now, dear lady, I have some idea of the shape and size of what it is we are looking for.' He opened a polished teak drawer beneath the chart-table, took from it a number of charts and laid them on the table. 'These are large scale charts of the various island groups. They give a good picture of the problem that confronts us.'

Mrs Clutterbutt nodded agreement. 'They do indeed. I have them at home. Checked them most thoroughly. I fear they'll give us little help.' She paused, looked at them pensively. 'Now tell me, Captain. Are you really interested? Do you think the search for White Island is quite hopeless? Please be frank.'

Stroking his beard, a habit he found soothing, Cassidy considered the question. 'I'd be no Irishman if I were not interested. Is it hopeless, you ask? I'd rather be asking, are we likely to find White Island? To be truthful, Mrs C, like Goosam, I have my doubts.'

'Oh dear.' For an instant Mrs Clutterbutt displayed symptoms of feminine helplessness. But only for an instant, then she was her normal, determined self. 'I am not prepared to give up easily, Captain. I believe the search to be worth pursuing.'

There was a twinkle of good humour in Cassidy's blue eyes. 'So do I, Mrs C,' he said. 'And what's more, so does Goosam. Maybe he's not hopeful, but as a man of business he *is* interested. You see . . .'

'I take it the fifty per cent has a good deal to do with that.'

'Ah, you're right there, Mrs C. Maybe Goosam wouldn't like me to be saying it, but he thinks your offer is generous.'

'It is,' said Mrs Clutterbutt quite simply. 'It was my solicitor's idea. He felt that if you had the same financial interest as I did it would ensure your commitment and –,' she hesitated, looked at the sea beyond the chartroom windows. '– and your discretion.'

'Meaning that I wouldn't talk?'

'Or do anything else indiscreet.'

'What would that be then?' Cassidy's expression was one of bland innocence.

'Dropping me overboard. Something like that. Once we've found the gold.'

The Irishman's deep throated laugh echoed round the chartroom. '*Me*, do that Mrs C? With all those passengers and crew around. Holy St Patrick! Now that would be a daft thing to do.'

'That's what my solicitor said.'

56

'He knows about White Island. About . . .' Cassidy flourished an arm. '. . . the chart, this cruise. The details?'

'Everything,' said Mrs Clutterbutt. 'Mr Abernethy is most interested.'

'Mr Abernethy?' enquired Captain Cassidy. 'Who is he, then?'

'My solicitor.'

'Now there's a coincidence for you, Mrs C. There's a passenger aboard of that name. The tall youngster with the red hair. He's at the starboard table.'

'It's no coincidence, Captain. He's my nephew. His father, Frank Abernethy, married my sister. She died not long ago. Jim has had rather a sad time. I thought this cruise would get him away from an unhappy environment. Help him to forget.'

'Poor lad.' Cassidy turned back to the chart-table, looked at the barograph. 'Steady it is,' he said absent-mindedly, as if the barometer reading was not what he was really thinking about. 'So your solicitor is your brother-in-law. A family affair.'

'Not quite, Captain. My solicitor is John Abernethy – Frank's brother.'

'Would you not like to have your nephew seated with you at my table?'

'Thank you, Captain. But no. I want Jim to stand on his own feet. To fend for himself. I think my sister tended to smother him with affection. She was, I fear, over-protective, and it has not helped him. Principally for these reasons, he and I have agreed that we will not reveal our relationship on this voyage. *Officially*, we are strangers who met at Heathrow when he helped me with my luggage. I must ask you, Captain, to respect our decision.'

'Well, and it's an odd arrangement, but I'll certainly not be mentioning it to anyone.'

'It is an arrangement, Captain, which has advantages you may well share. If it is known that Jim is my nephew, people may refrain from saying certain things in front of

57

him. Things that, as the voyage lengthens, you and I might like to hear.'

Cassidy took a cigar from the leather case on the chart-table. 'With your permission, Mrs C?'

'If you must; so bad for your health.'

When it was alight he said, 'And what is it then, that they might be saying?'

'Oh, at this point one cannot be specific. But let us assume that, for some reason or other, someone suspects that *Sunglow* – that is *we*, you and I – are engaged in some mysterious mission, the word might get around. Jim would hear it and be able to inform us. Sounds far-fetched, I know, but John Abernethy considered it important.'

Cassidy frowned at his thoughts, then smiled. 'Maybe he believed the arrangement would make me think twice before dumping you overboard.'

Mrs Clutterbutt was guilty of a rare chuckle. 'I'm sure that was not in his mind or he'd have mentioned it. In which case,' she added, 'I would certainly not have told you that Jim was my nephew.'

Cassidy tapped the end of his cigar on an ashtray. 'Does your nephew know of this project?'

'Yes. I told him last night when he came to my cabin. I stressed how vital confidentiality was, showed him the cutting from *The Times*, but not the chart. However, he knows enough now to be a useful ally. He thinks it's all terribly exciting. Wants to find White Island as much as we do.'

Cassidy blew smoke at the deckhead. 'Wise was it, Mrs C? That he should come to your cabin. Tongues wag, you know.'

'Perfectly wise. Officially he came to return a paperback I lent him on the journey out to Kenya. And I cannot believe tongues wag when boys of seventeen call on elderly ladies.'

Cassidy was about to say something. Instead he looked at the clock over the chart-table, smiled at Mrs Clutterbutt.

'Seven bells is not far off. There's things I shall have to be seeing to.'

She got up from the settee, returned Bannister's chart to the linen-backed envelope and put it in her handbag. 'There remain some important points to be discussed, Captain. The way in which you propose to conduct the search for White Island, for example.'

'Ah, and that's right. But there's time enough. There's another few days at least before we're in latitude nine and ten degrees south. That's when the search must begin. And we'll be discussing it before then. There's other things, too. Goosam had interesting thoughts about disposing of the . . .' Cassidy lowered his voice, looked quickly round the chartroom as if in that small space there might be those who should not hear. 'Let us call it "the goods" shall we?'

'Excellent suggestion, Captain. The other word is so emotive. Yes, I would very much like to hear of Goosam's ideas. And I think you'll be interested in my solicitor's suggestions.'

'Indeed, and I will, Mrs C.'

She moved towards the door, was about to leave, when Cassidy put a restraining hand on her arm. 'You'll not forget what I said in the note Mrs C.'

Her expression became mischievous. 'That your chairman, Mr Goosam Patel, had requested you to treat me as a very important person in view of my large shareholding in the Capricorn Islands Shipping and Trading Company. I thought it a most ingenious idea – even if not quite the truth.'

'It was Goosam's idea, not mine.' Cassidy was becomingly modest. 'A clever man is Goosam. He gave the letter to Gaston Pascal in an unsealed envelope. The story will soon be around the ship.'

That afternoon the wind fell away, the swell became more pronounced, and the direction from which it came shifted slowly to the east. Ranks of cirrus cloud gave way to dark layers of alto-cumulus, the sky and the sea taking on a grey, desolate aspect. The change in the weather, the long oily swell, the steel-like grey of the horizon, filled Said Obudo with an apprehension he could not rationalize until, in the second dog-watch, he heard a ship, the *Lake Taipa*, reporting the suspected presence of a tropical storm, possibly a cyclone. He at once informed Cassidy who came to the bridge. The second mate showed him the details he'd recorded. *Lake Taipa* had reported a corrected barometer reading of five millibars below the normal mean, wind force six to seven. Before the fall in barometric pressure the ship had experienced a heavy easterly swell in which direction her captain suspected lay the centre of a tropical storm. Bound for Mahé, speed eighteen knots, she gave her position as 3° 57′ S: 49° 30′ E. As a precautionary measure she was altering to a north-easterly course. She would make further reports as the situation developed.

Port Louis and Mahé had acknowledged the signal and re-broadcast it to shipping, adding that it was too early yet to predict the position and probable movement of the storm.

SEVEN

Cassidy's first action on reaching the chartroom was to plot *Lake Taipa*'s position. That done, he looked at the barograph trace: pressure had fallen since he'd last read it at 1800. He jotted down the reading, applied the diurnal variation and other corrections. It was three millibars below the normal mean for the time of year. That would not have worried him unduly but for *Lake Taipa*'s storm report. He knew from long experience in the Indian Ocean that a fall of three millibars was a warning of the proximity of a tropical storm. But he found it difficult to believe that *Lake Taipa*'s observations indicated a cyclone. More likely a localized storm, he decided. He had two good reasons for this: cyclones north of Madagascar were extremely rare in September – he had never experienced one in that month – and, as a general rule, they originated between latitudes 7° and 15° South, whereas *Lake Taipa* was in 4° South. Nevertheless, if that ship was recording winds of force six to seven, a barometer reading five millibars below normal, and a pronounced easterly swell, her master had very good reason to believe that a storm centre was approximately two hundred miles to the east of his ship.

Head in hand, Cassidy leant over the chart-table doing some hard thinking. In the southern hemisphere the track of a cyclone was usually west-south-west, curving to the south and, later, recurving to the south-east. Initially it would travel at from ten to fifteen knots, its speed increasing the further south it went. In his twenty years in those waters he had been in or close to a number of cyclones and the laws of revolving storms were well known to him. But so were the exceptions: notably, tropical storms sometimes failed to curve to the south and south-west, obstinately holding to a westerly course. Until more radio reports came in from ships in the disturbed area he would be in the dark. *Lake Taipa*'s master had done the prudent thing: steaming on an easterly course at eighteen knots towards a suspected cyclone travelling on a westerly one at ten to fifteen, gave a speed of approach of about thirty knots. That meant *Lake Taipa* could have been in the storm centre within seven hours if avoiding action had not been taken.

Cassidy considered other facts, made more assumptions and calculations: *Lake Taipa* was ninety-five miles to the north-east. That put the storm centre about three hundred miles east-north-east of *Sunglow*. With the coaster's ten knots and the cyclone's fifteen, the speed of approach was twenty-five knots. If *Sunglow* held her course, and the cyclone behaved normally, they'd meet within twelve hours. If it behaved abnormally, held to a westerly course, it would pass about sixty miles north of the ship. That would be too close. But he hadn't enough information yet to make a decision. If the storm reported by *Lake Taipa* was confirmed as a cyclone, and its path became known, he would be able to decide on a course of action. He went back to the bridge. 'There should be more storm reports soon,' he told Obudo. 'When we get them we'll be knowing what it is we have to deal with.' He paused. The second mate could hear the heavy breathing of the older man. 'In the meantime, tell Mbolwo I want him.'

'Aye, aye, sir.' The second mate picked up a phone, spoke into it. Soon afterwards Mbolwo came to the bridge.

'Tell Mr Pascal I won't be down to dinner. Bring up something on a tray at seven-thirty. And my compliments to Mr Scalatti. All awnings to be furled immediately.'

With a quiet 'yes, sir,' Mbolwo disappeared.

Strange, thought Obudo, how the old man says 'something on a tray', and Mbolwo always knows what he wants.

Cassidy went across to the wing of the bridge. It was an hour after sunset and the night sky was dark. Close ranks of cloud blackened the night, shutting out the stars. The sea was calm, the atmosphere still and windless, the only sounds the muted throb of the diesel, the lap of water along the side, and the creaking of the hull as the ship responded to the swell.

He sniffed the night air as though that might tell him something. For the Holy Mother's sake, he thought, let *Lake Taipa*'s master be wrong. With apprehension he thought of the passengers. How would that odd assortment of humanity stand up to a cyclone in a small ship?

At eight o'clock Scalatti came to the bridge to relieve the second mate. Cassidy told him of *Lake Taipa*'s report.

'I'll be staying up here for the time being, Mr Scalatti.

You'll find me in the chartroom. Sure, and there should be more reports soon.'

Cassidy was right. He'd not been in the chartroom long when the radio alarm sounded. He switched on. It was *Lake Taipa* reporting again to Port Louis and Mahé. As she steamed to the north-east the wind had eased to force six, the barometric pressure remained unchanged, and the direction of the swell was now east-south-east. Cassidy was not surprised. In the two hours since *Lake Taipa* had last reported she'd been drawing clear of the disturbed area. He envied her master the eighteen knots at his disposal.

During the next hour or so two more ships reported falling barometers, shifts of wind and other indications of unusual weather. The ships concerned appeared to be east of the disturbance and thus safely in its wake.

At 2200, Port Louis and Mahé re-broadcast a summary of the reports, warning shipping that an area of unusually low pressure, cyclonic in character, existed in approximately 4° South: 52° East, and would probably move in a westerly to south-westerly direction. There was not as yet, concluded the message, sufficient information on which any more specific predictions could reasonably be based.

'Holy St Patrick!' Cassidy muttered. 'It's the specific predictions we're needing. "Probably" is not enough.'

The problem for him was a difficult one. *Sunglow* was at best a twelve knot ship; in bad weather nothing like that speed would be possible. That severely limited any chance of keeping clear of the disturbance unless he knew, reasonably soon, the direction in which it was moving. On the chart he plotted the options open to him. Option one – alter course to the north-east and increase to twelve knots? That would take *Sunglow* north of the cyclone, and about ninety to ninety-five miles from its storm centre at 0600, the time of nearest approach *if* the cyclone behaved normally. If it did not, and held a westerly course, the storm centre would be seventy to seventy-five miles distant at 0600. That would be uncomfortably close. Advantage – in either event the ship would be in the navigable semi-circle, that was the safe half of the revolving storm. Disadvantage – altering to the north-east would increase the distance to the Amirante Islands by about eighty miles.

Option two – alter course to the south-east and increase to twelve knots. That would take *Sunglow* south of the cyclone and about ninety miles from the storm centre at 0600, the time of nearest approach – but again, only if the cyclone behaved normally. If it did not, and held a westerly course, the storm centre would be about 125 miles distant at 0600. Advantages – distances from the storm centre greater, and to the Amirantes less, than on a north-easterly heading. Disadvantage – the ship could find herself in the dangerous semi-circle, the most difficult half of the disturbance.

He decided that unless specific information about the course of the storm was forthcoming soon, he would have to assume its behaviour to be normal. While it was important to keep as far from its centre as possible, it was even more important to avoid the dangerous semi-circle. That would mean altering to the north-east. He looked at the barograph. The pressure had continued to fall. He steadied himself against a sudden lurch of the ship and realized that *Sunglow*'s movements were becoming more lively. He was under no illusions: each hour brought the cyclonic disturbance twenty-five miles closer. The chartroom clock showed twenty minutes past ten. Time, he knew, was not on his side.

During the next half hour wind and sea and the easterly swell increased steadily. Ahead of the ship the moon shone fitfully through banks of fast moving cloud. Against a darkened background of sea and sky, *Sunglow* lifted and plunged, her bows throwing up sheets of spray which blew back across the foredeck. It's later than I've been thinking, Cassidy told himself. He went to the centre of the bridge. The dim shape of the Italian showed up near the man at the wheel.

'Alter course to the north-east, Mr Scalatti,' Cassidy ordered. With the ship already making heavy weather of sea and swell, he'd decided against increasing speed.

After the alteration of course he told Scalatti to go round the ship with the bosun. 'See that everything on the upper deck is properly lashed and secured. Have an eye to the hatch covers. Check the lashings on those fuel drums on the port side forward. Take a couple of seamen with you. Be sharp about it. There's heavy weather coming, Mr Scalatti.'

When the mate had gone Cassidy sent for Kumar Gupta, the chief engineer. Gupta, a Bengali who'd been with him for many years, was soon on the bridge. Cassidy told him what was happening. 'Make sure that everything's secure in the engineroom, Chief. I'm hoping we'll be keeping clear of the worst of it, but it's better to be cautious.'

'A cyclone here? In September, Captain?' The pitch of Gupta's voice rose. 'Very strange.'

'Indeed, and it is, Chief. But there's been a strange change in the weather. Look for yourself. I don't like the feel of things.'

Some time later Port Louis reported that it was still not possible to predict accurately the path the cyclonic disturbance would take. Ships' reports most recently received, went on the Port Louis message, confirmed that the disturbance was a cyclone. All ships in the area were warned to take the necessary precautions.

When Said Obudo came to the bridge to take over the watch at midnight, Cassidy sent him down to see how Scalatti was getting on.

Obudo was soon back to make his report; he found the Captain in the chartroom. 'The mate says everything's okay on deck, sir. No need to worry.'

Hunched over the chart-table, the Captain's big body seemed to fill the small room. 'Have they not finished the job then?' he asked, measuring on the chart with dividers.

'Yes, sir.'

'Where is Mr Scalatti?'

'In his cabin, sir.'

Cassidy looked up, frowned. 'Doing what?'

'He's turned in, sir.'

Obudo saw the Captain's lips snap shut so that the moustache and beard became one. It was a well-known and much feared signal. The second mate waited for the explosion.

'Has he then?' To Obudo, the Captain's voice sounded like emery paper on a rough surface. 'You'll be telling him, Mr Obudo, that he will report to me on the bridge *at once*, d'you understand?'

'Aye, aye, sir.' The young Swahili made off as fast as he could.

Scalatti came to the wheelhouse some time after Obudo had returned from delivering the message.

'You want to see me, Captain?' asked the Italian, speaking to the dark shape by the binnacle.

'That I do. Follow me.' Cassidy led the way to the chartroom. There he stood against the port door, wedged between chart-table and settee. Scalatti faced him, a hand on the chart-table to steady himself, his grubby T-shirt and crumpled shorts curiously unsuited to the weather.

'Now Mr Scalatti, you will explain why you had the bloody impertinence to turn in before reporting to me that you'd seen to things on deck.'

Scalatti looked at the big Irishman with narrowed, hostile eyes. 'The things you told me to do were finished,

66

Captain. Everything okay. So not necessary to report. Anyway, I send you message by second mate.'

Cassidy thrust his bearded chin downwards at the Italian. 'Not necessary to report.' He ground out the words. '*You* sent *me* a message? Who the bloody hell d'you think you are, Mr Scalatti?' He stopped for a moment, eyes liquid with anger. 'Now you be listening to this – you know damn well that it was your duty to come back to the bridge and report to me. And don't you be forgetting that in future. Now get below.'

The muscles of Scalatti's face twitched and flexed, and the dark eyes gleamed with such ferocity that Cassidy thought the Italian might do something violent. But Scalatti did no more than shake his head before disappearing into the wind-swept night. For a moment Cassidy regretted the lack of violence – but only for a moment. Earlier in his life at sea he had killed a man in a fight. Gentle by nature in spite of his great strength, he had never been able to shed the sense of guilt. He had not begun the fight, and the man's death had been put down to misadventure; but the sense of guilt remained.

EIGHT

With the weather growing steadily worse, Cassidy once again checked the barometer. It had fallen five millibars below normal. During gusts the wind was reaching gale force, building up a confused sea through which *Sunglow* lurched and rolled, shipping broken water which foamed and cascaded down the well-deck, the wind screeching through the rigging and rattling the bridge windows. At times when she rode a big sea her propeller would come clear of the water and the engine would race, causing the whole ship to vibrate excessively.

Gaston Pascal came to the bridge to report that most of the passengers had gathered in the lounge. The others, suffering from seasickness he supposed, had gone to their cabins.

'We've had to stack and lash the lounge furniture. The passengers look worried. Frightened, I'm sure. They're huddled in the corners. That way they are not thrown about so much.'

'They're not showing panic, Gaston?'

'No, Captain. Just fear. The naval man, Commander Rollo, is helping things along. No more than an unseasonable gale, he's saying. Uncomfortable, of course, but nothing to worry about. That's what he's telling them.'

'Aye, and that's good. But they must go to their cabins, Gaston. It's safer for them there. Not so liable to be thrown about by the motion once they're bedded down. Tell them that's my orders. But use your tact.'

The chief steward looked through the bridge windows into the black, restless night. A white crest showed up in the darkness on the starboard beam, high above the ship, its advance menacing her as she slid sideways down the slope of the sea. To Pascal, the invisible wave beneath the crest seemed about to break over the ship, and fear gripped him. *Sunglow* rolled to port, and was lifted high by the advancing sea. Buffeted by its crest, she rolled to starboard and began a sideways lurch into the trough below.

'Like a roller coaster,' said Pascal, not wanting Cassidy to know that he was afraid. He had to raise his voice against the noise of the wind. All he could see of the Captain was the dark bulk beside him.

'Sure, and she's a fine seaboat, Gaston. A great little lady with the seas.' Cassidy's deep voice was comforting.

'D'you think the gale will last, Captain?'

'Not too long. We're on a north-easterly heading. We should be drawing away from it.'

'It's a cyclone, is it not?'

'It is that, Gaston. But don't be using the word in front of the passengers. Tell them it's a tropical storm – *if* they ask. Now get back along there. See they go to their cabins.'

It became apparent to Cassidy that *Sunglow* was not drawing away from the storm. The south-easterly wind was now holding steady. Earlier it had shown signs of backing; that had warned him that *Sunglow* was heading for the dangerous semi-circle. That the wind should now hold steady, indicated that the ship was directly in the path of the storm. So where, approximately, was its centre? He faced the wind, recalled the rule for the southern hemisphere . . . *if the observer faces the wind the storm centre will be nine to eleven points on his left hand when it is about two hundred miles distant . . . the nearer the storm centre, the nearer will the displacement of the wind be to eight points.*

That put the storm centre to the north-east. Directly ahead of *Sunglow* on her present course. Was it moving west-sou-west or holding to a westerly path? The answer was of vital importance. Cassidy went to the chartroom, checked the original position of the storm as reported by *Lake Taipa* shortly before eight o'clock that night, took into account the probable speed of advance of both *Sunglow* and the cyclone since that time, and plotted his estimate of the bearing and distance of the storm centre. It was, he reckoned, north-east, distant 150 to 160 miles. That meant the storm was not heading west-south-west as he'd hoped it would, but west. If he tried to go south of it now, the ship would steam into the dangerous semi-circle. That involved the risk of being sucked into the storm centre. He had to go north.

There was no chance of avoiding the cyclone – there never really had been with *Sunglow*'s limited speed – but at least he could make sure the ship would be in the navigable half of the storm, clear of its centre. To do that he'd have to steer about eight points to port of the present course. He

69

gave the order for port wheel. *Sunglow* came round slowly until the seas were astern, lifting and launching her forward, their white crests racing past in the darkness, leaving her to sink back into the valleys between. When the wind came full on the port quarter, Cassidy went to the steering compass, spoke to the Swahili at the wheel. 'What's her heading now, Achmed?'

'Nor-west by west, sir.'

'Good. Steady her on nor-west.' He patted the young man's shoulder. 'It's a fine job you're doing, Achmed. Takes a good man to hold a small ship on course in this weather.' He'd said that because he knew encouragement helped overcome fear, and in the brown face, illuminated dimly by the light of the binnacle, he'd seen fear.

A heavy squall swept over the ship driving swathes of rain against the bridge windows, reinforcing the blanket of darkness under scudding clouds. Though little could be seen, the gusting of the wind, the slap and wash of the sea, the corkscrewing motion of the ship, the vibrations when the engine raced, the shudder when a sea broke inboard, the squeaking and groaning of the super-structure – these were things Cassidy's senses could register.

He moved to the windward side of the bridge, gripped the coaming to steady himself against the gale, and saw in the green reflections of the starboard light the heaped seas coming up from astern, lumping as they met the swell.

Watching them, he visualized the cyclonic disturbance, the outer reaches of which had already caught up with *Sunglow*. It was a revolving storm, a great mass of disturbed air with a radius of several hundred miles, blowing clockwise at high speed round the storm centre, the area of low pressure – the eye of the storm. In the southern hemisphere the dangerous semi-circle was the southern half; the safe, or navigable semi-circle, the northern. That was where *Sunglow*'s nor-westerly course would take her. He would know when they'd entered the navigable half because the wind would then begin to veer. There could be

70

no question of heaving-to, putting the ship head on to the weather, for she was too close to the path of the storm. The nor-westerly course was taking her away from that path; it must be held at all costs.

He ran a hand through wet, matted hair, shook his head as if that might in some way help. There would be violent weather in the time that lay ahead, but the ship would be clear of the disturbed area sometime in the coming afternoon – *if* all went well. There could be no rest for him until then.

He remembered something: his duty to report *Sunglow*'s position, course and speed, and the weather she was experiencing. He went to the chartroom, switched on the radio, called Port Louis and Mahé. They acknowledged, and he made his report. He went back to the bridge. Mbolwo was talking to the second mate.

'What would you be doing here, Mbolwo?'

'Coffee, sir. You like it in the chartroom?'

'Yes. Thank you.'

The tall Swahili moved away in the darkness. He came back a moment later. 'Anything else, sir?'

'Nothing, Mbolwo. Get some sleep.'

'Yes, sir.' Mbolwo knew as well as the Captain that sleep would be impossible.

The radio alarm sounded, Cassidy went to the wheelhouse. It was Port Louis giving the approximate position of the storm centre. 'It is moving to the west at between ten and fifteen knots,' advised the anonymous voice.

Some passengers had already fallen from their chairs when Pascal and a steward came to the lounge to secure loose furniture. The chairs and tables had begun to slide and topple as the weather deteriorated and several passengers were hurt, among them Mrs Bruckner, the Rev. Arnold Bliss and Mr Cawson, all of whom suffered bruises.

With the loose furniture stacked and lashed, passengers huddled together on settees in the corners of the lounge.

71

What little conversation there was tended to be monosyllabic. Each time the ship did something alarming, as often as not accompanied by the heavy thud of a sea breaking on deck, or its crest slapping against the lounge windows, there would be a sudden silence in which frightened glances were exchanged.

By two o'clock in the morning the weather had grown worse and *Sunglow*'s movements more extravagant. At one stage her stern failed to lift in time to prevent a sea breaking over it with such violence that the whole ship whipped alarmingly. The lights in the lounge flickered before going out. Almost immediately the muffled beat of the diesel fell away, its vibrations ceased, and only the splash and roar of the sea, and the unending shriek of the wind remained.

The silence in the lounge was broken by the frightened cry of a woman. 'Oh no. For God's sake *no*.'

A male voice followed: 'It is not goot to stop the engine at this time.' The guttural accent identified Mr Bruckner.

'Can't somebody do something? We can't just sit here in the dark.' There was a suggestion of hysteria in Sandra Carter's voice.

Dean Carter said, 'Okay, honey. I'll go get a torch.'

'Oh my God! Why should this happen to us?' Mrs Kitson's voice was pitched higher than usual. Jim, sitting on a settee opposite her, felt helpless and inadequate. He should do something to help her, but what? He was scared, too. Really scared now that the lights had gone out and the engine no longer turned.

The Rev. Arnold Bliss said, 'Ladies and gentlemen, I would like to lead you in prayer.'

'Cor blimey. Come to that 'as it? Expect him to send a bleedin' lifeboat?' The identity of the hoarse voice was unmistakable.

An anonymous laugh from the darkness was muffled by the crash of a sea breaking over the ship.

'Yes, I think a prayer would be a very good thing.' The quiet, authoritative voice was Mrs Clutterbutt's.

'Whatever else you do, keep calm,' advised Commander Rollo. 'I'm going to the bridge. When I know what has happened, I'll let you know.'

The sound of the commander leaving the lounge, banging into something in the dark, muttering a faint 'damn', was followed by the Rev. Bliss's voice raised against the outside noises of the storm: 'Oh Lord, Almighty God, who orders the universe and controls the raging seas, we pray that you will grant Thy Almighty protection to us Thy humble servants, and to the ship in which we sail, in this time of peril from the sea. Deliver us safely, O Lord, to our destinations that we may praise and glorify Thy Holy name. Amen.'

A chorus of *amens* followed.

Arnold Bliss sat back in the darkness, hoping that his recollection of the authorized prayer for use at sea was approximately correct. He was worrying about this when Mrs Clutterbutt said, 'Thank you so much. That was a beautiful prayer. I'm sure we all feel better for it.'

There were scattered *hear-hears*.

Mrs Clutterbutt's fear was mixed with a sense of guilt. But for her insistence, Jim would not be in the ship. Before the lights had gone out she'd seen him looking tense, fearful questions in his eyes, though he smiled bravely. My poor darling Jim, she thought, what have I done to you? He was so young, his whole life ahead of him, and this had to happen.

It was Rollo's first visit to the bridge. Traversing the unfamiliar route in darkness, holding on and bracing himself as best he could against the violent and unpredictable movements of the ship, he experienced difficulty in finding his way. Once on the bridge the shriek of the wind, *Sunglow*'s gyrations, the blank wall of darkness, the rain lashing at the windows, all conspired to conceal the Captain. Rollo had to call 'Captain' several times before a torch beam was turned on him.

'Ah, it's you, Commander. What is it then?'

'Sorry to trouble you at a time like this, Captain, but it would help if I could tell the passengers why the engine has stopped?' Rollo had to shout to be heard.

Cassidy put a hand on his shoulder, led him to the chartroom. 'The automatic throttle control has fractured. That stopped the engine. The electric generator drive is off the main engine when we're at sea.' The emergency seemed to have robbed Cassidy of some of his Irish accent. 'That's why there's no lights. They'll be switching on to the auxiliary generator shortly. The lights will come on then.'

'I see. What is the automatic throttle control? Something new since my time I fancy?'

'It prevents the propeller from racing. Not entirely, but it reduces it. They're busy welding the broken part. Difficult in this weather.'

They went back to the bridge where gale-driven rain battered and buffeted the windows while the moon, showing briefly through a break in the clouds, turned spume and spray into veils of liquid silver. Looking through a clear-glass screen, Rollo saw great seas racing up to the ship, lifting it high, thrusting it down-wind as they passed, their surface streaked with white lines of foam. When the ship sank back into the valleys, he had the impression that she was moving astern. He knew that was because the gale was blowing the surface of the sea faster than the ship was moving, but the impression remained.

'Cyclone, isn't it?' he shouted.

Cassidy hesitated. 'Yes. Better not use the word, Commander. It's a frightening one for landfolk.'

Rollo nodded in the darkness. 'I know. Suspected it was a cyclone. I told them it was a tropical storm, nothing to worry about. They accepted that at first. Not now I'm afraid. Any real danger d'you think?'

'A lot less than if we'd got into the southern half. We're

in the navigable semi-circle. Wind's just beginning to veer. We'll follow round.'

Rollo's involuntary laugh was more relief than humour. 'I gather you know your laws of revolving storms, Captain.'

'And a poor day it would be if I didn't, Commander. I've been sailing in these waters for twenty years.'

'I can imagine what that means. I spent a short time on the East African coast in World War Two. We got near a cyclone once. In the Mozambique Channel. That was in a cruiser. The navigator rang down twenty-five knots. We were soon clear of it.'

Cassidy said, '*Sunglow* has twelve knots at best. With the wind on the quarter she'll maybe manage six or seven in this weather.' With a note of defensive pride, he added, 'But she's a fine seaboat, Commander. You can tell the passengers that. And do be trying to get them to their cabins.'

'I will do my best. Thank you for your confidences.' Rollo hesitated, anxious to avoid any show of emotion. 'And good luck, Captain. I'll get back to the others now.'

The two men had made conversation possible by shouting into each other's ears.

Rollo had returned to the lounge and begun telling its occupants of his talk with the Captain, when the lights came on. Soon afterwards the familiar thump of the diesel engine and its vibrations reached the saloon.

Henry Atkins, the blue yachting cap firmly on his head, called out, 'Come on folks. Round the bay for five bob.' The subdued laughter that provoked was followed by the arrival of the chief steward who made another appeal to passengers to observe the Captain's wishes and go to their cabins. 'It's well past two o'clock. You'll be more comfortable there – and you must be needing sleep.'

Rollo said, 'Now that we're under way again, I think that's the most sensible thing to do.' He turned to the doctor. 'Let's go below, Mark, and get some shut-eye.'

Mark Summers knew that the chances of sleep were remote, but he nodded agreement and the two men left the lounge. Others soon followed: reluctant, still frightened, but partially reassured by the switching on of the lights, the sound and feel of the ship's engines, and the example set by Rollo and the doctor.

When Scalatti got to his cabin at midnight he did not undress. The violence of the storm, its effect upon *Sunglow*, frightened him. He'd been in bad storms in big ships, but never in anything as small as the coaster. So he decided not to attempt sleep. If anything went wrong he didn't want to be asleep, to wake up trapped in the cabin. So he sat on the half settee, jammed between the cabin bulkhead and the wardrobe, the electric light on, his thoughts alternating between what he would do if the ship turned over, the bitter humiliation inflicted upon him in the chartroom by Cassidy, and regret that circumstances had landed him in this time-worn coaster which seemed to be making such heavy weather of a gale. The only comforting thought was his arrangement with Ali Patel. If the ship survived the storm – he was anything but optimistic about that – he'd be able to carry out his side of the bargain within the next two or three weeks. Fifty thousand US dollars would make all sorts of things possible. He'd fly back to Italy as soon as he got the money, leave the sea and buy a small store in a country village.

Most important of all, he would be able to take Maria away from their wretched little flat. It was in a ramshackle, foul smelling old building on the Via Marinella, in the heart of Naples slumland. Maria would like to be in the country. The clean air would be good for her lung trouble, and a country doctor would do more for her than an overburdened Neapolitan clinic could.

The stranding of *Sunglow* on a reef would serve another purpose. He'd get his own back on Cassidy. The loss of a ship usually ended a sea captain's career. Cassidy wouldn't get another command. He was too old, too many ships were being laid up.

Scalatti's thoughts went back to Maria. With all those dollars he'd be able to get her some really nice clothes. She had been a handsome young woman. Living in the country, away from the smog, grime and diesel fumes of the city, good health would return and bring back her looks. She was still only thirty-five. She could never have children, but that didn't matter. What was important was the chance for her of a better life. To make that possible, he'd used the savings of three long voyages to purchase a First Mate's certificate in Hong Kong; he'd been a seaman in big ships for many years, knew enough about officers' duties to get away with things. Not astro-nav and all that technical stuff, but enough of the rest of it to get by. He'd only had the certificate for a few months before he went sick in Mombasa, so there hadn't been time to save much money. His plan had been to save regularly for a few years, sending money to Maria until there was enough to make the move into the country. That wouldn't be necessary now.

This agreeable train of thought was brought to an end by the sudden impact of a big sea striking the ship somewhere aft. The hull whipped and shuddered, the cabin lights flickered before going off, and the main engines stopped.

Scalatti froze with terror. The ship would drift, turn beam on to the seas and capsize. Without power, the coaster could never survive in that weather. He fell on his knees beside the settee and began praying, recalling as best he could the prayers he'd learnt at his mother's knee.

The radio alarm sounded while Cassidy was drinking the coffee Mbolwo had brought him in a flask. He switched on the receiver: 'MAYDAY, MAYDAY, MAYDAY, this is *Solidaro* calling all ships and shore stations.' Without waiting for an acknowledgement the urgent, foreign voice continued, 'My position is . . .' The signal faltered and crackled before petering out. Almost immediately the air became alive: acknowledgements came from the naval station at Diego Garcia, from radio stations at Port Louis, Diego Suarez, Mombasa and Mahé, and from several ships at sea; all requested *Solidaro* to give her position. But there was no reply. The requests were repeated at regular intervals after that, but no word came from her.

Cassidy thought of her crew. Poor devils. The ship had probably been caught in the eye of the storm. Foundered suddenly. A capsize perhaps. In his mind's eye he saw a ship engulfed by the great, gale-torn seas. But if she had been in the disturbed area why hadn't she reported her position and the weather she was experiencing? It was mandatory for the master of a ship to do so. He realized he was assuming that *Solidaro* was somewhere in the cyclonic area. Perhaps she wasn't. Perhaps she'd met with some other disaster.

In the early hours of morning the wind began to shift slowly from south-east towards south. It was the veering Cassidy had been waiting for. It told him the ship was approaching the navigable semi-circle. A lingering doubt, a fear that his earlier predictions might have been incorrect, was dispelled. He altered *Sunglow*'s course to north-west-by-north. As the wind veered over the next twelve hours, the direction from which it came would move clockwise round the compass. *Sunglow*'s course would be altered in sympathy with the shifts of wind, so that it was always blowing on her port quarter while she was within the orbit of the storm.

Once clear of it, he would put her back on course for the Amirantes. But he had no illusions. For some time before that happened the ship would continue her struggle with gale force winds and huge, confused seas. It would be well into the coming afternoon before that ceased.

Scalatti came up at four o'clock in the morning to take over the watch from Obudo. Gaston Pascal had suggested that he should. 'I know the old man likes to keep the morning

78

watch,' he'd said. 'But he's been on the bridge now for more than twenty-four hours. He must have a rest.'

Scalatti agreed. In any case he'd rather be on the bridge than in the cabin where he'd felt blind and trapped, thrown about by the violent buffeting, terrified by the crash and thump of the seas, and the sickening noise and feel of the propeller racing.

Cassidy had no intention of leaving the bridge during the next four hours, nor of sharing it with the Italian, so he told him to go below. 'If necessary I'll send for you. In the meantime I'll look after things here.'

Scalatti, as little inclined as the Captain to share the bridge with him for four hours, but hurt by the rejection of his offer, and sensing an innuendo of contempt, decided he should do something about it. 'Maybe with no sleep you cannot manage, Captain.' His voice rasped like a file.

'That's a risk I'll take, Mister Scalatti. Thank you for your offer.'

Since there wasn't much he could say to that, Scalatti left the bridge.

If anything the severity of the weather increased during the morning watch. At six o'clock *Sunglow*'s speed was reduced to between four and five knots and Cassidy put the bosun, Moses Kibusu, on the wheel. Running before the storm with wind and sea on the quarter, he feared that the ship might broach-to. Kibusu, a first class seaman, had been with him for many years. If anybody could prevent a broach-to it was this gnarled and portly Swahili.

Cyclones could not interfere with Mbolwo's routine and at 6.30 he had come to the bridge with coffee and an apple.

'I bring again in the flask, sir,' he apologized as he wedged it on the chartroom table. 'But the ship is not too still.' It was a masterly understatement.

Cassidy shook his head in disbelief. 'It's a true saint you

are, Mbolwo. The good Lord will reward you. Your cattle will multiply and your children will prosper.'

Mbolwo grinned. He didn't know about the Blarney Stone, but he was no stranger to the Captain's way with words.

NINE

Daylight when it came revealed a desolate scene. The sky a dark mass of cloud racing with the storm, beneath it steep confused seas, white marbled with foam, liquid volcanoes rearing up alongside the ship, their pinnacles breaking onto it, the air filled with flying spindrift, endless white plumes in pursuit of the wind. At times visibility was reduced to nothing.

During the hours which followed there was little change. Cassidy, alone on the bridge but for the helmsman, endured the violence with a mixture of stoicism and anxiety, his head aching, a persistent buzzing in his ears, his vision blurred with fatigue. At eight o'clock Obudo had come to the bridge to take the watch. Cassidy was glad to have the second mate with him, but there was no possibility of rest. *Sunglow* was a small ship caught in a storm of exceptional ferocity, and though he was proud of the way she rode it, danger could never be far away. A broach-to, another and perhaps more devastating sea over the stern: these things could bring sudden disaster.

He sent the second mate off to check the extent of the damage the big sea had caused. Obudo came back to report that the starboard lifeboat had been lifted from its chocks and swept overboard, two engineroom ventilators had been smashed, a gravity tank had been wrenched from its seating and lost overboard, guardrails round the stern had broken and buckled. From the bridge Cassidy could see that the funnel and upperworks round it were coated with salt-rime as if some giant had gone berserk with an outsize whitewash brush.

He had sighed, shaken his head despondently, when he learnt the full extent of the damage. Repairs would cost money, and so would extra steaming time. The cyclone was responsible for a long detour. He estimated the increased distance to be 150 miles, the time factor at least another day, for in that weather speed was much reduced.

It could, he decided, have been worse. He thought of *Solidaro*. In all probability she'd foundered somewhere in the storm. Whatever the disaster, it must have been sudden; so sudden, so devastating, that there had been no time to complete the MAYDAY.

The wind had continued to veer over the last eight hours. Blowing now from south-south-west, it came with such fury that it was not possible to stand in the wings of the bridge facing it. Cassidy estimated its force to be twelve on the Beaufort scale – that was close to seventy miles an hour. With each shift of wind he had brought *Sunglow* round on to more northerly courses, always keeping the wind on the port quarter. Now her course was due north.

By eight o'clock that morning the barograph had recorded its lowest reading – 1019 millibars, six below the normal mean. Since then it had registered a slight rise. Cassidy's estimates had placed the ship within sixty-five to seventy miles due north of the storm centre at that time. As the cyclone moved away to the west, each hour would increase its distance from the ship. Sometime in the afternoon the worst of the weather should be well to the west. For that prospect he was grateful.

By three o'clock in the afternoon, conditions, though still bad, had improved sufficiently for course to be set for the Amirantes. The sky was too heavy with cloud for sun-sights, but by dead reckoning he put the ship 270 miles north-west of the islands. He estimated that the storm centre was now 150 miles to the south-west. The wind was blowing at force seven, the sea continued to be rough, but the barograph trace was rising.

After the alteration of course he saw a few passengers venture onto the sundeck, Mrs Clutterbutt among them. It pleased him. He knew they'd had a bad time. The last thing they would have bargained for was a cyclone when deciding on the adventure cruise. They would blame the Capricorn Company, they would blame him. That was human nature. But no one was to blame. A cyclone in that part of the Indian Ocean in September was almost unknown. In the chartroom he checked with *Admiralty Sailing Directions* – two cyclones had occurred in September in those waters in the last hundred years. 'Holy Mother O' God,' he said aloud. 'And we have to be the third.' He put the book back in the rack and went out to the bridge.

Despite improving weather there were a number of absentees from dinner that night, seasickness and lack of sleep having taken their toll. Those absent included Miss McLachlan, the Cawsons, the Rev. Bliss, and the Bruckners. Mrs Cawson had spent most of the day sleeping off the valium with which she had liberally dosed herself during the storm; Miss McLachlan, in spite of Dr Summers' exhortations, had not left her cabin since shortly after leaving Mombasa; the Bruckners, for their part, insisted that it was still too rough to eat below. Instead, they ordered sandwiches in the lounge, something the chief steward did his best to discourage, but Mrs Bruckner was adamant. 'You vont that vee should starf?' she protested.

'I fear I have no appetite,' was Arnold Bliss's humble admission to the steward who tried to interest him in lunch.

As on the previous night, Cassidy did not appear. In conveying his apologies to those at dinner, the chief steward remarked that the Captain liked to be on the bridge when the weather was not too good. It was the seaman's instinct, he'd explained.

'Not too good – you must be joking,' observed Henry Atkins.

The meal itself was a scratch affair; fiddles on moistened table-cloths to stop crockery sliding; stewards battling to remain on their feet and retain their loads; and an occasional crashing of pots and pans in the serving pantry, followed by expletives in Swahili and the patois of the Seychelles.

The rhythm of *Sunglow*'s pitching and rolling continued to be interrupted at times by the thump of a wave crest striking the ship, followed by a slap of sea against the saloon portholes. It was then that passengers would look at each other in alarm and shake their heads, fearing that another night of violence might lie ahead.

'Should it go on doing this?' Mrs Kitson's limpid eyes appealed to Commander Rollo who sat opposite her.

'We are most certainly over the worst. But this is a small, slow ship. It takes time to get clear. These storms often affect large areas.'

She smiled at him gratefully. 'Oh good. How useful to have a sailor at the table.'

'A naval officer.' The abrupt correction came from Mrs Clutterbutt who was sitting next to Rollo.

'Aren't naval officers sailors, Commander?' Mrs Kitson made a moué at Rollo.

'Yes,' he said distantly. 'They are. But I daresay "naval officer" is more appropriate. It's really quite unimportant.'

'I see. But don't you think . . .?'

A steep roll and pitch to port, as if *Sunglow* had missed her step, was followed by a crash of pots and pans in the serving pantry. A steward lost his footing and the food he was carrying ended up on Dr Summers' shoulder. As *Sunglow* came upright and began to roll to starboard, a sea struck the side of the saloon, a wall of water momentarily obscured the portholes, the ship trembled and faltered before continuing its roll.

83

'Oh my God!' The cry of alarm came from Mrs Van der Karst at the starboard table.

'Nothing to worry about,' the Commander called across to her. 'Just the top of a sea.'

'*You* should be worrying if a hot stew had come onto your lap,' complained Mrs Van der Karst. With the assistance of an embarrassed steward she began to mop up the damage.

'No good.' She looked despairingly at her husband. 'The new frock. It is ruined. I have to go to change.'

'So what,' said Van der Karst. 'It's not the end of the world.'

That began the exodus. Well before nine o'clock the saloon had emptied, most of the passengers determined to catch up on lost sleep.

The following morning brought good weather, the sun shining down from a clear sky, the only remnant of the storm a confused swell which had movement without direction. What little wind there was came from the south-east and did no more than ruffle the surface of the sea. Most of the passengers appeared at breakfast, the cheerful atmosphere in the saloon now far removed from the anxieties of the last two days when impending disaster had hung over the ship.

Abandoning his normal routine, Cassidy came to the saloon for breakfast. This made the occasion even more notable for passengers, most of whom were there when he arrived. Half way through the meal Dr Summers rapped on the table, the buzz of conversation ceased, and Cassidy rose to address them.

'Ladies and gentlemen,' came from the big bearded figure. 'It's a difficult time, I fear, that you've been having in the last couple of days.' He paused, looked round the saloon with fatigue ringed eyes. 'But its happy indeed, I am, that the weather has improved.' *Hear-hears* greeted this. 'A very unusual and, indeed, a most worrying experience you have had. A cyclone at this time of year, in the doldrums, so close to the Equator, happens perhaps once in a hundred years. If there had been more warning we could have steamed round it, but the storm originated not far from us. By the time the first radio report came, well – it was too late then, to do more than keep away from the storm centre.' He paused, smiled. 'Fine it was the way you folk conducted yourselves. That was greatly to be admired.' He nodded several times as if confirming some fundamental truth. 'And the ship – the ship,' he repeated proudly. 'Did she not behave like the great little lady she is?' He looked up, as if fearful of disagreement. 'Though she suffered some damage, I fear.' Hastily, he added, 'But nothing that can interfere with her sea-worthiness.'

Cheerful *hear-hears* were mixed with exclamations of concern. The only dissonant note was Mrs Bruckner's. 'In the storm, the water is coming with leaks through the porthole.'

'Welsh water,' muttered Henry Atkins, patting his yachting cap more firmly onto his head.

Cassidy had been briefed by Gaston Pascal on the subject of Mrs Bruckner's porthole. 'I'm sorry about that, Madam,' he said. 'I understand the steward who had to check that portholes were properly secured was not permitted to enter your cabin. Your husband said he'd see to the porthole.'

'Naturally. It is not possible that the man should come in when I am not with my clothes. It is not goot. But the porthole . . .'

'Put a sock in it love.' Henry Atkins accompanied his interruption with a severe frown which silenced Mrs Bruckner.

Cassidy appeared not to have heard. 'We should sight the light on North Island, that's the northernmost of the Amirantes, about ten o'clock tonight. We'll head then for Eagle Islet, about fifteen miles further south. We'll lay off there until morning; go to an anchorage when daylight comes.' He was about to sit down when Mbolwo came into the saloon. The Swahili spoke to him in an undertone. Cassidy nodded, turned to the passengers at his table. 'Please excuse me,' he said. 'I have to go to the bridge.'

As he made his way up the staircase, followed by Mbolwo, Mrs Clutterbutt turned to Commander Rollo. 'Poor Captain Cassidy. He looks quite exhausted. Those deep rings under his eyes.'

The commander helped himself to another slice of toast. 'I imagine he's been on the bridge for most of the last twenty-four hours.'

'For most of the last thirty-six,' corrected Dr Summers. 'I offered him amphetamine tablets but he is rather uncomplimentary about that sort of thing.'

'Sensible fellow.' Rollo dabbed at his lips with a table napkin. 'I wonder what's taken him to the bridge.'

It was the first mate who'd sent the message to the Captain.

'What is it then?' Cassidy asked.

'Over there, Captain. On the port bow.' Scalatti pointed. 'A life-raft I think.'

Cassidy took binoculars from the rack, focused on the distant object. It was small, round and orange – visible only when it lifted on the swells.

'A life-raft it is, Mr Scalatti. A couple of miles away, I'd be saying. Tell Mr Obudo to make ready a skimmer for launching.'

Cassidy altered *Sunglow*'s course towards the life-raft. The coaster drew closer and a man in the canopy aperture could be seen waving.

Cassidy rang down *slow* on the engineroom telegraph. 'Keep the raft fine on the starboard bow,' he told the helmsman.

Before long, *Sunglow* had stopped to windward of the raft and a skimmer was lowered. Obudo and a seaman climbed down, the outboard engine was started, and the skimmer bumped and splashed its way across to the raft.

Alerted by the stopping of the ship's engines, passengers had gathered on the sundeck where the air buzzed with conversation and the click of cameras. The skimmer reached the raft and two figures could be seen being helped from it. The inflatable's engine burst into life again and soon it was heading back to *Sunglow* with the life-raft in tow. It came alongside and two men, haggard and unshaven, were helped up a rope ladder onto *Sunglow*'s after well-deck. The second mate and the Swahili seaman followed, and the skimmer and life-raft were hoisted on board.

On Cassidy's orders Scalatti rang down *full ahead*, and once again *Sunglow* made for the Amirantes.

The survivors were taken aft to the crew's quarters. The only accommodation available there was a four-berth cabin, already occupied by two of *Sunglow*'s crewmen.

Dr Summers attended the survivors. Both, he said, were suffering from shock and exposure but nothing that a day's rest and a few good meals wouldn't put right. Later, on Cassidy's instructions, the chief steward questioned them. They were, he reported, Nils Krol a Swede, and Luther Nelson, a West Indian, crewmen from a Liberian registered bulk carrier, the *Solidava*, on passage from Bombay to Baltimore via Cape Town. Their ship, Krol explained, had run into heavy weather. During the night, soon after encountering it, there had been an explosion and the ship had broken in two just forward of the bridge. Shortly before, he and Nelson had been sent to tighten lashings on some deck cargo near the foc'sle. They were doing this when the explosion occurred. That was about an hour after midnight. The afterpart of the ship had capsized and sunk almost immediately, but the forepart had remained afloat. When daylight came they realized they were probably the only survivors. Though the weather was improving, it was evident that the forepart of the ship could not remain afloat much longer. They took an inflatable life-raft from the racks under the foc'sle, launched it, jumped into the sea beside it and pulled themselves on board. Ten minutes later *Solidava*'s bow section sank. There were no provisions in the life-raft, no water, no flares and no emergency radio. They had drifted for two days, seen aircraft pass over, but, without flares, had been unable to attract attention.

Gaston Pascal reported these details to Cassidy who was in his cabin writing a report on the cyclone. 'The *Solidava*, you say.' He leant back in his chair, began to light a cigar. 'It must have been her MAYDAY we heard. I took it to be *Solidaro*.' He drew on the cigar. 'Did this man Krol have any theories about the explosion?'

'He thought it might have been in the tanks they'd been cleaning the day before. She'd carried bulk oil on the outward voyage. Gas fumes still in them, he said.'

Cassidy fondled his beard. 'She must have caught the tail of the cyclone. Strange that her master did not report his weather to Mahé or Port Louis. Did you ask Krol about that?'

The chief steward shook his head. 'No, Captain. Krol and Nelson were just crewmen. They didn't even know that the storm was a cyclone. But there was something Krol said. It could be the reason.'

'What was that, Gaston?'

'He said the captain and the mate had been drinking. Mexicans, he told me. They often had drinking sessions.'

Cassidy drew on his cigar, watched the chief steward with puzzled eyes. 'It's strange indeed, Gaston, the riff-raff these foreign registered ships have aboard these days. The sea is no place for them. It is too strong. It seeks out the weak and destroys them.' He shrugged. 'I'll have to give Mahé and Mombasa the news.'

The chief steward looked at the clipboard he was carrying. 'Well, I must get busy with making up the lists for the skimmers tomorrow.'

Cassidy took the cigar from his mouth, blew a smoke ring, watched it climb to the deck-head. 'Be sure to put like with like, Gaston. You know what I mean.'

The chief steward's dark face puckered in a smile. 'You mean, don't put Atkins and the Bruckner woman together. I'll do my best, Captain. It's not possible to please everyone.'

Cassidy sighed. 'They soon discover that one atoll is much like another, Gaston. Blue water, white beaches, coral reefs, waves breaking, coconut palms, casuarina trees, mangrove swamps, seabirds, turtles, creole labourers, fishermen, sometimes a white plantation manager. Sometimes no one – just the sea and the sky, the sand underfoot, and the hot sun above.' He shook his head, drew deeply on the cigar. 'It's the skimmer journeys that keeps them happy, Gaston. The scream of the engine, the sensation of speed over water, the bumping, the spray thrown back, shining in the sunlight, the snapshots to show to the folks at home – that's the real adventure for these landfolk.'

Cassidy in his more Celtic moods never failed to charm Gaston Pascal, whose French/Indian origins made him naively responsive to anything resembling romance.

'Ah, you describe it well, Captain. But imagine how different all those things must be from the lives our passengers lead, to the things they see. The cold grey skies, the busy cities, the traffic choked streets, the foul air they breathe. Our islands here must be Paradise to them.'

Cassidy's tired eyes managed a smile. 'Do they have cyclones in Paradise, then, Gaston?' He tipped the ash from his cigar. 'Now be along with you. I must see to that radio message. Then it's sleep I'm after.'

TEN

During the afternoon the south-easterly wind freshened, banks of cloud piled upon each other on the western horizon darkening the sky and bringing downpours of rain. Towards evening the sky cleared, the wind fell away, and *Sunglow*'s movements were again rhythmic and gentle. A spectacular sunset had drawn most of the passengers to the sundeck, their voices and laughter mingling with the fizz of syphons and clink of ice cubes in the nearby bar.

At the far end of the deck, Dr Summers and Commander Rollo were leaning against the rail, looking out to sea, chatting idly over whiskies and sodas. Dr Summers stopped in mid-sentence to say, 'Look out Dick! Your girl friend's approaching.'

'Hullo you two.' Mrs Kitson, smiling and incredibly chic for one so recently in a cyclone, joined them, glass in hand. The doctor said, 'You look fit.' The Commander, frowning apprehensively, was silent.

'I am,' she said. 'Frightfully fit. Have you seen the noticeboard? Most exciting.' She put a hand on Rollo's arm. 'We're in the same skimmer tomorrow, Commander. Isn't that marvellous? It should be such fun.'

'Are we really?' Rollo couldn't have sounded less enthusiastic. 'I haven't seen the board.'

'Nor have I,' said the doctor. 'Who have I drawn?'

Mrs Kitson's eyebrows arched mischievously. 'You, Dr Summers, are with our VIP – the fearsome Mrs C – *and* that nice young man, Jim Abernethy.'

The doctor turned to Rollo. 'You are a lucky devil, Dick. You always get the prettiest girl.'

The commander grunted something unintelligible.

Mrs Kitson tinkled with brief laughter. 'Oh, how sweet of you, doctor. But it is *you* who've got her. I kept that till last. Sandra Carter's in *your* boat – skimmer I mean. She's really lovely isn't she?' The ice in Mrs Kitson's empty glass rattled like a collection box.

The doctor took it from her. 'I'll get you the other half.' He made for the bar.

She moved along the rail, closer to Rollo. 'You were absolutely magnificent in that awful storm, Commander. It helped so much.' Her voice trailed into huskiness.

'I'm not quite sure what you're talking about,' he said. 'Unless you mean I didn't advertise my feelings. I was, of course, extremely frightened. One would have to be a half-wit not to have been.'

'Oh, you're so modest, Commander. So *typically* naval.'

Rollo looked at his watch. 'Hm. It's late. I must be off. Shower and change, you know.' He'd no sooner gone than a tall, slim figure came up beside her.

'Oh, Jim,' she cried. 'How lovely to see you. Isn't it a perfectly marvellous evening. So wonderful after that dreadful storm. Wasn't it too ghastly? Have you seen the noticeboard? You're in Skimmer Two, you know. With Dr Summers and the Carters. She's such a lovely person, isn't she?'

'I wish I was in your skimmer,' said Jim hoarsely. 'Much more fun.'

'You are sweet, Jim. I wish you were, too.'

'Can I get you a drink, Mrs Kitson?'

'Please call me Diana, Jim. Mrs Kitson makes me sound so awfully old. Thank you, but the doctor's getting me one.'

'Oh, I see,' he said sadly.

She touched his arm. 'I'd love to have a drink with you, Jim. I tell you what – let's meet here after dinner tonight. Shall we? At nine-thirty, say. Would you like that?'

'Yes. I would. Very much.'

Dr Summers arrived, carrying two glasses.

Jim said, 'I must go now.'

'Don't forget, Jim. Nine-thirty.'

'I won't forget, Diana.' He made for the lounge.

The doctor laughed. 'You leading him astray, Mrs Kitson?'

'Good heavens no. But do call me Diana, doctor. Mrs Kitson makes me sound so old.'

There was a knock on Scalatti's door. 'Yes. Okay,' he called out.

The door opened and a man in shorts and a singlet came into the cabin. He was deeply sun-tanned, his dark hair unkempt. The aggressive glint in his pale eyes, the flat nose and muscular body, suggested a pugilist. Several days growth of beard had done nothing to lessen the image. The Italian looked up in surprise. 'What do you want, Krol?'

Scalatti had met the *Solidava* survivors earlier in the day. He'd taken to Krol, if for no other reason than the Swedish seaman's colourful description of *Solidava*'s captain. 'Him?' Krol's pale eyes had narrowed. 'That bastard? Drunk Mexican shit. Captain Rodriquez – captain my arse.'

So instead of resenting the man's intrusion as he would normally have done, Scalatti – a man with strong opinions about ships' captains – pointed to the settee. 'Sit down. How you feel now? You and Nelson?'

'Okay. Not too bad. But this is not the trouble.'

'What is it then? Tell me.'

'The accommodation is no good. Cabin too small, not clean, four bunks. We are seamen. Why must we bunk with greasers? Also they are black men.'

Scalatti grinned. 'Your shipmate, Luther Nelson. He's a black man.'

Krol nodded. 'Yes. But he is a seaman. Also West Indian, not African. The messroom is dirty. Food no good. Plenty cockroaches. It is not right to treat survivors like this.'

'There is no other accommodation. The ship is small. You can see this for yourself.'

'Why not treat us same like passengers? The *Solidava* company will pay the price. I hear from the greasers that some of the two-berth passenger cabins have just one person. Why not possible for two passengers to share one cabin? This can make proper accommodation for me and Nelson. We are distressed seaman. The law says we must be treated properly. Also I have no clothes. Just this.' He looked down at his dirt stained singlet and shorts with a worried frown. 'How long before we are put ashore?'

Scalatti shook his head. 'Another seventeen days. Not possible to land you in the islands. Not allowed. And anyway, you can be there for some months before the next ship is coming. And that can be only a native schooner. Also, the chief steward says the Captain has radio orders that you stay on board until we are back to Mombasa.'

'For Chrissake You expect we must live so long like pigs. In the *Solidava* every crewman has own cabin and shower. Also proper lounge and messroom. And good food.'

Scalatti said nothing. The indications that the Swede was a sea lawyer had provoked an interesting train of thought.

'So,' Krol challenged. 'What is to do?'

'See the Captain,' said Scalatti. 'He is only man in ship who can do something. Make your complaint to him. I arrange it – for some time tomorrow. Okay? Also I arrange for chief steward to give you some clothes from the ship stores. He can make charge for this against your company.'

The Italian got up from his chair, went to the cupboard. From it he took a bottle of Martini and two glasses. He poured the Martini, passed a glass to Krol. 'Take this. Help forget your problem.'

Krol took a glass, looked at it doubtfully. 'Skol,' he said and gulped it.

Scalatti did the same. He refilled the glasses.

Krol said, 'The Captain? What sort of man?'

The Italian shrugged, held his glass to the light, squinted

at the vermouth. 'Irishman,' he said. 'Already old. Plenty bullshit. You will see.'

For some time after that they talked about ships and seaports, and women and drink, until Scalatti said, 'It is past nine. I must get some sleep now. The middle watch, you know.'

'Okay, okay.' Krol got up from the settee, stared at the Italian for a moment, unasked questions in his eyes. 'Thanks for the drink,' he said. 'Also for your help.'

He left the cabin.

About the time that Scalatti and Krol parted, passengers were gathering in the lounge for the briefing session. It was to be taken by Gaston Pascal who sat at a small table near the bar with clipboard and papers. Mrs Clutterbutt was a notable absentee, and Jim Abernethy, sitting in a corner with Henry Atkins, was wondering where his aunt was. It was unlike her to miss such an occasion. In fact Captain Cassidy was entertaining her in his day-cabin, where Mbolwo had brought coffee and liqueurs. During the afternoon Cassidy had sent her an invitation to take coffee with him after dinner: *I'll be giving you all the information – and more – that you'd be getting at the briefing*, he'd written, *so look forward to your company*.

Cassidy's sense of guilt had persuaded him to send the invitation. There had been a hiatus in the matter of Mrs Clutterbutt and her strange project. It was something which had quite gone out of his mind; pushed out, he supposed, by the more immediate problem of the cyclone.

The shadowy, rather illusory notion of searching for buried treasure on an unknown, unspecified island, in an area where there were literally hundreds of islands had, perhaps, been too easily displaced. But he liked and admired Mrs Clutterbutt and, notwithstanding scepticism about her project, his conscience was troubled by his neglect of what so concerned her.

Sunglow would, he now explained, anchor off Eagle Islet

soon after daybreak; he had a few letters for the people there and some stores; maybe copra would be loaded. It was a small settlement, only a handful of inhabitants. There would, he said, be an early breakfast, after which beach parties would leave the ship at 8.30.

'We hope to sail at eleven. That'll allow passengers time to look round and stretch their legs, you see.'

Mrs Clutterbutt eyed him thoughtfully. 'Will you be coming ashore, Captain?'

'No, Mrs C. It's not often that I do that. Too much to see to aboard. It's Said Obudo you'll be having in charge of your skimmer. He's a good seaman – a fine youngster. Your –' He checked himself. 'Young Abernethy is also in your party.'

Cassidy went on to explain that after Eagle Islet the ship would make for D'Arros and St Joseph Islands, twenty miles further south. 'You'll find them interesting,' he said. 'We'll anchor off D'Arros, put the skimmers in the water and they'll make for the St Joseph's Group, a few miles across the lagoon. There's half a dozen uninhabited islands in the Group, so it's the real thing you'll be seeing. We should reach D'Arros about lunch time. Passengers will have most of the afternoon to look around, swim and the like. There'll be a barbecue on the beach that night. *Sunglow* sails the next morning for Ile Desroches, another two or three hours of steaming. We'll spend a short time there, landing stores and mail and picking up any cargo that offers. There won't be time for beach landings, I'm afraid. After that it's a good run south towards Alphonse and François Islands – about ten hours of uninterrupted steaming. It'll be a nice change after the short runs.'

Mrs Clutterbutt raised her hands in mock despair. 'My dear Captain Cassidy, I cannot possibly remember all those names and times. But the programme sounds interesting. I really do look forward to it.' She paused, considered him with one of her disconcerting grey-eyed stares. 'And what about White Island?'

He drained his glass, looked into it as if seeking an answer there. 'Ah, and that's what I was coming to, Mrs C. It's on the run down to Alphonse and François Islands that you and meself will be getting together to talk of these things. François Island is about seven degrees south latitude. You'll remember that we don't have to look out for White Island until the ship is close to nine degrees south. There's more than time enough.'

'Yes, indeed. But there remains much to discuss, Captain. So I much look forward to that meeting.'

Jim Abernethy arrived on the sundeck for his appointment well before time, whereas Diana Kitson was half an hour late. He'd spent a miserable half hour wondering if she'd forgotten, or whether her absence was deliberate. At last she was there, touching his arm, saying, 'I'm most awfully sorry, Jim. Mr Pascal was telling me about the two sailors we picked up this morning. How their ship sank in the cyclone. A modern bulk carrier, he says. About twenty thousand tons. Apparently there was an explosion, and it broke in two and sank. Wasn't that ghastly? And yet our marvellous little *Sunglow* came safely through that awful storm. Wasn't she simply marvellous?'

Jim said, 'Yes. But I suppose Captain Cassidy had a lot to do with that.' He looked down at her, said awkwardly, 'Would you – I mean, what would you like to drink?'

'Oh, dear. Would you think it awful if I said rum and coke, with lots and lots of ice.'

When he came back with the drinks – his was a beer – she had moved to a corner at the after end of the sundeck where she'd been joined by the Cawsons. They'd no sooner gone than the Carters took their place, and Jim found himself more or less pushed aside. When the Americans moved on, Diana Kitson smiled at him over the rim of her glass. 'Let's finish our drinks and go up into the bows, Jim. It's marvellous there. Not all artificial and lit up like this – I mean, there you really have the feeling of the ship ploughing its way through the seas. I went up there on our first night out of Mombasa. It was heavenly.'

Jim experienced a surge of jealousy. 'Were you alone?'

She laughed. 'What a funny question. Actually, Mr Scalatti took me there. He's a nice man. He was showing me round the ship.'

'I see,' he said moodily. 'Well, shall *we* go now?'

'Yes. But let's not make it too obvious. You go first. I'll join you there in a few minutes.' She laughed again, squeezed his arm. 'We're conspirators, Jim, aren't we?'

The few minutes turned out to be ten, but when she arrived – breathless and apologetic, 'I simply had to spend a penny,' – he forgave her. She led him forward into the bows, past the windlass and the anchor cables. Once there they were able to look down *Sunglow*'s forefoot to where the phosphorescent bow-wave hissed and spluttered before falling back to bubble and murmur along the sides. Away to port the moon rode high, sharing the sky with stars and scattered banks of cloud. Fanned by the trade-wind, ruffled seas came in from the south-east, their frills like white lace in the path of the moon. The only sounds were those made by the sea, the distant thump of the engines and the occasional creaking of the hull.

The light breeze gusted for a moment and she teased back strands of hair from her eyes. How lovely she is, he thought. He felt her head touch his shoulder and supposed the movement of the ship was responsible. 'Isn't it beautiful,' she whispered.

He looked down, breathed in the fragrance of jasmine, resented the moonlight, knowing they could be seen from the bridge. A cloud drifted across the moon and darkness closed in on the night like a drawn curtain. He wondered if it was a response to his thoughts. Romantic tenderness overcame him. He leant down, tried to kiss her. She turned her head away, said, 'No, Jim. It's wrong. We mustn't,' but she made no attempt to leave his arms. Instead she looked up at him, her breath warm on his face. He tried again and this time her lips, soft and moist, met his. It was a long kiss, her hands reaching up to him, holding him tight. The magic of the moment was shattered by a voice behind them. 'Blimey! Talk about moonlight and roses!'

There was a brief silence then, until the cloud came clear of the moon, and they saw Henry Atkins standing by the windlass. 'Sorry if I scared you folks. It's me jogging sneakers. They don't allow no sound of footsteps.'

'Oh, it's Mr Atkins.' Mrs Kitson's voice was quite without embarrassment. 'No, you didn't scare us. It's simply marvellous up here isn't it. One really does feel at sea.'

'I felt that in the cyclone, luv. Wished I couldn't 'ave. 'Ullo, 'ullo, 'ullo,' he interrupted himself. 'What's that over there, then?' He pointed into the darkness ahead.

At first they couldn't see it, but soon their eyes adjusted to the distance and they picked up the faint speck of light. It showed twice for a few seconds, then was gone. Not long afterwards it showed again, two miniscule flashes, quickly swallowed by the night.

'Light'ouse,' said Henry Atkins. 'Must be the light on North Island. The skipper said ten o'clock. It's just gone ten.'

'Oh, isn't it thrilling. We've reached the islands at last.' Diana Kitson clapped her hands.

Jim said nothing. Inside, he was churning with a complex of emotions. The last five minutes had been the most unusual and exciting in his life. First a mature and lovely woman in his arms, then the distant light on a mysterious tropical island. Nothing, he decided, could be more wonderful. His thoughts were interrupted by Henry Atkins' voice. 'Good skipper we've got. Brings us safely through a cyclone, then finds that little light stuck away somewhere in the middle of the ocean. Marvellous, isn't it?'

'Yes, it is,' said Jim. But he wasn't thinking of Captain Cassidy.

ELEVEN

When the light at North Island was sighted Cassidy rang down *dead-slow* on the engineroom telegraph. There was no lighthouse on Eagle Islet, and many outlying shoals and hidden coral reefs made a night approach dangerous. For the rest of that night he kept *Sunglow* well away from the land, the distant light on North Island always in sight and within radar range.

At daybreak speed was increased, and course set for Eagle Islet. Some time later a familiar dark line appeared ahead, the cumulus clouds massed above it advertising the presence of an island. As the ship drew closer, the dark line resolved itself into trees, most of them coconut palms, their ranks extending along the low cliffs of coral, their bunching heads rustling in the south-east trades, their tall grey trunks leaning gracefully downwind.

Sunglow's anchor was dropped a few hundred yards off the northern side of the islet where blue-green sea lapped a sandy beach, white in strong sunlight. The dark hulls of *pirogues*, the native fishing craft, were drawn up above the high water mark; beyond them smoke curled into the sky from a woodfire. The beach led up to undergrowth and a clump of casuarina trees through which showed the roofs of the settlement. An old, barnacle encrusted schooner lay at anchor close offshore, her sails furled.

The gangway was lowered and before long a motorboat, small and time-worn, came chugging out to the ship. It came alongside, and a man in shorts, bushshirt and a white sun hat, portly and dignified, climbed the gangway. He was greeted by Pascal – they knew each other well – and taken to Cassidy's cabin.

99

After an early breakfast, passengers gathered on the upper deck to watch the skimmers being lowered into the water. Once afloat and manned, each came in turn to the gangway where Pascal stood, list in hand, supervising operations. The first names he called were those of the Carters, Henry Atkins, Mrs Clutterbutt, Dr Summers and Jim Abernethy. They followed each other down the gangway and were helped into Skimmer One by Said Obudo. A Swahili seaman in the bows shoved the little craft clear, its outboard engine crackled into life, and it drew away from the ship.

Hand on tiller, Obudo addressed his passengers. 'We'll have a look at the island from seaward first, then come back, land on the beach, and have a look around.' He opened the throttle wide and the skimmer leapt forward, spray flying, the engine screaming. With the exception of Mrs Clutterbutt, the passengers were in shorts, beach shirts and sunglasses. Some had cameras and most wore some sort of headgear as protection against a fierce sun which, they'd been warned, would be directly overhead at noon. Mrs Clutterbutt looked cool and elegant, though perhaps a trifle formal, in a cotton sun-frock, a wide brimmed straw hat, a rolled sunshade at her side. Her only concessions to the occasion were sandals and bare legs. But neither the skimmer – not the most comfortable of craft – nor the intensity of tropical heat, could detract from the air of authority and composure with which she regarded those about her as the little craft bumped and sprayed along the flank of the island. The noise of its outboard, much like the sound of tearing linen enormously amplified, made speech difficult – but other things were happening: Dean and Sandra Carter, cameras clicking, were leaning this way and that, shouting coded information to each other, adjusting focal lengths, changing lenses and bemoaning missed opportunities, like the silvery flashes of dorados leaping in pursuit of flying fish.

The main preoccupation of Henry Atkins, seated on a

thwart beside Jim, appeared to be keeping his yachting cap on his head. Dark glasses masked the sardonic expression, but shouted asides indicated that the Atkins brand of humour was alive and well. Dr Summers, silent but genial, appeared to be enjoying himself in a quiet, undemonstrative way.

When they had gone some distance down the western side of the island, Obudo stopped the outboard. 'We'll drift a bit, so you can see the bottom,' he told them. 'There are wonderful things down there.'

The high pitched whine of an outboard came up from behind them. It was Skimmer Two. It drew closer and they saw Commander Rollo, Mrs Kitson, Stephen Blake and the Van der Karsts on board, with Kibusu the bosun at the tiller. Far astern of it, Skimmer Three could be seen approaching. The three craft came within hailing distance of each other, stopped and drifted, while shouted messages were exchanged. But passengers were soon engrossed in what they saw beneath the surface, where the sandy bottom reflected shafts of sunlight dancing and quivering to the movement of the sea. At times the shafts settled like stage spotlights on brightly coloured fish, some swimming sedately with slowly twitching tails, others darting in sudden flashes of movement.

The skimmers drifted closer to the island's low grey cliffs, and the sandy bottom gave way to glimpses of a strange world far below, the thrusting shafts of sunlight revealing unexpected greens and pinks and mauves in coral forests where marine life was in constant motion. In the sky between the island and the sea, frigate birds wheeled and soared. Beneath them boobies dived on to shoals of fish, emerging heavy laden with their catches only to lose them to swooping frigate birds.

'It's fantastic – it's really unbelievable,' bubbled Sandra Carter between camera shots.

Said Obudo grinned. 'This is nothing,' he said. 'Wait till you have seen some of our other islands.'

'Which ones?' challenged Jim.

The second mate shook an admonitory finger. 'The itinerary is secret. Wait and see.'

Jim looked across to Skimmer Two where Diana Kitson was talking animatedly to Commander Rollo. He wondered what she was saying, hoped desperately that he might be in her skimmer next time. As it was she seemed to be ignoring him; he waved in her direction but it was his cabin mate, Stephen Blake, who waved back, held up binoculars, shouted, 'Aren't the seabirds fantastic?'

Jim nodded. 'Yes, terrific.'

Diana Kitson had not even turned her head.

'Any pubs ashore?' Henry Atkins pushed his cap onto the back of his head, removed the sunglasses and mopped his face with a large handkerchief. 'I could do with a jar. Bleedin' furnace, this is.'

Obudo started the outboard, shouted to the other skimmers, 'Right, let's go.' He opened the throttle and led the little flotilla in a race back towards the northern end of the island, three churning lines of foam in its wake.

Through a porthole in his day-cabin, Cassidy watched the approach of the antiquated wooden lighter. Loaded with sacks of copra, it was being towed by the motorboat which had brought off the plantation manager earlier in the morning. The two craft turned in a wide circle, the tow was slipped and the lighter drifted alongside. Lines were thrown and it was made fast opposite the foremost hold.

A shouted conversation followed between the lighter's creole labourers and *Sunglow*'s Swahili seamen. A derrick was swung out, guys secured, a winch rattled and loading began.

Cassidy was pleased. The copra load was larger than he'd expected at that time of year. He was thinking about that, wondering if it would be repeated at the other islands, when there was a knock on the door.

'Come in,' he called.

It was the first mate, Scalatti. 'Krol, the crewman from the *Solidava*, asks to see you, Captain.'

'See me? What about?'

'He is dissatisfied with the accommodation. Does not think we treat him right.'

Cassidy turned from the porthole, went to his desk. 'What's his story, then?'

Scalatti repeated what the Swede had told him on the previous night.

'The black man from the *Solidava*? Has he complained?'

'Not to me, Captain.'

Cassidy looked at the clock on the bulkhead. The time was close to nine. 'Right, I'll see them now.'

'Them? It's only the Swede that's asked.'

'It's them or no one. They're survivors from the same ship. Sharing the same accommodation, eating the same food. They see me together, right away, or not at all. Understand?'

The Italian shrugged his shoulders, spread his hands, and left the cabin.

Cassidy was at his desk writing when they came in, escorted by Scalatti. They were wearing clean white T-shirts and khaki shorts. 'The men from the *Solidava*, Captain,' he announced.

Cassidy stopped writing, the big bearded head came up and critical blue eyes examined the faces in front of him. 'You.' He stared at Krol. 'Your name and nationality?'

'Nils Krol. Swedish.'

Cassidy saw the glint of aggression in the pale eyes. 'How many years at sea?'

'Nine years.'

Cassidy nodded at the big black man, inches taller than the Swede who stood beside him. 'You. Your name and nationality?'

The West Indian's smile revealed strong white teeth. 'Luther Nelson, sir. West Indian from Antigua.'

'How many years at sea?'

'Twelve, sir. Since I was twenty-one.'

Cassidy put down the ballpoint he'd been holding. 'You've had the longer time at sea, Nelson. I'll hear you first. What's your complaint?'

The black man hesitated, looked at Krol. 'No complaint, Captain. Now that we have some clothes from the chief steward, it's okay.'

Cassidy turned to the Swede. 'You, Krol. What's your complaint?'

The Swede began to repeat, almost word for word, what he'd said to Scalatti the day before. When he wanted to know why two passengers in single cabins should not be made to share, so as to make a passenger cabin available to the survivors – at that point, Cassidy raised a large, peremptory hand. 'You want to know why you can't have a passenger cabin,' he challenged, his voice uncharacteristically harsh. 'I'll tell you why, Krol. You're not a passenger. You're a distressed seaman, a survivor from a sunken ship.' He stopped speaking for a moment, tapped with his fingers on the desk top. 'You are being treated in accordance with international maritime law. What's more, Krol,' he gave the man a hard look, 'you'd better be remembering who it is you have to thank for your rescue, instead of bellyaching about conditions here. And there's another thing you'd better be knowing. If you want passage back to Mombasa in this ship, you turn to and work. D'ye understand? I'm not carrying idlers. If you don't like that, there's an island not far away where I can land you. The people are not too friendly, they don't like strangers. And it's a long time that you'd be there.'

Krol managed a forced laugh. 'Work in *this* ship. You're joking.'

For a moment Cassidy regarded the Swede with a contempt that needed no words. Then he turned to the black man. 'You prepared to work your passage, Nelson?'

'Sure, I'll do that, Captain. I guess the time passes quicker that way.'

Krol turned on the West Indian with sudden violence. 'You goddam blackleg! Goes with the colour, I guess.'

'Cool it man . . .' Luther Nelson's eyes threatened.

Cassidy interrupted. 'You dare to use language like that, in front of *me*, Krol. In *my* cabin.' The Irishman stood up, left his desk, pointed to the door. 'Get to hell out of here before I have to teach you some manners.'

Krol's mouth set in a hard, tight lipped smile. 'You and who else, *old man*.' The aggressive eyes narrowed.

Cassidy moved to the door. With one hand he opened it, with the other he spun the Swede round and, with the whole force of his body, threw the man out. Krol landed heavily in the passageway. He got to his knees, stared at Cassidy with dazed, unbelieving eyes while Scalatti and Luther Nelson helped him to his feet. Cassidy slammed the door, went back to his desk. He sat there for some minutes, head in hands, body shaking. 'Holy Mother O' God,' he muttered at last. 'It's forgiveness I'm asking, for I have abused the strength you gave me.'

Loading had taken longer than expected. It was after eleven o'clock when *Sunglow* weighed anchor, gave a farewell blast on her siren and stood out to sea, making for the narrow passage west of Remire Reef. Once through it she altered to a southerly course and headed for D'Arros Island. The humid heat of the tropics grew steadily as the sun neared its zenith, and most of the passengers, wearing as little as their ages and tastes permitted, sought shelter on the sundeck where awnings and the south-easterly breeze gave some relief.

They had returned on board at 10.30 that morning, tired and dripping with perspiration, but enthusiastic about their first run ashore. Inevitably, conversation on the sundeck turned to the morning's activities.

105

'I don't know what you thought of it,' Mrs Kitson said to the Carters, 'but for me the skimmer was just heaven. Seeing that gorgeous little island rushing by as we raced over the water – the pale blue sea, the incredibly white sand, and those green topped palm trees looking like giant feather dusters. It was just fabulous.'

Dean Carter said, 'Yes. It was great. We got some fantastic pictures, didn't we, honey!' He patted his wife's bare knees. 'But walking around the island, seeing the creoles splitting coconut husks on those sharp wooden spikes, the youngster climbing that high coconut palm – I guess it was all of sixty feet – with just his hands and that piece of fibre between his ankles. Why, that was really something.'

Blake was in a nearby deck chair. Mrs Kitson turned to him. 'You haven't said a word, Mr Blake. What did you think of this morning's adventures?'

He inclined his chair towards her, frowned. 'Sorry, I didn't get that. What did you say?'

She shook her head, wagged a reproving finger. 'You didn't hear a word I said, Mr Blake. You've been day-dreaming, haven't you?' She repeated her question.

'Sorry. Now I'm with you. Well, I found it all interesting. For me the frigate birds and the boobies were the high lights.'

Sandra said, 'Do tell me. What are boobies?'

'Gannets. There are a number of varieties. Sailors gave them the name "booby".'

'You know a lot about birds, don't you Mr Blake?'

His smile was embarrassed. 'Not really. But bird-watching *is* my hobby.'

Diana Kitson was right, Blake admitted to himself, he hadn't heard a word she'd said. But it wasn't day-dreaming. He'd been absorbed in his own thoughts. Thinking about Kunwar Singh, J. G. Patel & Co's correspondence clerk, and the concertina. That had been the breakthrough. The missing piece in the jig-saw puzzle. They owed much to the bearded, turbanned young sikh; so quiet, so dignified. Of course, others had helped; some inadvertently, like Vera White – the intercepted letters – and Mrs Sugden, the indiscreet landlady. Tom Voi, too, had handled things in his conscientious, professional way. That was Voi, and that was as it should be. They were qualities Blake rated highly.

The matter was in no way concluded: the problem of identification remained, the last hurdle before the application for extradition. Much could still go wrong. For Duchescu the stakes were high. He'd invested everything in the project: the money, years of his life, the whole of his future. A man like that would not stand idly by if he thought those things threatened.

TWELVE

The Amirante Bank, all ninety miles of it, from North Island down to the southernmost of its many islands, Ile des Neufs, was a long strip of submerged coral and sand, within it a complex pattern of atolls, islets, shoals and sand cays. Some of the shoals were exposed at low water, others were not; some were accurately charted, the position of others was only rumoured. To east and west of the bank lay safe water, most of it many hundreds of fathoms deep.

The shoal waters of the Amirante Bank were the most hazardous into which *Sunglow*'s voyages took her. Of all the islands on the bank only North Island had a lighthouse. For these reasons Cassidy treated the area with respect, rarely undertook journeys between the islands in darkness, and in daylight seldom left the bridge. On those short, inter-island passages the coaster's radar and echo sounder were in constant use.

It was for these reasons that he kept *Sunglow* in deep

water, well to the west of the shoals, on the run down to D'Arros Island.

Like most of the islands, D'Arros, in origin a coral reef, was flat, its highest point no more than a dozen feet or so above the sea. Thus the clump of casuarina trees and the coconut plantation were sighted from *Sunglow*'s bridge well before the island itself showed up.

Passengers were finishing their lunch when the telegraph bells rang and the engine vibrations ceased. Some time later the bells sounded again; the noise of the engine going astern and the anchor cable running told of *Sunglow*'s arrival.

Cassidy had anchored several hundred yards to the north of the settlement, in water protected from the south-east trades. Not far from *Sunglow* another ship, smaller than the coaster and with a trawler-like hull, lay at anchor. Whatever its hull shape, any connection with fishing was discounted by the multiplicity of radar scanners, radio antennae and other electronic sensors which festooned its masts and upperworks.

It was by no means the first time Cassidy had seen a Soviet surveillance trawler in that part of the Indian Ocean. His confidential report, handed in to the British consul in Mombasa after *Sunglow*'s last voyage, had included photos he'd taken of two such vessels. It was the British consul who had told him that they were *Maya* class intelligence-collectors of the Soviet Navy.

'The US naval base at Diego Garcia is the target,' explained the consul. 'These surveillance trawlers record the movements and characteristics of warships, submarines, fleet auxiliaries and everything else that goes in and out of the base. They monitor the communication networks and every sort of electronic emission, whether it's to do with weapons or search systems. They monitor the underwater stuff, sonar transmissions, propeller signatures – the lot. Everything is recorded and sent to Soviet naval intelligence in Leningrad. Their boffins sniff it, analyse it, evaluate it, copy it, beaver away at breaking the codes and ciphers. You name it, the boys behind the iron curtain are at it.'

Cassidy had looked unhappy. 'And shouldn't something be done, then, to control their trawlers?'

The consul had shaken his head. 'There's no international maritime law – or any other law for that matter – which says it can't be done. It's perfectly legal, and of course our side does it too. I imagine the US Navy – and NATO ships generally – dish out a good deal of phoney stuff to confound the comrades.' He had sighed, looked gloomily out of the window. 'All at great expense and no doubt in the best interests of mankind.' He turned back to Cassidy with a smile. 'But keep up the good work, Captain. I'm sure your reports and photos are much appreciated.'

During the next forty-eight hours *Sunglow* had not only visited D'Arros Island, but made a brief stop at Ile Desroches before heading south for Alphonse and François Islands.

Quite the most interesting time for passengers had been the afternoon following the coaster's arrival off D'Arros Island. The short run in skimmers from the anchorage across to St Joseph Island had been made under ideal conditions, the south-easterly wind not much more than a breeze, and the sky clear but for a few layers of wispy cloud. Soon after leaving *Sunglow*, the three inflatables had made their way through a passage in the reef enclosing a large lagoon around the perimeter of which lay a number of small islands. St Joseph, by far the biggest, marked the lagoon's south-eastern end, and justified in every way the lyrical description in the Capricorn Company's brochure.

'We won't land on St Joseph,' Obudo had told his party. 'Just skim around it. Give it the once over from seaward. Then we'll go on to Fouquet and Resource Islands. There's nobody on them, so you really will be exploring uninhabited tropical islands.' He grinned. 'We'll land on Fouquet Island and you can swim there. The reef around the lagoon keeps out sharks. So don't worry on that account.'

There were smiles of relief.

Fouquet Island, less than half a mile in length, palm studded and uninhabited, was a happy choice for the swimmers. Once landed, changing presented few problems for most of them were wearing bathing gear under whatever else they had on.

Among those first into the lagoon was Mrs Kitson. Wearing the briefest of bikinis, she raced down to the water's edge and waded out, closely followed by the tall and muscular figure of Jim Abernethy. They were strong swimmers and had soon reached deep water, well beyond the other bathers. Jim, who'd responded to her challenge and taken the lead, stopped swimming, turned on his back and floated, relishing the lap of cool water which cushioned the heat of the sun. On his right Diana Kitson shouted something unintelligible. He turned in time to see her duck-dive. She must have swum under him, for later she surfaced to his left, turned on her back and floated beside him. During the dive she had shed her bikini top, and her firm, well-shaped breasts lay awash in translucent water. Jim, hardly believing what he saw, experienced a delicious shock, a curious mixture of boyish embarrassment and sexual excitement.

It made him laugh, feel self conscious, so that it became imperative to say something. 'Where's the top?' he asked her.

On the side away from him, a hand with scarlet tipped fingers held it up. 'Be a darling, Jim.' She was treading water. 'Tuck it in your trunks. I adore swimming topless. I promise to put it on again before we go in. Mustn't shock our friends.'

He tucked it into his trunks. 'You look great,' he said hoarsely. 'Really terrific.'

She spluttered, shook water from her head like a dog drying. 'For my next trick.' She laughed mischievously, made as if to duck-dive again.

'No, no, don't,' he warned. 'Look who's coming.' It was Dr Summers and Commander Rollo, their laboured, snorting breast-strokes bringing them steadily closer.

'Oh blast! Come on, Jim,' she called. 'Let's leave them behind.' With a powerful crawl she swam further out.

Filled with euphoria, and relief that Aunt Beryl couldn't see him, Jim followed. His fear that Diana had been avoiding him since the night they'd gone up to the foc'sle was, he realized, groundless.

In late afternoon the skimmers crossed the northern side of the lagoon to land on Resource Island. Only half a mile in length, it was soon explored and by nightfall the coxswains – Obudo, Pascal and the bosun – had brought the food and drink hampers ashore, and collected enough driftwood and dried palm leaves for the night's activities. A shallow trench was dug in the sand, the driftwood was laid in it, a short length of wiremesh placed over it, and the fire lit. Fillets of marlin and sharks' fins, bought from the islanders at Desroches, curried chupatties and potatoes in their jackets, were laid on the fire and the sizzling, spluttering business of a barbecue began. A salad of mangoes, pawpaws, bananas and limes, prepared on board by *Sunglow*'s chef, stood ready for serving in coconut shells. Quantities of *calao* were passed round for those who wanted it; the few who didn't were given the fresh juice of limes in iced water. Chatter about the food, the day's experiences, and the voyage in general was punctuated by sudden bursts of laughter.

Shafts of moonlight probed the shadows under the palms, lending an unreal quality to the figures round the fire. Somewhere in the background a man began to sing a West Indian folk song to the accompaniment of a guitar.

111

'My goodness,' shrilled Sandra Carter. 'Where's that coming from?'

'Wake up, honey. Never heard of taped music?' Dean Carter gave her bikini clad bottom a playful slap.

'Don't do that,' she snapped. 'You know I don't like it.'

Clicking noises came from Said Obudo. 'That's no taped music, sir. That's a genuine, hundred per cent human. And I guess it's my guitar he's playing.' He stepped away from the fire, looked towards the palms. 'Hey, black man. Come here. Show the folks you're not a cassette player.'

A dark shape, guitar in hand, came from the shadows and stood by the fire. It was Luther Nelson.

'Oh, lovely,' Sandra Carter clapped her hands. 'Please, *please* give us more.'

The West Indian's smile exposed even white teeth. 'Thank you lady.' He plucked the strings of the guitar again, and his deep voice picked up the song.

Sunglow arrived at and sailed from Ile Desroches during the morning after the lagoon party. Her stay had been too brief for the passengers to land. Once clear of the anchorage, Cassidy put her on course for Alphonse and St François Islands, some hundred miles to the south-west.

In the afternoon the wind freshened and banks of cumulus cloud built up on the horizon, a dark background to the moderate sea into which the coaster dipped and rolled, her rust streaked hull shining wetly in bright sunlight.

Cassidy had invited Mrs Clutterbutt to take tea with him that afternoon. Punctual as always, she arrived at the appointed time. She and Cassidy exchanged pleasantries, while Mbolwo poured the tea and handed round the sandwiches. When the steward had gone Cassidy broke the ice. 'Tell me, Mrs C, and how did you enjoy the visit to the lagoon?'

'It really was splendid, Captain. A most enjoyable occasion.'

He nodded. 'Well now, and that's good. Did you swim?'

'No, I much prefer walking, so I decided to explore. Mr Blake very kindly escorted me. He is an interesting man. There is simply nothing he doesn't know about the bird-life of the islands. He was most helpful and charming. So dull for him, you know, being saddled with an old lady.'

'Ah, Mrs C.' Cassidy looked into his teacup, shook his head emphatically. 'Now your worst enemy wouldn't be calling you that. Indeed, any man would regard himself as fortunate to be in your company.'

Mrs Clutterbutt looked away, apparently embarrassed by the compliment, before saying with some severity, 'Captain Cassidy, you have been kissing the Blarney Stone.' With that she changed the subject to White Island. What were his plans for the search?

He considered the question in silence, got up, transferred the tea-tray to his desk, took a chart from a drawer and spread it on the table.

'We are here.' He pointed to the chart. 'In latitude six degrees, thirty minutes south – half-way between Desroches and Alphonse Islands. Alphonse and François Islands are about a dozen miles apart. We'll be there around ten o'clock tonight. I had planned to call in at Alphonse, but we haven't the time. Must make up for what we lost in the cyclone. We'll hold this south-westerly course until we reach the Providence Group where we call before going on to the Farquhar Islands, about thirty miles to the south. Providence Island is close to nine degrees south latitude. Bannister's chart gives White Island's latitude as between nine and ten south. As I said last time, we should begin our search at about eight degrees thirty minutes south.' He made a pencilled cross on the chart, 'Right there,' he said.

'I see.' Mrs Clutterbutt squinted at the chart.

'After the Farquhar Group we'll be making for the Cosmoledos and Aldabras – another three hundred miles of steaming. With stops, that's about four or five days. All the islands in these groups lie between, or close to, the nine

113

and tenth parallels of south latitude. After the Aldabras we'll call at Dada's Island, then head for the East African coast. That'll be a long run, 360 miles, a day and a half's steaming. You'll see that the chart shows no islands along that stretch, but all the same we'll keep *Sunglow*'s course between the ninth and tenth parallels. After Farquhar Island we'll steer a broad zig-zag to increase radar coverage. In that way we should pick up any uncharted island close to or between those parallels.'

Mrs Clutterbutt looked at Cassidy with what seemed a hint of admiration. 'I must say, Captain, that sounds most thorough. Do you think there *are* any uncharted islands?'

'To be honest, Mrs C, I think it's unlikely. But that's not to say impossible. There are a lot of uninhabited islets and atolls in the groups we'll be visiting or passing through. The real problem, I'm thinking, is not to find an uncharted island but to identify White Island. Bannister landed on it, lived on it, the natives rescued him from it. So it must be there.'

Cassidy folded the chart and took it back to his desk where he made a pencilled note while Mrs Clutterbutt sat silent, chin in hand, her eyes on a porthole beyond which the sea appeared and disappeared in time with *Sunglow*'s gentle rolls.

It was she who took up the conversation. 'You may recall, Captain, that when last we discussed this you said Mr Goosam Patel had his doubts about our project, but nevertheless liked the idea of searching for a mysterious desert island because it would be something of unusual interest for the passengers.'

'Ah, indeed and that is correct.'

'Well, I feel I owe you an apology. I rather abruptly rejected that idea. On reflection, however, I feel we might well do with what you referred to as "more eyes and lookouts". What *is* important, Captain, is that we do not say a word about the chart, or Bannister, or the buried

114

gold. We must invent quite another story – a different reason for the search.' She paused, a glint of good humour in her grey eyes. 'What do you say to that?'

They were discussing the suggestion when four bells sounded on the bridge above them. Cassidy excused himself. 'I keep the second dog-watch this evening, Mrs C. Six to eight o'clock.'

She got up from the settee. 'Yes, of course. But we must sometime discuss the problem of getting the gold . . .'

'The *goods*, Mrs C. The *goods*,' Cassidy prompted good-humouredly.

'Oh dear. I'd forgotten. Getting the *goods* ashore.'

'Yes, indeed. Now that's something we shall have to talk about at our next meeting. By the way, Mrs C, I'd ask you not to mention the itinerary. We have to keep that for the briefings.' He winked. 'Keeps the interest alive, you know.'

Mrs Clutterbutt held out her hand. 'Of course. I shan't say a word. Thank you so much, Captain, for a delightful tea.'

He took her hand, held it for a moment. 'Ah, and wasn't the pleasure entirely mine.'

As she left she said, 'I must confess, Captain, that I always feel *Sunglow* is in the safest of hands when you are on the bridge.'

'Well, indeed, and who is it now that's been kissing the Blarney Stone?' he called after her.

She did not turn her head, but he heard the quiet chuckle.

A friendship had been growing between Scalatti and Krol since the Swede's humiliation in the Captain's cabin. On the night at D'Arros Island, when the passengers were enjoying themselves at the beach barbecue, Krol was drinking with Scalatti in the first mate's cabin. With Krol now working on deck as a seaman, there was a ready made excuse for his presence there. One drink had led to

115

another, and in the course of these Scalatti had encouraged the Swede's dislike of Cassidy.

During their talk that night they found other things in common apart from their intense dislike of the Captain. Both were anxious to leave the sea, to enjoy the fruits, real or imaginary, of life ashore. Like many sailors, they hankered after the rural life: for Scalatti, a corner shop in a village somewhere north of Naples; for Krol, a small lake farm, inland from Göteborg.

'But how?' Krol had rapped his knuckles against his forehead in a gesture of impotence. 'There is not the possibility to save enough money on a seaman's wages.'

Scalatti grunted assent. 'Without money nothing is possible.' His dark eyes settled on Krol. 'But sometimes the opportunity can come. Maybe once in a man's life. If he does not take it, then – pouf.' He shrugged. 'It will not come again. Of that you can be sure, my friend.'

'Let such a chance come my way.' Krol's shaggy head nodded in emphasis. 'I will not miss it.'

'It can come when a man is not expecting it. When it does, he must grab it with two hands.' The Italian went on to explain that money would not only enable him to leave the sea, but would help with his wife's health problems.

Krol expressed sympathy, said that he himself had never married. 'What's marriage for a man who lives at sea?'

That led to a general discussion about women. It had gone on, more specifically, to those on board. 'There's only two of them worth a look.' Krol pinched his nose, yawned. 'That Yankee girl and the English woman. That one's got it. Good looks, fine body.' He made a circle with a thumb and forefinger. 'She gives me a smile yesterday. Says something about the islands being great. You know how passengers are?'

'She's okay. I show her round the ship the night we leave Mombasa.' A sunken eye winked. 'Help her up and down ladders. That way you learn a lot.'

Krol nodded approval. 'Think she would?'

'Why not. If the opportunity comes. She is only human.'

'Is there a husband?'

'Divorced, she is telling me. She comes on the trip to forget.'

Krol's pale eyes settled on the bottle of vermouth. Scalatti took the hint, filled their glasses.

'So she tells you that,' said Krol. 'Soon as you show her round the ship. She must fancy you, Luigi.'

The Italian's hollow face creased into a smile. 'I guess so. She been up here to drink with me since then. Tells me plenty. She is lonely. Other passengers not friendly, not to her. She says married men all time watched by wives. The doctor and the navy man not interested, she says. Only guy who is friendly is the young man, Jim. The guy with the red hair. So, what's wrong with him, I ask her? She laughs, says he's sweet, but just a boy, you know.'

Krol ran a hand through tousled hair, grinned. 'So she wants a man, okay. What about you, Luigi. Could be she really fancies you.'

'Maybe. But I don't take chances like that with her, not with this bastard Cassidy waiting to fire me if he get half a chance.'

'That wouldn't worry me,' said Krol. 'I'm a distressed mariner. He can't fire me.' He lit a cigarette. 'But you say she's been to your cabin?'

'Sure. Pascal brought her here. That make it okay.' Scalatti sought refuge in silence, the frown over his sunken eyes suggesting deep thought.

Krol drained his glass of vermouth. 'Think I can have a chance with her?'

'How can you tell? Not just a man's looks that count.' Scalatti forced a laugh; then, aware that he'd been less than tactful, he added, 'I try to fix it she's here, next time you come. Okay, Nils?'

The Swede's sour look turned to one of pleasure. 'Sure. That's okay with me.'

When Krol had gone, Scalatti sat at his desk for some time thinking about their conversation. He was sure now that he had an ally. In due course he'd put the proposition to him. In general terms of course. Nothing specific until he had sounded the man out. Later, when Scalatti himself had settled details in his own mind – time, place and method – he'd put Krol in the picture. Not completely, but enough for the Swede to play his part. In the meantime it was important to develop a good relationship. It was that which had prompted him to say he'd fix things.

THIRTEEN

In late afternoon a squall swept over the ship. It was followed by thunder and lightning and a torrential down-pour which drove passengers off the sundeck where the awnings had been hurriedly furled. Despite its violence the storm was short lived, passing away to the westward, thunder and lightning marking its passage.

Mrs Clutterbutt gave a champagne party in the lounge that evening. It was, she said, to celebrate completion of the first week of *Sunglow*'s cruise.

After a hesitant start the party got into its stride. Formal conversation gave way before long to convivial chatter, bursts of laughter from the men, and occasional shrieks from the ladies. Canapés with a tropical flavour were handed round and the two stewards saw to it that empty glasses were soon filled. An hour later the ringing of the dinner gong was the signal for Commander Rollo to make a brief speech of thanks. When Mrs Clutterbutt rose to reply her smile was a mixture of pleasure and embarrassment. 'This first week has been so enjoyable – so full of interesting

118

things – I really felt it called for some sort of celebration,' she said.

'Cyclone an' all,' suggested Henry Atkins.

'Yes, indeed. Cyclone and all. It *was* frightening, but nevertheless interesting in a rather desperate way. Something, I daresay, we shall never forget – and I'm sure you would want me to say how deeply grateful we are to Captain Cassidy. But for his fine seamanship, his devotion to duty – all those hours on the bridge without sleep, in that terrible weather. But for him I doubt if we would be here tonight.' There was nothing restrained about the *hear-hears* and clapping which followed.

'And now what can I say, but thank you all for coming to this little celebration. I do hope you have enjoyed it.'

Mrs Clutterbutt was sad that Cassidy had not accepted her invitation, for she had wanted to thank him publicly, something she'd not let him know when he made his apologies. He'd said, 'It's a golden rule of mine, Mrs C, not to intrude at passengers' functions. It's fine for folk to be themselves. That's more easily done without the Captain's presence.'

'You are so wrong.' She had looked at him with mock severity. 'They would love to have you there. But like all men you're obstinate, so I suppose I shall have to accept your refusal.'

Cassidy had smiled disarmingly. 'You'll not be forgetting the dinner at Nyali Beach, Mrs C. Indeed, and I wasn't for refusing your invitation then.'

Between ten and twelve o'clock that night *Sunglow* passed Alphonse and St François Islands. Neither had lighthouses, but some of the passengers believed they had seen lights on Alphonse Island, presumably from the small settlement there.

Cassidy had given the islands a wide berth, keeping at least five miles to the westward. On many occasions he'd seen the three wrecks which lay rusted and forlorn on the reefs and shoals between Alphonse and St François. He had no intention of adding to their number.

The islands dropped astern, were swallowed by the darkness, and passengers drifted back to the lounge. Mrs Clutterbutt, the Cawsons and Jean McLachlan returned to their bridge table, as did the Bruckners and Van der Karsts; Commander Rollo and Dr Summers resumed a game of chess. Sandra Carter, Stephen Blake, Jim Abernethy and Henry Atkins were on the sundeck talking to Gaston Pascal who was describing the two islands they'd passed. He assured them there was little to see there. Mrs Kitson had gone off early pleading a headache, while Arnold Bliss was in the lounge reading a treatise on the work of missionaries in the Solomon Islands. Dean Carter was processing films in *Sunglow*'s dark room; a small, hot compartment next to the galley.

It was a dark night, the moon and the stars showing fitfully through gaps in the clouds, the sea moderate, the south-east trade wind helping to counter the heat. The coaster's hull creaked and groaned in muted but familiar complaint as she gave to the movement of the seas, but the passengers, inured now to her habits, scarcely noticed these things. By midnight, the bar having closed, most of them had gone to their cabins.

At dinner that night Gaston Pascal had announced that a briefing would take place in the lounge at ten o'clock the following morning. Captain Cassidy would then disclose the next stage of the itinerary.

At midnight the second mate took over the watch from Scalatti. The Italian reported the ship's course and speed, drew attention to the lights of a sailing vessel still some miles away – 'Can be an old island schooner,' he said – and was about to go below when the phone from the engine-room rang. It was Kumar Gupta, the chief engineer. 'Main engine bearing running hot,' he said. 'It is necessary to stop.'

Obudo had answered the phone. 'For how long, chief?' he asked.

'Only know when we look at it. An hour or so. Could be more if we must change it.'

'Right. I'll tell the old man.' He rang down *stop* on the engineroom telegraph. As he dialled the Captain's number, the beat of the diesel faded and the hull vibrations ceased.

The second mate was wondering why the phone was not answered when Cassidy himself appeared on the bridge. 'What's the trouble, Mr Obudo?'

The second mate told him. Cassidy ran a hand across ruffled, unruly hair. 'Main bearing is it, lad. That's all we need.' He made for the chartroom. Unused to seeing Cassidy out of uniform, Obudo was thinking how wild the bearded Irishman looked, his big body wrapped in a blue silk kimono around which a white dragon pursued its tail. Meanwhile, in the chartroom, Cassidy was plotting the position of the ship; something Scalatti had failed to do at the end of his watch. By radar, *Sunglow*'s position was twenty miles south-south-west of Alphonse Island. Wind and current would set the ship to the north-west where there was ample searoom and deep water. Cassidy had no worries on that account. He phoned the engineroom, spoke briefly to Kumar Gupta. Back on the bridge, he saw that Obudo had already switched off the steaming lights and seen to the hoisting of not-under-command lights on the fore-yardarm.

'Good lad,' he said. 'First things first. No man goes far wrong that way.'

He stayed talking to the second mate for some minutes. As he was about to leave the bridge, Mbolwo arrived, tray in hand.

'Holy St Patrick.' Cassidy shook his head. 'Do ye not ever sleep man?'

There was nothing but to watch and wait while the coaster lay in lifeless silence on the sea, the absence of familiar things, the thud of the diesel, the churn of the propeller, the vibrations of the hull, more noticeable than ever their presence had been.

Some six hours later the chief engineer reported that the crankshaft bearing had been replaced; *Sunglow*'s engines could, he announced, once again turn. During those six hours she had drifted before wind and sea, an awkward corkscrewing motion, the high sides of the bridge and deckhouse acting as a sail, causing her to lie across the wind. Concerned at the stopping of the engines for so long, a number of passengers had come up on deck to find out what was happening. The word soon got round that the engineers were replacing a worn bearing in the main diesel. Not serious, said Pascal, but might take a little time: ship perfectly safe, well clear of the land, get back to bed, have a good sleep, tomorrow's a busy day, was his reassuring advice.

Several passengers disregarded it, among them Rollo, Dr Summers and the Carters. Grateful for an excuse to escape from hot and stuffy cabins which were shut off from the wind on the leeward side, they sought refuge on the sundeck where the south-east trade wind, the splash and lap of the sea and occasional glimpses of the moon and the stars, made life more pleasant than below decks.

Jim Abernethy was leaning on the rail at the after end of the sundeck, looking out to sea and thinking of Diana Kitson. She had a two-berth cabin to herself. Number six, a couple of doors down from the cabin he shared with Stephen Blake. She'd said she had a headache. It would be marvellous if he could go to her cabin now and ask if the headache was better? Was there anything he could do to help? But of course there wasn't, and he couldn't. He tried to picture her lying on her bunk. What would she be wearing? Nothing, possibly. In his mind's eye he saw her floating alongside him in the lagoon.

His thoughts were interrupted by Sandra Carter's excited, 'Oh, gee! Now just look at this.'

He joined her on the starboard side, 'Hey, man,' she squealed. 'Isn't that just beautiful.' A school of dolphins was passing down the side, leaping and diving with regimental precision, the commonplace noises of the sea giving way to the swishing resonant sound of their passing, their course marked by phosphorescent trails.

Jim said, 'Yes. It's great,' and felt sad that Diana was not there to share the moment.

Sandra Carter was telling him something about dolphins when he interrupted. 'Hey, listen! Hear that?'

She listened and did, and the distant sound of engines drew steadily closer until the aircraft passed low overhead, its navigation lights flashing, the noise of its jets deafening.

Seconds later three lights, brilliantly luminous, appeared in the sky, windward of *Sunglow*. As they drifted downwind over the ship, they turned night into day. The sound of jet engines grew again in intensity as the aircraft flew round *Sunglow* in a wide circle, keeping low over the sea.

Dr Summers and Commander Rollo joined the others at the rail. 'Think that's a distress signal, Dick?' the doctor asked.

'No. Those are reconnaissance flares. It's somebody having a good look at us. US naval aircraft from Diego Garcia – or from a carrier, I daresay.

'Could it be Soviet?' asked the doctor.

'Quite possibly. I suppose the fact that we've been drifting for some hours with not-under-command lights makes us interesting.'

During the morning watch the chief engineer phoned Cassidy to report that all was well, but revolutions for *half-speed* should not be exceeded during the next hour or so. The time was 0610. Wind and current had pushed

Sunglow some twenty-five miles to the north-west while repairs were being carried out. Cassidy plotted her position once again before setting course for Providence Island, 130 miles to the south-west. He estimated their time of arrival there at about seven o'clock that evening, and was far from pleased. His plan to make up lost time by omitting calls at Alphonse and St François Islands had gone by the board. But for the breakdown, Providence Island would have been reached by midday and left again before dusk. That was no longer possible. On arriving off the island that night *Sunglow* would have to await daylight before delivering stores and mail, loading copra and sending passengers off on their jaunt ashore. He had no illusions. The nominal profit of the last voyage looked like becoming a substantial loss on the present one.

To add to Cassidy's problems, Gaston Pascal had reported that the ship's store of fresh fish was all but exhausted. Most of that obtained at Desroches had been used at the barbecue. Cancellation of the visit to St Joseph and François had precluded obtaining supplies there. Pascal had been hopeful, however, that he might stock up at Providence Island. In reporting the estimated time of arrival there by radiophone, Cassidy had learnt from the settlement manager that little or no fresh fish was available. So the problem remained, and it was a serious one. Locally caught fish was an important item on *Sunglow*'s menus.

Henry Atkins was one of those who had deserted his cabin in favour of the sundeck when *Sunglow*'s engine broke down. The persistent snoring of the Rev. Bliss, more noticeable with all extraneous noise gone, had more to do with this than the heat, for the cabin they shared was on the windward side. With the porthole open and the door on the latch, the strong sea breeze made conditions tolerable.

Lying in his deck chair well away from the others, he feigned sleep. He had no desire to become involved in small talk. There was too much to think about. Time was passing, the voyage was now more than a week old, and with each day achievement of his objective came closer. It was one for which he had waited a long time, done much to make possible. An anonymous note had triggered the idea; the idea had become a plan, its execution a mission, the mission an obsession.

The unsigned note had been left on the front seat of his car outside the Islington flat. He recalled its contents: *The Duke is on a wee corral island in the Indian Ocean. A ship from Mombasa calls there ocasional with letters and supplies. They say he has a nice set up, lasses and all. God bless.*

Atkins was pretty sure it was from McGott. The illiteracy, the crude lettering, the *wee*, the *lasses*, the spelling of *coral* and *occasional*, all fitted. McGott had lived with the Duke's sister until things went sour and she'd kicked him out. Maybe the anonymous note was his way of getting even with her. The man had a violent temper, it was the sort of thing he would do. He and McGott had been good friends. A man got to know who his friends were living like that. It would be like McGott to think he could put his conscience right about Vera by doing an old friend a good turn. Anyway, it was the note that started things.

It hadn't been easy making enquiries in Mombasa, all those thousands of miles away, and it had taken time. For a start he'd had to be discreet. Couldn't use his own name. His niece worked in an estate agency in Hampstead, so he'd asked her if she'd type the letters and sign them in her name. The first would be to the port authorities in Mombasa. 'Ask them,' he'd said, 'if there's a ship there that visits the atolls and islands of the Indian Ocean? What's its name, does it take passengers, how often does it go?'

She'd said, 'What on earth do you want to know all that for, Uncle Joe?'

'I fancy a trip down there, love,' he'd said. 'All them atolls and islands in the tropics. Palm trees and blue lagoons. Very romantic, Maureen. Time I had a good holiday.'

She had laughed in gentle derision. 'What'll you use for money, Uncle Joe?'

'No problem, Maureen. I've, er-well, actually I've a big deal coming through. Property syndicate, you know. Important development. There'll be plenty coming in.'

She'd winced, given him a despairing look, shaken her head. 'Oh, Uncle Joe. For God's sake. Whose property? You're not into villainy again, are you? It's just not worth it. Surely you know that.'

'What a suggestion to make to your favourite uncle, Maureen. Really, you do shock and disappoint me. Where's your gratitude? Who paid for your private schooling? No, Maureen. What I'm into is strictly L-E-G-A-L. That I promise you.'

'Well, that's a nice change, Uncle Joe.'

'And remember, Maureen,' he'd said by way of a final word, 'you *never* mention the name of Joseph Blunt in connection with this matter. Right?'

'There's a lot I disapprove of about you, Uncle Joe, but I wouldn't ever let you down.' With that she had smiled sweetly, kissed him, and undertaken to do the letters.

Some time later her enquiries yielded their first dividend. She called at his flat one night and handed him a brochure advertising *Capricorn Adventure Cruises*. Among other things it contained a picture of *Sunglow*, and a simple map of the islands the coaster visited. That was when the idea had become a plan, when he'd made his decision to go. Money, and travel documents in another name, were next on the list of things to be tackled. Having regard to the circles in which he moved, and the nature of his mission, neither had presented insoluble problems. But it had taken time to get things fixed, which was just as well because it made possible the growth of a decent beard.

Had it not been for the six hours of drifting which put *Sunglow* well to the west of her normal course, Wreck Island would not have been sighted. As it happened, it was no more than a few miles away when Cassidy came to the bridge that afternoon for the first dog-watch.

His immediate reaction was to send for Gaston Pascal. To him he said, 'Go down and tell the passengers all about Wreck Island. I'll be taking the ship close inshore so they can have a good look – photograph the wreck, etcetera. You know the story, Gaston. Be sure now that it loses nothing in the telling.'

Pascal smiled, tidied his moustache with a well-groomed forefinger. 'I'll do my best, Captain.'

The wreck to which Cassidy referred lay conspicuous and forlorn on the northern end of the island. Many years earlier, when on tow from Perth to Mombasa, the floating dock had broken away from its tug in a storm. Days later it had drifted on to the island which owed its name to a history of wrecks stretching back into the early days of sail.

Passengers were given a good view of the wreck, and photographs were taken, before Cassidy altered course to bring *Sunglow* down the leeward side of the island, keeping about a mile offshore. Apart from its wreck, the island, about a mile in length, had little to offer. There were the familiar wind bent ranks of coconut palms, the low grey cliffs of coral rising from the lagoon inside the reef, and the sky with its quota of frigate birds and boobies, wheeling, diving and screeching. An indentation in the coastline formed a small bay, its beach dazzling white in the setting sun. Beyond it a plume of smoke rose from the plantation, to hover uncertainly at treetop level before being carried away by the light breeze.

Searching with binoculars for the origin of the smoke, Cassidy saw a number of *pirogues* drawn up on the beach. Near them nylon fishing nets were draped over crude trestles; at the southernmost end of the beach a wooden jetty reached out into the bay; near it a cabin cruiser lay moored to a buoy. Cassidy was no stranger to Wreck Island. He had passed it a number of times over the years, and landed there twice within the last twelve months. On the first occasion to see if the guano deposits had been worked out – they had – and on the second, only four months earlier, he'd landed with Pascal to see if there'd been development since his last visit – there had not. On both occasions the island had been desolate and deserted but for the remains of a decaying hut near the wrecked floating dock. It had, he thought, been used by wreck scavengers from other islands.

The coconut plantation was too small, too remote, to be economically viable. So the island with its unsavoury history of wrecks, and situated off the main trading routes, had been left to itself to be washed by the rain and baked by the sun.

But things must have changed, he decided. Wreck Island had come alive: *pirogues*, a jetty, a cabin cruiser, smoke; a settlement it seemed. It was close to five o'clock. There was an hour of daylight left. A number of things persuaded him to investigate: the possibility of work for the ship, something of interest for the passengers, Pascal's need of fresh fish and, perhaps most importantly, his natural curiosity.

FOURTEEN

By the time Cassidy had made his decision and stopped the engines, *Sunglow*'s way had carried her on past the bay. Having checked the depth of water, he dropped anchor several cables south of the inlet. Undergrowth and coconut palms on the southern headland hid the view of the beach from seaward.

A skimmer was lowered and brought alongside the foredeck where a rope ladder had been put over the side. The second mate and a seaman climbed down, followed by

Pascal who was to check developments ashore and see if supplies of fish were obtainable. Cassidy was leaning over the gunwhale giving final instructions to the chief steward, when a voice from behind asked, 'Can I go with them, sir?'

He turned his head and saw that the voice was Jim Abernethy's. Cassidy hesitated before saying, 'Yes. Climb down. Make it smart, lad.' Had Jim not been Mrs Clutterbutt's nephew, he would have said no. It was too late for beach landing jaunts by passengers.

Jim went down the ladder, Obudo started the outboard engine and the skimmer speeded off, turned round the headland into the small bay and was soon lost to sight.

The second mate saw no signs of life as they made for the jetty. Just short of it he throttled back and the skimmer drifted alongside. They made fast, a seaman was left in charge, and the small party climbed on to the jetty and went along it to the beach. Led by Pascal, they headed for a path cut through thick undergrowth to the plantation beyond. They had barely reached it when a man with an automatic rifle slung over his shoulder stepped from the bushes. Brown skinned with Arabic features, he was wearing khaki slacks and a safari shirt, the metal letters IMMEC on its shoulder straps. He stood in their way, his manner challenging.

Speaking the *patois* of the islands, Pascal indicated that he wished to see the settlement manager. The brown man shook his head. Obudo took over, made the same request in Swahili. There was no response.

Pascal tried English. 'I want to see the boss-man. The manager.'

Again the man shook his head, said something unintelligible. With a warning gleam in his eye, he took from his pocket a cellophane covered card and handed it to Pascal. Printed in French, English and German it read: *Landing on this island is prohibited to all persons other than those carrying valid entry permits issued by the International Mineral and Marine Exploration Corporation Inc.*

Pascal read it aloud for the benefit of the others. They were discussing it when two white men came down the path through the undergrowth. Deeply tanned, they wore shorts, bush-shirts and sun-helmets. They stopped some distance away; the man with the rifle went back to them. A brief conversation followed, after which all three came forward. The older white man, shorter and thicker set than his companion, had a burn-scarred face. Staring with suspicion, he asked Pascal, 'What for you come here?'

The chief steward explained. They were from the coaster *Sunglow* of Mombasa, visiting the islands on her normal trading route; also carrying passengers. The ship was bound for Providence Island, last port of call Ile Desroches. The engine breakdown had pushed them way off course, otherwise they would not have passed Wreck Island. Was there now a settlement on the island? Were the coconut plantations and guano deposits being worked? Most important of all, was there any possibility of obtaining supplies of fresh fish?

The owner of the scarred face shook his head. The answer to all questions was 'no'. In hesitant but adequate English, with an accent Pascal could not place, the man said that he and his companion were members of a scientific expedition carrying out a geological, geophysical survey on behalf of the international corporation which had leased the island from the Seychelles government. There were no fish for sale; all that were caught were required by the survey team and its labourers.

'Okay. I understand,' said Pascal. With a smile, he added, 'You certainly aren't taking any chances.' He pointed at the brown man, pretended to aim a gun. 'Sentries with automatic rifles.'

For the first time the scarred man's hostile manner changed, and he smiled. The sentry, he said, carried a rifle more for effect than serious use. It helped to deter unwanted visitors. There were, he pointed out, other mineral and marine exploration groups – indeed other countries – which would be interested in the work being done on the island. That was why visitors were not welcome.

Pascal asked what country the two white men came from. The scarred man appeared not to understand. IMMEC was, he stressed, an international corporation.

'No, I mean you and your colleague personally. I can't place your accent. Russian?' he suggested with a grin.

The scarred man spoke to his companion in a foreign language. Both men laughed, shook their heads. 'No,' said the scarred man. 'But it is from next to the Soviet Union that we come – Finland.'

'Ah, you're Finns.' Pascal nodded in sudden understanding. 'No wonder I couldn't place the accent.'

A formal and friendly exchange followed: the weather, the latest news. Pascal asked if *Sunglow* could help in future with mail and stores. The scarred man thanked him. The expedition's requirements in that respect were, he explained, seen to by vessels from the Seychelles. He looked at his watch, then at the sky, remarked that the light would soon be going. Pascal took the hint. Accompanied by the Finns, he led his party back to the beach and out along the jetty. They climbed into the skimmer, the second mate started the outboard, the Finns waved goodbye, Pascal and his men responded, and the skimmer made for the open sea. It had soon cleared the bay, rounded the headland, and set course for *Sunglow*.

The skimmer was hoisted on board and Pascal made his report to the Captain. Not long afterwards *Sunglow*'s anchor was weighed. Steering a southerly course, she made down the palm fringed shoreline at half-speed. Once clear of the island, course was altered to the south-west. Providence Island, a hundred miles distant, was the next port of call. Steaming at half-speed *Sunglow* would, Cassidy estimated, arrive there at eight o'clock on the following morn-

131

ing. He hoped to load coconut oil and copra, the island's principal exports, and possibly mangrove poles, or *boriti* as they were known locally. It was a well-wooded island, there was a small village, and at low water there was safe bathing inside the reef. One way and another it would, he thought, appeal to the passengers, give them an interesting run ashore. These thoughts were interrupted by the ringing of the bridge phone. It was Kumar Gupta with unhappy news.

'New bearing run hot, Captain,' reported the chief engineer.

Cassidy exploded. 'Holy St Patrick! Not again, chief?'

'Sorry, sir. Is possible we make too tight. But we can fix it for sure. Maybe another six hours work.'

Cassidy did some quick thinking. The ship had just cleared the leeward side of Wreck Island, the southernmost extremity of which, a bush covered finger of desiccated coral curving round to the south-west, formed a small bay well sheltered from the south-east trade wind. It was still no more than a mile away.

He spoke into the phone. 'Can you give me another twenty minutes at half-speed, Chief?'

'Twenty minutes okay, Captain. Maybe thirty minutes. Not possible for more.'

Cassidy gave the order hard-a-starboard, the helmsman spun the wheel and *Sunglow*'s bows paid off to starboard. With Obudo calling the depths of water at the echosounder, Cassidy conned the ship in until, well within the twenty minutes Kumar Gupta had suggested, the coaster was swinging to an anchor in the small bay. Brief tropical twilight was already giving way to darkness, and on shore the rustling leaves of coconut palms were catching the last light of the sun.

Cassidy knew that the bearing trouble would delay *Sunglow*'s arrival at Providence Island to sometime on the following afternoon, and then only if she could steam at ten knots. Since there was a limit to the number of disappointments passengers could endure, he decided that something would have to be done. Ever an optimist, he sent for the chief steward. 'You'll have to be busy this night, Gaston,' he said. 'There's to be a beach party.'

Pascal's eyebrows rose, the elegant forehead wrinkled. 'On what beach, Captain?'

'Why Gaston, on this beach of course.'

'Landing on Wreck Island is not permitted. They told us so this afternoon.'

The big Irishman sank back in his chair, clasped his hands behind his head, thrust a bearded chin towards the deckhead and closed his eyes. Pascal knew the mood, read the danger signals.

'Oh, and to the devil with that, Gaston. The settlement is the best part of a mile to the north. It'll be dark shortly and, anyway, *Sunglow* can't be seen in here. It's only the beach we'll be using. No harm in that, man. If they do find our passengers there and clear them out, well, that's surely adventure enough.' Cassidy leant forward, poured himself two fingers of Irish whisky.

The chief steward shook his head. 'There are problems, Captain. We have no fish.'

'Ah, and to blazes with that, Gaston. Begorrah and be damned if I'll let a few fish interfere with me plans. It's a genius with food you are. You and that chef of yours – Pierre. Put your heads together, man. Come up with something special. Give it a fancy name – make up a story – a traditional *ilois* dish, you might call it. There's mangoes, pawpaws, limes, bananas, avocados, lychees and coconuts a-plenty in the cold chamber. And there's no shortage in the bar of rum, brandy, whisky, gin, beer, cola and other such delicacies.' Cassidy tasted the whisky, smacked his lips, nodded approval.

'And what time will they land, Captain?' The chief steward's voice lacked enthusiasm.

'Well, now, and what shall we say?' Cassidy pulled at his beard and looked at the clock on the bulkhead. 'Seven-fifteen. Does that give you time enough, Gaston?'

133

'Yes, Captain. It can be done.' With an air of preoccupation the chief steward hurried away. Cassidy's next move was to send for the second mate whom he told to pass the word among passengers that there would be a beach party that night, briefing in the lounge at 6.30, skimmers alongside at 7.15.

At Cassidy's request Mrs Clutterbutt had not joined the beach party. 'It's a fine chance for a talk tonight,' he'd explained. 'And it's honoured I'd be if you would take coffee with me after dinner.'

Others who decided not to go ashore were the Bruckners and Van der Karsts. 'We like better to play bridge,' Mrs Bruckner told the chief steward. 'To play beach games in the night is not goot.'

Mrs Kitson had volunteered for the beach party but changed her mind at the last moment. 'I've suddenly got the most awful headache,' she told Sandra Carter. 'It's a nightmare thing. Hateful thought, but early bed is my penance.'

'You poor dear. Ask Dr Summers for something. I'm sure he can help.' Sandra permitted herself a private smile. 'Too bad you have to miss the party. You do so love swimming, don't you?'

'I adore it. Especially in these gorgeously warm lagoons.'

'– and especially topless.'

'How d'you know that, Sandra?'

'Dean got a lovely picture of you and Jim floating side by side at Fouquet Island.'

'The beast,' said Mrs Kitson. 'That telephoto lens I suppose.'

Commander Rollo and Dr Summers, too, had decided to stay on board. Ostensibly because they had a chess game to finish but actually because Rollo, a model of good discipline, had been disturbed by Cassidy's statement at the briefing that the island was leased to an international corporation whose officials were making some sort of survey. He'd said that security in the island was tight. 'Understandably, they don't want visitors at the work site. But the beach you'll be landing on is a mile south of the site. Remain on the beach, don't go inland, and there'll be no problems.'

The other passengers had gone off in the skimmers, most of them more intrigued than frightened by what Cassidy had said. Jim Abernethy was certainly one of these. When he'd landed with Pascal and Said Obudo that afternoon he'd sensed that the *Sunglow* party had blundered into something peculiar; secretive, even dangerous. The two white men, foreigners with strange accents and suspicious, hostile stares, had heightened that impression. The man with the burn-scarred face and threatening eyes had looked sinister. For Jim, a romantic, the prospect of returning to the island that night, landing on a remote beach, promised high adventure. Not that he'd confided his beliefs to anyone, nor formulated any sort of plan, but deep inside he felt ripples of excitement he could scarcely explain.

Passengers were landed in two skimmers with the second mate, Pascal, Kibusu the bosun, Luther Nelson and a steward in attendance. Dry wood and palm leaves were collected and a bonfire lit. A few passengers went off along the beach, but most stayed by the fire while the meal was being made ready. Obudo had insisted that the tide was not yet low enough for swimming inside the reef. He intended to keep things that way. A dark night with no moon could be dangerous in strange waters, particularly for older people.

'No barbecue tonight,' Pascal had announced. 'Instead we have a traditional dish of the islands. Tropical fruits, drenched with a sauce made from *calao* and the fresh juice of limes. The natives call this *La Salade du Paradis* – the Salad of Paradise. A beautiful name, is it not?'

There were murmurs of approval. Sandra Carter squeaked with pleasure. 'Now isn't that cute?'

'For those who do not like the salad,' continued Pascal, 'we have Pirates' Pleasure. This also is traditional. A wholemeal sandwich of spiced minced meats with thinly sliced gammon.'

'Fantastic,' said Henry Atkins. 'It's what I usually ask for at the Ritz. Makes the old lady hopping mad it does. But it's great nosh. They call it sausages and bacon there.'

Drink flowed easily, tongues were loosened, inhibitions forgotten, and *La Salade du Paradis* quickly demolished. As the party got noisier and more cheerful, little groups of passengers drifted along the beach, pleased to get away from the fire on what was an oppressively hot night under a clouded sky.

Jim Abernethy was among the first to disappear into the surrounding darkness. It had been announced at the briefing that the last skimmer would leave the beach at midnight, but passengers who wished to do so could go off earlier. With this in mind he'd checked the time as he left the fire. It was ten past nine. That gave him the best part of three hours.

He reached the western end of the beach and made his way towards the plantation above it, climbing a fissure in the low coral cliff to get there. Once through the undergrowth which fringed the plantation he walked northwards, keeping as close to the sea as he could. Though the island was flat the going was not easy in the dark, and he often stumbled. Towards the northern end of the island he slowed his pace, trod warily; silence was important.

At times he would go through the undergrowth to the edge of the cliffs to see if there was any sign of the jetty on which he'd landed that afternoon. In the opaque darkness he all but missed it. About to go back into the plantation, he heard far off voices and the sound of water splashing. Staring into the night he saw phosphorescent flashes on the dark surface of the sea and realized they came from the paddles of a *pirogue*.

The voices grew louder, the paddling fainter, and he heard the squeak of wood against wood. It was followed by the sound of footsteps and planks creaking. People on the jetty.

He went back to the plantation and began to work his way cautiously round the area from which, that afternoon, the two white men had come. The rancid smell of cooking oil drew him towards the clearing. Soon afterwards he heard voices, saw the subdued glow of open fires. He went closer, moving tentatively, taking cover behind palm trunks, an outthrust foot testing the surface for dry timber.

He got within a few yards of the clearing before hiding himself in the undergrowth. When his eyes had adjusted to the dim light cast by the fires, he saw that rows of wooden huts stood between him and the far side of the clearing. Through the gaps between them he caught glimpses of machinery: camouflaged bulldozers, tractors, earth movers and generators. Groups of black men squatted on their haunches round open fires. A white man came from one of the larger huts, went behind it and urinated against a palm trunk. He was too far off for Jim to see if he was one of the men he'd met that afternoon.

The overhead reflections of the light from the fires puzzled him until he saw that the entire area was covered with camouflage nets. They were spread over a web of wire cables secured high in the trunks of palm trees, some fifty feet above the ground.

During the half hour he stayed there watching, nothing of interest occurred. It was getting late. Reluctantly, he decided to make his way back to the southern end of the island. Following the route by which he'd come, still moving warily, he covered about half the journey in the next twenty minutes. Wet with perspiration and suffering from thirst, he decided to rest for a few moments in a gap in the undergrowth. It was a good place, on the edge of a low cliff against the foot of which lapped the sea. Partly because it

137

had been a long day with a good deal of tension, and partly because the murmur of the sea was a powerful sedative – whatever the reasons – he dozed off.

Diana Kitson was standing in the inglenook fireplace in his father's house. Talking to someone he could not see, she had her back to him, nor could he hear what she was saying. He called her name and she turned slowly, smiled, beckoned to him, but he couldn't move. She turned away again and he was for the first time aware that she was naked. Again he tried to go to her; but it was hopeless, his limbs simply would not respond.

A deep voice intruded – his father's, of course – and a hand clasped his shoulder. The voice sounded again, closer now, and he looked up to see a dark shape standing over him, shining a torch in his eyes. He knew, then, that it was no longer a dream.

FIFTEEN

Cassidy spoke over his shoulder as he busied himself at the tray. 'Will you be taking milk or sugar, Mrs C?'

'Neither, thank you, Captain.'

He passed the coffee to her, poured his own, dropped in three sugar lumps and sat down. 'Good of you it is to have come,' he said. 'Missing all the pleasures of the beach party.'

Mrs Clutterbutt smiled. 'I think, perhaps, I'm a little old for moonlight picnics, Captain. And we have important matters to discuss.'

'Indeed we have, Mrs C.' He tasted the coffee. 'Now, it was this question of getting the goods ashore if we were fortunate enough to find them.'

'Yes. That is a most important matter. I did some

138

research before leaving England. Had most helpful advice from my solicitor. Perhaps I should tell you about it.'

'Indeed now, and that would be a good idea, Mrs C.' Cassidy put down the coffee cup, fidgeted with his cigar case. 'And would you be minding at all if I were to have me cigar?'

Mrs Clutterbutt shrugged. 'If you must. However, let me begin. The *Koolamagee* was owned by the Bannister family. Actually by Captain Bannister and his father . . .' Mrs Clutterbutt hesitated, a faraway look in her eyes. 'That would be my *great*-great-grandfather. When the barque foundered, Lloyds made good the loss to the Bannister family. Indeed, those funds became a substantial part of the Bannister assets, most of which . . .' she spread her hands, smiled apologetically, '. . . in due course came to me.'

'Ah, and it's an ill wind that blows nobody any good.' Cassidy sighed, examined the glowing end of the cigar.

'When I made my enquiries all those years afterwards, no details could be found of *Koolamagee*'s cargo. No manifests, no consignment notes, no records whatever of what she was carrying. Other, of course, than the cutting from *The Times*. As you know, all it said was "her cargo included a number of gold ingots". John Abernethy, my solicitor, looked closely into the legal aspects. He told me that since there was no record of the cargo, but for *The Times* report, and since the owners of the cargo she was carrying when she foundered could be presumed to have claimed on their insurers – such being the case – the treasure, if subsequently found, would be deemed to belong to the carrier, the carrier being the owners of the vessel. Since *Koolamgee* belonged to Harvey Bannister and his father, they were the carriers. In other words the ingots belonged – still belong – to the Bannister family. That, said my solicitor, was his interpretation of the legal position in England.'

Cassidy nodded. 'Interesting indeed, Mrs C, but the

islands hereabouts do not belong to England. Mostly they fall under the Seychelles.'

'Of course, and that is the problem. John Abernethy was well aware of it. His advice was quite simple, however. He believed that, whatever the foreign law might be, the Bannisters at least had moral entitlement to the treasure. "If you find it take possession – that's nine-tenths of any law," he told me. "Keep the finding as confidential as you can. Then, on return to Mombasa, consign the treasure to the RNLI and place it in a bonded warehouse, inform the RNLI, quote me as a reference, and leave it to them to settle the matter with the authorities concerned." That was his advice. Not that he thought we'd ever need it. On the contrary.' She frowned. 'He was highly sceptical.'

'And why would it happen to be the RNLI, then?'

'Because, Captain, as you must know, the Institution renders such wonderful service. The lifeboatmen are so splendidly brave, so selfless. Volunteers, unpaid, they risk their lives for others – and, sadly, not infrequently lose them.'

'Ah, and that's true.' He nodded several times in an understanding way, before adding, 'You'll not be keeping any of the money for yourself, then?'

'I'm a wealthy woman, Captain. Money is not something I need. Adventure is. Both for myself and Jim.' She closed her eyes, breathed deeply. 'There is perhaps one point I've not made clear. Though I shall be giving my half to the RNLI, yours will not be involved. John Abernethy would arrange with the RNLI for that to be sent to you and Mr Patel in terms of our agreement.'

'Indeed, and to be honest I was wondering about that meself.' Cassidy tipped cigar ash into a seashell. 'When I spoke to Goosam about these things we got on to the question of disposal of the goods. He is a clever man, Mrs C. Knows what can and cannot be done in Mombasa. Now I'm not saying that his advice is any better than Mr Abernethy's, but it is indeed practical.'

140

'Then I should much like to know what it is, Captain.'

Cassidy looked away from the disconcerting challenge of Mrs Clutterbutt's grey eyes. 'A little more coffee, Mrs C?'

'No thank you, Captain. It does not help sleep.'

'Ah, and that's true.' He mopped his face with a handkerchief before going on. 'Now, about Goosam Patel. Like your solicitor, he did not think we'd ever be finding White Island – or the *goods*. But very sure he was about what we should do if we did. "Avoid the legal jungle," he told me. "Keep it aboard until we can arrange for its transfer in harbour, or at sea, to a dhow bound for India. We'll consign it," he said, "to my brother's business in Bombay, Hadji Patel and Company, that is." Goosam explained that his brother would see to its landing and sale there, and the distribution of the proceeds.' Cassidy drew on his cigar. 'You'll be wondering, Mrs C, if Goosam's brother can be trusted.'

'I certainly am, Captain.' Mrs Clutterbutt's tone hardened.

'Well now, and let me tell you that there's no more trustworthy man than Goosam. It's twenty years and more that I've known him. I would trust him with my life, Mrs C, let alone my worldly goods. Sure, and I'm thinking his brother must be the same, or Goosam wouldn't be trusting him.'

He went over to the coffee tray, refilled his cup. Mrs Clutterbutt left the settee, moved to the front of the cabin and stood by an open porthole. In the distance the darkness was broken by the flickering light of the beach party's bonfire. Her thoughts softened as she pictured Jim there. How much more exciting and interesting for him than the house in Hampstead, with his father and that dreadful step-mother Leonie forever expressing disapproval: his clothes, his manners, his friends, the way he spoke, his lack of ambition. Nothing was spared. She'd heard them at it. Mrs Clutterbutt sighed with new-found content. It didn't really matter a damn whether they found White Island or

Harvey Bannister's gold. The real importance of those things was that they'd made possible Jim's escape from an unhappy environment into a most interesting and exciting one.

Turning to Cassidy, she said, 'You know, Captain, even if we never find White Island I shall not regret having come on this cruise. It is a wonderful experience – both for me and my nephew. I would not have missed it.'

Cassidy came back, coffee in hand, and stood beside her at the porthole. 'Ah, and that's good to hear, Mrs C, for those certainly are my sentiments.' He laughed. 'And it's no Blarney Stone I've been kissing. When you've been at sea as long as I have, one voyage is much like another. But the search for White Island, the interesting story behind it –' he hesitated, looked down at her, and there was no mistaking the warmth and affection in his smile, 'and the company of the most charming lady who told it to me. Well – such things make this a different sort of voyage for me. And, indeed, a very happy one.'

For the first time since they'd met, Mrs Clutterbutt blushed. 'You really are a truly Irish Irishman, Captain Cassidy.' She looked at him, smiled contentedly. 'And a very nice one, too.'

In the discussion which followed they agreed that it would be sensible to defer a decision about getting the gold ashore until they'd found it. 'The problem may never arise,' said Mrs Clutterbutt, dismissing it in her common-sense way.

They talked about a number of things after that, including the announcement Cassidy would shortly be making to enlist the support of passengers in finding White Island, and the reward she had authorized him to offer. It was not, she insisted, to be known that she was the donor. Some time after 10.30 he escorted her to the lounge.

Passing along the passageway through the officers' quarters on his way back to his cabin, he heard voices in Scalatti's cabin; one of them was a woman's. So she's there

142

again, he thought. Well, there's nothing I can do about that, unless they create a disturbance.

Alone in her cabin, Mrs Clutterbutt thought of her conversation with Cassidy. The more she saw of him the more she liked him. Indeed, she confessed to herself, I do believe it has become more than just liking him. But that is absurd. I must be sensible, remember my age, and behave accordingly.

She wondered what his feelings were? There seemed to her to have been genuine warmth, even affection, in the way he had looked at her when he said she'd made the voyage a different one for him.

But he's Irish, she reminded herself. They have an inborn charm, a gift for saying the right thing. And what of his motives? Was she really attractive to him'. She was, after all, a rich woman. Was it that?

With such doubts in her mind, she fell asleep.

'Why don't you go on these beach parties, Luigi? Don't you like them?' Mrs Kitson's frown of inquiry was directed at the Italian over the rim of her glass.

Scalatti, perched on a bunk higher than the settee she shared with Krol, shook his head. 'Last cruise I was three times on beach parties. Very nice. Lot of fun. This cruise nothing.' He pointed in the direction of the Captain's cabin. 'He not like me. Wish to make trouble for me. So no beach party for Luigi. You will see. If ship is loading or unloading I can understand. Chief mate must be on board. But no cargo work tonight, and he is not sending me to the beach. Now always it is Obudo and Pascal.' He shrugged his shoulders. 'Anyway. What the hell. I like better to be here with you, Diana – an' this louzy Swedish fellow.' Scalatti made a pistol with fist and forefinger, and pretended to fire at Krol.

The Swede said, 'Forget your goddam captain, man. We want to enjoy ourselves.'

Scalatti slid off the bunk, took the bottle of vermouth from the corner cupboard. 'Sure. Have another drink.'

'Not for me, Luigi.' Mrs Kitson held up a hand in protest. 'Had too much already.' Her speech was uncertain, her voice pitched rather higher than usual.

'Come on, Diana.' Krol took her glass. 'This is a party, enjoy yourself lady. Have fun.'

She took a deep breath, raised her eyes in mock despair. 'All right. Goodness knows what it'll do to me.'

Scalatti filled her glass, added ice. 'I know what Nils like it to do, Diana. Watch him. He likes ladies too much.'

Krol's pale eyes blinked, the flat nose between them glistened with perspiration. 'He talks rubbish, Diana. Don't listen. Come on Eyetie. Some more drinks for your Swedish friend.' Krol held out his glass. Scalatti filled it, then his own.

The Swede raised his glass to Diana Kitson. 'Skol,' he said. 'To the most beautiful lady on board.'

She stood up, swaying uncertainly, glass in hand. 'Thank you Nils.' She bowed. 'S'lovely compliment, Skol to you, too, dear.' She drank from her glass, swayed again. 'Oh dear, I think I'm drunk,' she said, sitting down heavily and spilling vermouth.

Krol put an arm round her shoulders. 'You are not drunk. You are happy, Diana. Nothing wrong with that.'

She put her head on his shoulder. 'Oh, Nils, you are a sweetie. So kind.'

Scalatti put down his glass, went to the door. 'I must check the anchor cable. Also look around the decks.'

'Oh, Luigi, must you?' The corners of her mouth drooped, but she snuggled closer to Krol, her head under his chin.

'In half an hour I will be back.' Scalatti stopped at the door, held a finger to his lips, a conspiratorial grin on the sunken face. 'Be good, *bambinos* and quiet. *Il Capitano*,' he warned, closing the door and making off down the passageway.

It was a nuisance having to waste half an hour, but it was important to humour Krol, to put the Swede under some sort of obligation.

The dark shape growled something, prodded him in the ribs with what felt like a gun barrel.

Jim jumped up, all drowsiness banished by fear. He was bigger than the man with the gun and for a moment thought of tackling him. Then, realizing that his chances were better if he were compliant, he raised a hand to shield his eyes from the torch. His captor mistook the gesture, jumped back, shouted a warning. Jim dropped his hand. 'Okay,' he said and forced a laugh. Somehow tension had to be relieved. The man must be another IMMEC sentry.

In what sounded like an African language his captor repeated something several times. Jim assumed it to be a question – probably, 'What are you doing here?' Since there was no way of answering it, he pointed south, to where he'd landed with the beach party. The sentry grunted something, turned Jim round until he was facing the southern end of the island and pushed him forward. So the man wanted to be taken to the beach party? Happy to comply with that, Jim led the way.

They had not gone far when the light of the bonfire showed up in the distance. They reached the end of the plantation, went through the undergrowth and down to the beach. Making their way along it towards the fire they almost bumped into Obudo and Dean Carter in the darkness.

The second mate berated Jim for leaving the beach: 'The Captain warned you not to – we've been searching all over the place – thought you must have drowned – you're crazy, man. You've made a lot of trouble – now look what's happened.'

Having got that off his chest, Obudo spoke to the sentry in Kiswahili. It was evident that this was the appropriate language, for what sounded like an emotional conversation followed. At the end of it, Obudo led the little group to the fire. There it could be seen that the Swahili was wearing the same uniform, carrying the same pattern automatic rifle, as the IMMEC sentry encountered near the jetty earlier that day.

'His name is Aziz Agojo, he wants to come back to *Sunglow* with us,' Obudo explained to Pascal. 'He is a coast African from one of the small islands south of Zanzibar. He has a young wife and two children there. He says he and the others were brought to this island to work as labourers. They were told the island was on the East African coast and the work was for a few weeks only. Already they have been here nine weeks. The pay promised was good, but so far they've had no money. It would be paid when the work was finished, the white men told them. But they would not say when that would be. 'Not long now' is the only answer they get. The work is very hard. Agojo says he complained to the boss man and was then beaten by an African foreman. Tonight he ran away from the camp. He was hiding in the plantation when a sentry found him. He knocked out the sentry, took his gun and uniform and was making for the southern end of the island when he found me.' Obudo turned to Agojo, said something in Kiswahili. The African took off his safari shirt and turned his back to the fire. They saw the livid weals and broken skin.

'My God,' Sandra Carter protested. 'That's simply terrible. It's just too wicked. It's barbaric. They're treating these people like slaves.'

'Poor wretch,' said Mrs Cawson. 'Can't we help him?'

The Reverend Bliss said, 'I've no doubt it is our Christian duty to rescue this man. His evidence – his condition – will certainly persuade the authorities to investigage conditions on the island.' There were murmurs of approval. With UNO-like indignation, Jean McLachlan said, 'It's a flagrant violation of human rights.'

After a further exchange between Agojo and Obudo,

the second mate again addressed the worried group round the bonfire. 'He says he and some other labourers come from a small island not far south of Zanzibar. They were brought by ship to this island. He doesn't know its name or where it is. They boarded the ship at night and were kept below decks throughout the voyage. They were offloaded here at night, after three days at sea. If we don't take him, he says he fears for his life.'

Pascal was dubious. Captain Cassidy would be far from pleased. The second mate asked Kibusu for his opinion. The bosun said he was convinced the man's story was genuine. 'I know Captain long time already. He is good man. Will help this man Aziz Agojo. We can put him ashore in Zanzibar. Fishermen will take him to his island.'

There followed a general discussion in which several passengers took part. Eventually Pascal and Obudo agreed to take the man on the understanding that the Captain would make the final decision.

The bonfire was doused with sea water and the beach party gathered up its belongings. Soon the three skimmers were bumping and spraying their way through the darkness to *Sunglow*.

At sunrise next morning Kumar Gupta reported that *Sunglow*'s engine repairs were completed. Anchor was weighed and course once more set for Providence Island. The south-easterly wind had freshened, rolling before it ranks of small seas topped with lace-like frills which foamed and sparked in the path of the rising sun.

At first Cassidy had been unwilling to take Agojo, but after interviewing the man, and seeing the injuries for himself, he gave way to the pleas of Arnold Bliss and others who'd been on the beach party. But, said Cassidy, Agojo would have to work his passage, and live makeshift under the foc's'le with the creole deck passengers. To these terms the Swahili readily agreed.

The coaster was half an hour's steaming south of Wreck Island when a small vessel was sighted astern. It was coming up fast. Cassidy focussed binoculars on it, recognized the cabin-cruiser seen moored near the jetty on the previous afternoon. His first thought was that it was making for the islands to the south. Then he realized it was unlikely to be doing so at such high speed. Was it pursuing *Sunglow*? And if so, why? If it had a message to pass it could long ago have done so by radio. Was Agojo's desertion the trouble?

To Obudo he said, 'See that Agojo keeps below decks until we know what this craft is up to. And brief the passengers. Make it sharp, lad.'

Cassidy focussed the binoculars again. The cabin-cruiser was little over a mile away now, her flared bows plunging into the short seas, throwing up sheets of spray, then rising high, poised to plunge again, white water streaming from them.

He took a loud-hailer from the rack, waited in the wing of the bridge. Before long the cabin-cruiser had all but drawn level, and the throb of its diesels dropped to a lower key as it took station to starboard of the coaster.

A man came from the wheelhouse and stood at the guardrail, his binoculars trained on *Sunglow*'s bridge. Obudo touched Cassidy's arm. 'That's the man with the scarred face, sir. The Finnish scientist who did the talking yesterday.'

Cassidy nodded. 'Well, then, I'll be hearing what he has to say today.'

The man at the guardrail lowered his binoculars, picked up a loud-hailer. 'Our man – Agojo – you have him there, yes?'

'Don't know what you're talking about,' Cassidy's voice boomed across the water.

'Persons of your ship come to the south beach last night. We see the tracks they make. Also the fire they make. It is not permitted to land on the island. Already we tell you this yesterday. Now you take our man Agojo. This is very serious, you understand, Captain.'

'We had engine trouble,' Cassidy shouted back. 'Had to anchor off the south beach for the night. Some passengers landed for a picnic there. No harm done. Nobody saw your man, whatever his name was, and . . .'

The scientist interrupted. 'His tracks, and also another's. We find them. They come to where the passengers were on the beach. Then they disappear. The man Agojo was taken away by the passengers.'

Cassidy turned to Obudo, who was immediately behind him. 'Keep talking to me for a minute or so, lad. Say what you like. As long as that Finn sees us talking, it's okay.'

Obudo said, 'His English is a lot better today. I'll give him a lip-reading problem.' The second mate broke into Kiswahili. He was in full stride when Cassidy said 'That'll do, lad.'

He put the loud-hailer to his mouth. 'My second mate was in charge of the passengers. He tells me they saw those tracks. Wondered whose they might be. He says the tracks were fresh. Must have been made shortly before our passengers landed. He and the passengers discussed them. Reckoned somebody must have come ashore from a *pirogue*, walked inland a bit, then come back with another man. That would be your man, I don't doubt. Looks like he was taken off in the *pirogue*.'

The burn-scarred face looked uncertain, spoke to someone in the cabin-cruiser's wheelhouse before saying, 'The nearest land from Wreck Island is too far for a *pirogue*.'

The loud-hailer amplified Cassidy's derisive laugh. 'Too far? You can't have been in these waters long. The natives travel hundreds of miles in *pirogues*.' The big Irishman shook his head. 'Sorry. We can't help you. He's certainly not here. I don't take runaways on board. This is a cruise ship. Costs money to travel with me.'

The twenty feet of water between the cabin-cruiser and *Sunglow* were not enough to conceal the puzzled, unhappy

149

expression on the face of the Finnish scientist. Its owner shrugged his shoulders, turned again to speak to the man in the wheelhouse. The cabin-cruiser drew away from *Sunglow*, pitching and rolling in the short seas as she turned to head back to the island. The rumble of her diesels grew stronger and *Sunglow*'s passengers, who'd been lining the side while the shouted conversation took place, waved a cheerful farewell.

SIXTEEN

Later that morning Cassidy presided at a briefing in the lounge. Attended by Gaston Pascal carrying a clipboard and frowning with preoccupation, the Captain seated himself at a table near the bar. On it he placed his notes and a sealed envelope.

'Well now, ladies and gentlemen,' he began. 'I trust it was a good time you had ashore last night, and that our troubles with the engines did not unduly inconvenience you.' He looked at his notes, stroked his beard, had a quick word with Pascal. 'We should be reaching Providence Island soon after lunch today. There the skimmers will be taking you ashore to see around the island, to swim and so forth.' Having described somewhat perfunctorily, and with a certain lack of conviction, the principal features of Providence Island and its small community, he opened the sealed envelope. 'Ah, so that's it.' He looked up understandingly. 'This is interesting indeed. We are now approaching latitude nine degrees south. In the belt between nine and ten degrees, extending from Providence Island and the Farquhar Group across to the African coast, there are many atolls, islands and groups of islands. Some are inhabited, others not. All are believed to be charted, yet a few that lie off the main shipping routes may not be.' With a grave expression he considered the faces in front of him before glancing once more at his notes. 'Now one of these may well be a certain mysterious island, the whereabouts of which the *ilois* treat as a close secret. They call it Ile Blanche, White Island,' he explained. 'Sure and I couldn't say why. Maybe it looks white – a long line of surf breaking on a reef can give that impression. Perhaps its existence is no more than a legend, handed down through the generations. The natives, if you could be getting them to talk, will tell you there are palms there that give out an oil with famous healing properties.' Raising his head, Cassidy added, 'For such complaints as fevers and rheumatism. Their story has it that these, and more, can be cured with White Island's palm oil. Superstitious folk they are, and sure it takes a lot of believing.'

'Excuse me, Captain,' interrupted the shrill voice of Miss McLachlan. She was sitting in the back row, her hand raised in scholarly fashion. 'Their belief may have nothing to do with superstition. Quite the contrary. There is a strong body of medical opinion which believes that certain vegetable matter contains chemicals which can be used as protective agents against, for example, cancer.'

Cassidy nodded. 'Thank you, Miss McLachlan. Very interesting, I'm sure. Now if I may continue.'

'I've not yet finished.' Miss McLachlan frowned. 'Research scientists are showing particular interest in a remote community in El Salvador which appears to be free of cancer. That community has for generations used a red palm oil containing beta carolene, a major source of Vitamin A. It is not impossible that the palm trees on White Island produce an oil with similar properties. In which case the natives' belief in its healing qualities is well founded.' Miss McLachlan fiddled with her pebble-lens glasses, coughed nervously, and sat down.

Welcoming an unexpected ally, Cassidy favoured her with a blue-eyed beam of approval. 'Ah, and that's indeed most interesting, Miss McLachlan. It makes what I have to tell you folk all the more important. But first let me say that there is no island shown on the charts with the name Ile Blanche or White Island. Nor, so far as I know, has any white man ever found it. So what the truth of the matter is, I can't be saying. All the same . . .'

At this point the Rev. Bliss entered the discussion. 'It occurs to me that possibly it is *Huile Blanche*, not *Ile Blanche*,' he suggested.

'Why now, Reverend. What's the difference then? They sound the same to me.'

'In French *Ile* is island, *huile* is oil. The H is not sounded, you see, so it is pronounced the same way.'

'Trust the French.' Cassidy made a face, pulled at his beard. 'Indeed and it's a difficult lot they are.'

'That palm oil could be white, you see,' prompted the Rev. Bliss. He smiled apologetically at Miss McLachlan. 'Not red as in El Salvador.'

'Thank you, Reverend.' Cassidy's manner implied that the subject had been sufficiently discussed. 'Now if you'll allow me, I must tell you that my owners, the Capricorn Islands Shipping and Trading Company, would very much like to find that island.' He emphasized the point he was about to make with an exaggerated wink. 'It's the commercial possibilities you see. The Patels always have an eye to that. Clever business people, the Hindus. So on every voyage I keep a weather eye lifted for Ile Blanche. At each island we visit, I ask the natives if they know of its whereabouts. Usually I get no more than sly grins or tight lips, but some have spoken and from them I have formed this mental picture. It's a small island, no more than a mile in length, lying on a north-south axis. At its northern end a lone palm tree stands on a finger of land jutting into a lagoon which lies inside an offshore reef. There are many palm trees in the central and southern parts of the island.'

Cassidy paused, drank from a glass of water, looked across the saloon to where Mrs Clutterbutt shared a settee with Jim Abernethy. Her face was quite expressionless, but he thought he detected a glimmer of approval in the unflinching grey eyes. He glanced at his notes.

'Now, I'm going to ask you all to help in the search for White Island. The more eyes, the more lookouts we have, the greater the chances of finding it. And so,' he paused for effect, 'it gives me much pleasure to announce a prize of one thousand US dollars to the passenger who first sights White Island.'

There was a stir of interest, a sudden buzz of conversation. Cassidy held up a restraining hand. 'The competition, for that indeed is what it is, begins at noon today. Only passengers, not crew, are eligible for entry. One final point – any passenger who believes that he or she has sighted White Island must at once report to the bridge in order that the claim may be verified.' Slowly, methodically, Cassidy folded his notes and placed them in a shirt pocket. He leant sideways to say something to Pascal. The murmur of conversation between passengers stopped when Henry Atkins rose to ask how such a claim could be verified. 'I mean an island could look like what you've described Captain, and still not be White Island. Maybe, after what the Reverend said, it's name could be Oil Island in English.'

'Sure, and those are good points, Mr Atkins.' Cassidy began an unrehearsed improvisation. 'I forgot to mention that the natives say the palm trees on White Island are tapped for oil at the tops of their trunks, rather than at the bottom. Now I've never in my life seen such a thing in these parts, so I think there'll be no mistaking the island – *if* we do find it.' He stood up, made much of looking at his watch. 'I'll have to be leaving now, ladies and gentlemen. Mr Pascal will give you the detailed briefing for our activities over the next few days.'

As he passed Mrs Clutterbutt on his way out of the saloon, her nod of approval was accompanied by the slightest of smiles.

153

Sunglow reached Providence Island in early afternoon, and anchored on the north-western side, well protected from the prevailing south-easterly wind. The skimmers took the passengers off to explore the wooded island and swim, while the coaster landed stores and provisions and loaded coconut oil. The skimmers returned just before sunset. Loading completed, and a number of creole deck passengers embarked for the journey to the islands ahead, *Sunglow* weighed anchor and put out to sea as darkness fell.

That night the ship steamed slowly south; Cerf Island was passed and passengers awoke to find the ship anchored off the entrance to the inner harbour of North Island. During the forenoon they were taken on visits to both North and South Islands, the principal elements of the Farquhar Group. They were back on board for lunch and in early afternoon *Sunglow* sailed again, bound now for the Cosmoledos some 220 miles to the west. It was the 5th October, eleven days since the departure from Mombasa. The cruise had reached its half-way mark and with the ship now westward bound, each additional mile bringing it nearer to the East African coast, passengers began to feel they were at last homeward bound; for some this came as a relief.

'Have you had that chat with Agojo yet?' Jim Abernethy asked Said Obudo in whose cabin they were discussing the cruise. The second mate nodded. 'Yes. He says the two Finns we saw near the jetty, the guy with the scarred face and the other one, belong to a party of ten white men. They all speak the same language. There are four Ethiopian foremen. Agojo says the white men have a lot of strange instruments like telescopes standing on legs. Theodolites, I guess. And a lot of heavy earth moving and excavating gear. Also drums of diesel oil and big dumps of stores. He says these are brought to the island by ship. It has come there twice during his time. It arrives and unloads at night.

154

The Swahili labourers have to do the heavy work. There are no islanders, no creoles. For this reason the Swahilis also do the fishing. They like this because they are themselves fishermen, used to handling catamarans which are much the same as *pirogues*. But always the cabin-cruiser goes with them, an armed foreman on board. There are also Ethiopian sentries on duty day and night, patrolling the island. Agojo says it is not possible to escape.' The second mate snapped open a coke tin. 'More Jim?'

'No thanks. I've still got some.'

The second mate drank from the tin. A strict Muslim, he didn't touch alcohol.

Jim said, 'Did Agojo say what the work was?'

'Yes. He says that at first many pegs had to be driven in the ground in long lines from the beach up to the plantation. That's from the beach where the jetty is. And palms had to be ringed with white paint. Also in straight lines across the island, but at right angles to those from the beach. He doesn't know what for. The bulldozers are digging big holes in the ground. At night the earth movers take the excavated soil to other parts of the island and dump it. He thinks . . .'

The whistle on the voice-pipe next to the second-mate's bunk sounded. Scalatti's voice came through. 'Ten minute call.'

Obudo replied, 'Okay, I'll be up.' To Jim he said, 'I go on watch in ten minutes. Must get myself ready.'

The young Englishman stood up, ran a hand through thick red hair. 'Okay. Did Agojo say anything else about the work?'

'He told me that after rigging those camouflage nets – that took nearly a week – they had to crush coral and mix it with sand and cement in big machines. Concrete mixers, I guess. He says it was used for making hard places on the beach where the lines of pegs ended. I asked him what the hard places were for. He didn't know. Said that when the tide was high it came up to the hard places.' Obudo looked round the cabin, put on his uniform cap. 'Must go up now. See you.'

Jim Abernethy followed him out of the cabin.

The relationship between Scalatti and Krol was growing apace. Though they were careful to conceal this when on deck, Scalatti took care to foster it when the Swede came to his cabin for a drink in the evenings. It was while *Sunglow* was on passage between the Farquhar Islands and the Cosmoledos, that Scalatti used one such opportunity to further his plans. He had learnt a good deal about Krol during these nocturnal get-togethers, when vermouth loosened the Swede's tongue. The man was tough. He'd confessed to five years in a Swedish gaol for robbery with violence. That, and Krol's hatred of Cassidy, convinced the Italian that here was a man upon whom he could depend, a reliable and willing accomplice. So the Italian implied that he'd been offered a sizeable sum of money if he could arrange for the ship to be lost. He'd laughed. 'Not too difficult with this old barge. Plates thin now, you know. And plenty atolls and coral reefs around on these voyages.'

Krol had nodded, shown no surprise. 'For how much, Luigi? What was the offer?' He watched the first mate with narrowed eyes.

Scalatti hesitated. He'd not expected such a direct question at that stage. Krol had nothing like the tact or delicacy of Ali Patel in such matters. But Scalatti had no intention of letting the Swede know the amount Ali had promised. It would have to be something substantially less. 'I can get thirty thousand US dollars for the job,' he said in a low voice.

Krol's eyes gleamed. 'That's good money. You tell me this, Luigi, because you want help. Right?'

'Right.'

'So what's the plan?'

'You like to work with me on this, Nils?'

'Sure. If the plan's okay. *And* you give me fifteen thousand dollars.'

'Jesus – you think you can get half?' Scalatti's deepset eyes burned with indignation. 'Half, when I must do ninety percent of the job. You must be crazy, man.'

Krol shrugged. 'Tell me the plan, Luigi. When I know what I must do, we can talk about the money.'

Scalatti's manner became conspiratorial. He leant forward, lowered his voice. 'Right I tell you. You can see the schedule on the noticeboard. On the last day of the cruise we leave Zanzibar late evening October 13, arrive off Mombasa daylight October 14. Ship must keep this schedule. After Zanzibar we steam along the coast. There will be many islands and reefs west of *Sunglow*'s course. The current at this time will set ship to the west. That is onto the land.' Scalatti stopped, lit a cigarette, passed it to Krol, lit another for himself.

Krol grinned. 'I see you do good homework, Luigi.' He blew a smoke ring at the deckhead. 'What about *il capitano*? You can fix him?'

'I have middle-watch. He comes up at four o'clock, for the morning watch. Ship hits reef in my watch, say two o'clock. The old man will be sleeping then.'

Krol scratched his shaggy head. 'At this time wind and sea are from the south-east. What happens if the weather is bad that morning? Can be dangerous, you know, to make a wreck in such conditions. I had one bad shipwreck already, in *Solidava*. Maybe I don't make it another time. You figured this problem, Luigi?'

'Sure, sure, Nils.' Scalatti waved a dismissive hand. 'If weather is bad, we run ship ashore on leeward side of island.'

'You say we. Who is *we*?' Cigarette in mouth, leaning back on the settee, Krol looked away, stretched his arms with studied nonchalance.

'You, Nils – and myself. That is *we*. I will be on watch

navigating the ship. You will be quartermaster and look-out. I fix it so you are on the wheel. Okay?'

'The plan is good.' Krol nodded approval. 'Now – how much for me? In US dollars,' he added quietly.

The haggling took some time. Eventually it was agreed that Krol would get $12,500 and Scalatti, as principal, the lion's share of $17,500. Krol had insisted on knowing who was putting up the money. With some reluctance, Scalatti had told him. The arrangement was sealed with tumblers of vermouth, the Italian having impressed upon his accomplice that secrecy and discretion were paramount. 'Otherwise we can be doing time in Mombasa,' he warned.

Before he left the first mate's cabin Krol said, 'You fix with Diana for another visit here?'

'Yes. She will come the night before Aldabra. After eight o'clock.' He frowned at the Swede. 'We must be careful. If *il capitano* knows you come here too much, he can make trouble.'

'Bugger *il capitano*. Only four times now that I come here. He don't see me anyway.'

'Maybe he can hear. We must be careful, Nils.'

'Okay. 'bye now, Luigi.' Krol went, closing the door behind him.

Scalatti was well satisfied. The Swede's share wasn't going to make too much of a dent in the $50,000 Ali Patel had promised.

Alone in his cabin after dinner, Cassidy fell into an uncharacteristically pessimistic mood. Were they on a wild goose chase, he asked himself? Could Bannister's chart, authentic though it seemed, be taken seriously? Wasn't it, perhaps, fantasy, the work of a man who'd been through a long period of suffering and delirium? No man could remain normal under those circumstances. Drifting on a raft for weeks, one companion going mad and jumping over the side, the other dying in his arms soon after the landing on

White Island. How he must have suffered there. A series of macabre pictures drifted through Cassidy's mind, so vivid that the reality of Bannister's privations distressed him.

'It's me Irish imagination,' he muttered, hoisting himself out of the armchair and making for the refrigerator. From it he took two tins of Carlsberg lager, opened one, filled a pewter tankard and went back to the armchair. But if the chart was a figment of Bannister's imagination, the cutting from *The Times* was not. *Koolamagee* had foundered somewhere north of Madagascar. She *had* been carrying gold ingots.

Reminded of these realities, Cassidy's spirits rose and his thoughts about the barque's cargo developed. Gold ingots were heavy. For Bannister to have got a few onto the raft would have been possible. But how had he kept them there in all those days of drifting, with bad weather thrown in? They must have been in something that was lashed to the raft – a sea chest perhaps? He wasn't sure what an ingot weighed. Mrs C had told him that her research suggested one hundred pounds in the days when *Koolamagee* sank. At today's prices, say four hundred dollars an ounce, that was $640,000 – or £420,000. Half of that was £210,000 – Goosam would take half of that again. That would be the proceeds from one ingot. There might be more. Holy Saint Patrick! Cassidy refilled the empty tankard. Pity I can't get the lot, he thought. Indeed, and he could, with Mbolwo's help. The big Irishman worked at an imaginary plan, chuckled at his thoughts. Arrive back in Mombasa at night, anchor in Kilindini port, go alongside in the morning. Fix things that night. Gold and Mbolwo gone in the morning. Give Goosam his cut and things would be looked after ashore. No problem. He belly-laughed, hit a knee, choked on the lager. He'd clear out, leave the sea. Go back to where he'd come from. Buy himself a fine house with a thatched roof, overlooking Killarney Lough. Find a buxom woman to mind the place. A widow, not too young, not too old. She'd cook and clean and keep his bed warm. Dear

159

Mother O' God! He laughed again, wiped a tear from the corner of an eye, took another Carlsberg from the refrigerator. Indeed, and it was a fine fantasy. He looked at himself in the mirror. He'd never do it, of course. It was out of character. That was why he'd been laughing. The idea of Shamus Cassidy and Goosam Patel behaving in such a fashion. He filled the tankard again. £100,000 more or less was money enough. Mrs C was a fine lady, a strong character, and an unselfish one too. He had a great admiration for her. Why should he want to steal from her? After all it was her project, it was she who'd offered him and Goosam a half share? That was a generous act. And, as if that were not enough, she was giving her half to the RNLI. He was more than content with things as they were. The problem was to find White Island. If he couldn't do it this voyage, maybe he could the next. And if that didn't work, then on another. There'd be plenty of time. Maybe Mrs C would come along too, though he doubted that. But leave *Sunglow* and the sea? How could he possibly do that? There was nothing, there could be nothing, that meant more to him than *Sunglow* and the sea.

SEVENTEEN

At daybreak *Sunglow* reached Menai, the principal island of the Cosmoledo Group. Anchor was dropped and as the day progressed the normal routine of the cruise swung into gear; it was a routine which had become as familar to passengers as it was to the crew. It was evident from remarks made by several of the former that evening that the Cosmoledos had been disappointing. "Perhaps I'd expected too much," said one: "These islands are all rather alike," complained another; "When it isn't unbearably hot, we're soaked in tropical downpours," observed a third. Mrs Bruckner had sprained an ankle when getting out of a skimmer, a misfortune which no one was permitted to forget, and which was in no way improved by Henry Atkins' admonition at dinner that night: 'There's too bleedin' much of you, love. That's the trouble. Can't expect to be nippy on yer pins if you overload yer stomach. Know what I mean?'

It was while *Sunglow* was on passage between the Cosmoledos and Aldabra atoll that Gaston went to the Captain's cabin to report signs of flagging interest among the passengers – and some discontent. 'It was the same on the last cruise, Captain,' he said unhappily. 'At first there is much enthusiasm, then they get used to the islands and the routine, and the grumblers begin to make themselves felt. Now they complain that the islands are all alike, that the routine's too repetitive, the food not varied enough, cabins too hot, too much sea time at night, etcetera.'

Cassidy sighed, ran a hand across his forehead, helped himself to a cigar. 'Well now, and that's nothing new, Gaston. I've always said one island is much like the other. It's only the skimmers, the noise, and the sense of adventure that keeps things going.' He lit the cigar. 'And who is it then, that's for making trouble?'

Pascal fidgeted with the underside of his moustache. 'Mrs Bruckner of course. She is full of complaints. Lately also the Van der Karsts and the Cawsons – even Mrs Carter, who is young, complains that a three week voyage is too long, that it should be two weeks at most. She says the facilities on board . . .'

Cassidy growled. 'We are forever telling them this is a working vessel going about her lawful trade, not a cruise liner. Mother O' God. What is it they're expecting?' He leant back in his chair, blew smoke at the deckhead. 'At tonight's briefing I'll be talking of Aldabra. That should help things along. Now tell me, Gaston. You took on supplies of fresh fish in the Cosmoledos?'

'Yes. From Menai Island. Good quality. Prices reasonable.'

'Well, and at least that's good news.' Cassidy got up, took an ashtray from his desk, put it next to his chair and sat down again. 'The White Island competition, Gaston. Is that not doing something to hold their interest?'

Watching Cassidy for some sign of uneasiness, some indication that this was a delicate matter, Pascal said, 'A few, perhaps, are interested. Others seem to think – well to be frank, Captain – they think that White Island may exist only in your imagination.'

'You mean, Pascal, they believe I manufactured the story?' There was an embarrassing silence. Cassidy's bearded face, cigar sprouting from it, thrust forward aggressively. 'Are you, maybe, thinking that?'

Pascal turned away from the challenging eyes, hesitated before replying. 'I have been with you for many years, Captain. You have never mentioned White Island. Does it exist? Is there really a legend about it?'

Tapping his cigar against the rim of the ashtray, seeming to play for time, Cassidy looked at the chief steward in a calm, contemplative manner. Pascal was a man for whom he had a considerable regard. 'Yes,' he said eventually. 'I do believe White Island exists. More than that, I'll not be saying.'

After his talk with the second mate, Jim lay awake for a long time thinking about Agojo's story. There were so many questions which called for an answer. Why did the supply ship arrive and discharge stores – and the Swahili labourers – at night? Why did the earth movers do their dumping at night? What was the purpose of the long lines of pegs, the lines of white ringed palms, and the 'hard places' on the beach? Why were the foremen and the sentries Ethiopian? Why had the Finns chased *Sunglow* in the cabin-cruiser? Would they have gone to such lengths to retrieve one Swahili labourer?

Instinctively, he felt that something strange was happening on Wreck Island and, being an imaginative young man, that strangeness took many shapes in his mind. He remembered Commander Rollo's remarks about the activities of pirates and corsairs in the islands and how they had buried their treasure. Perhaps IMMEC was an international corporation of sorts, but the scientist's story of geological and geophysical research was probably a cover for a large scale hunt for buried treasure. Uninhabited, with its dangerous off-lying reefs and unsavoury reputation among mariners, Wreck Island would have been an ideal place for burying treasure.

The next night, with the ship somewhere between the Cosmoledos and Aldabra, he again found he couldn't sleep, his brain too active with the problem of Wreck Island. It was wretchedly hot in the cabin so he went to the sundeck, stretched himself out on a deck-chair, and continued to worry away at the treasure island theory. He thought so hard, and for so long, that his head throbbed and later began to ache. He was about to give up when suddenly, in what seemed a flash of revelation, another solution presented itself; a much more likely one, he decided. Perhaps it was Cuba all over again? Maybe the scientists were Russians not Finns. They were preparing a track from the beach into the palms. Whatever came up that track would be concealed in the plantation. What would come up the track? Amphibious tracked vehicles, probably. They'd be unloaded from a ship offshore at night, make their way to the lagoon, climb out of the water and up onto the beach by way of the 'hard places', motor up the track into the palms. There they'd be housed in the excavations under the camouflage nets, well protected from air and satellite observation. What sort of amphibious tracked vehicles would they be? Mobile missile launchers, of course. And the white ringed palms Agojo had spoken of. What was their purpose? Surely to mark a track still to be cleared through the plantation – a track at right angles to the one from the beach? What was that for? To give the launchers three cardinal points from which to fire: north, east and west? Jim's thoughts raced on: the targets? The US naval base at Diego Garcia, ships using the Mozambique Channel, the main sea-route north and south along the East African coast – the strategically vital oil route from the Persian Gulf to the West – and ports like Mogadishu, Mombasa, Dar-es-Salaam, and even Durban, well to the south. All could be reached by land based, intermediate range nuclear missiles.

It was a solution which explained everything. Next day, when he was fit and fresh, he would decide what to do. He couldn't leave things as they were. He'd have to confide in someone. Satisfied at last he went back to the cabin, climbed onto his bunk and fell asleep.

As the curtain of rain lifted, great banks of cumulus cloud could be seen over a smudge on the horizon. It was South Island, largest of those on the Aldabra atoll. It had been on *Sunglow*'s radar display for some time, but for Cassidy, despite his many years at sea, the sighting of land was always an occasion. It was the ultimate step in the solution of a familiar problem: the chart and sailing directions told that the land was there – sometimes, as now, no more than a speck in a vast ocean – the compass pointed the way, sextant and chronometer kept the mariner on it, radar gave early warning of approach, and the human eye, seeing the land and so confirming the correctness of the equation, triggered a glow of achievement.

On this morning, as so often, for *Sunglow*'s landfalls were mostly at dawn, the moment was improved by the arrival of Mbolwo carrying the customary tray. 'Coffee in the chartroom, sir,' he reported to Cassidy soon afterwards, his African intonation implying neither inquiry nor intention.

'Ah, and that's fine,' replied Cassidy, playing his part in the ritual, yet not lowering his binoculars.

'Aldabra, sir?' Mbolwo, in the act of leaving the bridge, had stopped beside him for a moment.

'Yes. South Island.'

The steward searched the sea beyond the bridge's rain streaked windows. 'Too much rain, sir,' he observed.

'The south-easter will be blowing it away.'

Mbolwo nodded, looked at Cassidy with grave eyes. 'The clean uniform is on the bunk, sir.'

Cassidy thanked him, and the tall African slipped silently away.

During the first hours of daylight *Sunglow* headed westwards down the cliff-lined coast of South Island, reached its end and swung north along the western flank of West Island until the houses of the settlement showed up, set among trees above a long sandy beach.

The coaster came to an anchor opposite the settlement, some distance to seaward of the beach. There were few signs of activity ashore, but Cassidy had spoken to the manager by radiophone and knew that he would come off to the ship soon. Used to the leisurely pace of life in the islands, the Irishman was happy to wait. He had stores and mail to discharge and had been promised a useful load of *boriti* – the mangrove poles much in demand by furniture makers in Kenya and Arabia.

For those passengers who'd been on deck for the arrival at what promised to be the most interesting of the islands, the business of the day was soon begun. The rain had stopped and the sun was shining through the clouds when skimmers were lowered and their human cargo embarked on a day which already shimmered with heat. Apart from inspecting West Island's settlement, the only permanent one in the Aldabras, much of the day was to be spent

165

exploring the islands and observing underwater life on the reefs.

At a breakfast briefing passengers had been warned by Pascal that walking on the islands was hard work; and damaging to footwear because of the *champignon* – the jagged, eroded land surface – and the dense and often impenetrable scrub. Other than the Bruckners, who remained on board because of her sprained ankle, passengers were undaunted by the chief steward's warning. They went off in high spirits, cameras, packed lunches and light waterproofs much in evidence.

The Aldabra atoll, its lagoon and islands, turned out to be all that Cassidy had promised. The skimmer parties returned to *Sunglow* that evening exhausted, foot weary and shoe worn, but brimming with stories of an exciting and sometimes hilarious day: like when Obudo, standing in the stern-sheets to point to a rare species of tree, had lost his balance and fallen into the lagoon. Jim had taken the helm and brought the inflatable round to pick up the embarrassed second mate who was standing up to his waist in water.

The giant land tortoises were just incredible, enthused Dean Carter. Four feet long, and almost three feet high. There were many hundreds of them, he said, and they studded the landscape like smooth boulders. He'd got a fabulous shot of Sandra riding one. By day, explained Jean McLachlan, the tortoises rested, sleeping in what shade they could find. At night, when it was cooler, they became active and their foraging began.

Stephen Blake, the quiet man of the cruise, emerged from behind his crust of reserve to talk with animation about the birds he'd seen. Most exciting, he confessed over his third scotch-on-the-rocks, was the flightless White Throated Rail. He thought he'd heard the flutelike note of the False Cuckoo but, sadly, had not seen the bird. All in all, it had been a tremendous day.

Commander Rollo had enjoyed it with customary reticence, his only real show of enthusiasm accompanying the story he told of the German cruiser *Koningsberg* evading the Royal Navy in the First World War by concealing herself for weeks at the western end of the lagoon, before making her dash to the Rufiji River in what was then German East Africa. There, he explained with unconcealed pride, her days were ended by *HMS Chatham*.

While exploring the Aldabras, Jim Abernethy had acted as self appointed escort and willing slave to Diana Kitson, a role which made the day for him. For her part, Diana, though unusually preoccupied, seemed grateful for his company and attentions; he was always helping her in and out of the skimmer, giving her a hand over awkward terrain, and leading the way through undergrowth and scrub. On several occasions they were separated from the others and once, when she stopped to deal with a troublesome shoe, they were left some distance behind. Whether she had manufactured the opportunity was not clear, but quite suddenly she looked up from the hummock where she was sitting to say, 'Something very unpleasant happened on board last night, Jim. I'm frightened out of my wits.'

All he could manage was an incredulous, 'What?'

'I can't tell you now. It's too confusing.' She turned away. 'Take too long. Can you – do you think you could possibly come to my cabin tonight – after midnight – when the watches have changed, and there's no one about.' She turned to look at him again and he saw that she really was worried – and yet still lovely. What she'd said, the way she looked, made his heart thump against his rib-cage.

'Yes, of course I'll come.' He'd gone suddenly hoarse.

'Be careful, Jim. You know how people talk.'

He said, 'Yes, I do,' helped her to her feet, and they set off after the rest of the party.

In the lounge soon after the return of the day's explorers, Pascal announced that the ship would sail at midnight and not eight o'clock as shown on the noticeboard. 'The chief engineer wishes to undertake certain preventive maintenance work,' he explained.

'Another bleedin' breakdown if you ask me,' was Henry Atkins' hoarse observation to Jim Abernethy.

During dinner, Gaston Pascal came into the saloon, went across to the officers' table and tapped on it with a spoon. Affecting a worried frown, speaking slowly, he said, 'It is my duty, ladies and gentlemen, to extend to you on behalf of Captain Cassidy an invitation to a surprise briefing.' He placed a finger against the side of his nose, arched his eyebrows. 'Yes, indeed, a *surprise* briefing – surprise because drinks will be on the Company' – he paused for the laughter which followed – 'and because of what the Captain will tell you. It will take place on the sundeck at nine o'clock tonight.'

The surprise briefing had been the Captain's idea. 'We'll have to do something to take their minds off this confounded delay, Gaston. Sure and they'll be thinking the old lady's engines are not what they should be.'

'They'll be right,' said Pascal.

'Well now, we must make allowances, for it is a lot of hard work those engines have done in their time.' Cassidy looked up from the desk, his blue eyes twinkling. 'There's nothing that cheers folks like drinks on the house, Gaston. So make yourself busy will you, lad.' Relaxing momentarily, he leant back in the chair and applied gentle, therapeutic touches to his beard. 'When they've had a few drinks I'll be telling them the tale of Dada's Island. This afternoon I called Dada on radiophone. He likes the idea of a beach party. Promises full support. His young folk will be there in strength, and with plenty of *calao*.'

'Not surprised he likes the idea,' Pascal spoke with asperity. 'He got completely stoned last time. Just about raped that nice French girl we took along.'

'Hard words, Gaston. No more than a flirtation, he told

me. And indeed, did he not apologize to her for being a little strenuous. Ah, and it's fine to be young.' The Irishman sighed for lost youth. 'Our arrival there is always an event. Natural it is that he likes to celebrate.'

Before he left the Captain's cabin, Pascal had complained that drinks on the house would be an expensive item.

'Indeed, and that's true, Gaston. But water down the spirits, lad. When they've had a few, they'll not be noticing. And better for their health, too.'

Pascal forebore to mention that his earnings wouldn't be what they were had he not regularly practised what the Captain advocated.

EIGHTEEN

The 'surprise' briefing on a hot, starless night attracted a full house, but for Mrs Bruckner. Beyond the awnings under which the passengers sat, the lights of the settlement winked through a wall of darkness from which came the sound of surf breaking on a reef. Cassidy, arriving as always with Pascal in tow, lost no time in opening the proceedings. 'Tomorrow,' he began, 'you will be visiting Dada's Island. It is a most unusual one. Far from the tracks of inter-island schooners it is more or less unknown. It exports nothing; its coconut palms and fish are required for its own needs. *Sunglow* calls there at three-monthly intervals with supplies and mail. That is the island's only connection with the outside world. It was uninhabited until the arrival of its present community. Now let me tell you something about them.' He stopped, not to consult notes for this was a briefing he could well handle without them, but to mop his face and make time for the stewards who were darting about among passengers seeing to their drinks. When this activity had quietened down, he put away his handkerchief and continued. 'There are no creoles, no natives on Dada's Island – only thirty or so men and women who live there in a commune. I suppose they'd be called drop-outs. Talk to them and they'll be telling you they've repudiated the values of Western society. Oh, yes, it's high flown language they use. They have, they'll say, exchanged the materialism of the West and the threat of the bomb, for the simple, back-to-nature life possible on a desert island. Who is to say they are wrong?' Cassidy's fine beard emphasized the challenging thrust of his chin. 'You'll find them a decent enough lot of young people, and it's certainly happy they seem to be.'

He went on to say that the leader of the community, Dada, after whom the island was named, was a former British industrialist who'd long nourished the idea of abandoning his business interests and finding a tropical island where he could settle with a group of people who, like him, wanted to escape from the complex industrialised life of the West.

'You could,' Cassidy enlarged, 'call him a middle-aged drop-out. In fact he's a man who made a fortune and used it to realize a dream.'

It took Dada years to find the island, went on Cassidy. He bought a yacht, took a few young people as crew and began his search. First in the Pacific where he hunted around for a long time without finding anything suitable. The search was then shifted to the Indian Ocean. Beginning in the north with the Maldives, Dada worked his way south through the Chagos Archipelago and on, westwards, to the Seychelles. From there he went south and west through the Amirantes to the Cosmoledos and Aldabra Groups, checking as he went on the adjoining islands, of which there were many. It was after leaving the Aldabras that a great storm swept him northwards, and it was then that his persistence was rewarded. He found an uninhabited islet north-west of the Asquith Bank, and about eighty miles from the Aldabras.

It lay on the eastern flank of a typical atoll, a ring-shaped coral reef enclosing a lagoon. It was very small, but in every way what Dada had in mind. He could not buy it, but the Seychelles Government, under whose sovereignty it fell, leased it to him.

His next move was to recruit a group of young people of like mind. He'd gone to Amsterdam for that purpose because of its large drop-out community. He chose carefully, having in mind the individual skills, backgrounds and personalities of the men and women concerned, and the probability of pairing. Having got the equipment, stores and other gear needed, he flew out to the Seychelles with his party. There he hired a schooner for the journey to the island. Before leaving Mahé he recruited two Seychellois for the commune, bought several *pirogues*, some fishing gear, a few pigs, goats and poultry. Having landed Dada and his people on the atoll, the schooner sailed back to the Seychelles and his dream began to take shape. They set about building huts, a community centre and a rain-catchment area, and saw to their other needs. From the Seychellois they learnt how to use the *pirogues* for fishing, how to climb coconut palms, and make use of the nuts, and other regional skills.

'The commune has been going for about seven years,' said Cassidy. 'And it seems well settled. Indeed it's grown a bit for there's a few children been born there in the time *Sunglow* has been calling – and that's the last few years.'

Mr Van der Karst interrupted to ask about the economics of the commune. It was expensive to maintain a community of thirty or so people. Where did the money come from?

'Dada is a millionaire,' replied Cassidy. 'He financed the whole project and continues to do so. The supplies we are carrying for the island, anything needed, is paid for by him. Not that their needs are that great. They live on fish and

171

coconuts, they keep pigs, goats and poultry, and they grow casavas, bananas and other food. In this climate few clothes are necessary.' He grinned. 'As you will see.'

Miss McLachlan wished to know the structure for decision making. 'I trust it is democratic? That Dada does not enjoy dictatorial powers?'

Cassidy shook his head. 'From what I've seen of him, decision making wouldn't be much like the House of Commons. None of those shenanigans. More like a ship, I'd say, with him the captain. Don't forget, young lady, he foots the bills.'

Miss McLachlan blinked at Cassidy, the pebble lenses making small marbles of her eyes. 'That sounds thoroughly undemocratic.'

'Like a ship,' Cassidy conceded cheerfully. 'You'll have to be watching Dada,' he added, 'for he's a great one with the ladies, they say. Ah well, none of us is perfect.'

Miss McLachlan frowned her disapproval. Mr Bruckner held up a hand. Cassidy forestalled him. 'We will be on Dada's Island tomorrow. There is to be a beach party that night, and a real good one it should be. Dada himself is coming with his young people. You'll be talking to them about life in the commune, I've no doubt. And you'll find it interesting for it's not often the Robinson Crusoe story comes true.' He got up from his chair. 'And now, ladies and gentlemen, I'll bid you good night for I'm sure you'd like to be filling your glasses?' With that the proceedings ended.

Cassidy was pleasantly surprised when Kumar Gupta came to his cabin to report that the worn thrust-block bearings had been replaced, a task which had occupied most of the day.

'The engines are now ready for sea,' announced the chief engineer, mopping his face with cotton waste.

'Good news that is, chief. Well done. Tell Mr Scalatti and the second mate we'll be getting under way in half an hour.'

Thus *Sunglow*'s anchor was weighed at half past ten that night, instead of at midnight as originally intended. When well clear of the land, Cassidy put the coaster on course for Dada's Island, eighty miles to the north, and handed over the watch to the second mate.

Jim had turned in at eleven o'clock; not to sleep, he was too tense for that, but to wait for Stephen Blake to fall asleep. He filled in the time thinking about Diana. What was it she wanted to tell him that was so secret? Was it an excuse for something else? She was a strange woman, a little wild really. But she had looked genuinely upset. As the time passed he began to worry. If he left going to her cabin too late, she might decide he wasn't coming, lock the door and go to sleep. It wouldn't be possible to knock loudly because his aunt's cabin was opposite hers.

At last solid snores came from the other bunk. The luminous digits of his watch showed nine minutes past one. He tip-toed into the shower-room, slipped on shorts and a T-shirt, and slipped quietly out of the cabin. Hers was number six, two doors from his. He knocked gently and waited. Nothing happened. He tried again, knocked a little harder, but there was no response. He was about to give up, when the door opened. He went in, brushed against her in the darkness, smelt the jasmine. She closed the door behind him and switched on the light. With a delicious sense of shock he saw that she was wearing a flimsy pink wrap, almost transparent. It hung loosely from her shoulders, finishing just above her knees. The combination of what his heart was doing and the buzzing in his head made him feel strange. It was an exciting feeling.

She pointed to the cabin's only easy chair. 'We'll have to be very quiet,' she warned.

'No, you take it,' he whispered, going to the settee.

She looked at him with querulous, worried eyes. 'Thank God you've come, Jim. I was beginning to think you wouldn't.'

'Sorry I'm late. Had to wait for Stephen to fall asleep.'

'Yes, of course.' She smiled wanly. 'It's very kind of you. I need someone –' she hesitated '–someone to confide in.'

Jim said, 'Yes. Go ahead.' He tried hard not to look at the neckline of her garment which revealed most of two firmly rounded breasts.

'You're very young, Jim – I hope you'll understand what I'm going to tell you.' She gave him a quick look of enquiry. 'I've been up to the first mate's cabin several times this voyage. To chat and have a drink, you know the sort of thing. Luigi Scalatti is good company. Very Italian and quite attractive really, in a foreign way. That accent. He's kind, too, and – well – he admires me, and that's important to a woman.'

'So would any man,' Jim blurted out, feeling curiously guilty about the admission.

'Oh, you are sweet, Jim.' She gave him a little smile, sighed and went on. 'Sometimes Nils Krol was there. At first he seemed nice. He's a Swede, you know, and it's always difficult to place a foreigner. To know what he's really like, I mean. But now I know that Nils is a horrible man – a ruthless one, I think.'

Jim frowned. 'Is he the trouble?'

'Part of it – yes.' She regarded him with puzzled eyes. 'I've been rather foolish with Nils, I suppose. The trouble is – or was – Luigi's rather generous with his vermouth. It all came to a head the night before last. I'd had two or three drinks on the sundeck. With the Carters and the Cawsons. I'd promised Luigi that I'd have a drink with him and Nils soon after eight o'clock that night. Stupidly, for fun, I thought I'd play a trick on them. Get to Luigi's cabin early – I knew he was on watch until eight – and hide in the clothes cupboard. Wait until he and Nils arrived, listen to their chat – they'd be likely to talk about me if I was late, and that way I'd know what they thought of me – something a woman wants to know, especially if she's been indiscreet.

174

And even if they didn't talk about me, I'd have the fun of bursting out of the cupboard and giving them a fright. Sounds childish, Jim – foolish – I know but –'. She shrugged, looked towards the porthole. 'After a few drinks I'm afraid I can be rather foolish.'

Jim winced. She was so lovely, too nice altogether for the sort of things she was hinting at. 'So what happened?' he asked dismally.

'Well, I hid in the cupboard. It was all dark and stuffy, and awfully hot. I heard someone come into the cabin not long afterwards. I didn't know who it was, of course. A few minutes later someone else came in and said, "Hullo Nils", and then I knew it was Luigi. I heard him bring out the vermouth, and they began to chat.'

'About you?'

'Not really. Nils asked where I was. Luigi said, "Late as usual." Then they got on to other things. Something funny, something I couldn't understand. It was rather garbled. Difficult to hear in that cupboard. Krol wanted to know where it would be? Luigi said, "Not settled yet, I'll let you know in good time." Krol went on about money. What was the guarantee? Something like that. There was more then that I couldn't follow. The last things I remember hearing were Luigi saying, "if he lets us down what can I do?" Nils then said, "kill the bastard" – and at that moment I sneezed. Couldn't help it. There was masses of dust in that cupboard. Seconds later Nils opened the door, dragged me out and pushed me against the bunk. There was an awful moment then, those two men just looking at each other in deadly silence. Their faces were quite horrible, Jim. I can't tell you. A mixture of fear and anger and suspicion, and even hatred, all mixed up together. Somebody had to do something, so I forced a laugh, said I'd hidden there for a joke. To give them a surprise and hear what they said about me, because men always talked about women. Nils Krol looked at me in a horrible sinister way. He wanted to know what I'd heard them say about me. I said he'd asked Luigi

175

where I was, and Luigi had said late as usual. Nils gave Luigi a knowing sort of look, asked what else I'd heard. I made a stupid mistake then – I was terribly scared you see – I said I couldn't make out what they'd been saying, it was gibberish to me. Not possible to hear properly in that cupboard, I explained. Nils said, "You're lying, lady. You heard what we said about you, okay. You just told us." I said that was different. It made sense. What they'd said after that didn't, as far as I was concerned. I just couldn't understand, so I stopped listening. I said I was about to come out of the cupboard – and say "boo" or something idiotic – when I sneezed. I could see Nils didn't believe me. He took me by the shoulders, put his face close to mine, breathed vermouth all over me. "You'd better keep that red mouth of yours shut, lady or . . ." He didn't finish the sentence, just stared at me with that dreadful look in his eyes.'

'What about Scalatti,' Jim said. 'Didn't he say anything?'

'I was coming to that. Nils Krol had his hands on my shoulders, the knuckles of his thumbs pressing into my neck – like this.' She got up, put her hands on Jim's shoulders and demonstrated what Krol had done. She sat down again. 'Then he shook me – terribly roughly – said, "Know what I mean, lady?" I said, "Don't, you're hurting me."'

'Luigi pulled Krol away from me and said, "Cut it out, Nils. What the hell does it matter if she did hear what we said?" Nils said, "You must be mad, Luigi." Luigi laughed, a sort of cackle. "I'm not mad," he said. "Just listen to what I say." After that he turned to me, explained that they'd been talking about something confidential, something that could get them both into real trouble. Krol looked furious at that. He said, "Stop, you stupid bastard." Luigi said, "I'm not stupid. For Chrissake listen before you talk." Luigi turned back to me again and said they'd been talking about a drugs deal. The second engineer, Bashi Menon, had bought the stuff in Mombasa for some people on

Dada's Island. It had to be smuggled ashore because Dada wouldn't allow drugs on the island. Luigi said Bashi Menon had asked him to arrange for Krol to go ashore on one of the skimmer trips to make the delivery. That was because neither he nor the second engineer would be going ashore at Dada's Island. He said that was a privilege the Captain and chief engineer kept for themselves. Bashi Menon had promised to pay a good sum for the delivery. Under Seychelles and Kenyan law drug dealing was a criminal offence. Although it was not a big deal, Luigi said there could be serious trouble for them if I talked. So I . . .'

Jim interrupted. 'Promised not to talk?'

'Yes. I swore I wouldn't. And, except for you, I won't. But I'm frightened, Jim. I can't really explain why, but somehow I don't believe Luigi was telling the truth. He kept on stopping as he told me the story – as if he were making it up as he went. And the way Nils Krol looked, angry, puzzled, dangerous – oh, just terribly sinister – that made me think there was something else. When I got ready to leave Luigi's cabin that night, Nils gave me a hard look, shook a fist at me. "You'd better watch it, lady," he said. No smile or anything like that.' She stopped, her hands clasped on her lap, looked at Jim inquiringly. 'Do you believe Luigi's story?'

Jim said, 'Yes, I do. We all stop to think for words, how to put our thoughts into words, when we're making a long explanation. They must have had a nasty shock when they found you in that cupboard. Put yourself in their place. Of course they were worried, frightened that you'd talk, and that the word would get back to Captain Cassidy.'

'Why did Nils Krol say, "kill the bastard"?'

'When I was small my mother used to say, "If you do that again, Jim, I'll kill you." Then she'd pick me up and hug me. I bet you've said it, too. It's just something people say. It isn't meant literally.'

She threw out her arms in a gesture of relief. 'Oh, Jim, you are a darling. That's so comforting. Lots of commonsense in what you say. But I had to confide in someone, and you were the only person I really liked and trusted.'

Jim watched her, undisciplined thoughts troubling him. 'In your own interests, Diana, you must keep the promise you made. Don't talk of this to anyone. Be friendly, as if nothing had happened, with those,' – his voice hardened – 'those guys. If they give you any trouble come to me. They've frightened you. I reckon I can frighten them, if they're really looking for trouble.'

She stood up, pulled the wrap more tightly about her. 'You've been wonderful, Jim. Absolutely marvellous.'

He left the settee, stood facing her. 'I'd do anything for you.' His voice struck him as absurdly husky.

She stood on her toes, placed her hands on his shoulders, raised her mouth to his and kissed him. 'You must go now, Jim – before I do anything silly.' She paused. 'Like crying.'

He saw the searching look in her eyes, felt an overwhelming desire to take her in his arms, but knew he wouldn't. She was in trouble and it would be taking advantage of her. In a hoarse whisper he said, 'Good night, Diana. Turn off the light and I'll go.' Conscious of the clumsy anti-climax, he felt foolish.

For a moment they stood looking at each other, the wildest thoughts going through Jim's mind. She switched off the light, opened the door and he stepped out into the passageway.

When he got back to the cabin, Stephen Blake was still snoring; if anything more noisily than before.

NINETEEN

During the night the wind dropped and the white horses of the trade wind gave way to a long swell from the south-east. In the deck-log he wrote up at midnight, the second mate described the weather as *doldrums*. When Scalatti came to take over, Obudo reported course and speed, mentioned that there was nothing in sight, and confirmed that the ship was on auto-steering. With that he went below.

Scalatti told the standby helmsman to keep a good lookout. 'I'll be in the chartroom,' he said. There he began examining the Admiralty chart of the East African coast between Zanzibar and Mombasa. A number of factors affected place and timing. Most importantly it had to happen during his watch. After almost an hour of working at the problem, he decided that the reefs and islets off Wasini Island, about forty-five miles south of Mombasa, would be the ideal place. Ali Patel had suggested stranding the coaster towards the end of her voyage: 'Not too far from Mombasa,' he'd advised. 'It'll keep down the cost of getting passengers and crew back here.'

A shrewd man was Ali Patel, reflected the Italian. Not difficult to see why he was rich – he'd be pleased with the choice of Wasini Island. Scalatti put away the chart and went back to the bridge. He crumpled the piece of paper on which he'd made his calculations and threw it over the side. He wouldn't tell Krol yet that he'd decided where it was to happen. Better to delay that until they left Zanzibar. It would be possible then to estimate the time more accurately.

179

Two hours after midnight the engines stopped. The bridge phone sounded. It was Bashi Menon, the second engineer, reporting that the fuel injector had packed up.

Scalatti laughed. '*Mama mia*! Not again. We shall be rowing soon. How long to stop this time, Bashi Menon?'

'This I cannot say, Luigi. I am calling the chief. He will know. Naturally it will be some hours.'

Scalatti put the engineroom telegraph to *stop* as Cassidy arrived on the bridge. To the Italian, apprehensive as always of the Captain's presence, the blue silk dressing gown with its dragon rampant gave the big, tousle-haired Irishman an even fiercer image. Fortunately, the frightening figure went straight into the chartroom.

Cassidy noted the ship's position as recorded by Obudo at midnight, glanced at the clock over the chart table, and with dividers and pencil set about plotting *Sunglow*'s position by dead reckoning. He made it more or less halfway between the Aldabras and Dada's Island; both outside the range of the coaster's aged radar.

There was no present danger. The equatorial current would set the ship to the north-west, well clear of any land. On most of her recent voyages *Sunglow* had suffered engineroom troubles of one sort or another, but for Cassidy three breakdowns on one voyage was too much. Delays cost money, and breakdowns were bad for passenger morale. The word soon got around. Goosam Patel would be extremely upset. Cassidy shied away from the direction in which his thoughts were taking him. The prospect of *Sunglow* being sold for scrap was one he refused to contemplate. Deeply concerned, he was about to return to the bridge when the chief engineer came into the chartroom, grease-streaked and wet with perspiration. The drive of the main fuel injector had fractured, he said. Stripping, dismantling, repairing and reassembling were involved. 'It can be anything up to eight hours, Captain. Maybe a little less.'

'Holy Mother O' God, chief. That's bad news indeed.

What's wrong with the engines these days?'

'We do our best, Captain. But the machinery is old. It is worked hard. Perhaps too hard for its age.'

Cassidy thought well of Kumar Gupta. He and the Bengali had been together for many years. He knew what problems old machinery created. In a gesture of understanding he touched the Indian's shoulder. 'It's not you I'm criticising, chief. It's your best you do – and a very good best it is. Now get along with you, and fix that damned injector.'

Throughout the remaining hours of darkness the coaster drifted beam on to the swell, rolling gently, her upperworks creaking in protest, dissonances in a silence broken at time by metallic sounds from the engineroom. Occasionally passengers would appear on the sundeck, awakened by the absence of engine noise and vibrations, and the heat, more evident in the cabins now that there was neither wind nor ship's movement to set the air in motion.

At four o'clock in the morning Cassidy took over the watch from the first mate. Scalatti was more than happy to go; the Captain had come to the bridge at intervals ever since the ship stopped, and the Italian's nerves were frayed.

Cassidy got a radar contact soon after Scalatti had gone. It showed on the display as a luminescent speck, fifteen miles to the north-east, so small that he took it to be a ship. As time passed the speck grew larger and he noted that the distance was closing at about three knots. With *Sunglow* drifting to the north-west, the contact could be a schooner on a closing course.

Daylight came, followed by a rising sun which brushed the clouds with washes of bronze and gold. With it, too, came Mbolwo, tray in hand, and a phone call from Kumar Gupta to report that work on the fuel injector was going well. 'Another two hours, Captain, and the job will be finished.'

181

As eight bells struck, Cassidy heard the main engines come alive, and a great burden lifted from his mind. Kumar Gupta phoned to say all was well.

'Thanks be to the Holy Mother,' said Cassidy, ringing down *slow ahead* on the telegraph. The coaster trembled into life, began to move slowly through the water. The bearing of the radar contact had moved round to the north. Now ten miles distant, it was too large for a ship. Cassidy searched along the bearing with binoculars, but a thick curtain of rain shut down visibility. If his dead reckoning position was correct, there should be no land within radar range.

He switched on the echo sounder. The depth of water was under a thousand metres. Had the equatorial current carried *Sunglow* to the north-west, as it should have done, the depth would have been several times greater. With a growing sense of disorientation he went to the chartroom and consulted the chart. The only place where the depth was under a thousand metres was on the Asquith Bank. In that case the ship was something like twenty miles east of the position he'd plotted by dead reckoning. There was only one explanation: a counter-current had set *Sunglow* to the east instead of north-west. The shoaling of water on the Asquith Bank could have been responsible for that. He ran a hand through unruly hair, expressed his dismay with a 'well I'll be damned'. But his discovery made sense of the radar blip. It could only be the nameless islet on the northern side of the Asquith Bank, marked on the chart by a tiny speck on a blue ground. He'd never before picked it up on radar; it was too far to the east of the course line from the Aldabras to Dada's Island.

With the range and bearing of the islet, he was now able to plot *Sunglow*'s position. From it he saw that Dada's Island was thirty miles to the north-west. In the six hours of drifting the counter-current had carried *Sunglow* twenty-one miles to the east. Certain now that he knew where the ship was, he rang down *full ahead* and put *Sunglow* on course for Dada's Island. Estimated time of arrival there, 11.30 a.m.

The line squall came steadily closer, bringing with it torrential rain, whipping the sea into a frenzy of white water. Obudo shouted to the bosun to trim ventilators and furl the sundeck awning. Aided by three seamen the bosun set to with a will, but the awning was only part furled when the squall hit the ship. Sounds like gunshots came from the billowing canvas which finally carried away with an explosive boom, its tattered ends flapping in the wind.

As suddenly as it had come the squall passed over the ship, the sea became smooth again, the sky cleared, and the sun drew wisps of steam from rain drenched decks. Cassidy went below to bath and change. 'I'll be back shortly,' he told Obudo.

As the rain clouds moved away to the west, visibility improved slowly. Ahead of the ship to port, boobies were diving on a shoal of fish, big black frigate birds circling above them. A school of dolphins passed across *Sunglow*'s bows, heading for the shoal with joyous leaps and dives. Fascinated, the second mate was watching their progress when he heard footsteps on the bridge ladder. It was Dean Carter, binoculars in hand, face alive with excitement. 'I guess that's it, Said. Just has to be,' he shouted.

Said Obudo shook his head. 'What are you talking about?'

'That! Look!' Dean Carter pointed to the horizon on the starboard side, trained his binoculars there. 'Must be the island.'

'What island?'

'White Island, man. Take a look. Jeez, one thousand dollars.' Dean Carter snorted with happiness.

Obudo focussed binoculars on the starboard horizon, picked up the line of surf, above it the dark streak of trees. A compass bearing confirmed that it was the blip on the radar screen. Seen through binoculars, the island's features now showed clearly. Obudo checked the distance by radar. It was five miles.

Dean Carter, still highly excited, rambled on. 'D'you see, man? It's just how the Captain described it. A small island, less than a mile long. Lying on a north-south axis. A lone palm tree on a finger of land jutting into the lagoon on the northern end. Many palm trees on the central and southern parts. It's all there, Said. Can't you see? I guess there's nothing there that doesn't fit his description.'

The second mate had a feeling that the American was right. Certainly the features of the small island were remarkably like those the Captain had described. Cautious by nature, he said, 'You could be right, Mr Carter. But it's a matter for the Captain to decide. I'll report to him right away. You stay here.'

TWENTY

In spite of affected nonchalance, Cassidy found it difficult to restrain his excitement. With binoculars to his eyes he said, 'Begorrah, and indeed it might be White Island. But there'll be no knowing until we've steamed round it.'

It was an hour later when, that manoeuvre completed, he conceded that it probably was White Island. 'We'll be sending beach parties in shortly,' he announced. Throughout the journey round the island Dean Carter had remained on the bridge where he was joined later by Mrs Clutterbutt who was there at Cassidy's request. 'So clever of you to recognize it, Mr Carter,' she said, throwing off her customary reserve by clapping her hands and doing a little jig. 'How very exciting it all is.'

Alerted by Sandra Carter who had been broadcasting the news – 'my Dean has found White Island' – passengers gathered on the sundeck with binoculars and cameras. Even the off-duty crew, infected by the general enthusiasm, had taken up vantage points on the stern casing. To Mrs Clutterbutt, who was with him in the chartroom, Cassidy confessed that they'd never have found White Island but for the engineroom breakdown. 'The Holy Mother looks after her own in wondrous ways,' he said, spoiling the moment for Mrs Clutterbutt with a ponderous wink. 'I've only one doubt though, Mrs C. The latitude of this island is eight degrees thirty-five minutes south. That's a bit north of the nine to ten degrees Harvey Bannister indicated on his chart. But navigating the way he was, from a raft, and I don't doubt without a nautical almanac, half a degree was no great error.' He paused, nodded as if acknowledging the unasked question. 'It's plain to me that he named it White Island because of that long line of surf breaking on the reef. It must have been the first thing he saw from the raft.'

'I must confess, Captain, that I am more excited than I would have thought possible. To be quite honest, I had given up any hope of finding the island. Particularly when the competition didn't seem to be catching on. I found that most depressing.'

'Ah, and it was the same with Shamus Cassidy. I didn't want to sadden you, but it was small store that I set on our chances of success.' He patted her arm affectionately. 'Well, now, Mrs C. I must be getting back to the bridge. There's much that needs doing.'

Cassidy anchored *Sunglow* four cables off the western side of the island, well clear of the reef which ran parallel with the shoreline. The ship had no sooner swung to her anchor than he went down to the sundeck to talk to the passengers.

Raising a hand for silence, smiling broadly, he said, 'You can congratulate Mr Carter, for I think it's White Island he's discovered.' There was a noisy cheerful response. Dean Carter stood up, looked at his fellow passengers with the cautious but pleased expression of a passer-by caught on television. 'Thank you, folks.' He flashed his teeth in a brief smile. 'I guess I was lucky to be looking that way when the rain lifted.'

'The next thing is to explore, and for that we'll be sending in the skimmers,' continued Cassidy. 'I'll be handing you over to the chief steward shortly and he will detail skimmers' parties and the section of the island allocated to the . . .', he hesitated, '. . . shall we call them the search teams. Number One Team will explore the middle section of the island, Number Two Team will take the southern section . . .'

Mr Cawson raised a hand. 'What about the northern section, Captain?'

'I'll be taking that for meself,' said Cassidy. 'As you can see, it's mostly in the middle and southern parts that the palm trees are situated, and that's where the majority of you will be going. There are only a few palms in the north. I'll be taking a small team in Skimmer Three – a couple of passengers and my steward. That should be more than enough.'

'One final point.' He stared until there was silence. 'Each team must elect a leader. Do it on the journey into the beach. When you've landed, it will be the leader's duty to organize the search in your section.'

Skimmers One and Two with Obudo and the bosun in charge left the ship shortly afterwards, each carrying seven passengers. They headed for a break in the reef midway down the western side. A few minutes later Skimmer Three, with Cassidy at the tiller, made off towards the northern end of the island. On board with him were Mrs Clutterbutt, Jim Abernethy and Mbolwo. The only passengers to remain on board were Mrs Bruckner, her sprained ankle not yet healed, and Henry Atkins, who'd decided to have a day of rest. 'Me stomach's playing up,' he explained.

Prior to leaving the ship, Cassidy and Mrs Clutterbutt

186

held an urgent discussion on bringing off the gold if it were found. It would, they agreed, be important to conceal the finding.

'I've told Obudo and the bosun not to bring their skimmers back to the ship before three o'clock this afternoon. We must get back an hour before them. That'll give us the best part of four hours ashore. Should be time enough.'

The equipment taken on board Cassidy's skimmer included two spades, a pickaxe, a steel rod for probing, and a couple of canvas gunny bags with rope handles. 'For carrying *the goods*,' Cassidy told Mrs Clutterbutt with a wary smile. 'We'll fill up with sand on top of them. That'll help explain the weight. Clean sand is always needed for holystoning the sundeck.' He had with him a two-way radio for keeping in touch with Pascal who was to remain on board with Scalatti.

With its outboard high-whining, Skimmer Three bounced and sprayed its way up the windward side of the island. Sitting in the sternsheets, hand on tiller, bearded chin thrust forward, Cassidy in white tropical kit looked bigger, more formidable than ever. On the thwart ahead of him sat Mrs Clutterbutt, calm and dignified, dressed as usual on these occasions in a cotton sun-frock. One hand clutched the crown of her straw hat, the other the gunwhale handrail. Her eyes gave no hint of emotion as the palm-clad island slid by, indigo seas breaking into foam on the reef, beyond it a strip of white sand shimmering in tropical sunlight.

With Harvey Bannister's chart firmly imprinted on his mind, Cassidy took the skimmer round the northern end of the island. He kept to seaward of Wreck Reef until he saw the tell-tale gap at its eastern end, and headed for it. Keeping clear of breaking surf he steered the skimmer through the turbulent waters of the narrow channel. Once inside the reef he throttled back and headed for the spit of sand which reached into the lagoon. At the beach end, quite by itself, stood a tall coconut palm. Cassidy pointed to it with a flourish. 'Lone Palm Point,' he announced, an unfamiliar tremor in his voice. 'See it, Mrs C?'

'Oh, Captain. I don't really know what to say. This is such an incredible moment for me.' Mrs Clutterbutt had to raise her voice to be heard above the sound of the engine. 'Harvey Bannister's little chart come alive. One thinks of the poor man – his raft wrecked on that reef – the struggle to get ashore with the injured cabin-boy – all those weeks of privation . . .' She broke off, evidently embarrassed by her display of emotion.

Cassidy said, 'Indeed, and it is a great moment. A dream come true, one might say.'

The skimmer drifted slowly across the lagoon towards the sandspit until with a final burst of throttle, he ran its bows on to the sand. Mbolwo and Jim climbed out, helped the others ashore, pulled the inflatable further up the sandspit, and took the spades, gunny bags and other equipment from it.

Led by Cassidy, pocket compass in hand, they walked towards the lone palm where it stood guard over the sandspit. Stooped seawards by the trade wind, its fronds rustled in ceaseless movement.

Cassidy went to its foot, bent down and put the compass on the sand. He turned it gently until the magnetic needle settled on north.

'Twenty paces to the east,' he said solemnly, moving off in that direction with large strides, counting as he went. At twenty paces he stopped and with his foot made a cross in the sand. The surface there, well above high water mark, was undisturbed. He began probing with the metal rod, but without result. 'It's not long enough,' he complained. 'We shall have to be digging. Come on, Mbolwo. Get busy. Make a start here.' Cassidy pointed to the mark in the sand. Mbolwo took off his singlet and began digging, his brown shoulders gleaming with sweat.

Mrs Clutterbutt went over to Cassidy, spoke in a low

voice. 'You said *we*, Captain. There are two spades. Shouldn't someone be helping him?'

Cassidy shook his head. 'It's not work for a white man in the tropics, Mrs C. The Sons of Ham shall be the hewers of wood and the drawers of water.'

'Racist rubbish, Captain. Jim shall help.' She beckoned to her nephew who was probing with the metal rod, pointed to the second spade. 'I think you should help.'

Jim brushed strands of hair from his eyes, looked at the sun. 'In this heat?' He managed a good natured grin. 'I could get a stroke.'

'Nonsense, Jim. What you'll get is exercise. You need it. You've put on weight. Too much easy living.'

He took the spade and began to dig.

During the next hour a number of holes were dug, the sandspit taking on the character of an alluvial diamond digging. But the sweated labours of Mbolwo and Jim produced nothing. At about three feet down in each hole the sand gave way to coral, hard and unyielding.

There was a long silence while Cassidy considered the problem. Slapping his thigh, he exclaimed, 'Holy St Patrick, and it's stupid I am! Bannister would have reckoned *east* from the position of the sun at sunrise. *The Times* report was April. He must have been on the island at least a few months before that. Say, January. The sun would have been well south of the Equator then – it's almost into October we are now. The sun's close to the Equator. Bannister's east would have been more like east-south-east by compass.' Once again the big Irishman stepped out the twenty paces, and once again Mbolwo and Jim – stripped to the waist, wet with perspiration, and close to exhaustion – began shovelling sand. Mbolwo had dug deep into a third hole when his spade struck something solid. He took it to be coral but knelt down, cleared the sand from it and found that the object was wooden. He went on clearing the sand until he was able to pull out an old, weather worn slat of timber. He threw it aside, went on digging. Soon afterwards he stepped back, wide eyed, his spade raised. 'No good to dig more, Captain,' he called to Cassidy in a startled voice. 'Bad things here.'

Cassidy, some distance away and talking to Mrs Clutterbutt, at once went over to the Swahili who pointed to the hole he'd been digging. Cassidy looked down, saw the human skull, white and grinning. Bones and pieces of rotted material showed through the sand.

Cassidy stared at the skull in silence. When he spoke his voice was hoarse. 'Ah, and that will be it, I'm thinking.'

Mbolwo shook his head. 'No good to dig here, Captain. Very bad. Can make trouble with the spirits.' He stood back from the excavation.

Cassidy fingered his beard, growled at the Swahili, turned to Jim. 'You carry on, lad. Harvey Bannister was no fool. Clever it was, to bury the boy on top of it. He must have known the native superstition. They'll not disturb the dead, you know.' He looked round. 'We've found it, Mrs C.' There was a tremor of excitement in the Irishman's voice. 'Twenty full paces from the lone palm. As sure as Saint Patrick it's under the skeleton it'll be.'

While Cassidy was talking, Jim had turned over the timber plank. With a handful of grass he brushed the sand from it. Frowning at what he saw, he said, 'It won't, you know.'

'Won't what, lad?' Cassidy was mopping his face.

'It won't be under the skeleton.' Jim ran a finger over the inscription carved into the time hardened wood. 'Look at this.'

Cassidy knelt, peered at the inscription:

HERE LIES JACK GOLD
BOY SEAMAN FROM THE
BARQUE KOOLAMAGEE OF
BRISTOL LOST AT SEA
17 DECEMBER 1880

He got to his feet, turned his back on the grave. 'Holy Mother O' God – all these shenanigans for nothing, then.' His gesture of disappointment, both arms raised, fists clenched, eyes lifted to the sky, gave way to a sudden burst of laughter.

Mrs Clutterbutt, who had retained her customary calm, regarded him with disapproval. 'Do control yourself, Captain. You are standing at that unfortunate boy's grave. It should be treated with respect.'

'Control meself, Mrs C? Holy Saint Patrick!' He laughed again, wiped the tears from his eyes. 'Surely to goodness yourself will be seeing the humour of it all. As for Shamus Cassidy, why – a fine house overlooking Killarney Lough – indeed, and is that not funny enough.' His deep laugh carried across the lagoon.

Mbolwo looked at him in astonishment, wondering, perhaps, if the evil spirits were already at work.

Mrs Clutterbutt shook her head. 'I don't know what you're talking about, Captain.' She went to the sandy grave, looked down at the skull and what could be seen of the skeleton. 'How sad, yet how remarkable, and now so very obvious. Stupid of me not to have suspected something of the sort.' She turned to Cassidy. 'What can I say, but that I am deeply sorry to have put you to so much trouble.'

'Ah, now, and don't be blaming yeself, Mrs C. The evidence seemed all one way. That chart, and the cutting from *The Times*. How could we be thinking otherwise?'

Mrs Clutterbutt began to say something but was interrupted by a shouted, 'Hi, there, folks.' It was Dean Carter, emerging from the undergrowth beyond the sandspit, camera at the ready.

'Oh dear.' Mrs Clutterbutt looked at Cassidy. 'What shall we do?'

'Leave it to me.' He produced his cigar case from a trouser pocket. By the time the Carters arrived the cigar was alight.

Sandra Carter took in the scene with bewildered eyes. 'What on earth have you people been digging for? The secret treasure of Commander Rollo's corsairs?' She giggled. 'Buried gold?'

'Ah, and you're right there, Mrs Carter. Gold it is. Come and see for yourself.'

Her eyes grew larger. 'Hey, Dean. Just come and see this,' she shrieked to her husband who was flitting from one vantage point to another, camera clicking, as he recorded the occasion for the folks at home. 'Can you believe it, hun? They've found gold.'

Cassidy pointed his cigar at the hole in the sand beside which Jim leant on a spade. 'In there,' he said.

The Carters looked at each other. Dean nodded, held his camera at the ready. Sandra moved forward, passed the mound of sand, peered down. She squeaked with surprise. 'My goodness! It's a skeleton – a pirate's I guess.' She looked across to Cassidy. 'But where's the gold, Captain?'

'You're looking at gold, lass. See what's on this.' He touched the timber slat with his foot. 'From the raft I'd say.'

With a look of disbelief, she knelt and examined the timber. She stood up, laughed self consciously. 'You're a wicked old tease, Captain. But how interesting.' She looked round. 'All those other holes. Why did you dig them?'

'To find the grave.'

'But this bit of wood. Surely it was on it?'

'No,' said Cassidy. 'It was buried *in* it.'

Dean Carter had an idea. 'Say, how did you know there was a grave here anyway?'

'It's a long story,' said Cassidy. 'You'll be hearing it later. Now tell me, any sign of those palms with the healing oil?'

'Not when we left our team. They're still searching, I guess. We wanted to make pictures, so we came this way. Also to see how you folks were getting on.'

Sandra Carter looked at the gunny bags. 'You came well prepared. What are those for, Captain?'

'We'll be taking sand back to the ship. For holystoning the decks, ye know.'

After further small talk with the Americans, Cassidy stepped forward and looked once more into the sandy grave. The eye sockets of Jack Gold's skull were staring at him with what seemed to be a sardonic grin. He picked up a spade. 'We cannot be leaving the poor lad like this. Come Mbolwo. Let us cover him. Unlucky it is to desecrate a grave.'

The African began shovelling back the sand. Cassidy stood watching, spade in hand. He looked up at the sun, took a handkerchief from his pocket, wiped the sweat from his forehead. He beckoned to Jim who was talking to Mrs Clutterbutt on the far side of the grave.

The young man came across. Cassidy held out the spade. 'Get busy, lad. Give Mbolwo a hand. Terrible hot it is for a man to be digging.'

Mrs Clutterbutt's nephew raised his eyebrows in a quizzical frown, took the spade, brushed sweat soaked hair from his eyes, and got to work.

Impossible old humbug, thought Mrs Clutterbutt, but a dear man in spite of it. How sad that I should have so disappointed him.

Perhaps Sandra Carter was able to read her thoughts. 'Isn't Captain Cassidy a darling,' she whispered to the older woman. 'Right out of some cute Irish folk tale, I'd say.'

'Would you,' said Mrs Clutterbutt in an offhand, distant fashion. She put up a hand to straighten her hat, before walking across to where Cassidy stood watching Mbolwo and Jim fill in the grave.

TWENTY-ONE

Cassidy and his party got back to *Sunglow* an hour before the other skimmers returned. Twenty minutes later the coaster weighed anchor and course was set for Dada's Island, three hours steaming to the north-west.

The word had been passed that search teams were to meet in the lounge at 4.30 to report on the day's activities. With Cassidy in the chair, proceedings began promptly at that time. Commander Rollo and Stephen Blake, leaders of their search teams, duly made their reports; the sections of White Island allocated to them had been thoroughly searched. No coconut palms with tapping incisions at the tops of their trunks had been found. A number of palms had been tapped by the search parties. The sap was colourless, but samples had been taken and were in Dr Summers' care. The doctor said he very much doubted if the fluid collected had any special healing properties, since the coconut palms on White Island appeared to be indistinguishable from those on the other islands they'd visited. He expressed interest, however, in Miss McLachlan's earlier report about the red palm oil used by a cancer free community in El Salvador.

At this stage Mrs Clutterbutt intervened to tell the story she and Cassidy had improvised for the occasion. Beginning with some diffidence, she said, 'I must confess that I am responsible for Captain Cassidy's account of an uncharted island, known to the natives as Ile Blanche. And I am, I fear, the sponsor of the thousand dollar prize which has, of course, been won by Mr Dean Carter.' Sandra Carter's delighted squeak could not blanket the murmurs of surprise.

194

'Not quite cricket, Madam, if I may say so,' observed Commander Rollo. 'I think you might . . .'

'I must explain,' went on Mrs Clutterbutt, 'my reasons for inventing the story.' She then read aloud the cutting from *The Times* of April 1881, reporting the loss at sea of the barque *Koolamagee* while under the command of her great-grandfather, Captain Harvey Bannister. She told them the story of how he and a cabin boy, the sole survivors, had drifted for weeks on a raft in the Indian Ocean until they reached a desert island which he had called Ile Blanche; though neither that name, nor its English version, White Island, could be found on any chart. She presumed that it was known to the native fishermen who'd rescued him as Ile Blanche. The cabin boy died soon after reaching the island, and her great-grandfather had recorded burying him 'twenty full paces east' of the lone palm tree on the sandspit.

'So that's why Skimmer Three took the northern section?' Mr Cawson's eyes accused Cassidy.

'Yes, it was,' said Mrs Clutterbutt with some asperity. 'Over the years, for sentimental reasons I suppose, my desire to find that island has become an obsession. It was that, and my love of ships and the sea, which brought me on this cruise. But I was quite sure that neither *Sunglow*'s passengers nor Captain Cassidy would be interested in searching for a cabin boy's grave, however important it might be to me. So I invented something of more general interest – the mystical healing qualities of Ile Blanche's palm oil!' Mrs Clutterbutt stopped to consider with unflinching eyes the faces of her listeners. 'You may disapprove of my action – regard it as presumptuous – but the search *has* been interesting. It *has* taken you to a really remote desert island, uninhabited, nameless and unknown except, perhaps, to a few native fishermen. That surely was adventure – and it was for adventure that you came on this cruise.'

Mrs Clutterbutt's explanations apparently accepted,

Cassidy declared the meeting closed, having reminded passengers that the ship would arrive at Dada's Island at 6.30 that evening. Skimmers to take them to the beach would be at the gangway at seven p.m.

The discovery of White Island, coming on top of Diana Kitson's trouble with Krol, had deflected Jim Abernethy from his Wreck Island problem. But it remained his intention to tell Cassidy of his suspicions once he'd had an opportunity of discussing matters with Jean McLachlan. The stumbling block in his theory was, he was aware, the possibility that the IMMEC scientists were in fact carrying out some sort of geological survey. When *Sunglow*'s passengers were exploring the Aldabras, he'd heard Jean McLachlan explaining the geological processes which led to the formation of atolls. When someone expressed surprise at her considerable knowledge, she'd admitted with modesty that she was a graduate in geology and marine biology. It was her interest in those subjects, she said, which had brought her to the islands which Darwin had explored in the *Beagle* when busy with his *Origin of Species*.

It was that overheard conversation which had persuaded him to have a talk with her before going to Cassidy.

An opportunity arose soon after leaving White Island. He found her reading in a corner of the lounge. 'Mind if I ask you something?' he said.

She put down her book. 'No, of course not. Do sit down.' She patted the settee beside her.

'It's about Wreck Island,' he said. 'Those Finnish scientists said they were carrying out geological surveys for the company which leased the island – the International Mineral and Marine Exploration Corporation. They had a bit set up there – bulldozers, earth movers, etcetera. What I'd like to ask you is, what sort of minerals could they be

196

looking for? I mean, could there actually *be* minerals in a place like that?'

She nodded. 'Oh, yes. Most certainly, Jim. Don't forget that seventy per cent of the earth's surface is covered by water. There are many minerals and chemicals beneath it. About a fifth of the world's oil and gas already come from under the sea. There are immense deposits of manganese on the ocean floor, and other minerals like nickel and copper and cobalt. Far more under the water than has ever been found above it.'

Jim frowned. 'Yes. But would there be, on one of those islands?'

'One doesn't know what IMMEC are looking for, or how deep those excavations may go. They've probably carried out seismic tests. They may be planning to drill beneath the island. To sample the geological formation. Could be gas or oil they're after, apart from minerals.'

'I see.' Jim tried to conceal his disappointment. 'So you think they might really find something.'

'Quite possibly. This is a potentially exciting region. Oil searches are already under way in the Comores and Seychelles area. There are scientific indications that a vast oil lake once existed off the Madagascar coast. It is believed to have moved, over millions of years, towards the Seychelles. The IMMEC people may be establishing a base on Wreck Island from which to carry out exploratory work in that area.'

'I see.' He stood up, ran a hand through untidy red hair. 'Well, thank you, Jean. That was really interesting. Let's hope they find something useful.' He left her to get on with her book. Though his theory had received a battering, he was still not convinced. He went out to the sundeck, leant on the taffrail and watched the sea sliding by, his mind still grappling with what looked like an insoluble problem now that Wreck Island had been left so far behind.

All the same, he decided, in spite of what Jean McLachlan had said, he'd see the Captain about it. He wasn't going

197

to abandon his theory yet. Why had the scientists troubled to chase *Sunglow* in their cabin cruiser? Would they have done that to get back one African labourer?

Deep in thought, he was scarcely aware of someone immediately behind him until a familiar voice said, 'Hullo, Jim,' and he smelt jasmine. Her presence had its usual electric effect.

'Hullo, Diana,' he said awkwardly. 'I didn't know you were there.'

'Because your thoughts were miles away, weren't they. I wonder what they were about?'

'Nothing much.' He smiled sheepishly, as if hiding a secret.

'Jim, I must tell you something.' She lowered her voice. 'Luigi spoke to me this morning. Before we landed. He said Nils Krol had asked him to apologize for his behaviour the other night. Apparently he'd had a few drinks in the crew's quarters before coming to Luigi's cabin. Luigi says that Nils got a bad fright when he found me in the cupboard – quite lost his head. He's terribly anxious to get back to Sweden, you see, and was scared stiff of ending up in an African gaol if I'd talked. Luigi was worried about that too.'

'I see.' Jim was guarded. 'What else did he say?'

'He said the drugs deal was off. Nils Krol will have nothing to do with it now – *in case* I talk. One can't blame him really, can one?'

'I suppose not.'

'Luigi begged me not to breathe a word about this to anyone.' She stopped, stared at Jim as if aware of the anomaly. 'And of course I won't, except for you.' She smiled, touched his hand. 'Luigi says that Captain Cassidy is very strict with the crew. If ever a rumour about a drugs deal reached him, Luigi and Bashi Menon would get the sack. So please, Jim. Never mention it, will you?'

'No, I won't.'

'Promise.'

'Of course I do.' He turned to see if anyone was near

them. There wasn't. 'Will *you* promise me something?'

'What, Jim?'

'That you won't get involved with Krol again – I mean do anything silly. You're too good for him – and for Scalatti. They're not your sort.' He felt presumptuous and awkward, talking to her like that; but someone had to.

'Oh, Jim, you are a nice man.' She put her hand on his where it rested on the rail. 'You've been such a comfort. Got me over a most horrible patch. Yes, I promise not to get involved. But even if I didn't promise, I wouldn't. Nils Krol gave me such a fright.' She hesitated. 'I feel a lot better now that I know the drugs deal is off. That's good news isn't it?'

With sudden caution, Jim said, 'Look out. We're being joined.'

The dumpy figure of Henry Atkins ranged up alongside them. ' 'ullo, 'ullo, 'ullo. You two together again. What's this then, Mrs Kitson? Cradle snatching?'

Jim wondered if the little man was getting at them. As always, Atkins' dark glasses and generous beard concealed his face.

Diana Kitson laughed. 'You horrible man! Jim may be half my age, but he's quite the nicest man in the ship – *and* quite the most reliable.

'Tell me, Mr Atkins – why didn't you come ashore with us today?' She affected a frown. 'We had such fun. White Island was gorgeous. A real one hundred per cent desert island. Uninhabited and unknown. And fancy Mrs Clutterbutt finding the grave of her great-grandfather's cabin boy – so sad and yet so romantic.'

Henry Atkins pulled at the peak of his yachting cap. 'To tell the truth, Mrs Kitson, I've had me fill of tropical islands. As for today's lark, well, I never did believe all that jazz about the healing powers of palm oil. Anyway, climbing palm trees is not for 'enery Atkins. So I had a nice quiet day, thank you. A good old feets up, you might say. Keeping me energies for the beach party tonight. Lookin' forward to that, I am. All them young drop-outs. Blimey! Wouldn't mind being a drop-out meself. Not that the missus would take too kindly to that.'

'You're incorrigible, Mr Atkins. I give up.' She looked towards the lounge. 'Let's go and get some tea.'

A soft wind ruffled the palms along the shoreline. Beyond it, ripples from the lagoon lapped the beach where the fire cast patterns of light and shade on those around it. From somewhere in the darkness came the sound of music: guitars, drums and flutes in a gently flowing melody, drowned at times by the hubbub of voices and laughter. There was constant movement, a steady coming and going to and from the firelight, the shadowy figures like moths round candlelight.

Pascal was pleased, the barbecue was a success, most of the food had been eaten, much of the *calao* swallowed, its remains still in brisk demand. The party had broken up into cheerful noisy groups. Dada's young men and women – he called them 'my children', they called him 'Dada' – had been on the beach tending the fire when the skimmers first came in. Dada himself, like Cassidy, had arrived later, by which time the barbecue was well under way.

Both men were now the centre of a group near the fire: it included Mrs Clutterbutt, Commander Rollo, Stephen Blake and Dr Summers. Conversation was brisk.

Dada was a rotund man in his middle fifties; bald, with a barrel of a chest which matched the ample stomach beneath it. Wide blue eyes, set well apart, looked out from a bearded, suntanned face with a mixture of humour and surprise. He wore khaki slacks, a cotton shirt, and a gold chain with a shark's tooth pendant. The razor sharp tooth, set in gold was, explained one of the commune, Dada's emblem of authority. Commenting on this to Stephen Blake, Pascal said he felt the emblem was unnecessary: the shirt and slacks were enough to set the man apart, since the rest of the commune, men and women, wore nothing but palmleaf skirts beneath which, in the manner of the best Highland regiments, no other garment was worn.

When Pascal joined them, Dada was talking to Dr Summers. 'I'd be grateful if you'd see Mandy's child,' Dada was saying. 'The kid's weak, running a temperature. Too much sun I expect. But Mandy's worried. Says it's more than that. There's a lot of pain.' Dada looked towards two men standing nearby. Both were tall, with shining, clean shaven heads which reflected the light from the fire. 'Hey JackKnife,' he called. The man came over. 'Take Dr Summers down to Mandy's hut. He's going to look at the kid.'

The doctor and the tall man walked off into the darkness.

'What an extraordinary name,' said Mrs Clutterbutt. 'Do tell me, Mr Dada, how he got it?'

As the night went on and the *calao* flowed, the barbecue became more lively. Inhibitions were forgotten and the beach resounded to the shouts and shrieks of laughter of those around the fire. The tempo of the music changed, a saxophone took over from the flute, drums and a banjo joined the guitars and the dancing grew wilder. People came and went, disappearing into the night, emerging from it, the bonfire the magnet.

Before eleven o'clock Cassidy left the party to return to *Sunglow*, taking with him Mrs Clutterbutt, Commander Rollo, Dr Summers and others among the older passengers. Dada had gone down to the lagoon's edge to see them off.

'I'll be landing your stores in the morning,' Cassidy told him. 'We sail at 9.30.'

'Good,' said Dada. 'I'll hand over our mail to your men then. Thanks for a great party, Captain.' He pointed to the bonfire. 'Looks like they're still enjoying it.'

'Ah well, Dada. Your people were the making of it.' He laughed. 'And the *calao*, maybe. See you in three months.'

201

The two men shook hands. 'Bon voyage, Captain. Look after yourself.'

'Same to you, Dada.'

Cassidy climbed into the skimmer where the others were waiting. The second mate started the outboard and the inflatable raced across the lagoon, heading for the break in the reef.

It was after midnight when Said Obudo tapped Jim Abernethy's shoulder. 'Look over there. That dishy bird with the Carters is Moonflower. She's great. Let's join them.'

They'd been watching the musicians, Luther Nelson among them, until instruments were put down for a *calao* break. It was by no means the first of the evening.

For Jim the attraction was not the tall girl wearing a white flower in her hair, but Diana Kitson who'd been prancing barefoot on the sand with Knuckleboy until the music stopped.

'Hi, Said, Jim.' Sandra Carter pointed to them in turn. 'Meet Moonflower.'

The girl with a frangipani in her hair and a skin like satinwood smiled. 'I know Said. He's an old friend. Hullo Jim.'

'Hullo.' Jim laughed self-consciously. 'Is your name really Moonflower?' He hoped she didn't think he was looking at her satinwood breasts.

She nodded. 'Yes. It is the name Dada gave me. He names us all. It is to break our last link with the world we left.'

'Do you really enjoy life here?' There was disbelief in Sandra Carter's brash question.

'Of course. We *live* here. In Europe we *existed*. It is not possible' – the accent was German, decided Jim – 'to understand the difference unless you have lived as we do.'

Diana Kitson said, 'I do believe that. All of you I've met tonight seem so natural, so happy. I do envy you.'

'Okay, it's a simple existence.' Dean Carter affected a

patronizing smile. 'But you're trying to put the clock back. This is – ah – the space age, Moonflower. Not pre-history. You're cut off from the state of the art in just about everything – high tech, medicine, communications, art forms. You name it, lady, you don't have it.' He shook his head. 'Why there could be a nuclear exchange and you folk just wouldn't know it had happened.'

Moonflower regarded Dean Carter with dark, serious eyes. 'You would *not* know it. We would know *of* it, but not experience it. We do have radio.'

'Big deal! I bet it's plenty used.'

'Not too much. It is in the community centre. Dada has the only switch key. He is very strict about this. He says television and radio are used to anaesthetize and trivialize society, to make non-participating morons of the masses. *Our* radio is used only on Sunday nights, for the BBC's news summary. Absolutely nothing else.'

'Good grief, I can't believe it,' wailed Sandra. 'No plays, no cinema, no music, no documentaries, no natural history – not even Dallas. How can you *exist*?'

'We *live*,' corrected Moonflower. 'We make our own music, paint our own pictures, provide our own entertainment, build our houses, make our furniture.' She touched her palmleaf skirt. 'Also our clothes – and we produce our foods.' She paused. 'You talk of natural history. There is much of it here. You have not heard of Darwin?' Arched eyebrows underlined the note of disbelief.

Diana Kitson said, 'Do most of you marry, have children?'

Moonflower raised her hands as if to ward off evil. 'Ah, the hypocrisy of the West. No, we do not marry. It is not necessary. We are all one family. Not just one man and one woman making improbable promises of fidelity. Marriage is monogamous, people are polygamous. Our commune recognizes this. If a child comes it is the responsibility of all of us – and it is loved by all of us.'

'Sounds like paradise.' Diana Kitson chuckled guiltily.

203

Jim did not know what to think. Did she really mean she liked that sort of thing?

Dean Carter returned to the attack. 'What sort of man is this guy, Dada? You say he's strict about radio. Is he a sort of dictator? Have you any rights. Can you leave the island if you wish?'

'Dada is a good man. Firm is perhaps a better word than strict. It is necessary to have a firm leader in a commune. Yes, we have rights – also obligations. One is not possible without the other. In seven years only three people have left. That is less than one in ten. One was very ill, two wished to marry. That is not possible here. They have since divorced.'

Jim asked his first question. 'Who are the two guys with shaven heads?'

'You mean JackKnife and Knuckleboy. They are Dada's prefects.'

'Prefects,' echoed Sandra Carter incredulously. 'What on earth does he need them for?'

'For the same reason that you need policemen. They are the outward and visible symbol of law and order. Dada is not young, not as strong as most of our young men. Sometimes when they have too much *calao*, or quarrel about women, or the division of work – then Dada has to lay down the law. JackKnife and Knuckleboy enforce it. They are seldom needed.'

'Marvellous,' said Diana Kitson. 'Simply marvellous. I'm thirsty. More *calao* please, someone.' She held up an empty coconut shell.

Jim took it from her. 'I'll get it.'

'Oh, you darling man.' She squeezed his hand before turning back to the others.

Sandra Carter said, 'One for me too, please Jim.'

Moonflower said, 'Look, Dada is coming over to join us. You will like him. He is very amusing.'

Jim made for the trestle-table beyond the fire.

He joined the queue for the *calao*, had the two coconuts filled, and set out on the return journey. Because he wanted to get back to Diana he hurried and, because the night was dark, he tripped over a log, fell awkwardly, and got up with two empty coconut shells. Angry with himself, but glad that darkness had hidden his humiliation, he rejoined the queue, had the empty shells refilled, and made once more for the knot of people round Moonflower.

To his disappointment neither Diana nor Dada were there. 'Where are they?' he asked.

'Diana stole him from us,' complained Sandra in a voice which suggested a pout.

'Be fair, honey,' corrected her husband. 'Dada hadn't been here more than a couple of minutes before *he invited* her to go with him to see how Dr Summers was getting on with the sick child.'

Jim handed Sandra her shell of *calao*, looked disconsolately at the one he'd brought for Diana before swallowing it in a long gulp. He was thinking of Cassidy's light hearted remark at the briefing about Dada being a great one with the ladies. What was the good of trying to protect Diana if she took risks like that with a stranger? Feeling miserable and diminished, he wandered back to where the skimmers were hauled up on the beach.

TWENTY-TWO

It had been Cassidy's intention to sail at 9.30, but the day worked out very differently. Before *Sunglow* had begun unloading stores, a *pirogue* driven by an outboard motor came alongside.

Two men hurried up the gangway and were greeted by

Scalatti who did not know them. It was *Sunglow*'s first visit to the island since he'd joined, and he'd not gone ashore the previous night.

To Scalatti they were a strange sight; muscular bodies, browned by years in the sun, naked but for the palmleaf skirts which rustled as they moved. The older man introduced himself as Balthazar. He had a jet black beard, and black shoulder-length hair tied with a red headband. Beneath it a fringe all but reached his eyebrows. The lobes of his ears were pierced, and from them hung what Scalatti took to be brass curtain rings. By contrast, Balthazar's companion – 'I'm Speargun,' he'd announced – was a light eyed blond with a mop of sunbleached hair, his only ornament a gold chain with a Pisces pendant.

Balthazar wasted no time; they must see the Captain at once. Scalatti looked at his watch and explained that Cassidy was probably in his shower. They could not wait, Balthazar insisted. 'Tell the Captain we have serious news for him, and that we cannot wait.' The dark eyes were so compelling that Scalatti gave in.

He took the two men to the lounge, and from there phoned Cassidy. Yes, he would see them, bring them along right away. Scalatti knocked, opened the door and put his head in to announce their names. They went in, he closed the door behind them and went down to the main deck. In spite of his curiosity, he was glad to have no part in whatever was afoot in the Captain's cabin.

From calls he'd made at the island over the years Cassidy knew both men, particularly Balthazar, who was Dada's deputy and one of those who had crewed his yacht throughout the long voyages in the Pacific and Indian Oceans. Speargun, too, had been a member of that crew. Wearing a towel round his waist Cassidy greeted the islanders, got them seated, and regarded them with narrowed eyes. 'Now lads, what's the trouble?' he demanded.

'Dada is dead.'

'Holy Mother O' God. What was it, then?' Cassidy all but rose from his chair.

'Murder,' said Balthazar. 'Moonflower waited for him in his hut last night after the last of your party had left the beach. That was past one o'clock this morning. When he didn't turn up, she assumed he'd gone to another hut. He'd had a good few *calaos* at the barbecue. So had Moonflower, and she soon fell asleep. Roll call this morning was at 6.30 as usual. As you know, Dada was very strict about that, party or no party the night before. The only absentees were Dada, and Mandy who was nursing her child. We carried out a quick search; huts, community centre, loos, the lot. No sign of him. We thought he might have gone back to the beach. Fallen asleep there . . .'

Cassidy nodded understandingly. 'There's no knowing what the *calao* will do.'

'He wasn't on the beach,' went on Balthazar. 'So we decided to search either side of the path on the way back to the settlement. JackKnife found his body in the plantation, halfway between the beach and the settlement. About thirty yards clear of the path. He'd been stabbed in the neck and heart.'

Cassidy shook his head, held up a hand in a gesture of despair. 'Mother O' God. What a terrible end to a life that was.'

'He was a great guy,' said Speargun. 'Had his faults, but he did everything for us. Just about everything. God knows what'll happen to the commune without him. It'll never be the same.'

'No, it never will be – without him. But it'll go on,' said Balthazar firmly. 'The commune is provided for in his will. Subject to it continuing to operate in the same way, it will not have any financial problems. That's what he told us. But Christ! Who'd want to kill Dada? Of course he had his weaknesses. Who hasn't. But he was a great leader. Kind but firm – and very just.'

'Where's the body?' asked Cassidy.

'Still where we found it.'

'What is it then, that you want from me, lad?'

'I know *Sunglow*'s due to sail this morning –' Balthazar's eyes focussed on Cassidy with such intensity that the Irishman wondered if he was about to be the subject of hypnosis – 'but we want you to delay that Captain. So that there can be a proper inquiry into Dada's death.'

'What do you mean by that?'

'Two things. As captain of a ship you have certain powers, I believe – marriage, burial, inquest.'

'Only at sea. In port, those things are for the authorities ashore.'

'There are no authorities here, sir. We have to look to you. There is another important point. We don't know at what time Dada was murdered. Nobody seems to remember seeing him after about twelve-thirty last night.'

'What's on your mind, then, lad?' Cassidy took a cigar from the leather case on his desk. With deft, caring touches he set about preparing it.

'It is possible, Sir, that somebody from *Sunglow* killed Dada. That's not an allegation. Just the statement of a possibility. But it *is* why we want you to delay sailing and conduct the inquiry. That is best done when all who might be concerned are here – and when the events of last night are still fresh in people's minds.'

'And the evidence,' prompted Speargun. 'Like Dada – I mean the body – still lying where it happened. The time of death? You have a doctor on board. He may be able to help with that.'

Cassidy drew on the cigar, exhaled little whorls of blue smoke. 'It would have to be – will be – a matter for the police. But it could be weeks, maybe longer, before they'll be arriving here, if at all. And there's no way the poor man's body would be keeping in this climate.' He stopped, looked out to the sea beyond the porthole as if seeking some solution there. He turned back to Balthazar. 'You wouldn't be having a big refrigerator or a cold chamber large enough for that, would you?'

Balthazar shook his head. 'Nothing like that.'

Cassidy lapsed into thought, drummed with his fingers on the desk. At last he looked up. 'Very well then. It seems there is no answer to the problem. I'll delay sailing until late afternoon. More than that I cannot do. Delays cost the Capricorn Company money. But you shall have your inquiry.'

For the first time that morning Balthazar smiled and it quite changed the dark intensity of the man. 'That's very good of you, sir. It is what the commune wants. It is the least we can do for Dada.'

The inquiry was held in the community centre, known to the islanders as The Chatterbox. It was an open shelter, its large, palm thatched roof supported by the trunks of felled coconut palms, the floor hardened with desiccated coral, its edges marked with large cockleshells. Beyond it, the thatched huts of the settlement lay in haphazard patterns around a clearing in which poultry scratched. Pigs and goats rested in the shade.

As presiding officer, Cassidy sat at a trestle table, with Commander Rollo and Mrs Cawson on his right, and Dr Summers and Mr Cawson on his left. Cassidy had asked Rollo to sit with him as assessor, the commander having admitted to some knowledge of legal procedures gained during his time in the Royal Navy.

Mrs Cawson had offered to record the proceedings with her tape recorder. She would type the transcript, once back on board. It was an offer Cassidy had gladly accepted.

Dr Summers sat at the table as medical expert, while Mr Cawson was clerk of the court; an appointment made by Cassidy in recognition of Mrs Cawson's valuable service. No one, including Mr Cawson, had the slightest idea what his duties were. This was not surprising since neither Cassidy nor the commander had experience of inquest proceedings. Both, however, were familiar with naval and maritime courts of inquiry, and it was with these in mind that the court was constituted.

Cassidy had appointed as officials only those who had returned to *Sunglow* with him before eleven o'clock on the previous night. They had been seen off at the beach by Dada himself, and thus could not be under suspicion.

The other passengers sat on benches facing the top table, with them the entire island community, but for Mandy and her child, and other children of the settlement who'd been sent to play on the eastern beach.

Opening the proceedings, Cassidy announced that the purpose of the court was to inquire into the death of Robert John Aspen, known as Dada, and the circumstances surrounding it. It was not, he said, the function of the inquiry to make allegations of guilt, nor to conduct a trial. That was a matter for the Seychelles authorities under whose jurisdiction the island fell.

And so the unorthodox court with its oddly assorted audience set to work, the brown bodies of the islanders, naked but for their skirts, setting them apart from the passengers.

Beyond the plantation the sea, shimmering mirage-like in the sun, suggested a coolness far removed from the heat beneath the palm thatched roof where the air barely stirred. It was a stifling day.

Cassidy, huge and resplendent in tropical uniform, shoulder straps glistening with gold lace, hair and beard groomed for the occasion, dominated the proceedings. 'The court,' he affirmed, 'has already visited the site where the deceased's body was found. Dr Summers . . .' Cassidy paused, temporarily lost for words. 'That is to say our *medical expert*, Dr Summers, has examined it and, under his supervision, polaroid pictures have been taken by Mr Dean Carter – one of our passengers – who has kindly volunteered to act as official photographer. The photos are before the court.' He tapped a brown envelope on the table in front of him. 'They will be attached to our report.' Cassidy's serious demeanour concealed the pleasure his important role afforded him. 'I will now ask Dr Summers to report on his findings.'

The doctor proceeded to describe, in predictably obscure terms, the injuries he had found on the body. The stab wounds were deep and must in his view have been inflicted by a sharp knife or dagger, its blade between four and six inches in length and probably serrated. There were two wounds in the neck, one having severed the jugular vein; the other, at the base of the skull, would have caused immediate loss of consciousness. The stab in the heart appeared to have been administered when the victim was lying on the ground, presumably after infliction of the neck wounds. Dr Summers said he had not the forensic means to establish the time of death, but the indications were that it was probably within an hour or so either side of midnight.

In matter of fact terms, rather like a London policeman, JackKnife then described how he'd found the body. There was an almost explosive ripple of interest from commune members when he ended his statement with, 'His badge of authority, the shark tooth pendant, was missing. I searched the area round where he was lying, but there was no sign of it.'

Cassidy nodded, wrote several lines on his notepad. He then announced that it was necessary to determine when Dada had last been seen alive. He asked that anyone present who could give information on the subject should do so.

A woman with a frangipani in her sleek dark hair, raised her hand.

Cassidy nodded to her. 'Yes, Moonflower.'

With long fingers she brushed strands of hair from a face which was so drawn, the shadowed eyes so inflamed, that her beauty of the night before seemed all but gone. In a low uncertain voice she said, 'At about eleven-forty Dada came

211

to where I was talking to some of the people from the ship. That was near the fire.'

Cassidy looked up from the notes he was making. 'Ah, and who would they be, then?'

'Said Obudo, Dean and Sandra Carter, the tall guy with the red hair – I think his name is Jim – and the other woman.'

'Her name?'

'I do not know but she is here.' Moonflower turned, pointed to Diana Kitson who was sitting between Jean McLachlan and the Rev. Bliss, several rows from the front.

Commander Rollo leant towards Cassidy, spoke quietly.

'You say Dada came to where you were with these people. How long did he stay?' asked Cassidy.

'About ten minutes, I think.'

Cassidy clasped his hands on the table, leant forward, beard jutting. 'About ten minutes to twelve that would be. Would you be knowing where he went?'

Moonflower shook her head. 'Ask her.' She pointed again to Diana Kitson. 'She went off with him.'

'Mrs Kitson, can you help?'

Looking as brown as the islanders in her scanty sun blouse and denim shorts, and as handsome as ever in a fragile way, Diana Kitson stood up.

Cassidy smiled. 'You don't need to be standing, Mrs Kitson.'

'I prefer to.' She dabbed the perspiration from her forehead with a tissue. 'Dada asked me if I would like to see the settlement. I said I would. We left the fire and went down there. He took me round the huts, showed me this centre, took me to the radio room' – she waved a hand towards the small hut built on to one end of the centre. 'We looked at the rainwater catchment area, and the poultry and animals. Then we went to Mandy's hut to see her – but she and her daughter were asleep. It was late. I was terribly tired. I told him I had to get back to the barbecue . . .'

Cassidy interrupted. 'What time was that?'

212

'I didn't take the time. After midnight, I imagine. So we set off along the path through the plantation. We were about half way – I could see the light from the bonfire – when he said he'd left the concertina in the hut.' She paused, frowned as if trying to recall something. 'He wanted Luther Nelson to play it. Anyway, he told me to go on to the fire. I said, "Are you coming back?" He said, "Yes of course." He left me then, and I joined up with the others.'

Again Rollo leant over to say something to Cassidy who nodded before turning back to Mrs Kitson. 'How long would you say it was between leaving Mandy's hut and getting back to the fire?'

Diana Kitson hesitated, a fist against her forehead. 'I'd say about ten minutes at most. When I got to the fire I chatted with the Carters.'

'So the last time you saw Robert Aspen was about half an hour after midnight.'

'Yes, I suppose it would have been something like that.'

Dean Carter jumped up. 'I can help there, Captain. It was 12.40 when Mrs Kitson rejoined us. I happen to know that because I asked her where Dada was, and she said he'd gone back for something and would be along later. It was then that I checked the time. Obudo can bear me out because, right after that, I asked him when we'd be going off to the ship. He said about 1.20, and I said "Okay, so we've got another forty minutes."' The American produced one of his neighing laughs. 'I guess we – that's Sandra and myself – were ready for bed. All that dancing in the sand, right – and too much *calao*, I guess.'

Sandra Carter was not pleased. 'Speak for yourself, Dean Carter,' she muttered fiercely. 'You may have had too much, I certainly didn't. And I wasn't all that tired.'

Cassidy bowed to Diana Kitson. 'It's helpful indeed your evidence has been. There's just one more question I'll be asking. Did you happen to notice if Dada was wearing the shark's tooth pendant when you last saw him?'

'Yes, he was.'

'Ah, and how could you be seeing that? It was a dark night.'

'There were lights in the radio room.'

Cassidy said, 'Thank you, Mrs Kitson.' He looked at the faces in front of him. 'You'll have heard that Mrs Kitson saw Aspen at about thirty minutes after midnight. Is there any of you who saw him at a later time? For example, when he got back to the settlement to fetch the concertina?'

Those on the benches looked at each other, those in front turning their heads to see if there was any response from behind. There was not, no hand was raised, no one spoke, until Balthazar stood up. The muscular, bronzed body, the jet black beard and hair, red headband, absurdly large gold earrings and dark fiery eyes, suggested a pirate in fantasy, if not in being. He confirmed having seen Dada and Diana Kitson leave the settlement some time in the half hour after midnight. He'd not noted the time. There was no reason to do so.

'Where were you when you saw them?'

Balthazar hesitated. 'Standing in the doorway of a hut on the far side of the settlement.'

'Which hut would that be?'

Balthazar's mouth tightened, the bushy eyebrows gathered in a frown. 'Moonflower's.' He spoke with reluctance. 'I had to see her about something – but she was not there.'

Cassidy looked at him, nodded slowly as if in affirmation of something unsaid. Cawson spoke to the Irishman in a whispered aside. Cassidy shook his head. Balthazar sat down. Cassidy announced that there would be a break for lunch, the inquiry to assemble at 2.30 that afternoon. He asked all present to attend at that time.

Gaston Pascal had provided packed lunches for *Sunglow*'s passengers who picnicked in a clearing on the side of the plantation overlooking the lagoon. The midday sun made a

214

dazzling white line of the surf breaking on the reef beyond which *Sunglow* rode to her anchor, grey diesel smoke puffing from the squat funnel.

After lunch the Carters, Diana Kitson, Jim Abernethy and Said Obudo changed in the undergrowth and went down to the lagoon to swim. Jim and Obudo put on goggles and snorkels, and swam out to the reef. Diana Kitson had more or less ignored Jim that morning, and he was in a retaliatory mood. If she wanted to do the hard-to-get act, he'd show her it was something two could play at. Quite apart from that, he was worried and confused about her involvement with Dada so close to the time of his death. There was, he felt, something unpleasant about that. Perhaps she'd not told the whole story at the inquiry that morning.

Cassidy began the afternoon's proceedings by recalling JackKnife. 'When you found the deceased's body did you see the concertina?'

'Yes. It was a few feet from him.'

'I see. Thank you.'

Cassidy then asked if anyone could help the inquiry with information about where they were, and what they were doing, between midnight and one o'clock that morning. After a hesitant start, hands were raised and over the next hour or so a number of commune members and *Sunglow* passengers volunteered information. Most of them had been at the bonfire on the beach at the times involved, but there were exceptions: Dean Carter, for example, said that he and his wife had gone down to the settlement at about midnight. They'd seen all they wanted to in about fifteen minutes. Coming back on the path through the plantation they'd met Henry Atkins. He'd walked back to the fire with them. There, he and Atkins had drunk more *calao*.

Atkins confirmed Carter's story. 'Being not a dancing man – and, well, to tell the truth, having had a skinful of *calao* – I go down the path to relieve meself. The Carters

215

come up it from the settlement just as I'm sorting out me flies. We chat, I walk back to the fire with them and, before you can Bob's-me-Uncle, there's young Dean passing me another *calao*. We stay by the fire for some time, then I go down to the beach and hang around, waiting for the skimmer to take us back to the ship.'

Atkins was followed by Jim Abernethy. He said he'd been at the bonfire with the Carters, Moonflower and Obudo shortly before Dada joined them. He'd left it to get *calao* for Sandra and Mrs Kitson. When he got back to the fire they told him that Dada and Mrs Kitson had gone down to the settlement. 'I felt a bit dizzy then, so I went down to the water's edge, to where the skimmers were. I sat in one for a bit. After a while I walked along the beach, keeping close to the water where the sand was firm. It was dark. I'd gone quite a way when I bumped into Stephen Blake coming from the opposite direction. We chatted for a bit. He said he'd left the barbecue when the dancing began – wasn't his scene, he reckoned. So he'd gone for a walk along the beach. He was on his way back when we met. We kept together after that, went to the skimmers and sat in one talking until some time after midnight when he left me. I stayed in the skimmer until the other passengers came down to the beach with the second mate and Mr Pascal to take us back to *Sunglow*.'

Said Obudo and Gaston Pascal then described their movements. At no time had Pascal left the beach; Obudo had done so only to take the Captain and some passengers back to *Sunglow*.

Cassidy asked Stephen Blake if he had anything to say.

Blake was brief. 'Jim Abernethy's account is correct in so far as it concerns me. After I left him in the skimmers, I walked towards the fire, saw that the dancing was still going on: I was tired, so I sat on a grass hummock near the edge of the plantation, about a hundred yards from the fire. I stayed there until I saw our people moving towards the beach. I joined up with them and went out to the ship in Mr

216

Pascal's skimmer. We got back on board at about one-thirty this morning.'

Cassidy thanked Blake, looked rather pointedly at his watch. 'Would anyone else be wanting to speak?' His manner suggested he hoped they wouldn't. No one did, and he declared the inquiry closed. 'The officials of this court,' he said with some importance, 'will be staying on a while to discuss what we have heard. If the rest of you will now leave, I'd be grateful. A copy of our findings will be given to the commune prefects before *Sunglow* sails this evening. The originals, together with the transcript of these proceedings, and the photographs, will be sent to the Seychelles Government. No doubt they will be taking whatever action they consider necessary. When I get back to the ship I'll inform Mahé of Dada's death and the manner of it.' He looked at a note he'd made, smiled, and finished with, 'Thank you ladies and gentlemen.'

The time was four-fifty p.m. It had been a long day.

TWENTY-THREE

Late that afternoon Cassidy handed a signed copy of the court's findings to JackKnife and Knuckleboy on the understanding that it would be displayed on the notice-board in the community centre. It read:

A duly constituted Court of Inquiry was held in the Community Centre, Dada's Island, on 10 October 1983, to inquire into the death of Robert John Aspen, known as Dada to the island community of which he was founder and leader.

The officials of the Court were: President, Captain Shamus Cassidy, master of MV Sunglow, assisted by Commander Richard Fortescue Rollo, RN (retd), Mr

Frederick George Cawson, and Doctor Mark Summers MD, passengers in the aforesaid ship.

The Court found that the deceased died of stab wounds inflicted by a person or persons unknown, some time after midnight on the 10th October, 1983.

A transcript of the tape-recorded proceedings is in course of preparation and will be forwarded with relevant photographs to the Government of the Seychelles upon return of MV Sunglow *to Mombasa on or about 14 October, 1983.*

Signed,   *Shamus Cassidy*
          R. F. Rollo
          M. G. Cawson
10 October 1983   *M. Summers*

Sunglow's last contact with Dada's Island came shortly before sailing when a motorized *pirogue* brought off Mandy and her daughter for passage to Mombasa. Dr Summers had told Cassidy that the four year-old child was seriously ill and in urgent need of medical attention. He suspected a burst appendix and peritonitis. Several islanders had come out with Mandy and the child to see them off: one was the father, another was Moonflower, and the third Balthazar, who'd been at the tiller in the *pirogue*. The father, Nicodemus, was a dour, bearded Hollander who wore his long blond hair in a pigtail.

Prior to the *pirogue's* arrival, Pascal had discussed the accommodation problem with Mrs Kitson and Jean McLachlan. There was, he said, no empty cabin, whereas they had double berth cabins to themselves. Having thrown out that hint, he explained that whatever arrangement was made would be for three days only since *Sunglow* was due in Mombasa on 14 October. Because of her age, he added, he had not approached Mrs Clutterbutt, the only other single occupant of a double berth cabin.

Jean McLachlan blinked myopically. 'I'll certainly help.

218

I've had the advantage of a double cabin to myself without having to pay the premium. Perhaps I could move in with Diana for those few days? If she doesn't mind.'

Mrs Kitson had shrugged her shoulders. 'It's not ideal, of course. But I gather that the poor child is very ill. We must help. Yes, do share my cabin, Jean.'

In thanking them, Gaston Pascal paid the warmest of tributes to their kindness and generosity. Mrs Kitson would, he said, have the single cabin premium refunded. Mwanaisha, the Swahili stewardess, would help Miss McLachlan move her things as soon as she was ready. That problem settled, he hurried back to his office to deal with the next one; a written and strongly worded complaint about copra beetles from Mrs Bruckner.

Having said goodbye to Mandy, Balthazar left it to Nicodemus and Moonflower to settle her into the cabin vacated by Jean McLachlan. 'Give me a shout when you're ready to leave,' he told them. 'I'm off to have a word with Captain Cassidy. Meet you in the lounge.'

The sun was setting against salmon and copper backcloths when *Sunglow* began to weigh anchor, her cable rumbling noisily around the windlass.

Scalatti turned from the foc'sle rail, waved to the bridge. 'Anchor's aweigh, Sir,' he shouted, his mind more involved with the Wasini Channel than the anchor. There wouldn't be any more weighing of anchors after that.

Cassidy rang down *slow ahead*, ordered, 'Hard-a-port.' The helmsman repeated the order. *Sunglow*'s bows swung to port until she was stern-on to the island. 'Steady as you go,' said Cassidy.

'Steady on west-by-north, sir.' Shakari, the African on the wheel, grinned; they were homeward bound.

Cassidy put the telegraph to *full ahead*; the coaster trembled and the bridge windows rattled. From the wing of the bridge he watched the bow-wave creaming and spreading, heard the splash and suck of the sea along the ship's side. *Sunglow* drew clear of the Island and began a gentle pitch and roll, the weather now on her port quarter. Once again Cassidy felt secure and at home in his habitual environment. For him the south-east trade wind was an elixir, a cleansing agent, blowing away the evil of the land; a belief reinforced by his experiences that day.

The inquiry into Dada's death, the near contact with murder, the knowledge that at least one of the faces in front of him was that of a killer, had shocked him. Involvement with such evil was, he felt, somehow soiling. His emotion was in no sense grief. Dada the eccentric, agreeable enough socially, meant little to him. He'd met the man often, but always under the circumstance of *Sunglow*'s visits to the island. Cassidy deplored his killing in the way that he deplored all violence. Every man had to die and there was, in his view, much to be said for sudden death; but not at the hands of a murderer.

With these thoughts in mind he thanked the Holy Mother that he was a sailor and not a landsman, and prayed that it might always be so. Thinking that it would be no bad thing to die at sea, his thoughts turned to his own burial: the body stitched tightly into its canvas shroud, fire-irons secured to the feet, the Red Ensign over the parcelled corpse, *Sunglow*'s engines stopped, Pascal – who else? – conducting the service, the solemn tipping of the burial plank, the corpse sliding over the side, the splash as it struck the sea, the slow sinking of it beneath the waves. Ah, and a fine ceremony that would be. These congenial thoughts were disturbed by the arrival on the bridge of Said Obudo, come to stand the second dog-watch.

That first night at sea found *Sunglow*'s passengers and crew much sobered by the day's events. Who had done it and why became the main topic of conversation. Whispered speculation and veiled insinuation led to the general view that somebody in the commune had settled a grudge.

In Cassidy's cabin after dinner, when Commander

Rollo, Dr Summers and Mr Cawson had gathered there at his invitation, the subject was discussed over coffee and liqueurs.

'It's my impression,' said Rollo, 'that he had his young people under a pretty tight rein.'

Summers nodded. 'I'm inclined to agree. Mandy tells me he was a strict disciplinarian. Could be unpleasant. A number of commune members feared him, she says.'

'On a remote island like Dada's there has to be good discipline, firm leadership. Much like a ship it is.' The liqueur glass Cassidy put to his lips all but disappeared between beard and moustache.

'If they didn't like his methods, why didn't they do something about it?' Cawson complained.

'I would have thought they did,' said Summers. 'After all, he *was* murdered.'

'I think Cawson means why didn't they do something before it came to that.' Rollo looked at Cawson for confirmation.

'I suppose there were several reasons,' went on Summers. 'They liked the life they were leading. Dada made it possible. Two of the toughest young men acted as his bodyguards. That's what JackKnife and Knuckleboy actually were, though he called them prefects.'

Cassidy said, 'How would you be knowing that?'

'Mandy told me. She also said he was liked by most, in spite of everything. Some sort of love-hate relationship existed between him and his little community.'

'How is Mandy, then?' Cassidy reached for his cigar case.

'Fit in herself, but very worried about the child. So am I. Things have been left too long. The girl's in danger.'

'Could they have taken action earlier?' Rollo looked doubtful.

Cassidy nodded. 'Dada had two-way radio. He could have asked for medical assistance. Diego Suarez was only two hundred miles to the south. War and supply ships must

221

quite often have been within a hundred miles or so. The base at Diego Garcia has made this part of the Indian Ocean a busy one.'

'I'd rather overlooked that,' conceded Rollo. 'I wonder, then, why he didn't ask for help.'

Summers shrugged his shoulders. 'Nicodemus, the father of the small girl, told me this afternoon that he'd begged him to send for assistance. Dada wouldn't hear of it. "We have to fend for ourselves", he told Nicodemus. "If we don't we destroy the whole concept on which this commune is founded. We must take the good with the bad." Something like that, I gather.'

Cassidy offered cigars. He and Summers were the only takers. While they were fussing with them, Cawson said, 'By the end of the inquiry I had the feeling, more instinct I suppose, that the guilty man had to be Balthazar. He was deputy-leader. That seemed motive enough.'

'I think there was even more to it than that.' Summers leant back on the settee, cigar in hand. 'Did you see his eyes when he said he'd gone to Moonflower's hut and found she wasn't there? I saw hatred then, fierce and uncontrollable. He knew she was waiting for Dada.'

'It was a long wait she was to have.' Cassidy's laugh was forced. 'Talking of hatred, did you notice her face when she said, "Ask Mrs Kitson. She went off with him." There was a lot of emotion around last night.'

Rollo held his liqueur glass to the light, peered at the Cointreau with narrowed eyes. 'I wonder if the Seychelles people will ever solve the mystery?'

'I doubt it,' said Summers. 'For my part, it could be Balthazar, or even Nicodemus. Revenge for Dada's refusal to get help for the child. Or, for that matter, Moonflower herself. You know, Hell hath no fury . . .'

'I doubt if it will ever be solved, unless a positive clue is found, like the knife or the shark's tooth pendant. But there you are.' Rollo's tone suggested there was little point in further speculation. Cassidy must have felt that, too, for

222

he led the conversation round to the goings on at Greenham Common, the principal item in the latest radio news.

During the night the south-easterly wind increased and the coaster's movements became more lively. Daylight revealed endless lines of foam-ridged seas following and overtaking *Sunglow*, nudging her unceremoniously on her way. On the sundeck, still wet from its early morning scrubbing, Jim Abernethy was going through his daily keep-fit routine. It was one much encouraged by his aunt. On this fine morning, alone on the sundeck but for a sailor using a squeegee, he decided that, after all, life had a lot going for it.

When seven bells struck he abandoned his press-ups and pulled on a T-shirt. He was about to go below when he saw Cassidy standing in the wing of the bridge looking in his direction. In that instant he made his decision. After his talk with Jean McLachlan he had decided to put his theory to Cassidy at the first opportunity. And here it was: the ship at sea, the time just after seven and the Captain on the bridge until eight.

When Jim reached the bridge, the Captain was nowhere to be seen.

'In the chartroom,' said the standby helmsman who was cleaning bridge windows with the leisurely motions of one who has time to spare.

Jim went to the chartroom, looked in through the open door. Cassidy was there, hands on the chart table, his back to it. Commander Rollo was sitting on the settee facing the Captain. Cassidy, in the middle of saying something, interrupted himself with a frowning, 'What is it, then, lad?'

Jim said, 'Sorry sir, I didn't know you were busy. I had something to tell you.'

Rollo smiled. 'Like me to go, young man?'

'No, no.' Jim shook his head. 'I think you'd be interested. It could affect the Royal Navy in a big way.'

'Come on then, lad. Let's be hearing what it is you have to say. The commander and meself were chatting about the old days.' Cassidy pointed to the settee. 'Take a seat.'

Jim began by sketching in the background; how his suspicions were aroused on the first visit to Wreck Island when they'd been told by the Finnish scientists that visitors were not permitted on the island. After that had come his second visit, secretly at night, when he'd watched the area under the camouflage nets, seen the bulldozers and other signs of large-scale activity. Having set the stage, Jim proceeded to outline his theory. Anxious to avoid a later charge of failure to tell the whole story, he told of his talk with Jean McLachlan and gave a fair summary of what she'd said.

Cassidy and Rollo had listened in silence to the tall young man who spoke so hurriedly, yet assuredly. When he'd finished, they looked at each other with inquiring eyes. Cassidy nodded to Rollo. 'You're a naval man, commander. What d'you say to that?'

'A neat theory, and full marks to Jim for developing it. And for putting the case so well.'

Jim experienced momentary excitement: it looked as if he'd convinced them.

'But,' continued Rollo. 'The explanation given by the Finns – and from what Jim says, reinforced by Miss McLachlan – is, I believe, a valid one. Nothing that he saw, nothing that Agojo says they're doing there is, I believe, inconsistent with some sort of geological survey. The hardened pad down at the beach was probably for use when the bulldozers and earth movers were brought ashore.'

Cassidy said, 'I think I'd have to be agreeing with the commander, lad.'

Jim went back to the attack. 'The big excavations in the coconut plantation?'

'I don't pretend to know anything about geology,' confessed Rollo. 'But surely it must involve excavations – even large ones.'

There was more general discussion after that, Jim posing the questions and the older men answering them. To all his queries they seemed to have a rational reply. His impression grew that these two elderly men had from the beginning decided that he was wrong. They resented a young man trying to convince them of something which disturbed their peace of mind.

Towards the end of the discussion Rollo introduced the political aspect: 'In any event I don't think the Soviets would risk anything so provocative as putting missile launchers on an island in the Indian Ocean belonging to another country – an island, incidentally, within a few hundred miles of the US naval base at Diego Garcia.'

'But surely that's why they'd put it there?' Jim's voice rose. 'They've leased the island. I imagine they can put missiles there without breaking any laws. The US have missiles in Britain and Europe. Castro was prepared to let the Soviets put them in Cuba. The Seychelles Government owns Wreck Island and it's known . . .'

'The Seychelles Government is very much opposed to the use of nuclear weapons,' interrupted Rollo. 'That's why US and British warships haven't visited Mahé since 1980.'

'Well I don't know how opposed they are,' – Jim was a stubborn young man, and his mood was hardening – 'but I do know that the Seychelles is a one party socialist state, and they have good relations with Moscow. I read that in our newspapers not long ago.'

'Ah, and that's a point, lad. When we get to Mombasa you'll be able to have a chat with the British Consul. I'm sure he'll be passing your ideas along to the right quarters.' Cassidy looked at the chartroom clock. 'And now I'll have to be getting the decklog written up. Close to eight o'clock, it is. Can't have the second mate thinking I've not handed over the watch in ship-shape fashion.'

225

'The Captain is right, Jim.' Rollo's smile was sympathetic. 'See the British Consul in Mombasa.'

Jim realized that the buck had been passed to him. That fitted in with his views on youth and old age. The old men made wars, the young men fought them. That was where the buck always stopped – with the young men. Yes, he told himself, feeling decidedly bloody-minded, I *will* see the consul and give him a written report – copies to Whitehall and the Pentagon. That'll get him off his arse.

Cassidy, in underpants, was at the washbasin in his sleeping cabin when he heard a discreet knock. Putting aside the scissors with which he was trimming his beard, he called 'Come.' The door of the outer cabin opened and through a chink in the curtain he saw the gangling, awkward figure of Jean McLachlan step into the day-cabin. Irritated by her intrusion at that hour, he called out, 'What is it, then?'

'It's me, Jean McLachlan,' she said. 'Forgive me, Captain, for arriving unannounced. I would not have done so if it were not so urgent. Something most disturbing has happened. I did not want to report through Mr Pascal, or any other intermediary.'

'Hold on there a moment, Miss McLachlan. I was not expecting visitors.'

Cassidy, caught at a disadvantage, was not pleased. He put on a uniform shirt, white slacks, and rope soled sandals, and did what he could with his hair before going into the day cabin. Miss McLachlan was standing on front of a porthole, her back to him.

He said a perfunctory, 'Good morning.' She turned and he pointed to the settee, sitting himself down at the desk.

For some time they looked at each other, the only sounds the creaking and groaning of the superstructure, and the distant beat of the engines. Cassidy broke the silence. 'What is it then?'

'It's about Mrs Kitson.'

Holy St Patrick, he thought. What is it now? Has she

226

disturbed me because of trouble with another woman? 'About Mrs Kitson,' he repeated.

Miss McLachlan looked away to avoid the displeasure in the Captain's eyes. 'We are sharing a cabin – as from yesterday.'

'I know.' Cassidy sighed, feared the worst.

'She came down to the cabin some time after midnight. I was half asleep, very tired, so I gave no indication of being awake. It was too late for conversation. She began rummaging for something in a suitcase. Presumably she found what she wanted, for minutes later she left the cabin. When the steward brought our tea this morning – that was at about seven – she was not there. Nor had her bunk been slept in. I got up and dressed, stayed in the cabin writing up my diary until eight o'clock. She has still not returned, Captain. So I've come to see you. It is most worrying. What on earth could have happened to her?'

Cassidy's irritation left him; this young woman was so clearly concerned, so genuinely upset. 'Why now, Miss McLachlan, and don't trouble yourself at all.' He got up from the chair, patted her shoulder reassuringly. 'Sure and she'll be showing up soon. You'll be seeing her at breakfast, I dare say, and she'll have some tale to tell. Couldn't sleep maybe. Too hot or . . .' He managed a quizzical smile. 'Maybe she'll be saying you snore.' Hurriedly, he repaired the damage. 'A lie of course, it would be. But you know how it is when a lady has to explain things.'

'A lady? Are you so sure, Captain Cassidy.' Miss McLachlan's mouth set in a hard line.

TWENTY-FOUR

Mrs Kitson did not appear for breakfast, nor could she be found later when the ship was searched from bow to stern.

Her disappearance confirmed, Cassidy at once reversed *Sunglow*'s course and posted lookouts. Not that he believed for a moment that she would be found, but it was the unwritten law of the sea. He broadcast a MAYDAY message giving the coaster's position, present course and speed, and those for the preceding twelve hours, and appealed to all ships in the area to keep a sharp lookout for a passenger lost overboard during the night.

Mahé, Diego Suarez, Mombasa, Diego Garcia and a number of ships at sea at once acknowledged. A frigate, *HMS Amphiberon*, on passage from Diego Garcia to Dar-es-Salaam, reported that she was sixty miles north-east of *Sunglow* and would fly off her helicopter to assist in the search.

These urgent things done, Cassidy informed passengers that Mrs Kitson was missing and must be presumed to have gone overboard at some time after midnight. He told them of the action being taken, stressed the importance of *Amphiberon*'s helicopter, and left the lounge having said that he was needed on the bridge. The passengers, so recently engrossed in the unpleasant business of Dada's murder, turned now to the more immediate, tantalizing and mysterious matter of Mrs Kitson's disappearance.

Mrs Bruckner was in an aggressive mood. 'How should it be possible,' she demanded, 'that this lady can from the side fall over?'

'Pushed, I guess,' whispered Sandra Carter to her husband.

228

'Shucks, honey,' was the shocked reply.

In an aside to Stephen Blake, Atkins said, 'Stoned I'd say.' He pulled at the peak of his yachting cap. 'Has a few with 'er friends up there.' He raised his eyes in the general direction of the officers' quarters. 'Goes on deck for a breather, ship rolls . . .' With an exaggerated movement of his hand, he sketched a fall. '. . . and, before you can say mine's-a-Guinness, she's in the bleedin' drink.'

'Poor Mrs Kitson,' said the Rev. Bliss. 'What a fate. I understand these waters are shark infested.'

'Lucky sharks. Wouldn't 've minded a nibble meself.'

From Mrs Clutterbutt, sitting immediately behind him, came a vehement, 'Do please show some respect for the dead, Mr Atkins.'

Ducking his head, pulling at his damaged ear, he mumbled an apology.

An utterly shocked passenger who said nothing was Jim Abernethy. Despite doubts about Diana Kitson which had grown as the voyage progressed, she was still for him the most beautiful and romantic of women, the subject of continuing fantasy. Because his emotions were adolescent they were all the more powerful. He could not bear the thought of her alone at night in that dark sea. What indescribable terrors must she have undergone?

Aware that he could do nothing to help in a search which his commonsense told him was no more than a formality – how could she possibly have survived? – he concentrated his mind on something which he could do. He remembered how frightened she'd been; her demonstration of the Swede's grip on her throat, her imitation of his threatening voice and manner. It was puzzling, though, because Krol had not gone ashore on Dada's Island, which seemed to confirm Scalatti's story that the drugs deal was off. Why then would Krol want to get rid of her? To that Jim had no answer, but lack of one in no way diminished his determination to do something. Some time before Mombasa he

229

would see Cassidy, tell him all he knew. That might get things moving.

In the meantime he couldn't just sit about doing nothing, just thinking about the god-awful thing that had happened to her. He'd go nuts if he did. Instead, he'd get down to it and write the report about Wreck Island. That, at least, would occupy his mind and keep him clear of the sordid gossip going on among the passengers.

The MAYDAY presented Roger Mallinson with a problem. The frigate he commanded was on passage to Dar-es-Salaam where it was due on the following afternoon, its mission to fly the flag. On leaving the Tanzanian port three days later, *Amphiberon* was to carry out exercises with US naval units at the northern end of the Mozambique Channel. Since several official functions had been arranged for the ship's visit, it was imperative that she arrive on time. His problem, then, was to give *Sunglow* the greatest possible assistance in the limited time available. Mallinson, like Cassidy, believed there was only the remotest chance of finding the passenger, but there had been isolated instances where a person overboard in warm water had been rescued many hours afterwards. In one case he knew of, some twenty-four hours later.

The frigate's navigator had plotted *Sunglow*'s position and the course she'd steered at ten knots since midnight, after which time the woman was deemed to have gone overboard. The coaster had already reversed course and was steaming back towards the midnight position which the navigator had marked on the chart as X. Given her slow speed, it would take her nine and a half hours to reach position X. That was a long time, almost certainly too long for the woman to survive, even if she were a strong swimmer and not taken by sharks. To that time, too, had to be added the hours already spent in the water. Nevertheless assistance must be given, decided Mallinson. *Amphiberon*, on a converging course with the coaster, had the most practical and speedy means of doing so. Thus, fifteen minutes after the MAYDAY had been broadcast, *Amphiberon*'s helicopter was airborne. Well under an hour later it had reached position X, and begun a search along the course line which *Sunglow* had been steering between midnight and her MAYDAY position.

Throughout that morning *Sunglow* steamed back along her course. Cassidy had posted lookouts, their number augmented at times by passengers with binoculars who acted as voluntary lookouts until the novelty wore off. As far as the eye could see rows of white horses came tumbling in from the south-east, making remote the chances of seeing anything as small as a swimmer. With the reversal of course wind and sea were now ahead, and at times the coaster's bows would throw up clouds of spray which glittered crystal-like in sunlight before they were swept away by the wind.

Several times during the morning Cassidy and Mallinson discussed progress by radiophone, the latter passing on reports from the helicopter which was working on a frequency outside the capability of *Sunglow*'s radio. On the last of these occasions Dr Summers was in the chartroom with Cassidy, to whom he was explaining how rapidly the condition of Mandy's child had been deteriorating. They were interrupted by the automatic radio alarm; Cassidy picked up the handset, spoke into the mouthpiece. '*Sunglow* answering. Go ahead *Amphiberon*.'

While he listened to the incoming voice, his eyes searched the sea beyond the chartroom windows.

'In twenty minutes,' he said. 'Ah, and that's fine, Captain. Over and out.' He replaced the handset. 'That was the frigate's Captain. He says *Amphiberon*'s helicopter should pass over us in about twenty minutes.'

'Splendid,' said Summers. 'It's just occurred to me.'

'What is that, then?'

'Mandy and her daughter. *Amphiberon*'s sickbay will

have a surgeon, medical assistants, X-rays, operating table, the lot. That's where the child must go.' Summers must have seen the doubt in Cassidy's eyes. 'The helicopter can winch them up, take them across.' There was an irresistible urgency in the doctor's voice. 'If I can speak to *Amphiberon*'s doctor right away I'm sure they'll co-operate. A life's at stake.'

'Holy St Patrick,' exploded Cassidy. 'Not another one.' He picked up the handset, looked at it doubtfully. 'Very well. I'll ask Captain Mallinson if you can have a word with his doctor.'

It took only a few minutes to settle the matter: all was well, Captain Mallinson would instruct the helicopter pilot to transfer mother and child to *Amphiberon*. His last words to Summers were, 'My helicopter will winch them up from *Sunglow*'s foc'sle in about fifteen minutes time. They *must* be ready. The chopper's endurance doesn't permit delay.'

'They'll be ready, Captain. Goodbye and thank you.' Summers hung up the handset, grinned at Cassidy, and left the chartroom at the double.

News of the helicopter's impending arrival spread quickly through the ship. Passengers were not permitted on the foc'sle, but they soon occupied other vantage points. Mrs Clutterbutt, Commander Rollo and Mr Cawson had been invited to the bridge, some passengers had gathered on top of No 1 hatch, but most were at windows in the dining saloon, safe from the occasional dousings of spray.

It took Pascal, Jean McLachlan and Mrs Cawson ten minutes to get Mandy and her daughter ready, and several more to escort them to the foredeck, Pascal carrying the child. As Mandy reached the foc'sle ladder, Stephen Blake and Jim Abernethy were seen to hand her envelopes which she put in her shoulder-bag. A few words were exchanged, after which she went up the ladder.

232

When Jim heard *Amphiberon*'s helicopter would be lifting off Mandy, he'd decided to give her the note. He wrote it in the lounge so that he'd hear the helicopter. As it was, he got to the foredeck shortly before a faint *floppa-chopper-floppa-chopper* gave notice of its approach, and the distant sound became a speck on the horizon which grew steadily larger.

Flying low over the sea, the helicopter passed down the coaster to starboard, crossed astern, and came slowly up the port side. When abreast the foc'sle it hovered, keeping station on the ship.

'He's making sure there's nothing to foul the winch wire,' said Rollo, raising his voice.

'Ah, and wise that is,' Cassidy shouted. 'There was a time when ships had forestays. Thanks be to God we've no such thing.'

To those on the foc'sle the down-draught from the helicopter's rotors was like a gale of wind. Mandy clutched her hair with one hand, held on to the guardrail with the other; Pascal, the small girl in his arms, pressed his bottom against the windlass drum to steady himself, while Dr Summers crouched like a track athlete waiting for the start.

In a brief moment of action the winchman dropped down on the lifting wire, picked up the child and was winched back to the fuselage where helping hands pulled her to safety. The winchman came down again, Mandy was lifted off, winched up and she and her rescuer disappeared into the helicopter. Turning steeply, it headed north.

Passengers cheered and waved and, for a moment, the loss of Diana Kitson seemed forgotten. But not by all, for as the helicopter once more grew small with distance, Jim realized that the search had ended. It was a conclusion confirmed by the ship's turn to starboard; one which continued until she was again on course for Zanzibar. *Sunglow* and the helicopter had covered the area of search. It was all over now.

He went back to the sundeck, sat by himself in silent

misery, one gloomy thought giving way to another, until the sound of a familiar voice broke in.

'Good morning, Jim. Wasn't that interesting? The helicopter's mercy mission so swiftly and efficiently done.' She cleared her throat, became very much the Beryl Clutterbutt who chaired an RNLI branch in Somerset. 'D'you realize, Jim, what an extraordinary difference helicopters have made to saving life at sea?'

He looked up from the deckchair, hands clasped behind his head. 'I suppose they have,' he said in a flat voice, adding, 'Can I get you something to sit on?'

'No thank you. Rather too much wind for me.' She looked at him in silence. 'What was it you handed her, Jim? Before she went up the ladder?'

'Oh, that. A sort of get well soon note.' He'd prepared himself for the question. 'There was a little money in it, too,' he admitted.

'How very kind of you, Jim. But you scarcely know her.'

He shrugged, looked out to sea. 'I think good wishes help if people are in trouble. Even from strangers. And I don't suppose she has much money.'

'I do agree. And so must Mr Blake.'

She'd seen that, too, had she?

Later in the day Blake joined him where he was sunbathing on the after hatch. He was wondering about the envelope Blake had given to Mandy when the older man said, 'Funny, both of us giving Mandy a letter.' He paused. 'Mine was to one of *Amphiberon*'s officers. He's a member of our bird watching lot in Cumbria.'

'Oh, I see.' Jim rolled over on his side so that he could see Blake's face. 'Mine was a get well soon card for the little girl. Had one in my writing case.' He shielded the sun from his eyes. 'Don't you think good wishes help if someone's in trouble? Even from a stranger?'

'Yes, I do. Very considerate of you.'

During the afternoon a sick-bay attendant handed two envelopes to *Amphiberon*'s captain. One was addressed to *The Commanding Officer, HMS 'Amphiberon'*, the other to *The Captain of the 'Amphiberon'*. They were accompanied by a scribbled note:

Dear Captain, these were handed to me just before I left 'Sunglow'. They were inside envelopes addressed to me personally. I'm sorry about the delay but I was worried and forgot. What you have done for my daughter and me is simply marvellous. We are most grateful.

Yours sincerely,
Mandy (Doris Wilson)

Roger Mallinson opened the envelopes, took out the letters and read them, his face expressionless. The one signed 'Stephen Blake' gave cause for thought, but little else. He'd have no hesitation in ordering the signals officer to transmit it in code as requested. It was the letter signed 'James Abernethy' which made him sit at his desk staring at the silver framed photograph of his wife and children without really seeing them. Who on earth was Abernethy? What was he? Congenital crank? Media man making a story for his paper? Would Roger Mallinson make a bloody fool of himself by giving the message the cypher and transmission priorities it seemed to deserve.

He looked at it once again:

To: The Captain of the Amphiberon
From: James Abernethy, passenger M.V. Sunglow.

THIS IS VERY URGENT

A week ago I landed twice on Wreck Island, about half way between Alphonse Island and Wizard Reef. The first time openly in daylight – the second secretly at night. Wreck Island has been uninhabited for years, but now there are twelve white foreigners and a big black labour force. From what I saw I believe that a Soviet missile site is being prepared. Look at the chart and see

235

*what it threatens, including Diego Garcia. Huge
camouflage nets in the coconut plantation cover the
work site and the bulldozers, earth movers, scientific
instruments, etc – and supply ship(s) arrive only at
night.*

*I am writing a report giving the whole story, but it's
not nearly ready so I can't send it to you, but hope you'll
be able to do something about Wreck Island before it's
too late.*

Sorry about the scrawl. In great haste.

James Abernethy.

Roger Mallinson shook his head. 'One little coaster gives
me two big headaches,' he muttered. First thing was to get
the navigator to show him where Wreck Island was – if
there was such a place. Next, he'd have a chat with the
young woman. What was her name? Mandy. She might be
able to tell him something about Abernethy. Only then
would he decide.

TWENTY-FIVE

The search for Mrs Kitson had delayed the coaster for more
than four hours. During the afternoon Pascal posted the
amended times of arrival and departure on the noticeboard: *Sunglow* would arrive in Zanzibar at 0900 on the
following morning, and depart at 1430 that afternoon.
There would be a guided tour of the town, passengers to
return on board for lunch. *Sunglow* would arrive in Mombasa at the end of her voyage at 0800 on the 14th October,
passengers to have disembarked with their luggage by
1100.

'Oh well, I shan't be sorry to see home again.' Mrs

Cawson put her hand over her mouth to stifle a yawn. She was one of a group who'd gathered in the lobby to read the notice.

'It's been a great experience,' said Dean Carter. 'And Zanzibar still to come. One of the oldest and most romantic seaports on the African coast. D'you realize that Arab slave traders used to come there in their dhows for . . .'

'Forget the history lesson,' snapped Sandra Carter. 'We've all got the brochure. As far as I'm concerned I'd never have come on this cruise if I'd known it would be like this – I mean the awful things that have happened.'

Henry Atkins turned towards her. 'Don't know what you're complaining about, love.' He grinned, and the two gold fillings in his mouth reflected the light in the deckhead above him. 'The ads promised an adventure cruise. You can't say they 'aven't delivered.'

Sandra regarded him with contempt. 'I don't call murder and suicide *adventures*.'

Under his breath the Rev. Arnold Bliss muttered, 'Could have been murder *and* murder.' For no apparent reason he glanced anxiously down the passageway.

Mr Cawson took his wife's arm. 'Come, dear. Tea time.'

'You're not doing very well, Arnold. That's the second time running I've defeated you.' Miss McLachlan dropped the Scrabble letters into the bag.

Arnold Bliss shrugged his shoulders, sighed. 'Sorry, Jean. Perhaps I'll do better next time.'

'You *must* concentrate.' She shook the bag vigorously. 'You're usually rather good. So many clergymen are. Like crosswords. You do the *Guardian*'s, I suppose?'

'*The Times* actually.'

'Surprised it's not the *Telegraph*. Anyway, notwithstanding what's on your mind, Arnold, *please* concentrate.' She regarded him with mock severity, adding, 'And forget all the unpleasantnesses of the immediate past. No point in

237

brooding over them.' She held out the bag, he put a hand in it, and the ritual of the new game began.

There was, indeed, a great deal on Arnold Bliss's mind. Mrs Kitson's loss overboard had confronted him with what he regarded as the most serious problem of his life. It had begun with his inability to sleep on the previous night: the cabin hot and stuffy, Atkins' snoring loud and persistent, and Balthazar's uncouth retort sounding in his mind like a stuck pick-up arm: *the last thing Dada would want is a stranger nattering over his grave.* All because of Bliss's offer to perform the last rites. Nicodemus had tried to repair the damage, pointing out that burial would not take place until the following day by which time *Sunglow* would have sailed. Why hadn't Balthazar said that himself, instead of offering the gratuitous insult, Bliss kept asking himself. At last he had given up the attempt at sleep, left the cabin and gone to the sundeck where it was cooler under the awnings. There he'd fallen asleep in a deckchair. He had woken later and seen that it was after one o'clock. Feeling stiff and uncomfortable, he'd gone to the after end of the sundeck, leant over the rail and watched the sternlight on the mainmast rising and falling against the dark background of the sea. The acrid smell of diesel fumes and the noise of the engines came down to him in the following wind. With Balthazar's remark still nagging at his mind, he'd thought over the unpleasant events of the day. Cassidy's conduct of the inquiry had been irreproachable, shown what a decent, open minded man the Irishman was but ... Bliss's thoughts had been interrupted by the distant sound of a splash. He had taken it to be a crewman throwing galley refuse over the side? It was something that happened regularly in the night watches, so he'd thought no more of it.

Soon afterwards he'd heard footsteps. Somebody was moving along the deck on the port side. A dark shape came round the corner of the deckhouse and passed by a light beneath the sundeck. Bliss saw that it was a man, though he couldn't see who for the man hadn't looked up. The suntanned body was naked but for khaki shorts. In that brief instant, Bliss had noticed that the man was gripping his right bicep with his left hand. Seconds later he had gone through the deckhouse entrance into the passageway. Bliss had noted the time, gone back to the deckchair and fallen asleep until four o'clock when the change of watches had disturbed him and he had returned to his cabin. Atkins was still asleep, an example Bliss had soon followed.

It was not until Cassidy's after breakfast announcement that Mrs Kitson was missing and presumed overboard, that the possible implications of what he'd seen and heard in the early hours of the morning began to dawn on him. His first reaction was that he should ask to see Cassidy, tell him of the incident, unlikely though it was to have been in any way relevant. The ship had just reversed course, the extra lookouts had been posted, and the Captain's preoccupation was the search for Mrs Kitson; something which Bliss knew his report could in no way assist. Unconsciously, perhaps, he had seized upon this as a reason for delay. But as time went on his reasons for delay became more complex, and fear became a factor. Might he not attract suspicion upon himself? Would not his reasons for being on the sundeck at such an unusual time appear dubious in the light of what had happened? It was quite possible that he'd not been seen there while he was asleep; if so there would be no one to corroborate his story. Would they believe him when he said he could not identify the man who'd passed by a decklight less than ten feet beneath him?

The more he thought about these things the more fearful he became. In short, Arnold Bliss panicked and, as the day grew older, conscience, commonsense and fear became locked in stultifying conflict. Despite his awareness that the longer he delayed the more he might incriminate himself, he simply could not summon the will to act.

239

Soon after taking over the watch at eight o'clock Scalatti, secure in the knowledge that Cassidy was at dinner, discussed with Krol the amended times of arrival and departure posted on the noticeboard that afternoon.

'So what's the difference?' asked Krol, who was duty helmsman.

'When we come on watch at midnight, after Zanzibar, the ship is already about one hour past the Wasini Channel. So that plan is no good. Right?' Scalatti had dropped his voice to a hoarse whisper.

'Jesus Christ,' said Krol. 'You telling me the plan is already finished?'

'When you talk, Nils, don't make so loud. Right?'

Nils lowered his voice and repeated the question.

'*That* plan is finished,' corrected Scalatti. 'I have other plan now. I tell you. Listen. At midnight we shall be past Funzi Island. Seven miles after that is Chale Island, with plenty reefs.'

Krol said, 'Okay. So Chale Island is the new plan, hey?'

'Chale Island is no good, Nils. There is lighthouse there. How can I say I'm not knowing ship is close to reef, if there is lighthouse?'

'What the hell, then?'

Scalatti grinned in the darkness, shook a finger at the Swede. 'What you take me for, Nils? Bloody fool? I tell you what's then. Five, seven miles after Chale Island. That is the place, my friend. Big reef runs along the coast there, about one mile offshore. Okay?'

Krol laughed. 'You are clever bastard, Luigi. That's for sure. Lucky it's first mate's job to fix watch rosters.'

'Sure, sure,' said Scalatti. 'Now you go do some fixing. Like fix coffee for us. Right?'

It had taken Jim Abernethy most of the afternoon to make up his mind. The reason for the delay was his recent experience of confiding in the Captain. The buck passing exercise. But this was different, more immediate, more

240

serious; something which only he could do. As always, his mind once made up was not easily changed. He had that evening asked Pascal if he could see the Captain about a private matter. The chief steward wanted details.

'No,' said Jim. 'It's strictly private. But it's urgent. I must see him some time tonight. After eight o'clock.'

Pascal had brushed the underside of his moustache with a ringed finger, a puzzled look in the dark eyes. 'Very well,' he said. 'I will ask the Captain at what time he can see you.'

'Will you ask him now?'

Pascal, a man of some self-importance, did not like being pressed. 'A little later,' he said in a dismissive tone. 'I will let you know.'

In due course he did. The Captain would see Jim in his cabin at 9.30 that night. That suited Jim well. Scalatti and Krol would be on watch. That was why he'd asked for a time after eight o'clock.

'Sit down.' Cassidy pointed to the settee with his cigar. 'And what is it this time, lad?'

'It's about Mrs Kitson, sir. I know something which may be important.'

Cassidy nodded slowly, several times, as if conferring with himself. 'Ah, well. You'd better be telling me.'

Jim told the story of what had happened in Scalatti's cabin when she'd hidden in the clothes cupboard; the angry scene when she'd been found, and Krol's threats; the subsequent apology by Scalatti, and his explanation that they'd been discussing the delivery of drugs, an assignment which he later told her they'd abandoned.

'She seemed quite happy after that,' explained Jim. 'With the drugs deal off, and her promise of silence, she was no longer afraid.'

Cassidy removed his cigar, considered its burning tip. When he looked up there was a hardness in his eyes. Wondering what the Captain was thinking, Jim went on. 'I don't know whether they had anything to do with her disappearance. But she was a good friend to me. It's the least I can do for her.'

Cassidy said, 'What you have told me is important, lad. When we reach Mombasa we'll be anchoring in the road-stead before going alongside. A police launch will come off to the ship. I'll be seeing to that. It's then you shall have to be telling them what you know. In the meantime, keep a tight mouth. No word to anyone.' Cassidy appeared to study the picture of Killarney Lough on the opposite bulkhead. 'How a lady like that could be getting mixed up with such . . .' He left the sentence unfinished.

'She was an unhappy woman, sir. She still loved her husband but he'd gone off with someone else. They divorced not long before she came on the cruise.'

The Captain asked a number of questions which Jim answered as best he could. By the time they'd finished, it was well past 10.30. Cassidy thanked him and once again stressed the importance of secrecy. 'If these men know what you know, Jim – well, it's your own life that might not be safe.'

Young, strong, and sure of his ability to look after himself, Jim said nothing. They shook hands and he left the cabin.

A rainstorm earlier in the watch had soon passed over. Astern in the western sky there were breaks in the clouds through which the moon shone fitfully. Cassidy looked along its luminous path, saw the seas fanned by the trade wind pursuing the ship, their tumbling crests white where the moonlight touched them. How clean and fresh it was, he thought, that wind blown sea; so different from the sordid human frailties of the last few days.

When taking over the watch from Scalatti at midnight he'd had difficulty in concealing his repugnance for the man. As for Krol, standby helmsman in the first mate's watch, Cassidy had seen in him the embodiment of evil. That such riff-raff should consider themselves seamen was, to him, an affront. They were human offal afloat. No more than that.

It had been an ill-starred voyage. Where was it all to end? He turned his mind to more immediate problems: under no circumstances must Scalatti or Krol be allowed ashore in Zanzibar, not even as members of skimmer crews. He would see Obudo and Pascal about that.

There was the problem of requesting Mombasa by radiophone to have a police launch come off to the ship on arrival. Fortunately, the approach to Mombasa would take place during his watch. It was then, with the Italian and the Swede asleep below decks, that he would pass the message. In spite of his contempt for the two men, he realized there was a weakness in the case against them. Would they have killed her for a drugs deal that had not taken place? Not that he'd really believed that story. Bashi Menon, who'd been with him for years, was a devout Muslim, had never been ashore on Dada's Island and could not have had any contacts there. But, if not a drugs deal, what could it be that had meant taking a life? Had she known something about the killing of Robert Aspen? In that case how could they be concerned; they'd not gone ashore on Dada's Island? There were other possibilities: an accident, suicide – the voyage nearing its end, the woman unhappy? He abandoned the problem. It was something the police would have to sort out.

He went and adjusted the radar's display hood, put his face to the viewer, turned up the brilliance and watched the sweep circling the screen. No land echoes yet. The three ships were still there; one northbound, one southbound, the third, by its relative motion since last he'd looked, was probably a sailing vessel. A dhow or schooner heading north-east. He turned down the brilliance, reset the display hood, and made for the chartroom. The clock showed twelve minutes past five. He checked the distance from the 0400 position to Ras Kzimkazi, the southernmost tip of Zanzibar Island. It was twenty-five miles. To the port on the island's west coast, fifty-two miles. With the current setting to the north, *Sunglow* would make the ETA of 0900. He crossed to the starboard side of the bridge. It was a hot night, but cooler out there than in the wheelhouse. With night glasses he searched the darkness ahead, picked up the steaming lights of the southbound ship but nothing else.

In the east, clear now of cloud, the stars were fading, the night sky growing lighter, revealing the sea beneath it. *Sunglow* would be back in Kilindini harbour within the next twenty-four hours, and he'd be making his customary call at the Head Office of J. G. Patel & Co Ltd. It would be good to see Goosam again, to exchange news and pleasantries. But how would the old man react to the weather damage, the cost of repairs, the delays entailed, the less than average cargoes, and the loss of a passenger overboard? Cassidy felt a deep apprehension. Ali Patel was anxious to get rid of *Sunglow*, regarded the ship as an unnecessary liability. Goosam had told him as much. Was this not Ali's chance? What was *Sunglow*'s future? The old coaster was more than a ship to him, she was a way of life; his past, present and future.

Soon after Ras Makunduchi had shown up on the radar display, a neon smudge glowing and fading with each sweep of the scanner, the lookout reported the sighting of the light fine on the starboard bow. Cassidy picked it up with binoculars: a faint pinpoint of light, twin flashes stabbing the darkness at regular intervals. In the chartroom he recorded the time of sighting – 0527.

After a restless night, half way between sleep and wakefulness, harassed by nightmares and hallucinations of his own making, Arnold Bliss arrived at a decision. He must see Cassidy. The Captain kept the morning watch. It would be full daylight by six o'clock.

Mbolwo had already brought Cassidy's coffee and apple to the chartroom when Arnold Bliss appeared on the bridge. There were dark rings under the clergyman's eyes and his round face seemed longer. As usual, he was wearing a clerical collar under his safari jacket; a garment which was too large, as were the knee-length shorts beneath it. Ever since the days of the cyclone, Cassidy had taken a liking to the meek parson from Norfolk. Bliss had thrown himself into the voyage's activities with a will, had only once missed an expedition ashore, had got himself severely sunburnt in the first week, suffered occasional rebuffs for which he was an easy target, and yet never complained.

He was a rare visitor to the bridge, and though Cassidy had not seen much of him he admired Bliss's simple, unaffected humility; if all Protestants were like that, Ireland would have been a better place, decided the Irishman.

Now, with Bliss sitting upright on the chartroom settee, his hands awkwardly at his sides, Cassidy wondered what had brought him to the bridge so early in the morning. 'It's a fine morning, Reverend,' he said. 'We've already sighted Zanzibar Island. Not long now before we shall be steaming around it.'

'Yes, indeed.' Bliss looked away from the Captain's questioning eyes.

'And what is it that brings you here, Reverend?'

Having said how sorry he was to disturb Cassidy at such a time, Bliss told the story of what he'd seen on the sundeck during the early hours of the previous day. Apologizing most humbly for his delay in coming forward, he said it was due to fear that he might be thought to have been involved in Mrs Kitson's disappearance: the longer he'd delayed, the more fearful he'd become.

'I have been weak and cowardly, Captain, and deeply troubled. Now that I have at last done what my conscience demands, I place my trust in the Almighty, and ask for his forgiveness.'

'Ah, and I'm sure he'll be giving that,' said Cassidy

cheerfully. 'Just as sure as I am that no suspicion will be falling upon you.' He put a reassuring hand on Bliss's shoulder. 'There's just two questions I'll be asking you, Reverend. You say it was after one o'clock. How long after would that be?'

'I did look at my watch. It was seventeen minutes after one o'clock.'

'Good, and you are certain you could not identify the man?'

'I could not, Captain.'

Stroking his beard, thoughtful, Cassidy was silent until he said, 'Tell me, Reverend. Was the man white?'

Bliss considered the question, looked unhappy.

'European, African or Indian?' prompted the Captain.

'It is difficult to be sure. In poor light how does one distinguish between suntanned white and natural brown?' As an afterthought Bliss added, 'But the hair was not African. Of that I'm sure.'

'Colour of the hair?'

'Dark. So far as I could see.'

'Well, and that maybe could help. Now you'd better be getting along,' said Cassidy. 'Not a word to anyone, Reverend. In the interests of your own safety, and to assist the police, keep a tight mouth on it. First thing tomorrow morning we shall drop anchor in Kilindini harbour and the police will come off. They'll be asking you to tell them all you know.'

Confused but reassured, a mortifying burden shed, Arnold Bliss went back to the cabin where Atkins was still asleep.

Before the end of Cassidy's watch, *Sunglow* had rounded Ras Kzimkazi and begun her journey to the north-east, following the broken, palm-studded coastline which led to the port of Zanzibar. There, true to her ETA of 0900, she dropped anchor, and the boats of officialdom, quarantine, immigration, customs and police, came off to see to the requirements of bureaucracy at a pace proper to a revolutionary state in a tropical climate.

Some time after 10.30 permission was granted for passengers to land. The coaster was not permitted, however, to use her skimmers. Instead, an old oil-stained launch with a weather-worn canopy took *Sunglow*'s passengers ashore. With Obudo at his side, Cassidy had been at the head of the gangway while they embarked. When the launch was on its way inshore, he turned to the second mate. 'I want you to remain on the upper deck until the ship sails this afternoon, Mr Obudo. Under no circumstances is any member of the crew, officers or otherwise, to go ashore without my permission.' Observing the second mate's look of surprise, he added, 'You must not ask why, nor must you tell anyone of my orders, unless it is essential to do so. Is that understood?'

The second mate nodded. 'It is, sir.'

Cassidy had absolute confidence in the young Swahili; not only because he was Mbolwo's nephew, but because he'd shown determination and steadfastness throughout the years he'd served in *Sunglow* as apprentice and second mate. Before the end of the year he would be sitting for his mate's certificate. That hurdle safely negotiated, he would become the coaster's first mate. He'd not been told this, but Cassidy had long decided that it should be so.

The Captain was in his day-cabin awaiting a visit by the local agent, when a familiar knock on the door was followed by the arrival of Pascal, envelope in hand. Cassidy observed the wrinkled forehead and the knitted eyebrows. Whatever the Seychellois was about to say would be a matter of some concern, for Gaston Pascal was a calm, unflappable man whose features rarely betrayed emotion.

He stood in front of Cassidy, staring, before saying, 'I have just come from the cabin where I was watching Mwanaisha pack Mrs Kitson's clothes. In a pocket, in the inside of one of the suitcases, she found this.'

Gingerly, between thumb and forefinger, he took from the envelope a gold chain from which hung a shark's tooth pendant.

Seconds passed while Cassidy stared at it. 'Holy Mother O' God,' he said at last. 'Would you be believing it?'

TWENTY-SIX

Sunglow's departure from Zanzibar was delayed by officialdom for some twenty minutes. Apart from small consignments of copra and cloves, and a few African deck passengers for Mombasa, little cargo had offered. And so, shortly before three o'clock, anchor was weighed and she headed out to sea, following the buoyed channel through out-lying reefs.

It was a windless night, the moon climbing above the low banks of cloud, the sky bright with stars, their reflections dappling the smooth sea. To port the distant light in Tanga Bay flashed intermittently. When it came abeam, Said Obudo took its bearing and distance and plotted the coaster's position on the chart, inscribing a neat *2235* against it. From where he stood on the bridge he could hear voices and laughter on the sundeck, the sound of distant music and the steady rumble of the diesel. Occasionally the darkness ahead was broken by the flickering torches of native fishermen, lit at short notice to warn the approaching ship that their catamarans lay in its path. Sometimes luminescent splashes and trails marked the passage of dolphins.

Close to midnight the radiophone alarm sounded. Mombasa had a message for the ship, announced the disembodied voice. 'Go ahead,' said the second mate. He picked up a pencil, nudged the signal pad into position:

To: Captain Cassidy, MV 'Sunglow'. From Miss Panjee. Deeply regret inform you Mr Ali Patel died in hospital tonight after car accident yesterday.

Obudo repeated the message, thanked the sender and hung up. He had not liked Ali, found him too smooth, too devious, the Hindu's questions at the end of a voyage suggesting that, behind the Captain's back, he was seeking information about the running of the ship. Nevertheless, the news shocked him. Only three weeks ago Ali Patel had come on board looking as healthy and prosperous as always.

Obudo was about to phone the Captain's cabin when he remembered that the first mate would be on the bridge in a few minutes to relieve him. It would be better to deliver the message to the Captain in person. He got back to the wheelhouse as Scalatti and Krol came up the bridge ladder. He was pleased to see the first mate; it had been a long day in Zanzibar, much of it in the hot sun on the upper deck. He couldn't wait to get his head down.

The routine of reporting course and speed, ship's position, other vessels in sight, having been attended to, Obudo turned to go below.

'What time we arrive at Mombasa?' asked Scalatti. They were on the port side of the bridge where the second mate had drawn attention to the flashing light on Wasini Island, now seven miles astern.

'At three-fifteen. We've about thirty-five miles to go,' said Obudo. 'By the way, the old man's night order book wants speed reduced to six knots at one-thirty. He is to be called at three o'clock. We should be five miles south of the port by then.'

Scalatti put a cigarette in his mouth, cupped his hands round the lighter, got it going. 'Okay, Said. I've got her. You can get some sleep now.'

249

'That's what I need, man.' Obudo went to the bridge ladder, turned, his hands on the rails. 'I've a job to do first.'

'What's that?'

'Deliver a radio message to the old man. Just come through.'

'Better not wake him now.' Scalatti's cigarette glowed in the darkness. 'He can be a bastard if you break his sleep for nothing.'

The second mate laughed. 'You think I would do that for nothing. This message is urgent, man.'

'What's it about?'

'Ali Patel, the boss's son. He's dead. Car accident.'

'Christ,' said Scalatti. 'Jesus Christ.'

As he went down the ladder the second mate called out, 'Bye now. Have a good watch.'

Speechless, numbed, Scalatti gripped the bridge coaming, stared into the darkness, his heart beat accelerating, an icy chill in his stomach. Ali Patel dead, Chale Point and the reef at Kinondo less than two hours away. It just couldn't have happened. It didn't make sense. Ali Patel dead. All the planning, the organization of watches, the worrying that things might go wrong, the constant fear of discovery, the corner shop in the village beyond Naples, the new life for Maria, for himself – all for nothing – all gone. Ali Patel dead.

He looked towards the wheelhouse, saw Krol against the dim light of the steering compass. He feared the Swede, feared the violence of the man's anger. Yet he would have to tell him. There was no escaping that. Reluctantly, his feet dragging, he made for the wheelhouse. Krol was in a corner, leaning down.

'The news is bad, Nils.' Scalatti spoke quietly.

'What you mean, bad?'

'The second mate just told me. Radio message from Mombasa for the Captain. Short time ago. Very bad news,' he repeated woodenly. His knees were trembling.

250

Krol straightened up from plugging in the kettle, took two mugs from the corner cupboard. 'Don't go on like bloody parrot, Luigi. What news?'

'Ali Patel is dead.'

'Dead, Ali Patel?' Krol dropped a mug. It rolled noisily across the wheelhouse. 'You make fucking joke, Luigi.'

'No. No joke. Ali is dead. Car accident. Died in hospital today.' The light from the binnacle played on the Italian's face, made silver lines of slowly falling tears.

'Jesus bloody Christ,' said Krol. 'Everything for nothing.'

Scalatti picked up the bridge phone, dialled the Captain's number, waited nervously for the response.

'What is it, then?' Cassidy's voice was hoarse.

'Three o'clock, Captain.'

'Good. I'll be up.' The phone clicked off.

Scalatti hung up the handset. 'He's coming,' he said to Krol. 'Call the second mate. Also Shakari.'

Krol grunted.

The lights of Mombasa glittered in the distance, the sky above the island luminous with their reflections. To north and south, scattered lights marked the suburbs.

Cassidy was on the bridge soon after the first mate's call. At the radar display he checked *Sunglow*'s position. The ship was three miles south-east of the point at Ras Serani. There was no sign of the pilot launch. During the night he'd called the port by radiophone to ask for a pilot at 0315.

The engineroom telegraph showed *slow ahead*. 'Ring down half ahead,' he ordered.

Scalatti repeated the order, pushed the telegraph. The wheelhouse windows rattled as the note of the engine rose.

'Port wheel,' said Cassidy.

Krol repeated the order, put the wheel to port.

When the light at Ras Serani was dead ahead, Cassidy ordered, 'Midships – steady as you go.'

251

There was the sound of footsteps on the bridge ladder. It was the second mate, with Shakari the helmsman, come to relieve the watch. As the Italian left the bridge Cassidy said, 'Make ready for the pilot, Mr Scalatti. Starboard side. We'll be anchoring. They can't give us a berth until seven o'clock.' To Obudo he said, 'Stop engines when you see the pilot launch. I'll be in the chartroom for a few minutes.'

The lights of the pilot launch showed up on the port bow. Obudo rang down *stop*, and made for the chartroom. Cassidy, talking on the radiophone, looked up, put his hand over the mouthpiece, his eyebrows raised in interrogation.

'Pilot launch, sir.'

'Right. I'll be there shortly.' He waved a dismissive hand. The second mate went back to the bridge. Down on the foredeck Scalatti and Krol were putting the pilot ladder over the side.

It was almost four o'clock when *Sunglow* dropped anchor in Kilindini harbour. Navigation lights were switched off, anchor lights switched on, and the pilot left the bridge to board his launch. Across the water from the anchorage arc lights shone on the ships alongside the quay; some were working cargo. The noise of cranes and the shouts of stevedores drifted down to the coaster.

When the pilot had gone Cassidy went to his cabin. He had told Obudo to let him know if a launch was seen approaching the ship. 'Quarantine people and port authorities,' he said. 'They may come off before daylight.' Strange, thought the second mate. 'They usually wait until we're alongside.'

To fill in time Cassidy sat at his desk checking through the schedule of deck and engineroom repairs prepared by the chief engineer. Reading it made him wince. In terms of work done and delays, the cost would be high. He'd begun making notes of possible savings when there was a knock on the door. He called out, it opened, and Stephen Blake came in. Never before had the man come to his cabin. One of the most reserved of passengers, he'd seldom spoken to the Captain.

Before Cassidy could do more than register inward surprise, the uninvited visitor had taken a small, black leather folder from his pocket and flicked it open. 'My warrant card,' he said.

Cassidy peered at it, frowned. 'So you're CID. It's not what your passport said.'

Blake pressed steel rimmed spectacles more firmly onto his nose, replaced the folder in his pocket. 'There are passports and passports in our business, Captain. Mind if I sit down?'

Cassidy nodded towards the settee. Blake sat down, the critical eyes of the Irishman upon him. 'Well now, Chief Inspector, it's unfortunate you didn't introduce yourself earlier. There's been work enough for a detective in these past few days. Even for one on leave.'

'Leave, Captain?' Blake forced a laugh. 'A Yard assignment brought me here. It was important that my identity wasn't known – even to you. Detective Superintendent Voi – Kenya CID – will be coming on board shortly. I wanted to have a word with you before he arrives.'

With sudden sharpness Cassidy said, 'How did you know I'd asked the police to come off?'

'I didn't.' Blake gave him a look, searching and uncertain. 'I sent a message to Tom Voi a few days ago. Asked him to meet me on board on *Sunglow*'s arrival. He'll ask for you.'

'A message. We've transmitted no such message for you, Chief Inspector.'

'I gave Mandy a note for *Amphiberon*'s captain. It requested transmission of my message to Scotland Yard, via Whitehall. Copy for Tom Voi. He's been working on the case with me.'

'Well indeed. And its full of surprises you are. What is the assignment, then?'

Blake was telling Cassidy about it when the phone rang. It was Obudo reporting the approach of a launch.

'Good.' As he spoke into the phone Cassidy watched Blake with curious eyes. 'There'll likely be someone in it asking for me. Bring him up as soon as he gets on deck.' He put the handset on its cradle.

Blake turned from the picture of Killarney Lough. 'Before we take matters further, Tom Voi and I will have to discuss things. Look through what he's bringing from the Yard. Mind if we do it here? Better that we're not seen in the lounge. Even at this time. Never know who's about.'

Cassidy looked at the clock on the bulkhead: twenty-seven minutes past four. 'You're welcome to use the cabin.' He re-arranged papers on his desk, playing for time to think, before saying, 'I've certain information about Robert Aspen and Mrs Kitson. Things you'd better be knowing. Maybe I should wait until Mr Voi is here before telling you. Then there's the inquiry report into Aspen's death. You'd like to be seeing that wouldn't you?'

'It won't tell me anything new, you know. I was at the inquiry.'

Cassidy rubbed an eye, smiled. 'Of course you were. But I daresay your man Voi would like to see it.'

'Don't say *my* man, Captain.' There was a hint of humour in Blake's manner. 'Tom wouldn't like that. His lot co-operate closely with the Yard when necessary, but Kenyans are proud of their independence.'

'Like the Irish.' Cassidy's eyes twinkled. 'And quite right, too. Pity the Protestants don't see it that way.'

The conversation was interrupted by the arrival of Obudo with a tall African; a thin man, with hooded eyes and a lined face. 'Mr Voi,' said the second mate.

Voi had a brown envelope in his hand. He smiled at Blake. 'Hullo Steve.' Blake introduced them, and the African bowed slightly in Cassidy's direction.

254

'Will you need me, sir?' asked the second mate.

'Standby in the chartroom, Mr Obudo. I'll be calling you if necessary.'

'Aye, aye, sir.' Obudo gave a last puzzled look at those in the cabin before closing the door behind him.

Superintendent Voi handed the brown envelope to Blake. 'Telex – it came yesterday afternoon. Pictures and all. You can thank hi-tech.'

Blake took it, nodded. 'Hi-tech helps both sides, Tom. The villains use it.'

The next half hour was a busy one, Voi paging through the inquiry report while Blake examined the contents of the envelope. Those tasks completed, they discussed Aspen's murder and Mrs Kitson's disappearance. They seemed to regard the two incidents as related. Warned by Cassidy that Scalatti's cabin was only a door away, they spoke in undertones, Voi's African intonation falling pleasantly on the Irishman's ears. Not like the Gaelic, he'd long ago decided, but a deal more agreeable than the clipped English a man was forever hearing.

At first the big Irishman did most of the listening, but his back-seat role ended when he broke in to suggest it was time they learnt what he knew. At that Blake and Voi exchanged patronizing smiles, after which Voi said, 'Of course. Go ahead, Captain.'

Cassidy was soon in his stride with lively accounts of what Jim Abernethy and the Rev. Bliss had told him. He mentioned, too, what Mandy had said to Dr Summers about Dada's relationship with the commune. When he'd finished he took from a safe Pascal's envelope – in it the shark's tooth pendant.

As Cassidy's story unfolded the detectives, pragmatic and objective by training, interjected flat-voiced questions for which, almost always, he had a rational and often colourful answer. At the end they thanked him: generously for men of their trade, and not surprisingly, for though it

255

had lost nothing in the telling his contribution had been invaluable. Behind Cassidy's bluff Irish exterior there was, his listeners had realized, a keen brain.

Within an hour of Voi's arrival they were ready to interview witnesses. At the Kenyan's request it was decided to begin with Arnold Bliss. Cassidy phoned the chartroom, told Obudo to call him. 'Do it quietly, apologize for the disturbance at this hour, say he must see me right away. No more than that, lad. While you're down there, wake Jim Abernethy. Tell him I'll be wanting to see him shortly.'

Bliss came soon afterwards: bleary eyed and apprehensive, wearing a T-shirt and pyjama shorts, peering uncertainly through his spectacles at those in the day-cabin. Cassidy did his best to put him at ease, introducing Superintendent Voi and explaining Blake's police role. It would, said Cassidy, be of great assistance if Bliss would tell them what he'd seen the night Mrs Kitson disappeared. Bliss responded nervously, hesitantly, sometimes faltering, always pausing before answering questions. When he'd finished Voi thanked him, told him to treat the matter as strictly confidential, and allowed him to go.

Jim Abernethy came next, red hair in disarray, half awake, wholly puzzled. Cassidy asked him to repeat what he'd told him about Mrs Kitson. Jim did so, answered questions put by the detectives, and was thanked for the help he'd given. Before he left the cabin he, too, was warned not to talk.

Pascal followed. He gave his account of the finding of the shark's tooth pendant. There was a brief exchange of question and answer, whereafter his offer of coffee and biscuits was accepted, and he went on his way. When he'd gone Voi said, 'I'm not so sure now that Aspen's murder and Mrs Kitson's disappearance are related. They may well be, but it's too early to decide. I think we may be dealing with unrelated incidents. Aspen's murder is a matter for the Seychelles authorities, since the island falls under their jurisdiction. On the other hand, Mrs Kitson was lost overboard from a Kenyan registered ship, subject to the laws of Kenya. The investigation into her death is a Kenyan responsibility.'

'Agreed.' Blake adjusted his spectacles.

'Let's have a word with Krol and Scalatti.'

Cassidy said, 'You'd be meaning here and now, would you, Inspector?'

'Superintendent,' corrected Voi briskly. 'Yes – I'd like to begin with Krol.'

TWENTY-SEVEN

Krol, hair dark and unkempt, pale eyes flickering, stood with his back to the door facing the Kenyan who was taller by inches though physically less formidable. From the beginning Krol's manner had been abrasive: what right had they to send for him in his watch below? Why couldn't they wait until the ship was alongside? What was Voi's authority? Where was the warrant? On what grounds could he be held?

A sea lawyer, a born trouble maker, thought Cassidy, who'd come to regard the *Solidava* survivor with almost obsessive contempt. But Voi soon tamed the Swede. Having delivered the statutory warning that anything Krol might say could be used against him, the Kenyan added, 'I'm not arresting you – yet.' The hooded eyes outstared Krol. 'I'm questioning you in connection with the death of Mrs Kitson. Right? Now, where were you between midnight and four o'clock on the morning of Wednesday last?'

Krol thrust his unshaven chin forward. 'On the bridge. Standby helmsman and lookout for the middle watch.'

'Who with?'

'The first mate, Mr Scalatti.'

'Did you hear or see anything unusual during that time? Sounds of a struggle on deck? Somebody falling in the water?'

'No. Nothing.'

'Did you leave the bridge at any time?'

'No.'

'Did the first mate?'

'He went to the chartroom a few times.'

'Did he leave the bridge?'

'Not as far as I know.'

'How d'you mean, not as far as you know?'

'If a man is on the port wing of the bridge, it is not possible to see somebody using the starboard ladder.'

Voi's expression was surgically cold. 'So, when the first mate was in the chartroom you could have left the bridge – for say five minutes – without him knowing it. Right?'

'I tell you already I did not leave the bridge.'

The Superintendent turned away, seemed to have finished with Krol. But he hadn't. He swung round, his face close to Krol's. With sudden ferocity he barked, 'Pull up the sleeve on your right arm.'

Krol blinked, stiffened, his eyes swivelled to his right arm, then back to Voi. 'What's the game?'

'Never mind the game, Krol. Roll back the sleeve of that T-shirt.'

Slowly, sullen eyed, the Swede rolled back the short sleeve until the bicep was exposed. With studied bravado he flexed the muscle; a bruiser showing off his stock in trade.

Voi took the arm, raised it, examined both sides of the bicep. 'Right,' he said. 'You can go now. I may be needing you later.' He opened the door, Krol glared hostility, went through the doorway and down the passage. Voi watched him until he'd disappeared through the far door, before turning to the others. 'Now for Scalatti,' he said.

Mbolwo arrived with coffee and biscuits. The steward was as impassive as always, appearing not to notice the men in the Captain's cabin, as if visitors at that time were in no way unusual. He put the tray on the desk, withdrew silently. While they waited for the Italian they discussed Krol's answers. 'A man doesn't have to be a detective,' suggested Cassidy, 'to realize it's a powerful motive that drives men to murder. What now would you gentlemen be saying, as to the motive?'

Blake said, 'For Krol and Scalatti, you mean?' He hesitated, thoughtful, ran a thumbnail across his teeth. 'One would have to know what it was they were discussing when she was in that cupboard. If they – or one of them – killed her, it was because of that. And it would have to be a lot more than protecting a drugs deal that never took place.'

'It can be that we'll never know the motive,' Voi said. 'We cannot yet be sure that these men had anything to do with what happened to her. It's still early days, but we will . . .'

Whatever it was that Voi intended to say was cut short by the arrival of Scalatti. The Italian's hair was dishevelled, his gaunt face drawn. The clouded, pouched eyes darted uncertainly from one face to the other, the hands clenching and unclenching. He was wearing a short-sleeved khaki shirt, grubby white shorts, and sandals.

'You want to see me, Captain?' The hoarse voice was subdued.

As he had done with Krol, Voi left Scalatti standing, back to the door. Cassidy explained who Voi and Blake were.

Voi said, 'I'd like your help. I'm investigating the disappearance of Mrs Kitson.'

Scalatti showed no surprise. Cassidy's explanation must have prepared him for what was to come.

'How can I help with this?' The Italian held up his hands, shrugged his shoulders. The stale smell of vermouth spread through the cabin.

'By answering my questions,' said Voi, following up the remark with the statutory warning. The pattern of Scalatti's interrogation was much the same as that which Voi had used for the Swede, and the Italian's answers were little different. Yes, he'd kept the middle watch. No, he had not left the bridge at any time between midnight and four o'clock, except to go to the chartroom two or three times. No, he had not seen Krol leave the bridge. Yes, Krol could have done so while he, Scalatti, was in the chartroom. No, he'd not seen or heard anything unusual during his watch.

Voi closed his eyes, ran a hand across his forehead, breathed wheezily as if affected by bronchial trouble. He turned, moved close to the Italian, their faces almost touching. With sudden sharpness he said, 'Let's see more of your arm, Mr Scalatti. Push that sleeve up to the shoulder, will you?'

The Italian recoiled, wavered, seemed uncertain at first what he'd heard. He began to push up a shirt sleeve with his right hand.

'No,' said Voi. 'Right arm, not left.'

Scalatti hesitated, shrugged, pushed the right hand sleeve up onto his shoulder. A band of plaster lay along the bicep.

Voi pointed to it. 'What happened there?'

'I slip on deck, fall against the stanchion. Cut myself.'

'When and at what time?'

Scalatti looked at the floor, chin in hand, the picture of a man deep in thought. The shirt sleeve had dropped back over the plaster. 'The night we are at Dada's Island. When they have the beach party. About ten o'clock on that night I make the fall.'

Voi took a cigarette from a crumpled packet, lit it, blew smoke in the Italian's face. 'Healing well is it? Let's get that plaster off. Have a look.'

Scalatti shook his head. 'Is not ready yet. It can take scab away.'

260

The line of Voi's mouth tightened. 'You do it, Scalatti – or I do it for you.'

'It's not right, Captain.' Scalatti turned, appealed to Cassidy. 'He must not make like this with me.'

Cassidy said, 'Better do as he tells you, Mr Scalatti. If not, it may seem you have something to hide.'

'Me.' The Italian's eyes narrowed, he tapped his chest, shook his head vigorously. 'For what must I hide something?' Slowly, reluctantly, he peeled off the plaster. The flesh was broken by two small parallel wounds, curving towards each other, an inch or less apart. Pinpoints of fresh blood glistened in places where the scab had lifted with the plaster. Voi took the Italian's arm, looked closely at the wound. 'Right. You can put it back.'

Scalatti tried to replace the plaster. 'No good.' He winced. 'Not want to stick now.'

Cassidy said, 'When you go, see Mr Pascal. He'll give you a new one.' The Captain's manner was sympathetic. He'd not liked the Italian's humiliation, the forced removal of the plaster.

Voi pressed on. 'Did anyone see you fall?'

'No. I was alone. Very quick, you know. I fall, then I get up.'

Voi stubbed out his cigarette. 'Right. Now we'll go and look at that stanchion.' There was no sympathy in the African's voice, just a dogged unrelenting determination.

Led by Scalatti, the four men went down in the darkness to the maindeck. They walked forward until the Italian stopped at a bulwark stanchion not far from a deck light. It was on the port side, abreast the saloon's serving pantry. 'This is where it happens.' Scalatti pointed to the stanchion. 'I slip, fall heavy. It makes the cut in the arm.'

Voi took a pencil torch from his pocket, bent down, examined the stanchion. He straightened up, shone the torch in the Italian's face. 'How does a stanchion with a round edge make two sharp incisions like those on your arm?'

'How can I say? A fall in the dark. Anything can happen.'

'Are you sure of the time?'

'Yes. About ten o'clock. It is hot in the cabin, so I go to walk on the deck.'

'And you have said you did not leave the bridge between midnight and four o'clock.'

'You mean . . .' Scalatti hesitated, frowned at the trap question. '. . . in the next night. Yes, that is correct.'

Voi switched off the torch.

Cassidy broke the silence. 'What was it that made you slip, Mr Scalatti?'

'How can I say. Dark, the ship can move, you know. Easy to fall.'

'But the stanchion's near a deck light, Mr Scalatti. A ship at anchor, in the lee of an island in a dead calm, does not move.'

The beam of Voi's torch settled again on the Italian's face. 'What would you say if I told you someone saw you on the main deck at seventeen minutes past one, last Wednesday morning. That is, during the middle watch.'

Scalatti put up a hand to shield his eyes from the torch. 'I will say it is not a possibility. I stay on the bridge for all the time. Twelve to four. I tell you this already.'

The Kenya CID man switched off the torch. 'Right. That will do. Let us return to your cabin, Captain. You too, Scalatti. You come along with us . . .'

The sentence was broken by Voi's sudden, shouted, 'Hey! Look out!' as the Italian jumped to one side, spun round and dived over the bulwark into the sea.

The splash of the impact was followed by the sound of swimming, but darkness beyond the range of Voi's small torch had soon swallowed the scene. Cassidy and Blake made for the bridge. Voi ran round the deckhouse to the starboard side to see if the police launch had returned early. It had not.

From *Sunglow*'s bridge Cassidy picked up the swimmer in the beam of an Aldis lamp, saw that he was making for the shore on the Mtongwe side, away from the island. Hearing voices on the bridge, Obudo had come from the chartroom. Cassidy saw him. 'Get a skimmer over the side double quick. Pick up that man. Take a seaman with you,' he shouted. Obudo made off at the double, the bridge ladder clattering under his feet as he raced down it.

An eerie sound, a sudden scream that choked into silence, drifted across the water. In the beam of the Aldis lamp the sea round the Italian could be seen to boil as a small dark obelisk moved round him.

'A shark it is.' Cassidy crossed himself. 'Ah, and it's a terrible fate to befall a man.'

'Poor bastard.' There was emotion in Blake's voice. 'I wonder if we'll ever know what it was all about.'

The sound of an engine bursting into life reached the bridge. Soon afterwards the phosphorescent glow of the skimmer's wake showed up through the darkness as it made for the distant scene.

Cassidy and the two detectives were back in the day-cabin when Obudo returned to report that a cigarette packet and a letter were the only things he'd found in the blood-stained patch of water where Scalatti had disappeared. He handed the sodden envelope to Cassidy, and left the cabin.

Cassidy glanced at the envelope. The ink had run, but the writing was still legible:

Sra Maria Scalatti,
Via Lampadora 46a
Napoli XVI
Italia

'Letter to his wife – or mother.' He passed it to Voi. 'It's not yet stamped. He would be wanting to post it when he got ashore, poor man.'

Voi took the envelope, removed the soggy letter, spread the single blue sheet on the desk blotter. 'In this heat it won't take long to dry,' he said. 'By the way, either of you speak Italian?' Neither of them did.

Voi raised his eyes in mock despair. 'I didn't think you would. My office will see to its translation.'

Cassidy rang for Mbolwo, asked him to bring more coffee.

Voi lit another cigarette. 'I was going to hold him for investigation. The evidence was largely circumstantial. There was much to be done before we could bring him to trial. Now he's convicted himself. Decided the punishment.' The Kenyan leant back on the settee, held the cigarette between thumb and forefinger, inhaled deeply before letting the smoke drift from his nostrils. 'But we shall hold Krol. Maybe he can tell us something.' The hooded eyes flickered. 'After a day or so they like to help, you know.'

'We find that, too.' Blake's face was expressionless.

'A man is helping the police . . .,' quoted Cassidy. 'Ah, and it's often enough we read that.' He went on. 'Those two cuts on his bicep. Now what did you make of those?'

'Teeth marks. An arm round her neck. They struggle. She does the only thing she can. Bites.' Voi pulled his right arm across his face, went through the motions of biting into the bicep.

'When Bliss saw him he had no shirt,' said Blake. 'What d'you make of that?'

Cassidy took it on himself to answer. 'In the middle watch, on a hot night in the tropics? That's not unusual.'

Blake said, 'Until tonight I was pretty sure I knew who'd got rid of Mrs Kitson – and it wasn't Scalatti. But I was wrong. Things are not always what they seem.'

264

'Didn't Shakespeare say that?' Voi squinted through a pall of cigarette smoke.

'He could have.'

'What exactly was your Yard assignment, Mr Blake?' Cassidy, in the act of lighting a cigar, had stopped to ask the question.

'To identify Robert Aspen without letting him know who I was. Once I'd made certain he was the man we'd been looking for we could arrange extradition proceedings with the Seychelles Government. His murder, hours after I'd found him, set another problem. Who killed him, and why? As Tom says, that's a matter for the Seychelles authorities. But not altogether. Scotland Yard is an interested party.'

Mbolwo arrived with the fresh pot of coffee. When he'd gone Cassidy began pouring. 'What was it, then, that Robert Aspen was wanted for?'

'Bank robbery,' said Blake. 'Four million pounds. He was the gang leader. There were six of them. We'd got all but one within a week. Thanks to him. He shopped them – anonymous letter after he'd cleared out with the loot. He's still got most of it. Stashed away in numbered accounts in Zurich, Lichenstein and the Caribbean I imagine. It must have been laundered and recycled out of all recognition by now.'

'Holy Saint Patrick, and I'll be damned.' Cassidy chuckled, pulled at his cigar. 'So that's how Robert Aspen made his money.'

Blake stood up, stretched his arms widely, yawned. 'God, I'm tired.'

Voi yawned in sympathy, looked at the clock over the desk. 'My launch should be back shortly. I told them six o'clock.'

'Ah well,' Cassidy sighed. 'It's not much sleep that I've had meself. There's a long day ahead.'

'Sorry, Captain.' Blake smiled sympathetically at the older man. 'But we're not quite finished.'

'And what's it now, Mr Blake?'

'I'd like to have a chat with Henry Atkins. Ask young Obudo to tell him – in the most friendly fashion – that you'd like a word with him in your cabin. Right away. You need his help.'

Cassidy looked puzzled, took the cigar from his mouth. 'Atkins? Very well.' He shrugged, went to the desk, picked up the phone. A brief conversation followed before he put the phone down. He turned to Voi. 'Your launch is alongside.'

Henry Atkins arrived wearing his yachting cap, dark glasses, pyjama trousers and the MINE'S A GUINNESS T-shirt. Cassidy thanked him for coming at such an awkward hour, adding that it was easier to discuss things now rather than in the hustle and bustle which would follow when the ship got alongside.

'You already know Mr Blake. This is Mr Tom Voi from the office ashore.' In making the introductions he avoided any reference to police rank. That had been Blake's idea. 'Hullos' were exchanged, Atkins joined Voi on the settee, Cassidy sat at his desk and Blake, arms folded, stood with his back to the door.

The stubby, bearded Londoner glanced at the faces round him. 'What's this, then? Deputation from the TUC.'

Cassidy said, 'Coffee for you, Mr Atkins?'

'Don't mind if I do. Milk and three lumps, please.'

Cassidy poured the coffee, put the cup on the low table by the settee. Atkins tried the coffee, put it down. 'Cor, it's 'ot.' He sucked his teeth. 'Sad about Mrs Kitson – and the first mate. Not that I worry too much about the Eyetie. Never took to 'im.'

'You know what's happened, then?' Cassidy showed surprise.

'Blimey. With all that commotion going on outside me cabin. It'd be a bleedin' miracle if I didn't. Wonder what the trouble was? People don't get killed for nothing, do they?'

'Very true.' Blake took the warrant card from his pocket, passed it to Atkins.

The Londoner looked at it, then at Blake. 'So the bird man turns out to be the fuzz. Well I never. Who's the dark gentleman, then?' He looked at Voi.

Blake said, 'More fuzz, I'm afraid. Detective Superintendent Voi, Kenya CID.'

Atkins nodded in sudden understanding. 'It's about Mrs Kitson going over the side, is it? Well, gents, that's something I'm afraid I can't help you with. Good lookin' lady she was, but we didn't hit it off. Bit up-market for me. Going strong with the Eyetie she was. At least that was the buzz. And then there's young Jim Abernethy. Nice boy. He was hanging around her. Love struck, I'd say. Perhaps you should have a word with 'im.'

Blake shook his head. 'Not as easy as that, I'm afraid. Sorry to have to do this to you.' He looked unhappy, took a deep breath. 'Joseph Blunt, I have to question you about the murder of Michel Duchescu, alias Robert Aspen, on Dada's Island on the night of . . .'

'You have to be joking,' interrupted Atkins cheerfully. 'I'm not Joseph Blunt and no way could I have killed Aspen. Ask Captain Cassidy. He conducted a full scale inquiry. Why would I want to kill a stranger? You're daft.'

Cassidy noticed that the Cockney accent had faded, the aspirates now more often in place.

'He was no stranger to you, Blunt. He was the leader of your gang. You were get-away driver. Duchescu cleared off with the loot. Shopped your lot and disappeared. That was why you killed him.'

Atkins held up his hands, laughed good humouredly. 'I just don't know what you're talking about. You're trying it on with the wrong bloke, Chief.'

'Am I? Take a look at this.' Blake took the big envelope from Cassidy's desk, slid its contents on to the low table. He passed a photo to Atkins. 'You, ten years ago. Immediately after arrest. No beard then, but the profile shows the damaged ear. That was before you wore your hair long enough to cover it. Then there are these. Your mate's pictures.' He passed them over. 'Nasty looking lot of villains, aren't they.' He took another single photo from the table. 'And here's Robert Aspen – alias Michel Duchescu – the Duke. Looking quite chirpy. The Yard took that some time ago – before the bank robbery – so he looks a lot younger, doesn't he. Here's one of you taken just before your release from Parkhurst. Aged a bit during those years inside, didn't you, Jo?'

Atkins glanced at them perfunctorily, passed them back. 'Never seen any of those blokes before. Including the one you say is me.' He rubbed a finger against his nose. 'Too bad you've been wasting your time.'

'Well now, Blunt, if you insist on being unco-operative, we'll have a little ID.' Blake picked up a sheet of typed paper, began to read from it. 'Lower portion of left earlobe missing, lateral scar on top of bald pate . . .' He looked up, smiled. 'That means the scar on your bald patch. The one you didn't want the Duke to see, so you cultivated the yachting cap. Like you did the beard and hair style, and the dark glasses.' Blake began to read again. 'Gold fillings in eye teeth, distinctive tattoo design on abdomen and buttocks – as per sketch annexed – and now the crunch.' Blake looked up, held up a white board the size of a playing card. 'Your finger prints, Jo.'

Atkins tipped back the yachting cap, ran his tongue round his lips, pushed the dark glasses firmly on to the bridge of his nose. 'Not bad, Inspector. Not bad at all.' He took out a handkerchief, sneezed into it several times. 'Okay. So I'm Jo Blunt. But you'll never succeed in pinning the Duke's death on me. Reason, I didn't do it, couldn't have done it, and it won't be too difficult to prove that I didn't.'

Blake turned to Voi. 'Over to you, Tom.'

The Kenyan got up from the settee; almost languidly, as if it were of little importance, he said, 'Joseph Blunt, on behalf of the Seychelles authorities, I intend to hold you for questioning in connection with the murder of Michel Duchescu.' Voi switched his attention to Cassidy. 'Get your second mate to send up my men. They'll be in the launch.'

TWENTY-EIGHT

Before Voi's men arrived Cassidy had gone through to the sleeping-cabin on some pretext or other. He'd done so rather than witness Atkins' humiliation; but that didn't prevent him hearing the metallic snap and rattle, and the little Londoner's, 'For Christ's sake, you don't have to handcuff me,' followed by Voi's, 'Take it easy, Blunt. They won't be on for long.' The Kenyan had added, 'Your gear will be brought ashore later.'

Only when he'd heard the door shut behind them did Cassidy go back to the day-cabin. Outside the windows it was growing lighter, the Mombasa skyline etched in black against an eastern sky which glowed with the promise of the coming sun. As he lowered himself into the chair by the desk he asked himself how much longer his uninvited guests would stay.

As if reading the Irishman's thoughts, Blake smiled apologetically. 'Sorry about all this, Captain. But thank you for your cooperation.'

'Well it certainly was a surprise. Not that the morning's been short of them.' Yawning, Cassidy patted his mouth with an open hand. 'You knew about this when you came on board did you, Mr Blake?'

'No. Until your inquiry on the island I'd not thought of Atkins in relation to Duchescu. Atkins was an odd ball, I reckoned – the Roller, the rag-to-riches story, you know – a

269

con man, perhaps. You get them on cruises.' He rubbed his chin, puffed out his cheeks. 'Well – then came the inquiry. It eliminated certain people, left a number of suspects. Who were they?' He paused before answering the rhetorical question. 'There had to be motive, opportunity and, beyond that, a reason why the killing took place during *Sunglow*'s visit. Among the islanders who could have had a motive, and whose movements that night were not fully explained, were Balthazar, Moonflower and Nicodemus. Among the passengers, the only two who seemed to fulfil the requirements of motive and opportunity were Mrs Kitson and Atkins. Why was the man killed during *Sunglow*'s visit? Probably because there was a barbecue, a late night party, plenty of alcohol, strangers present and, well – you know – all the rest that goes with that sort of party. If an islander did it, *Sunglow*'s passengers gave him cover. If a passenger did it, the reverse. Mrs Kitson? She *was* the last person to see him alive, remember? That was enough, prima facie, to invite suspicion. But she didn't seem to me to be strong enough physically or mentally to kill Duchescu. So that left Atkins – a possible, *if* he had a motive. Michel Duchescu had cleared out with the loot and shopped his gang. That's like signing your death warrant if they ever find you. It seemed to me there was just an outside chance that Henry Atkins could have been one of the gang. He fitted the part. If he had been, the motive was strong. My message to the Yard, via *Amphiberon*, requested a check on Henry Atkins at 279b Chester Square, Belgravia, with particular reference to the Duchescu bank robbery. Tom Voi brought the answer this morning.'

'So that was no blarney – the Chester Square address, the Rolls Royce, and so forth?' Cassidy's eyebrows lifted in inquiry.

'Not altogether. He lived in Islington, but Chester Square was his work place. Chauffeur to a big man in the City. That's where the Rolls Royce came in.'

'Ah, well.' Cassidy tapped the ash from his cigar. 'He

270

wasn't altogether untruthful then.' Something occurred to him. 'Mrs Kitson and the shark's tooth pendant. What of that?'

Blake shrugged. 'Atkins could have put it in her suitcase after she'd gone overboard. Good red herring.'

'And if Balthazar or Moonflower or Nicodemus had the pendant . . .?' Cassidy hesitated, '. . . could not one of them have put it in the suitcase, when they saw Mandy off?'

Blake stretched, yawned again. 'That may well be raised in Blunt's defence. If ever he's brought to trial. It's by no means an open and shut case, you know. I admit that. But why was Blunt – a member of Duchescu's gang – on the cruise? Why did he go to so much trouble to hide his identity? I was watching him at the barbecue. He kept away from Duchescu. Never, as far as I could see, spoke to the man. Yet he knew him intimately. The answers to those questions have to be more than coincidence.'

Voi wanted to know what the distinctive tattoo was.

Blake raised a quizzical eyebrow, smiled. 'Hounds chasing a fox round his abdomen and buttocks.'

Voi grinned. 'Did they ever catch the fox?'

'No. It had gone to earth. Brush sticking out of Blunt's arse.'

At seven o'clock the pilot came aboard, *Sunglow* weighed anchor and went slowly alongside; ropes were thrown and she was safely secured. A crane placed a gangway across from quay to sundeck, African stevedores came up it, hatches were opened and unloading began.

The forenoon was a busy one for Cassidy: port officials, police, forwarding and shipping agents, the representatives of ship's chandlers, victualling firms and others came and went. A number of passengers called on him to say goodbye, among them Mrs Clutterbutt whose invitation to dinner that night at the Nyali Beach Hotel he'd gladly accepted. In the ebb and flow of drama over the last few

271

days, she had remained for him the embodiment of all that was decent and dependable.

Among the mail that came to his desk on arrival was a note from Miss Panjee: Mr Goosam Patel would not be available that day – it was a Saturday – nor on the Sunday when Mr Ali Patel's funeral was to take place. Would Captain Cassidy kindly make his call at the offices on Monday. Mr Goosam had dictated an important letter, the transcription of which had been delayed by pressure of work consequent upon Mr Ali's death. She would, however, get it down to the ship as soon as possible.

It was Cassidy's instinct that the letter would have to do with *Sunglow*'s future. It was unlike Goosam to write a few days before seeing him. It was likely to be bad news; something Goosam didn't want to have to tell him in person. Depressed, insecure, he went to the sleeping cabin where Mbolwo had laid out the white linen shirt, white suit, spotted silk handkerchief, matching bow-tie, Panama hat and Malacca cane – the clothes he'd last used on the day of sailing, three weeks earlier. Since there was no point in going to the office, he would drop in at the club for lunch. It was a Saturday, but some of his old cronies might be there.

He had a cold shower, trimmed his beard and moustache, and began to dress. Getting into those clothes after weeks in uniform was a ritual that always interested him. For reasons he couldn't understand it somehow changed his outlook, caused him to see things in a different perspective, to feel less sure of himself, as if he were acting the part of the sea captain ashore. With vigorous strokes of silver-backed brushes he got his hair the way he wanted it. That done, he tied the bow-tie, put on his coat, arranged the silk handkerchief in a breast pocket, appraised himself critically in the wardrobe mirror, took the Panama hat and Malacca cane and went into the day cabin. He filled the cigar case, put his wallet, diary, chequebook and gold pen into his pockets. He was lighting a cigar when there was a knock on the door. He called out, 'What is it?' The door

272

opened and Stephen Blake came in. It was almost noon.

'I've come to thank you for a most interesting cruise.' With a smile Blake added, 'I don't mean the crime side. It was the islands. The bird life was fantastic. I wouldn't have missed it for anything.'

'Ah, and it's not much that I know about birds, but the islands are fine. I see them often, Mr Blake, and they never tire. The tropics get into a man's blood, you know. It's not easy to break with them after half a lifetime.'

'I can understand that. One other point, Captain. I'm afraid you'll be required to give evidence. Probably by deposition, since you're likely to be at sea when the time comes.'

Cassidy nodded. 'I expected that would be the case.'

There was further brief discussion after which they left the cabin together.

Among the mail delivered to *Sunglow* that morning was a letter for Jim Abernethy from his father. It welcomed him back from the cruise, gave some home and family news, and ended with:

I trust that this experience, made possible by your aunt's generosity, has proved valuable: broadened your mind, taught you how to get on with men and, more particularly, given you the ability to stand on your own feet. In short, I hope it has taught you something of life, its problems and realities. Leonie and I look forward to your return.

For some time Jim sat thinking about his home, his father and his stepmother Leonie, and the problems and realities of life. Then, tearing up the letter and dropping the pieces into a wastepaper basket, he muttered, 'I think it has, Father. It really has.' The reality that confronted him now was that the cruise was over and he had to go home. The problem was that he didn't want to go home. He had other plans for his return. He'd discovered that he liked the

273

sea. After all it was in his blood. His mother was a Bannister.

A more immediate and pleasant reality was that Said Obudo was taking him and Luther Nelson on a run of the town that night. He liked Said and Luther. They were really nice guys.

Cassidy felt it was much like the first time they'd dined together at Nyali Beach, except that she didn't seem quite so stern and dominant as she had on that occasion. There was a softer, warmer look now in those formidable grey eyes. But of course we know each other better, he reminded himself, and it is a lot we've been through together in these last few weeks.

She must have read his thoughts: 'It seems very much more than three weeks ago that we met here, Captain. So much has happened since. I must say it was a most exciting and adventurous cruise. Far beyond my expectations.'

'Ah, well now, Mrs C, and it's kind of you indeed to say that. I have to admit that I greatly enjoyed the search for White Island and the buried treasure at Lone Palm Point. Made me feel like a lad again. Doing the sort of things I used to read about at school.'

It was after dinner, and they were sitting in the same quiet corner they'd used the night they'd met. The waiter had brought them coffee, and an iced lager for Cassidy.

A sigh of regret came from Mrs Clutterbutt. 'Sad, though, that there were those, well – unpleasant incidents. I prefer to forget them, but you know what I mean.'

Cassidy nodded, raised his tankard to her. 'Ah well, Mrs C and that's the way of life, is it not? The good with the bad. All those terrible happenings and yet, at the end of the day, it's the good times we remember.'

She looked at him reflectively. 'I suppose you'll be setting out on another cruise quite soon, Captain?'

'There may be delays. Repairs to weather damage and

274

the engines, you know. I'll be getting the programme on Monday when I see Goosam.'

'Poor Mr Patel. How sad that his only son should have been killed in a car accident. So many people die like that nowadays. Such a waste of life, I always think.'

'Ah, yes. And a terrible blow it must be to him. Ali was to take over when he retires. The funeral is tomorrow. It's not something I look forward to.'

'They are sad occasions.'

The silence which followed was broken by Cassidy. 'And when is it you'll be going back to England, Mrs C?'

She watched him over the rim of her coffee cup. 'We fly to Nairobi tomorrow. Join the flight to London late that night.'

'You'll be glad to get back, I've no doubt.'

She looked away from him. 'For certain things, yes. But life will seem unbelievably dull at first – and lonely. Jim may stay with me for a few days. That will be pleasant. I'm quite sure most of our conversation will be about *Sunglow* and the islands.' She paused. 'You'll be off again before long. I wonder who your passengers will be next time?'

There was warmth in Cassidy's smile. 'There's no knowing. But it won't be the same. There'll be no substitute for Mrs C. Indeed, and I shall be missing her.'

Mrs Clutterbutt blushed, of that there was little doubt. 'How very sweet of you.' With a certain shyness, her eyes averted, she said, 'I shall certainly miss *Sunglow*'s charming Captain.'

Cassidy glanced at her, his expression a mixture of curiosity and surprise. He took a long draught of iced lager, dabbed at his lips with the silk handkerchief. 'Maybe you'll be coming on another cruise sometime?'

'I doubt it, Captain. Do you ever visit England?'

'Ah, and that's something I've not done these twenty years. Nor me own Ireland, for that matter.'

Mrs Clutterbutt looked away as if searching for something on the far side of the lounge. 'Your wife is here in Kenya, is she?'

'I've no wife, Mrs C.'

She turned back to him. With the slightest of frowns she said, 'Oh, I see. Have you always been a bachelor?'

He shook his head. 'No. When I was a young man on leave in Ireland, I married. A fine looking girl from Donegal. A few weeks later I was off to sea again. Third mate of an old cargo ship. Tramping the world looking for cargoes, we were. When I got back, two years later, she'd gone.'

'Oh dear, how sad.' Mrs Clutterbutt's eyes were clouded and uncertain.

'Ah, well, and I wasn't for blaming her. It was no life in those days for a girl married to a sailor. But after that I knew marriage was not for me.' He stroked his beard with thumb and forefinger. 'And that's the way it's been. My mother once said, "You'll be no use whatever to a wife, Shamus. Sure and you're too much in love with ships and the sea." She was right, you know.'

For some moments Mrs Clutterbutt was silent. 'More coffee, Captain?'

'Yes. Thank you kindly.'

She poured the coffee, passed it to him. 'Well, if you should ever come to England, do please let me know. It would be such a pleasure to see you again.'

'You can be sure I'd be letting you know, Mrs C.' It was easy to say, but knowing it would not happen he felt a sudden melancholy as if, for reasons he could not really comprehend, he was allowing something worthwhile in life to pass him by.

TWENTY-NINE

In the several days that had passed since the dinner at Nyali Beach a good deal had happened: Cassidy had attended Ali's funeral, said a few awkward but warmly felt words of sympathy to Goosam and his wife, and gone on to the club for a drink before returning to the ship.

On Monday he'd called at the company's offices to find that Goosam Patel had left for Nairobi that morning, en route to Bombay. Miss Panjee was out, so he left a note informing her that Goosam's letter had not yet reached him – would she please get it down to the ship as soon as possible. He was about to leave the office when Superintendent Voi telephoned to ask him to lunch on the following day. 'It's a Greek restaurant. The grilled prawns are exceptional.'

'Ah, and that's fine,' said Cassidy. 'There's nothing I like better.'

They met at Xenophon's the next day: a small, unpretentious restaurant in a back street facing the old dhow harbour. The grilled prawns were all that Voi had promised.

During lunch the conversation turned, inevitably, to the events of the last days of *Sunglow*'s cruise. So far, said the Superintendent, nothing of value had been elicited from Krol; but they intended to persevere. Cassidy asked if Scalatti's letter to Naples had revealed anything?

'Not really,' said Voi. 'It was the sort of letter a man writes to his wife. One point, though, on which you might be able to help.'

'And what is that?' Cassidy had suspected that the invitation to lunch was more than a courteous gesture.

'Had Scalatti handed in his resignation? Did you know he was leaving *Sunglow* on her return to Mombasa?'

Cassidy shook his head. 'No. There was no suggestion of that. I'd not have been sorry, mind you.'

'Strange,' said Voi. 'In the letter he told his wife he would not be making another voyage in *Sunglow*. He expected to be back in Naples soon.'

'Ah, and it's no surprise. The man knew I had no time for him. Must have made up his mind to clear out.'

They went on to discuss the murder of Duchescu.

Cassidy tapped with his fingers against the glass of iced lager. 'Sure and killing is a bad business, but I'm sorry for Atkins. He was an odd character, yet well liked on board. It's difficult I find it, to believe he was a murderer.'

'He could have been, but I'm not sure that he was,' said Voi.

'What makes you say that, Superintendent?'

The Kenyan delayed his answer, consulted his watch. 'If you can spare an hour after lunch, Captain, come back with me to my office. I think you'll find the answer to your question there.'

Left alone for a moment, Cassidy looked round the sparsely furnished office with its polished floor, filing cabinet, IN and OUT trays, PWD smell of officialdom, and framed photograph of Jomo Kenyatta.

The Superintendent was soon back, a tape cassette in his hand. He took a recorder from a cupboard, placed the cassette in it. 'Blunt was with me for two hours yesterday,' he said. 'Towards the end he came clean, admitted that he'd gone on the *Sunglow* cruise with the intention of finding and killing Duchescu. But as you'll hear shortly, things didn't turn out quite the way he planned.'

Voi sat down, switched on the recorder. The tape burbled through at speed until the Superintendent found what he wanted and switched off. 'I've skipped the account of how he discovered where Duchescu was. Quite a saga in

278

itself, that one. But this is what I think will interest you.'
Voi switched on the recorder again; the voice was Henry
Atkins': 'The Duke didn't recognize me. The beard, the
dark glasses, the cap, the way I stepped up the Cockney
accent. But I recognized him all right. Bigger, fatter, older
than I remembered, but definitely Michel Duchescu. Same
scar alongside the nose, same laugh and phoney smile.
There was no mistaking him. All that night at the barbecue
I kept my distance, though I watched him all I could. It had
to be that night or nothing; *Sunglow* was sailing next
morning. When he left the fire with Mrs Kitson and took
the path through the plantation, I followed at a distance. It
was dark, no moon. When they got to the settlement I
stayed in the plantation. I had no definite plan. Just had to
wait and see, and hope for an opportunity. They came back
about fifteen minutes later. Stopped not far from where I
was hiding. I heard him say, "You go back to the fire. I'll
join you soon. I've forgotten the concertina." That suited
me. My plan was to get him on the way back, nearer the
settlement. When Mrs Kitson had gone, I went back to the
path and nearly bumped into a couple coming up it. A torch
was flashed on me. It was Dean Carter with his wife, on
their way from the settlement. Like he told you at the
inquiry, he said "Hi. What are you doing here?" I said I'd
been having a pee. Put it politely of course, didn't want to
offend the lady. After that I joined up with them and we
returned to the fire. I reckoned I'd missed my chance, but I
wasn't giving up. After a while I wandered away from the
others into the dark. Went down the path, left it a few
hundred yards later and hid in the undergrowth. I waited
for a few minutes but nothing happened. So I rejoined the
path and went down towards the settlement. Thought he
might have decided not to come back to the barbecue. I'd
not gone far when I heard a noise behind me to the right. A
funny sort of choking, coughing sound. Bit like vomiting. I
thought it was him. He'd had a skinful that night. So I went
in quietly, slowly, and shone my torch that way. There was

this corpse, lying on the ground not far from the path. It was the Duke. There were stab wounds in the throat and chest, and fresh wet blood. I knew then that I had to clear out quick. He'd got what was coming to him, but it wasn't me that done it, and it wasn't the way I would've. I had a nylon cord in my pocket – a garotte – and it was to go round his throat. Stops any shouts for help, you know. Dead silent and not messy like a knife.' There was the sound of a mirthless chuckle, before the voice went on. 'But he was dead, throat cut, and there was I next to the body. If I said I'd found it, who'd have believed me? Not you, for one. Trouble was, I had a motive to kill the bastard. So I left him there. Went back to the barbecue. Had a couple of drinks to steady myself. Next day Captain Cassidy holds the inquiry. I expect you've seen the report. Anyway, I was okay. Nobody pointed a finger at me. So I thought that was the end of it.'

Voi switched off the tape. 'That's why I'm not at all sure that he killed Duchescu.' He took a cigarette from the crumpled packet on his blotter and lit it. 'And there's another reason.' He opened a drawer, took something from it, laid it on the desk. It was a white nylon cord, about thirty inches long, a wooden toggle at each end. 'It's a garotte,' said the Kenyan. 'We found it in his luggage.'

It was an October morning, crisp and fresh, and beneath a grey sky the countryside was painted in the warm colours of autumn. Seen through the French windows of her dining room, it was a view of rural Somerset to which Mrs Clutterbutt was much attached, for though its mood varied with the seasons, its charm was unchanged.

On her arrival at Heathrow the day before, she had phoned Frank Abernethy to ask if Jim might accompany her to Somerset and stay on for two or three days: 'To help me with my luggage, get the car started. That sort of thing.'

In his pompous, self-important way, and with a measure of sarcasm thrown in, Jim's father had agreed: 'Two days should be sufficient, Beryl. Leonie's feelings may well be hurt if he delays his return any longer.'

Mrs Clutterbutt had felt inclined to say damn Leonie's feelings, but instead she had thanked him. He'd asked to speak to Jim but she'd explained that he was getting her a taxi. That, mercifully, had ended the conversation. When she told Jim what had happened he'd grinned: 'We'll make two days into three, Aunt Beryl.'

Watching him over her newspaper as he worked his way through a large breakfast, she wished she could see more of him. He was a considerate, helpful young man, full of youthful enthusiasm, yet tempered by a certain dogged determination; a quality which reminded her of her father.

To Beryl Clutterbutt, who had no children, her nephew was of particular importance. Someone to look after and care for, an outlet for her warmth and affection, and a means of satisfying the desire to be useful and wanted. Her thoughts turned briefly to another man, one for whom she had grown unashamedly fond in recent weeks. Of course it was absurd at her age, she told herself, but she could not pretend it was otherwise. A man so striking in appearance, so natural in charm, so naively old-fashioned in manner, yet so genial a humbug when occasion demanded, would have made a wonderful companion. In her fantasies she had seen the big Irishman in that role, retired and happily settled with her in Somerset. But any hope that it might become more than fantasy had died on that last night at Nyali Beach. A woman of strong character, she put these thoughts from her, finished the gardening article in the *Daily Telegraph*, and put the paper aside.

'More toast, Jim?'

'Yes, please. I'll make it.' He got up, went to the sideboard. 'Any for you, Aunt Beryl?'

'No thank you.' She picked up the paper again, turned a page, glanced at the headlines.

'How very interesting.' It was said in a voice which was,

to her nephew, a signal that his aunt was about to read aloud.

'Do listen to this, Jim.' She gave him an affectionate smile, was about to begin, when the phone rang. 'Oh dear, that will be Joan Hilyard.' She stood, held the newspaper out to him. 'I must go. Read it yourself. There, that paragraph where my thumb is.'

He took the paper and she went to the phone.

Under the heading, SOVIET BUILD UP IN INDIAN OCEAN? it read:

Washington DC – Sources close to the Pentagon state US Navy investigating report of alleged Soviet construction project on formerly deserted atoll near the Amirante Group of islands north-east of Madagascar. Intermediate range ballistic missiles sited there would threaten US naval base at Diego Garcia, friendly ports on the East African coast, and tankers and other vessels using the oil route to the west.

Goosam's letter did not arrive until the Tuesday following the funeral, and then only in late evening.

When Mbolwo delivered it, Cassidy was in his day-cabin reading the day's paper, the tray with the bottle of Jamieson's whisky, his favourite crystal tumbler, the water jug and ice bucket, on the table beside him. The letter was accompanied by a note from Miss Panjee, profuse in its apologies.

I do hope you will forgive me, but Mr Ali's death, followed by Mr Goosam's departure for Bombay, has made formidable inroads upon my time.

Her postscript recorded that the letter had been dictated by Mr Goosam a few hours before the news of Mr Ali's car accident had reached him.

Cassidy slit the envelope, unfolded the letter, began reading.

My Dear Shamus,

I am writing to you in some haste because Ali and I have to leave for Bombay tomorrow at short notice. I will not therefore see you until my return; in the meantime there is important news.

During your absence my brother Hadji was here from Bombay. As you know his commercial interests in India are considerable. The purpose of his visit was to make a substantial investment in J. G. Patel & Co. Ltd. This injection of fresh capital will be of great assistance to the Company, and will make Hadji a major shareholder. He is a man of much influence with valuable connections in various parts of the world. Thanks to him we can now embark on the new project I refer to below.

First let me say that Sunglow *has been sold, probably for scrap, subject to delivery in Singapore by the 31st October. Thus, no repairs must be put in hand other than those necessary to get the ship to Singapore where you will hand her over to the purchasers. I know you will be sad to part with this little ship which has rendered such fine service, and been your home for so long. But she is old now and no longer profitable.*

Hadji has found an excellent replacement: a three thousand ton vessel with accommodation for seventy-five passengers and twenty crew. Built in Denmark six years ago, she is a seventeen knot, diesel engined vessel with an endurance of five thousand miles. She is at present undergoing a refit, including the alterations and additions necessary to enable her to fulfil the terms of the contract Hadji has negotiated with the US Defence Department. Namely, to carry US Defence stores and personnel, principally between African and Indian ports and the US naval base at Diego Garcia. The contract is for five years, with provision for renewal for a further five. It is an excellent one from our point of view.

*This will mean an end to the Capricorn Cruises. I am
sure you will not be sorry on that account.*

*In conclusion, I am happy to tell you that your new
command is to be renamed* Sunglow Two.

> *With all good wishes,*
> *Yours most sincerely,*

The letter had been signed by Miss Panjee on behalf of
Mr Goosam Patel.

Cassidy poured himself three fingers of whisky, added
ice and a little water and for some time sat thinking about
the letter and its implications. The new ship was twice the
size of *Sunglow*, considerably faster, a quarter of her age,
and no doubt easier to handle and more comfortable to live
in. 'African ports' presumably included Mombasa, so most
of his crew would remain with him.

But nothing could take the place of *Sunglow*: he and the
coaster had shared too many years of their lives, had been
through too many good and bad times together. The longer
a man stayed with a ship the less inanimate it became:
slowly but surely the seaman discerned the character and
personality of the vessel: the *it* became *she*, and the
relationship something beyond the understanding of lands-
men. The voyage to Singapore, the handing over, 'probably
for scrap', seemed to Cassidy an act of betrayal; but it was
one from which there was no escape. These were the
thoughts in his mind as he poured himself a third whisky,
added ice and a little water, and decided there was no profit
in dwelling upon the sadness of it all. The good and the
bad came and went and had to be accepted. That was
life.

'US Defence stores and personnel, principally between
African and Indian ports and Diego Garcia.' Well, there'd
be plenty of time in tropical seas, no lack of flying fish
weather, with fine rises and settings of the sun. Indeed, and
was that not something to be thankful for.

There wouldn't be any more adventures like the search

for White Island and gold at Lone Palm Point, and surely never another Mrs C. But there would be other things. There always were. That, too, was life.

Fontana Paperbacks: Fiction

Fontana is a leading paperback publisher of both non-fiction, popular and academic, and fiction. Below are some recent fiction titles.

- ☐ SEEDS OF YESTERDAY Virginia Andrews £2.50
- ☐ SONG OF RHANNA Christine Marion Fraser £2.50
- ☐ JEDDER'S LAND Maureen O'Donoghue £1.95
- ☐ THE WARLORD Malcolm Bosse £2.95
- ☐ TREASON'S HARBOUR Patrick O'Brian £2.50
- ☐ FUTURES Freda Bright £1.95
- ☐ THE DEMON LOVER Victoria Holt £2.50
- ☐ FIREPRINT Geoffrey Jenkins £2.50
- ☐ DEATH AND THE DANCING FOOTMAN Ngaio Marsh £1.75
- ☐ THE 'CAINE' MUTINY Herman Wouk £2.50
- ☐ LIVERPOOL DAISY Helen Forrester £1.95
- ☐ OUT OF A DREAM Diana Anthony £1.75
- ☐ SHARPE'S ENEMY Bernard Cornwell £1.95

You can buy Fontana paperbacks at your local bookshop or newsagent. Or you can order them from Fontana Paperbacks, Cash Sales Department, Box 29, Douglas, Isle of Man. Please send a cheque, postal or money order (not currency) worth the purchase price plus 15p per book for postage (maximum postage required is £3).

NAME (Block letters) _____

ADDRESS _____

_____

_____